TWO DARK REIGNS

KENDARE BLAKE

MACMILLAN

First published in the US 2018 by HarperTeen, an imprint of HarperCollins Publishers

First published in the UK 2018 by Macmillan Children's Books
an imprint of Pan Macmillan
20 New Wharf Road, London N1 9RR
Associated companies throughout the world
www.panmacmillan.com

ISBN 978-1-5098-7649-5

1 3 5 7 9 8 6 4 2

A CIP catalogue record for this book is available from
the British Library.

Typography by Aurora Parlagreco
Printed and bound by CPI Group (UK) Ltd, Croydon CR0 4YY

Kendare Blake is originally from South Korea, but was brought up in the United States. She has a BA in Business from Ithaca College in New York and an MA in Writing from Middlesex University in London. She is the author of *Anna Dressed in Blood*, *Girl of Nightmares* and *Antigoddess*, all published by Orchard Books. She lives with her husband in Kent, Washington.

Books by Kendare Blake from Macmillan

Three Dark Crowns
One Dark Throne
Queens of Fennbirn

'Roxane. An elemental.'

The Midwife repeated the final name and turned away, cleaning the baby before wrapping her in blue and placing her in the last bassinet. Philomene breathed heavily in the birthing bed. She had been right. She could feel it. The birth had killed her. Strong as she was, she might survive long enough to be bound up and put into the saddle, but it would be a body that Louis sailed home with, to be entombed in his family crypt or perhaps pushed overboard into the sea. Her duty to the island was finished, and the island would have no more say in her fate.

'Midwife!' Philomene groaned as another pain tore through her.

'Yes, yes,' the Midwife replied soothingly. 'It is only the afterbirth. It will pass.'

'It is not the afterbirth. It is not—'

She grimaced and bit her lip against one more push.

Another baby slipped out from the war queen's womb. Easily and without fuss. She opened her black eyes and took an enormous breath. Another baby born. Another queen.

'A blue queen,' the Midwife murmured. 'A fourth born.'

'Give her to me.'

The Midwife only stared.

'Give her to me now!'

She scooped the baby up, and Philomene snatched her from her hands.

'Illiann,' Philomene said. 'An elemental.' Her exhausted,

depleted face broke into a smile. Any disappointment of there being no new war queen vanished. For here was a great destiny. A blessing, for the entire island. And she, Philomene, had done it.

'Illiann,' the shocked Midwife repeated. 'An elemental. The Blue Queen.'

Philomene laughed. She raised the child in her arms.

'Illiann!' she shouted. 'The Blue Queen!'

The days spent waiting for someone to arrive at the Black Cottage were long. After the birth of the Blue Queen, the messengers raced back to their cities with the news. They had been at the Black Cottage, their horses saddled the moment the queen's labor began.

A fourth born. It was such a rare occurrence that it was thought by some to be mere legend. At the Midwife's announcement, none of the young messengers had known what to do. She had finally needed to screech at them.

'A Blue Queen!' she had shouted. 'Blessed of the Goddess! All must come. All the families! And the High Priestess as well! Ride!'

Had only the triplets been born, just three families and a small party of priestesses would have come to the cottage. The Traverses for the naturalist queen. The burgeoning Westwoods for the elemental. And the Lermonts for the poor little oracle queen, to oversee her drowning. But the arrival of a Blue Queen meant that the heads of the strongest families from all the island's gifts would come. The Vatros clan, who inhabited the capital and the war city of Bastian. And even the Arrons, the poisoners from Prynn.

Inside the cottage, beneath the dark brown beams supporting the ceiling, four bassinets sat beside the eastern wall to catch the sunlight of morning. All were quiet, except for the baby in the light gray blanket. The little oracle fussed almost constantly. Perhaps because, being an oracle, she knew what was to happen.

Poor little oracle queen. Her fate had always been sealed. Since the time of Mad Queen Elsabet, who used her prophecy gift to murder three whole families she said had plotted against her, oracle queens were immediately drowned. After wresting power away from Elsabet, the Black Council had made the decree. They would not risk such an unjust massacre again.

In the days following the birth, the Midwife burned the old queen's bedding. It could not be cleaned, so soaked through with blood. She did not wonder where the old queen was or how she fared. Looking at the state of the sheets, she could only assume Philomene was dead.

Just over a week past the birth, the first of the families arrived. The Lermonts, the oracles from the northwest city of Sunpool, nearest to the Black Cottage, though they also insisted they had foreseen the child's coming and had been ready to travel when the messenger arrived. They looked across the tops of the four black bassinets. They looked down gravely at the little oracle queen.

A day later came the Westwoods, new in their elemental dominance and foolish. They cooed over the elemental queen and brought her a gift of a blanket colored with bright blue dye.

'We had it made for her,' said Isabelle Westwood, the head of the family. 'There is no reason she should not have it, even though her life is short.'

After them, the Traverses arrived from Sealhead, and that same evening the Arrons and the hard-riding Vatroses arrived within minutes of each other to bear silent witness. The Vatroses, rich and well-gifted from the war queen's reign, brought the High Priestess with them from the capital.

The Midwife knelt before the High Priestess and gave the queens' names. When she said, 'Illiann,' the High Priestess clasped her hands together.

'A Blue Queen,' she murmured, and went toward the baby. 'I can scarcely believe it. I thought the messengers had gotten it wrong.' She reached down and took up the child, cradling her in the crook of her white-robed arms.

'An elemental Blue Queen,' said Isabelle Westwood, and the High Priestess shushed her with a look.

'The Blue Queen belongs to us all. She will not grow up in an elemental house. She will grow up in the capital. In Indrid Down. With me.'

'But—' the Midwife sputtered. Every head in the room turned toward her. They had forgotten the Midwife was even there.

Philomene glanced at the table of herbs and clean black cloths, jars of potions to dull the pain, all refused, of course. There were knives upon it as well. To cut the new queens free should the old one prove too weak. Philomene smiled. The Midwife was a small meek thing. Her trying to slice them out might be a feat worth watching.

The pain passed, and Philomene sighed.

'They are in a hurry,' she said. 'As I was. In a hurry since I was born, to make my mark. Perhaps I knew I would have a short time to do it in. Or perhaps it was the strain of rushing that shortened my life. You came from the temple, did you not? Before serving in solitude here?'

'I trained there, my queen. At the temple in Prynn. But I never took the oaths.'

'Of course not. I can see that there are no bracelets marked into your arms. I am not blind.' She strained again, and more blood gushed forth. The pains were coming faster.

The Midwife grasped her by the chin and pulled her eyelids back.

'You are weakening.'

'I am not.' Philomene fell back on the bed. She placed her hands atop her great distended belly in a near-motherly gesture. But she would not ask about the baby queens. They were not hers to wonder about. All belonged to the Goddess and the Goddess alone.

Philomene struggled back up onto her elbows. A look of grim determination set on her face. She snapped her fingers for the Midwife to take her place between her knees.

'You are ready to push,' the Midwife said. 'It will be all right; you are strong.'

'I thought you just said I was weakening,' Philomene grumbled.

The first queen born was born silent. Breathing, but she did not even cry when the Midwife slapped her across the back. She was small, and well-formed, and very pink for such a hard, messy birth. The Midwife held her up for Philomene to see, and for a moment, queens' blood flowed between them through the connection of the cord.

'Leonine,' Philomene said, giving the little queen her name. 'A naturalist.'

The Midwife repeated it aloud and took the baby away to be cleaned and placed in a bassinet, then covered in a blanket of bright green and embroidered with flowers. It was not long before the next baby came, screaming this time, and with tiny, clenched fists.

'Isadora,' the queen said, and the baby wailed and blinked her wide black eyes. 'An oracle.'

'Isadora. An oracle,' the Midwife repeated. And she took her away to be wrapped in a blanket of pale gray and yellow, the colors of the seers.

The third queen born arrived in a rush of blood, as if on a wave. It was so much and so gruesome that Philomene's mouth opened to announce a new war queen. But those were not the words that came out.

THE BLACK COTTAGE

400 YEARS BEFORE THE BIRTH OF
MIRABELLA, ARSINOE, AND KATHARINE

The labor, when it began, was hard and full of blood. Nothing less was to be expected from a war queen, especially one so battle-hardened as Queen Philomene.

The Midwife pressed a cool cloth to the queen's forehead, but the queen shoved it away.

'The pain is nothing,' Queen Philomene said. 'I welcome this last fight.'

'You think there will be no more war for you in Louis's country?' the Midwife asked. 'Even if your gift fades after you leave the island, I cannot imagine that.'

The queen looked toward the door, where Louis, her king-consort, could be glimpsed pacing back and forth. Her black eyes glittered from the excitement of the labor. Her black hair shone slick with sweat.

'He wants this to be over. He did not know what he was getting into when he got me.'

Nor did anyone. Queen Philomene's entire reign was marked

by battle. Under her, the capital city was overrun by warriors. She built long ships and plundered the coastal villages of every nation state except for that of her king-consort. But now, all that was over. Eight years of brutal, warrior rule. A short reign, even by war queen standards, but the island was exhausted by it nonetheless. War queens were glory and intimidation. Protection. It was not only her husband who was relieved when the Goddess sent the queen her triplets.

She strained as another pain struck her, and she turned her knee to see more blood darken the bedding.

'You are doing well,' the Midwife lied. But what did she really know? She was young and new in service at the Black Cottage. A poisoner by gift and therefore a clever healer, but though she had aided in many births, there was no true preparation for the birth of queens.

'I am,' Philomene agreed, and smiled. 'It is like a war queen to bleed so much. But I still think I will die of this.'

The Midwife dipped the cloth back into the cool water and wrung it out, ready in case Philomene should let her use it. Perhaps she would. After all, who would see? To the island, a queen was effectively dead once her triplets were born. The horses to take her and Louis to their river barge and on to their ship were already saddled and waiting, and once gone, Philomene and Louis would never return. Even the doting little Midwife would forget her the moment the babies were out. She put on a show of caring, but her only aim was to keep Philomene alive long enough to bear the triplets.

CAST OF CHARACTERS

INDRID DOWN

Capital City, Home of Queen Katharine

THE ARRONS

Natalia Arron

Matriarch of the Arron family. Head of the Black Council.

Genevieve Arron

Younger sister to Natalia

Antonin Arron

Younger brother to Natalia

Pietyr Renard

Natalia's nephew by her brother Christophe

ROLANTH

Home of Queen Mirabella

THE WESTWOODS

Sara Westwood

Matriarch of the Westwood family. Affinity: water

Bree Westwood

Daughter of Sara Westwood, friend to the queen. Affinity: fire

WOLF SPRING

Home of Queen Arsinoe

THE MILONES

Cait Milone
Matriarch of the Milone family. Familiar: Eva, a crow

Ellis Milone
Husband to Cait and father to her children. Familiar: Jake, a white spaniel

Caragh Milone
Elder daughter of Cait, banished to the Black Cottage. Familiar: Juniper, a brown hound

Madrigal Milone
Younger daughter of Cait. Familiar: Aria, a crow

Juillenne 'Jules' Milone
Daughter of Madrigal. The strongest naturalist in decades and friend to the queen. Familiar: Camden, a mountain cat

THE SANDRINS

Matthew Sandrin
Eldest of the Sandrin sons. Former betrothed of Caragh Milone

Joseph Sandrin
Middle Sandrin son. Friend of Arsinoe. Banished to the mainland for five years

OTHERS

Luke Gillespie
Proprietor of Gillespie's Bookshop. Friend of Arsinoe. Familiar: Hank, a black-and-green rooster

William 'Billy' Chatworth Jr.
Foster brother to Joseph Sandrin. Suitor to the queens.

Mrs. Chatworth

Jane

Emilia Vatros, *A warrior from Bastian City*

Mathilde, *An oracle*

THE TEMPLE

High Priestess Luca

Priestess Rho Murtra

Elizabeth, *Initiate and friend to Queen Mirabella*

THE BLACK COUNCIL

Natalia Arron, *poisoner*

Genevieve Arron, *poisoner*

Lucian Arron, *poisoner*

Antonin Arron, *poisoner*

Allegra Arron, *poisoner*

Paola Vend, *poisoner*

Lucian Marlowe, *poisoner*

Margaret Beaulin, *war-gifted*

Renata Hargrove, *giftless*

'You, Midwife, will cull the queen's sisters. And then you will come with us.'

The Midwife lowered her head.

The naturalist queen was left in the forest, for the earth and the animals. The little doomed oracle was drowned in the stream. By the time the elemental queen was placed on the tiny raft, to be pushed out into the water and on to the sea, both she and the Midwife were weeping. Leonine, Isadora, and Roxane. Returned to the Goddess, who had given them Illiann to rule instead.

Illiann, blessed and Blue.

THE VOLROY

Queen Katharine sits for her portrait painting in one of the high, west-facing rooms of the West Tower, just one floor below her own apartments. In her left hand, she holds an empty bottle, which in the painting will become a beautiful poison. Curled around her right is a coil of white rope that the painter's brush will turn into a likeness of Sweetheart.

She turns her head to the window to look out over Indrid Down: dark brown roofs of the north-end row houses and roads disappearing into the hills, the sky dotted with smoke from chimneys and cut through by the tall, finely built stone structures of the central city. It is a calm and beautiful day. Workers work. Families eat and laugh and play. And she woke up that morning in Pietyr's arms. All is well. Better than well, now that her troublesome sisters are dead.

'Please raise your chin, Queen Katharine. And straighten your back.'

She does as she is told, and the painter smiles a little fearfully.

He is the finest master painter in all of Indrid Down, quite used to painting poisoners and the common poisoner props. But this is no mere portrait. This is the Queen Crowned's portrait. And working on it makes even the finest master sweat.

They have set her so the view through the window behind her right shoulder will show Greavesdrake Manor. It was her idea, though the Arrons will take credit for it. She did not do it for them, but for Natalia, a small thing to honor the great head of the family, the woman who raised Katharine as if she were her own daughter. Because of her, Greavesdrake will always be present. A shadow of influence over her reign. She had wanted to set the urn of Natalia's ashes in her lap, but Pietyr had talked her out of it.

'Queen Katharine.' Pietyr strides into the room, looking handsome as always in a black jacket and a dove-gray shirt, his ice-blond hair pushed back from his temples. He pauses behind the painter. 'It is coming along nicely. You will be beautiful.'

'Beautiful.' She adjusts the empty bottle and rope in her hands. 'I feel ridiculous.'

Pietyr claps the painter on the shoulder. 'I need a moment with the queen, if you do not mind. Perhaps a short break?'

'Of course.' He sets down his brush, bows, and leaves, his eyes moving quickly over the bottle and rope, so he will know how to reset them.

'Is it truly good?' Katharine asks after the painter has gone. 'I cannot bring myself to look. Perhaps we should have brought in a master from Rolanth. That city is mine now, too, and you know they have better artists.'

'Not even the best master from Rolanth could be trusted not to sabotage the portrait so soon after a contentious Ascension.' Pietyr follows her to the west-facing window and slides his arms around her waist. 'A poisoner painter is best.' His arms tighten, fingers sliding across her bodice. 'Do you remember those first days at Greavesdrake? It seems so long ago now.'

'Everything seems so long ago,' Katharine murmurs. She remembers her manor bedroom, all the striped silk and soft pillows. How she sat as a child with those pillows pulled into her lap, listening to Natalia tell stories. She remembers the library and the floor-to-ceiling velvet drapes, whose folds she used to hide behind whenever Genevieve was sent to poison her.

'It feels like Natalia is still there, does it not, Pietyr? Like if we looked hard enough we could see her standing with her arms crossed before the window of her study.'

'It does, dearest.' He kisses her temple, her cheek, nibbles her earlobe so a shiver runs through her. 'But you must never speak so to anyone but me. I know you loved her. But you are a queen now. You are *the* queen, and there is no time for childhood longing. Come and look at these.' He leads her to a table and lays out a sheaf of papers for her to sign.

'What are they?'

'Work orders,' he says. 'For the ships we will provide as gifts to King-consort Nicolas's family. Six fine ships to ease their pain.'

'This is more than just ships,' Katharine says. But whatever they give is a small price to pay. The Martels had sent their favored son to become the king-consort of Fennbirn Island, and he had not even lasted a week before being killed in a fall from his horse. A bad fall, thrown down a shallow ravine. It took most of another week to find his body after his horse came back without its rider, and by then, poor Nicolas had been dead a long time.

If only they knew exactly how long. The story of the fall was a lie. A fabrication, worked up by Pietyr and Genevieve, so that none would ever know the truth: that Nicolas had died after consummating his marriage with Katharine. That she is a poisoner in the most literal sense, her whole body toxic to the touch. No one could ever know that. Not even the island, or they would also know that she can bear no mainland-fathered children. That she cannot bear the next triplet queens of Fennbirn.

Whenever she thinks of that, she nearly freezes in fear.

'What are we doing, Pietyr?' Her hand hangs over her half-finished signature. 'What is the point, if at the end of it all, I cannot provide my people with new queens?'

Pietyr sighs. 'Look at this with me, Kat.' He takes her hand, and they return to the portrait. There is not much to it yet. Shapes and impressions. The blackness of her gown. But the painter is gifted, and even at so early a stage, she can imagine what the finished painting will look like. '"Katharine, the fourth poisoner queen," it will be called. Katharine, of the poisoner dynasty. Who follows in the footsteps of the three previous poisoners: Queen Nicola, Queen Sandrine, and Queen Camille. It is who you are, and we have plenty of time to put things in place to ensure the future of the island.'

'My whole long reign.'

'Yes. Thirty, perhaps forty years.'

'Pietyr.' She laughs. 'Queens do not rule that long anymore.' She sighs and cocks her head at her unfinished image. Barely begun and unknown, much like she herself is. Who knows what she might do during her years as queen? Who knows the changes she might make? And Pietyr is right. The people will know what they need to know. Already they do not know that she was thrown down into the Breccia Domain, saved from death by the spirits of the dead sisters who were thrown down similarly when their Ascensions failed. The people do not know that she has no true gift of her own, and what strength she has is borrowed from those same dead queens, who even now race through her blood in a rotten current.

'Sometimes I wonder whose crown this is, Pietyr. Mine,' she whispers, 'or *theirs*. I could not have done it without them.'

'Perhaps. But you do not need them anymore. I thought . . . ,' he says, and clears his throat. 'I thought they might be gone. That they might leave you alone now that they have what they wanted.'

Katharine's stomach flutters. Her hunger for poison and her lust for blood have slackened since her sisters sailed into the mist to drown. So perhaps Pietyr is right. Perhaps the dead queens are finished. Perhaps now they will grow quiet and content.

She finishes signing the orders Pietyr brought and takes up her empty bottle and rope as the painter returns.

He wraps the rope again around her wrist, over and over until he has it just as it was. 'We must work quickly now, before I lose the light.' He lifts her chin with a finger and gently positions her head, daring one moment to look into her eyes.

'How many sets of eyes do you see?' she asks, and he blinks at her uncertainly.

'Only yours, my queen.'

The next morning, Genevieve arrives at the door of Katharine's chamber to escort her to the Black Council.

'Ah, Genevieve,' says Pietyr. 'Come in! Have you had your breakfast? We are just finishing.'

His voice is bright and smug; Genevieve's smile forced and closer to a grimace. But Katharine pretends not to notice. Natalia's murder has left a void that must be filled, and all Arrons will bicker among themselves to fill it. Besides, despite the hatred she still feels for Genevieve, Katharine has determined to judge her anew. She is Natalia's younger sister, after all, and now the Arron matriarch.

'I have already eaten.' Genevieve studies the queen's empty plate: a mess of cheese scraps and bits of boiled egg. Smears of a jam of poison fruit. 'I thought we had decided to limit her poison intake after what happened to the king-consort.'

'It is only a little jam.'

'Two days ago, I saw her shove belladonna berries and scorpions into her mouth faster than she could chew.'

Pietyr glances at Katharine, and she blushes. The dead warriors made her hands itch for blades, and the dead naturalist queens drew her to stroll in the garden. Sometimes the dead poisoners had their cravings.

'Well,' he says, 'limiting her intake may not reverse the condition anyway.'

'But it is worth trying, since we have time. And that is the only thing we do have, is it not?'

Katharine slips away to feed Sweetheart as they argue. The coral snake has molted and grown and has a lovely new enclosure filled with leaves to hide behind and rocks to sun herself on. Katharine reaches into another small cage and scoops out a baby rodent. She loves to watch Sweetheart race across the warm sand of her enclosure after it.

'Is there a particular reason you have come to escort me this morning, Genevieve?'

'There is. High Priestess Luca has returned.'

'So soon?' Pietyr wipes his lips with his napkin and stands. It has been only two weeks since the High Priestess departed for Rolanth to move her household from her quarters in Rolanth Temple to her old ones in Indrid Down. 'Kat, we should go.'

One on each side, Pietyr and Genevieve escort her down the many stairs of the West Tower, down and down until they reach the main floor of the Volroy and the council chamber. The other members have already assembled, chatting quietly over their tea. High Priestess Luca stands apart, drinking nothing and speaking to no one.

'High Priestess Luca,' Katharine greets her. She takes the old woman's hands. 'You have returned.'

'And so quickly,' says Genevieve with a frown.

'My household is traveling slowly behind me by wagon,' Luca replies. 'I have beaten them by a day or two.'

'You should install some of your belongings here in the West Tower.' Katharine smiles. 'It would be good to have another floor in residency. From a distance, it looks very grand; imagine my surprise to discover how many floors are taken up by kitchens and storage.'

She and the High Priestess both refuse to acknowledge the sour looks on the faces of the council, as well as their own discomfort. Katharine cannot say that she likes the old woman, and from the way Luca's eyes follow her, she knows the High Priestess neither likes nor trusts her either. But Natalia struck this bargain. Her last bargain. So Katharine will honor it.

She gestures to the long dark table, and the Black Council takes their seats as servants leave two fresh pots of tea, one poisoned with Natalia's beloved mangrove, and refresh the sugar and lemon bowls. They clear old cups and saucers littered with biscuit crumbs and brighten the lamps before closing the heavy doors. An extra seat has been added for Luca. Pietyr sits in Natalia's old seat, though he has not replaced her as Head.

As Cousin Lucian goes over the day's accounts—tax collections from the merchants for the Queens' Duel were higher than expected, and there is a fear over a lack of crop production in Wolf Spring—Katharine does her best to pay attention. But day-to-day matters on the island are not what is on everyone's mind.

'Oh, how long will you make us wait?' Renata Hargrove exclaims.

'Renata, be calm,' says Genevieve.

'I will not be calm! Natalia promised the temple three council seats. And you know whose seats those are.' She looks at Lucian Marlowe, Paola Vend, and Margaret Beaulin. They are the only other members of the council who are not Arrons. Marlowe and Vend at least are poisoners, but Margaret is war-gifted, and as for poor Renata, she is completely giftless.

'How can you know whose seats they are,' Katharine says mildly, 'when I do not?' She studies Renata from her chair, and Renata shrinks back. It is a good feeling, to be able to command such a reaction. Katharine does not look like much, small as she is from so many years of poisoning. Forever scarred and forever pale. But there is more to her than that. More to her even than the boost of a thousand years of vanquished queens, and the entire island will come to know it.

'However, Renata does have a point.' Katharine turns to Luca and smiles, all teeth. 'You have returned. And you must have given some thought to your choices while you were away.' She had hoped that the High Priestess would not be able to stomach staring into the eyes of the queen who had bested her beloved Mirabella. That Luca would not be able to bow to her and would never return. But she should have known better. Before Mirabella and Arsinoe sailed into the mist, Luca had agreed to preside over Mirabella's execution, after all.

'I have,' says Luca. 'And my choices are myself, the priestess Rho Murtra'—she lifts her chin—'and Bree Westwood.'

The cousins, Lucian and Allegra, make small pained noises. Pietyr scoffs. 'Never.'

Katharine frowns. The only real surprise is Bree Westwood. She had expected that Luca would choose Sara, the head of the elemental family. Not Bree, the flighty girl who played with fire. And of course, Mirabella's best friend.

'The High Priestess cannot serve on the Black Council,' Genevieve spits.

'It is uncommon, but in the old times, it was not unheard of.'

'The temple is meant to be neutral!'

'Neutral to the queens. Not to the affairs of the island.' Luca's gaze slides over Genevieve dismissively, and Genevieve's lip quivers with rage.

'So,' the High Priestess goes on. 'Queen Katharine. These are my choices. Who are yours, to be replaced?'

Katharine looks at the faces of her council. But they are not really her council. They are Natalia's. A few are even Queen Camille's. She feels the hostility coming off them, and beneath her skin, the dead queens prickle.

The Arrons expect that she will remove three of the others;

the others would say that she ought to keep them, to better represent all interests. Even the giftless. Genevieve would tell her to throw the High Priestess's selections back in her face. And no doubt they all think that she should replace Pietyr. She has seen the way they look at him, how their eyes narrow whenever he touches her.

But they can think what they like. Her Black Council will be hers alone.

'Lucian Marlowe and Margaret Beaulin, you are released. You have both been faithful servants of the crown, but Lucian, we have no shortage of poisoners here. And Margaret, I am sure you can understand my feelings about the war gift, given what happened to me at the hands of Juillenne Milone. Besides, there will be a war-gifted priestess on our council now, to look after the interests of Bastian City.'

Margaret stands and shoves her chair back from the table. She does not use her hands, but the movement is too quick for Katharine to tell whether she used her mind to push or her heel.

'A priestess has no gift,' she growls. 'Rho Murtra's voice will be for the temple and the temple alone.'

'Indeed,' says Lucian Marlowe. 'Do you mean to have an entire council of only Arrons and priestesses?'

'No,' Katharine replies, her tone clipped. 'Renata and Paola Vend will stay. Allegra Arron will yield the last place.'

Allegra opens her mouth. She looks at her brother, Lucian Arron, but he will not look at her, so finally she rises and bows her head, so low that Katharine can see the whole of the ice-blond bun piled high atop it. She looks so much like Natalia. And it is for that reason as much as anything else that Allegra is leaving.

'Will you stay on,' Katharine asks them, 'until my new council members arrive?'

Lucian Marlowe and Allegra nod. But Margaret slams her fist against the table.

'Do you want me to shine my chair for the priestess as well? Give her a tour of the Volroy? This is not the way to rule. Allowing the temple to invade the council space. Keeping your boy by your side as though it is his advice that you're interested in!'

Katharine reaches into her boot.

'Guards!' Genevieve calls. But Katharine leaps to her feet and throws one of her poisoned knives hard toward Margaret, so hard that it sinks into the tabletop.

'I need no guards,' she says softly, sliding another knife between her fingers.

'The first was a warning, Margaret. The next will go into your heart.'

BASTIAN CITY

Jules Milone places her hands on the stones of the city wall. Beneath her palms, the mortar is rough, warmed by the sun but cooling now in the early hours of twilight. Before her lie the sea and the beach, cast in gray by the stretching shadow. The sound of the waves and the smell of the salt air are a little like home, but nothing else is. The wind in Bastian is less wild, and the beach is not dark sand and flat black rock for the seals to lie on, but pale, fading into a beach of small red and white wave-polished stones. It is pretty. But it is not Wolf Spring.

Camden, her cougar familiar, rubs along the back of her, hard enough to press her to the wall, and Jules winds her fingers deep into the big cat's soft, golden coat.

Their companion on this walk is Emilia Vatros, the eldest daughter of the Vatros clan, warriors who have led Bastian City for as long as anyone can remember. Emilia looks at Camden and frowns. She would have rathered the cat stay behind, in hiding. But Jules is a naturalist, gifted to make fruit ripen and fish swim into her net. And she does not like to go anywhere without her cougar.

Camden hops up and places her good front paw atop the stones, to look out at the waves like Jules is. Jules moves quickly to drag her back down, careful to avoid the cat's bad shoulder, injured the past winter by an attacking bear.

'It is all right,' Emilia says. 'No one is here, and with the sun at her back, anyone looking will mistake her for a big dog.'

Camden cocks her head as though to say, *Big dog, my eye*, and swats at Emilia half-heartedly when the warrior girl leaps up onto the wall's edge. Jules gasps. The wall is high, and the ditch below full of unfriendly rocks.

'Don't do that,' Jules says. 'Do what?'

'Just jump up there like that. You're making me nervous.'

Emilia raises her eyebrows and hops from stone to stone. She spins on one foot.

'Be as nervous as you like. I've been running these walls since I was nine. The war gift gives balance. You could do it as well as I. Perhaps even better. Faster.' She smirks at Jules's doubtful face. 'Or perhaps you could had your naturalist mother not bound your war gift with low magic.'

Emilia spins away, miming sword slashes and dagger strikes with imaginary weapons. She has the grace of a bird. Of a cat.

Maybe Jules could do what Emilia does. She is legion cursed, after all. Cursed with two gifts: naturalist and war.

'Had Madrigal not bound the curse, I'd have been driven

insane and been drowned a long time ago.'

'Yet you can use your war gift now. It is weakened, but it is there. So maybe you would have been fine all along.' Emilia spins again and thrusts an imaginary sword at Jules's throat. 'Maybe the madness of the legion curse is nothing but a lie spread by the temple.'

'Why would they lie?'

'To keep anyone from being as powerful as you could be.'

Jules narrows her eyes, and Emilia shrugs.

'I see you think it is not worth the risk.' She shrugs again. 'Fine. You have the war gift, however muted, so I will hide you however long. Until you no longer want to hide.'

On tiptoe now, Emilia jumps to another stone. But the stone she lands on is loose, and she wobbles precariously.

'Emilia!'

Emilia grins and lowers her arms.

'I knew it was loose,' she says, and chuckles when Jules scowls. 'I know every step of this wall. Every crack in the mortar. Every creak in the gates. And I hate it.'

'Why do you hate it?' Jules looks back at Bastian City, the light and shadow slatted across it by the setting sun. To her it is a marvel, fortified and ordered, built-up buildings of gray brick and timber. The marketplace with stalls covered over in red cloth, the shades as differed as the offered goods as the dye fades with age.

'I love Bastian,' says Emilia. She jumps down. 'I hate the wall. We keep it up now because of the gift, because to be ever

24

prepared is our way. But a wall isn't needed when we have the mist. So it just seals us off.' She clenches a fist and pounds the stone. 'Until we forget the rest of the island. The wall makes the people turn their backs, lazy and safe, and who cares if the gift grows weak? Who cares that another poisoner wears the crown?' She watches Jules run her fingers along the mortar lines. 'I suppose there are no walls at all in Wolf Spring.'

'Not like these.' Only fences made of wood or pretty, piled rocks to mark the borders between farms. Easily jumped by a horse, or by a person with enough of a running start. 'When we rode into Indrid Down to save Mirabella from Katharine in the duel, we passed what was left of the wall that once enclosed the capital. It was overgrown with grasses and weeds. Half-buried. There's nothing else on the island like this. Not even the ramparts that protect the Volroy fortress.'

'I have heard they still have a fine border wall in Sunpool.' Emilia sighs. 'Oracles. They are a paranoid lot. Are you going to do what you came out here to do or what?'

'Can we go down to the beach?'

'Not today. I did not send scouts. There could be others down there in the dunes. Others to recognize you and your cat and send word back to the Volroy. The longer the poisoner queen thinks you left on that boat with her sisters, the better.'

'The longer the better.' Jules takes the pair of silver shears from her back pocket. 'How about forever?'

'Nothing lasts forever. Why do you want to go down to the beach?'

Jules pulls her long brown braid over her shoulder.

'I don't know. To cast it out into the water, I guess.'

Emilia laughs.

'Are all naturalists so sentimental?' She gestures toward the shore full of red and white stones. 'Throw it anywhere. The terns will tear strands of it to line their nests. That should please you. Though you don't have to do it at all. That braid is the last thing that will give you away. More likely are those two-colored eyes of yours.' She nods at Camden. 'Or that.'

'I'm never going to put Camden aside, so you can stop hinting about it,' Jules snaps.

'I'm not hinting about anything. I like her. Only a war-gifted naturalist would have a familiar so fierce. Now get on with it.'

Jules touches the end of her braid. She wonders how long Emilia's dark hair is. She always wears it pinned to her nape in two small rolled buns.

She sets the braid between the open blades of the shears, just below her chin. Arsinoe used to do this. Every season, she would hack off what had grown, anything to avoid the sleek, groomed beauty expected of the queens. One year she left it cut so crooked that it looked like her head was perpetually cocked. Her Arsinoe. She would be so proud.

Jules takes a deep breath and then cuts off her braid. She throws it out as far as she can, out toward the water her friend sailed away on.

* * *

The family house of the Vatros clan is tucked into the southeast quadrant of the city, along the wall. It is a large house, with many floors and rows of brown-shuttered windows. The shingles of the pitched roofs are deep red. And it is old, some parts older than others and made of the same gray stone as the wall. The newer additions have been constructed in white. It is one of the finest houses in Bastian City, but all houses seem quite fine to Jules, who is used to clapboard and paint faded by damp, salty breezes. The war gift may have diminished over the centuries, but they have done what they can to not let it show; it is only visible upon much closer inspection, in the patched masonry in the walls and the stitches over stitches in their clothing.

'Attack at half speed.'

Emilia turns the sparring stick over in her hands. It is a clever weapon: sturdy, oiled wood joined in the center as a long pole and able to be twisted apart quickly into two shorter staffs for dual striking.

Jules does as she is told, though her own sparring stick feels heavy and clumsy. She sweeps low for the legs twice, then blocks Emilia's attacks and dodges an attempt to pop her in the chest. Emilia nods, the only encouragement she ever gives.

'You never ask me to use my war gift,' Jules says. 'You never tell me when to use it.'

'You'll use it when you use it.' Emilia twists her pole into separate staffs. 'And you will know when.' She comes forward, still at half speed, but even so, Jules's arms cannot keep up. The poles crack against each other.

'Though it would come easier if we could get your mother to lift the binding.'

Jules lowers her staff. She flexes her fingers and tucks her hair behind her ear. When she cut it, she cut too short, and now it escapes from its ribbon. She does not like it. Camden does not either. The mountain cat licks it every night when they go to sleep as if she is trying to slick it back into a braid.

'Stop asking that,' Jules growls.

'I am only teasing.'

Except that she is not. At least not entirely. Jules rubs the ache in her poison-damaged legs. Bound gift or no, she might never be the warrior Emilia hopes she will be, thanks to that.

'Come on,' Emilia says. 'We don't have all day.'

They square off again. They do not have all day, but they have most of it; the afternoon sun burns bright and hot against the top of Jules's head. Emilia's dark hair shines like a mirror, and knowing how skilled Emilia is at combat she will probably figure out how to blind Jules with it.

As they circle, Jules's eye wanders to the tree. One lone tree in the private, walled-in courtyard of uneven bricks, not as full as it could be, as it *should* be, in the height of summer. She could make that happen. Make it bloom with leaves that instant. They would have shade, and Emilia might be distracted enough that Jules could land a decent hit.

'I never ask you to use your war gift,' Emilia says, and Jules looks away from the tree. 'But you never use your naturalist gift either. Why? Do you think the other gifts offend us?'

She strikes twice, and Jules blocks them.

'Maybe not.'

'Maybe not,' Emilia repeats. 'Maybe not normally, you mean. But in you it would, with your legion curse.' She moves in quick and effortlessly smacks Jules right between the eyes. Behind her, Camden begins to growl.

'Can you blame me?' Jules scowls. 'My own family feared the curse. My own town turned their backs on me for it. I still don't understand why you—and the warriors—don't.'

'We look past it because of what you have done. The great things that you will do. It was you who boosted the weak queen. Arsinoe,' Emilia adds when Jules's eyes narrow. 'And even bound, your war gift is as strong as mine. You could use it now. Push my staffs off course, if you wanted to. If you would.'

Something sharpens in Emilia's eyes, and she comes for Jules in a flurry. No longer fighting at half speed or half strength, she drives Jules back, using her advantage in skill to push Jules until her knees bend. And as her heel slides in against the gravel path, Jules feels a spark of familiar temper.

She dodges and pivots as Emilia keeps coming on. Jules waits until she is positioned just right. Until Emilia has allowed herself to put Camden in a blind spot.

Jules strikes out hard with her staff and Camden leaps. She had been crouched, waiting, to knock Emilia down and pin her to the grass.

'Oof!' Emilia says, and rolls faceup as Jules and the cougar look at her. For a moment, her jaw clenches and her face reddens even beneath her deep tan skin. Then she laughs. 'All right.' She grasps Camden fondly by the fur and pats her ribs. 'No need of a war gift when you have her.'

Emilia tosses Jules a light red cloak, like the ones the servants wear.

'Where are we going?' Jules asks. After a long afternoon of training, she is in no mood to go anywhere; she craves a hot bowl of stew and the softness of her pillow.

'There is a bard staying at the inn. Father told me she knows the song of Queen Aethiel, and I would hear it.'

'Can't you go without us? I'm likely to fall asleep in my ale, and I don't want to insult the bard.'

'No,' Emilia replies, 'I can't go without you. Camden will have to stay here, of course. Too many people not in our trust. We'll bring her back a nice fat leg of lamb.'

Camden lifts her head from her paws but only long enough to yawn. A leg of lamb and a quiet room suit her just fine.

As Jules walks beside Emilia through the city, she pulls the hood of the cloak down to shadow her eyes. Nearly everyone they pass acknowledges Emilia somehow, with a nod or a lowered gaze. The whole city knows the oldest daughter of Vatros by the jut of her chin and the bounce in her stride. They revere her, almost like the people of Wolf Spring used to revere Jules before they knew about the curse. Now if she were to return, they would march her to Indrid Down with her hands tied behind her back.

When they arrive at the inn, there is already a crowd and the bard has already started. Emilia frowns slightly, but the long spoken songs are known to go far into the night, with listeners coming and going as they hear their favorite parts.

'This isn't even the song of Aethiel,' Emilia says. 'It is the arming verse for the song of Queen Philomene. And it goes on *forever*. I'll get us some ale and food.'

Jules lets the hood slip back in the heat of the inn. No one is paying attention to her anyway. All eyes are on the bard, standing near the fireplace in a lovely tunic edged in gold thread. She is one of the youngest bards that Jules has seen, though she has not seen many. So few pass through Wolf Spring, tired perhaps of night after night of the song of Queen Bernadine and her wolf. This bard wears a light hood, not unlike the red one that Jules wears, and her voice is melodious even as she recites the arming passages: greaves and knives and leather to be buckled, on and on, dressing the long-dead war queen in her battle finery.

Jules finds an empty table along the rear wall and sits. By the time Emilia returns with two mugs, the bard has moved on to tell of the fierceness of the queen's army.

'What is there to eat?' Jules asks.

'A leg of lamb, like I told you. And boiled greens. We will eat what we can and bring the rest back to the cat.' Emilia's eyes dart around the inn and back to the bard. 'She will never get to Aethiel at this rate. Perhaps we can bring her to the table when she stops for food and get a few lines then.'

'Or you can wait. She'll be here for as many nights as people have coin to pay her. Besides, I don't want her so close. Bards travel all over the island. She could recognize me.'

'Even if she did, she would not say anything. For a people who speak so much, bards have very tight tongues.'

'How do you know?'

Emilia raises her eyebrows.

'Well, I've never had to cut one out, for a start.'

The food arrives, a great platter of it, a whole roasted lamb leg on a bed of greens and roasted potatoes besides.

'Thanks, Benji,' Emilia says to the server, a yellow-haired lad who will run the inn one day.

'An entire leg for two,' Benji remarks. 'I wouldn't think such a small thing would have such a large appetite.'

Jules looks up and finds him smiling at her. She lowers her eyes quickly.

'Nothing small about my stomach,' she says.

'Well, I hope you enjoy. I'll bring another jug of ale.'

'He is curious about you,' says Emilia.

Jules does not respond. She is bad company, pretending to listen to the bard and speaking only when she must. She supposes that she has been bad company since she came to Bastian City. But it is hard not to be, when every dish of food makes her think of Arsinoe and her famous appetite, and every boy with a crooked smile could be Joseph, for just one instant before she remembers that he is dead.

She forces herself to look back toward the bard and finds her staring directly at her, eyes fixed as her lips move over the words of the raid on the burned city. Jules stares right back, angry, though she cannot say why, and the woman turns her head just slightly so Jules can see the stark white streak running through her hair. The white strands have been gathered together into a braid that falls through the gold like an icicle.

Such white streaks are common marks amongst the seers.

'That is no mere bard,' Jules whispers. 'Emilia, what are you up to?'

Emilia does not deny it. She does not even look guilty.

'The warriors and the oracles have always had a strong bond. It is how we knew to come to your aid during the Queens' Duel. And now we would know what the Goddess has in store for you. What? Did you think we would just hide you here forever, like a prisoner?'

Jules watches as the bard bows to the crowd, taking a break for a meal and some wine. 'You said I was welcome for as long as was needed,' she mutters.

The bard stops before their table.

'Emilia Vatros. It is good to see you.'

'And you, Mathilde. Please, sit. Take some ale with us and food. There's plenty, as you can see.'

'You even know each other,' Jules says as Mathilde takes a seat. She is striking, up close. Not more than twenty years old perhaps, and the braid of white stands out so starkly against her bright blond waves that it is a wonder Jules did not notice it right off.

Emilia takes her knife from her belt and carves a thick slice of meat from the leg, piling it onto a plate along with the greens and potatoes. Benji arrives with a fresh jug of ale and a third cup.

'I would take some wine, also,' Mathilde says, and he nods before going to fetch it. 'It is an honor to meet you, Juillenne Milone.'

'Is it?' Jules asks suspiciously.

'Yes. But why are you looking at me like you hate me? We have not yet spoken.'

'I don't trust many these days. It's been a bad year.' She looks at Emilia. 'And she's saying my name awfully loud.'

Emilia and Mathilde share a pacifying look. If only Camden were there to swat both of their faces.

'I am aware of the need for discretion,' Mathilde says. 'Just as I am aware that your dislike of oracles stems from the prophecy surrounding your birth. That you were legion cursed. But that has turned out to be true, hasn't it?'

'That I was cursed, yes. Though I've heard that the oracle also said that I should be drowned. *That* is not true.'

Mathilde raises her eyebrows and tilts her head as if to say, *Maybe not*. Or just not yet. 'And is that all that you have heard?'

'What else is there?'

'We never knew the specifics of the portent. We see through another seer's eyes only that murky curse.'

'You never knew her, then?' Emilia asks. 'The oracle who

threw the bones when Jules was born?'

'I was still a child when Jules was born. If I knew her in Sunpool, I do not remember. And nor would many, anymore. For that oracle never returned.'

'What is that supposed to mean?' Jules snaps.

'That your family covered the truth of you well.'

That they killed the oracle is what Mathilde means. But seer or not, she does not know for sure. It is only conjecture. Accusation. And Jules will not imagine Grandma Cait or Ellis or even Madrigal putting a rock to an old oracle's head.

'And what is the truth of me now? Isn't that what you're here to tell us?'

Mathilde tears a sliver of meat off her plate. The lamb is succulent; there is no need for cutting. Even so, she takes forever to chew. Waiting, Jules vows that she will not believe a word out of the seer's mouth. And at the same time, she hopes to hear some other vision, some news about Arsinoe and Billy and how they fare on the mainland. Is Arsinoe happy there? Is she safe? Did they give Joseph a fine funeral? It seems an age since she left them that day, bobbing before the mainland. That day that the mist of Fennbirn swallowed her up again and brought her and Camden home.

She would even settle for news about Mirabella.

'The truth of you is yet to come,' Mathilde says finally. 'I know only that you were once a queen and may be again. Those words came into my head like a chant the moment that I looked at you.'

THE MAINLAND

At the sound of the bell, the horses take off from the starting line, hooves and tails flying. Arsinoe grips the rail in front of her seat and pulls herself nearly up and over it to watch as they thunder past, every horse shining and beautiful, and each with a tiny man clinging onto its back for dear life.

'There they go!' she shouts. 'They're rounding the . . . that turn that you said. . . .'

'The clubhouse turn.' Billy grasps her by the back of her dress, laughing. 'Now get down from there before you fall into the next row.'

With a sigh, she puts her feet back on solid ground. But she is not the only one out of her seat; plenty of others have stood to clap or hold clever little magnifying glasses up to their eyes. Even Mirabella has risen on the other side of Billy, crowding so close in her excitement that he can hardly breathe between the two sisters.

'Fun as this is,' Arsinoe says, 'it would be even more fun to be down there beside the track.' She takes a deep breath, smells roasted nuts, and her stomach growls.

'The view might not be as good,' says Mirabella, and Billy nods. His father paid good money every year for these fine seats, or so Billy had told them on the way to the track.

'How about from the back of a horse, then?'

'They don't allow girls to ride,' Billy says, and Arsinoe frowns. They would change their minds soon enough if only they could see Jules. Small, wiry Jules, who could weave her horse in and out of a herd as though the two were of one body.

On the racetrack, the horses cross the finish line to a chorus of mixed cheers and groans. The last race of the day, and none of the horses they had bet upon had won, but the three of them stand up, smiling. Arsinoe takes Billy's hand in her left, and pulls Mirabella along with her right as they make their way down from their seats, her ill-fitting gray dress riding up over the legs of the trousers she insists on always wearing underneath. By contrast, Mirabella looks lovely in white, full sleeves and lace to her throat. Before they left the island, neither had worn any color besides black, and Mirabella, a few colored jewels. But Mirabella, with her beauty, manages to look at home in anything.

Arsinoe takes a deep breath. It is pleasant to be out, even if the warm summer air smells like city instead of the sea. Sometimes Billy's family's brick row house—fine though it may be—can feel so stifling. As they turn down the avenue in the midst of the crowds, she bumps a shoulder into a passerby. Before she can apologize, he recoils at the sight of her scars, still bright pink and running down the right side of her face. Billy makes a fist, and Mirabella opens her mouth, but Arsinoe pulls them back.

'Never mind it. Let's just go.' They do but closer to her and just ahead, their shoulders protecting her shoulders, their scowls a barrier against anyone who might slight her. 'Good Goddess,' she says, and laughs. 'You lot are as bad as Jules.'

They walk on, navigating the crowds and watching the cabs and carriages pass. It is busier even than Indrid Down High Street, and never seems to slow. A cab dashes by, pulled by a poor bony horse, his back a wreck of whiplashes.

'Oi, go easy on him, will you!' Arsinoe shouts, but the cabbie only sneers.

'If only I had the fullness of my lightning,' Mirabella adds. 'Or my fire. I would start a cozy flame in the pocket of his pants.' But she does not. Away from the island, their gifts weaken and fade. Even if Arsinoe were a true naturalist instead of a poisoner, she may not have had enough left to comfort the horse anyway.

Billy shakes his head. 'Don't try to tell me that no one mistreated their horses on Fennbirn.' But his eyes lose focus as he tries to remember an example. Even in the capital, respect for the naturalist gift kept the worst of abuses in check.

Arsinoe curses when someone runs into her from behind. She does not know if she will ever get used to the crowds. And somehow, she is always the one jostled. Something in Mirabella is still regal, and no one comes within a foot.

'Oh no,' says Billy. They have reached the end of their street, the row of grand, red-brick houses with wrought iron gates and front steps of bright white stone. But clustered around their doorway is a gaggle of young ladies in dresses of pink and green and pale yellow. It can only be Christine Hollen, the governor's daughter, and her ever-present troupe of society friends.

Arsinoe looks up to the window of the third-floor room she shares with Mirabella. With four stories' worth of rooms in the town house, they had not really needed to share. But when she and Mirabella had arrived on the mainland, legs shaking and clothes still soaked from the storm, they had clung to each other's elbows and refused to let go. So Billy's mother, Mrs. Chatworth, had directed them, lips trembling, to one of the larger guest rooms.

'I don't know if I have the stomach for this today,' Arsinoe mutters. Christine Hollen had apparently 'set her cap' at Billy during the time he was away on the island, and no amount of Arsinoe's presence seemed able to deter her. If Arsinoe had to endure one more tea watching Christine paw and fawn over Billy, she was likely to behave in a way that Mrs. Chatworth would deem unladylike. Or even more unladylike than usual.

'There's no way we can scale the bricks and sneak in through our window?'

'Not without being seen,' Mirabella says with a smirk. She touches Arsinoe's shoulder. 'You go. Take off awhile until they have gone.'

'What?'

'Yes, what?' Billy asks. 'I've no desire to be left alone in there with my mother and Christine. If you go, Arsinoe, you might return to find me gagged and engaged.'

'Go,' Mirabella says again. 'Maybe . . . maybe you should visit Joseph.'

'Do you mean it?' Arsinoe asks.

'Of course I do. Why ruin a perfectly lovely day?'

'What about Miss Hollen and the governor's girls?'

Mirabella steps closer to Billy and slips her hand into the crook of his arm. Just that simple movement and change of posture: a subtle shift in her hips, a slight incline of her head, and anyone watching would think that she and Billy were madly in love. Well, were it not for the shocked look on Billy's face.

'You leave Christine Hollen to me.'

Arsinoe glances at the girls up the street. All are girls Mrs. Chatworth will gladly welcome into her home and would gladly marry her son to. Girls who are nothing like the strange, foreign ones she took in. They dress in proper skirts and do not have deep scars on their faces. Christine Hollen, in particular, is one of the prettiest people Arsinoe has ever seen. Golden hair and peach cheeks, a smile that dazzles. That she is also quite rich seems just plain unfair.

Arsinoe smiles at Mirabella gratefully. 'Poor Christine doesn't stand a chance.'

Arsinoe takes off through the city, skirting the row houses by way of alleys and side streets. She is relieved to not face another strained meeting with Christine, who looks at her as if she is some kind of a bug when she bothers to acknowledge her at all, but the farther away she gets, the more her relief is replaced by resentment. In the gray sack of a dress, with no friends or family save Billy and Mirabella, no fortune or prospects of her own, she is no match for Christine Hollen. She would be if things were different. If she were still herself in her black trousers and vest, a fierce black and red-slashed mask over the scars on her face. If she were still a queen.

Her legs hasten as she makes her way through the streets, heading for Joseph, ignoring the stares from people she passes by. Stares she attracts merely by running, by being a girl out on her own without the benefit of an escort or a parasol.

She should not have gone off alone. She should have stayed and choked down her tea. It is only when she is alone that the doubt creeps in, that feeling that she does not belong here and never will.

When they first arrived, both she and Mirabella had tried to charm Mrs. Chatworth. Arsinoe especially, had been prepared to like her or even love her. She was Billy's mother, after all. She had raised a boy who would stand by his friends. So when they met, she expected to find someone like Cait Milone: with a stern face and a stout heart, and strong arms for holding her children. Or even someone like Ellis: never serious but always ready with advice. Instead, Billy's mother was worse even than his father in some ways. She lacked substance, and her facial expressions vacillated between irritated and horrified.

By the time she reaches the cemetery gates, Arsinoe's legs burn from exertion, but her frustration has not been spent. She slows to a walk, respectful of those at rest, yet cannot help kicking feebly at pebbles on the path.

'Parasols,' she mutters. 'Frilly dresses and silly games. That is all there is for a girl to do here. Drink tea and twirl a parasol until she gets married.' And to be married on the mainland means to obey. If there is one word in the world sure to get Arsinoe's hackles up, it is that one.

Thank the Goddess, Billy does not want that. Her Billy, who only wants her to be what she is and for her and Mirabella to be happy. Which she is, most days. It is only when she is alone that she remembers that she is not one of them. Not even Mirabella will be accepted as one of them, and Mirabella follows all their rules.

Arsinoe pauses and takes a breath. The cemetery where Joseph is buried is set out on the edges of the city and surrounded by stone walls. It is quiet and sunlit, marked by gentle hills and groves of trees, and overlooks the deep blue water of the bay. It is a place Jules would have liked. Arsinoe likes it, too, for it is always nearly empty.

She follows the path through the northern entrance and past the loose bricks near the Richmond Family markers, then cuts through the grass toward the grove of elm trees. Their shade just reaches Joseph, where he rests near the top of the hill. Before she gets there, she slips into the shadow of the largest tree and strips off her gray sack of a dress. Then she shakes out her rough-cut hair and smooths her shirt—an old one that Billy grew out of—before she clears her throat and says:

'Hallo, Joseph.'

Hallo, Arsinoe, says the Joseph in her mind, and for a moment, her eyes blur. His grave marker is simple. Unadorned. No ornate carvings of ivy. No marble sculptures. It is not a fancy mausoleum with stained glass windows and its own private gate. It is a patch of grass and a dark, rounded stone. She blinks hard and runs her fingers along the inscription.

Here lies
Joseph Sandrin
Beloved of Jules
Brother to Billy
A friend to queens and cougars

It is what she told them to write. It does not matter that no one on the mainland will understand what it means, that in years to come, visitors to the cemetery might puzzle over it and think it a joke. The engraving took some time, and when they buried him, the grave had to go unmarked except for a white piece of wood. When the stone was ready, they returned and mourned all over again.

On the island, he would have been burned on a pyre and his ashes spread in Sealhead Cove. They would have stood together on the deck of the *Whistler* while the people of Wolf Spring threw petals and grain from the docks. Instead, he is here, under the dirt and far from home. But Arsinoe is glad of that now. At least buried, there is a place that she can come and talk to him.

'We went to the races today. We didn't win.' She lowers herself to the ground and balls up her gray dress for something to lie upon. 'And then I had to run away when Christine Hollen was at our door. Not that I wouldn't have come to see you anyway. Christine Hollen. The governor's daughter. Did you know her?' Arsinoe turns her head.

'I'm sure you knew her. She probably fancied you to begin with, didn't she? Probably fainted dead away at the sight of you; it doesn't take much. But you weren't from here, and you weren't staying. And Billy's rich and'—she clears her throat—'not *bad* to look at.'

In her mind, she hears Joseph's laughter. And then a low rumble of thunder as clouds begin to roll from over the sea.

'It's going to rain. I wonder if that means Mirabella's upset about something. She swears that her gift has all but left her, but I've seen her close her eyes, and then felt the coolness of a breeze. And then there's the fact that her melancholy days always seem to wind up overcast.' She snorts. 'A gift like hers is too strong to be stifled. Even by the mainland.'

She looks up at the sky. She has nothing but time now. Time to wait for Billy to make a life for them, and the thought of his needing to do that sends her stomach into knots. Who is she here? Not Queen Arsinoe, raised as a naturalist and discovered to be a poisoner. Now she is nothing. A rogue queen with no crown.

She turns toward Joseph's marker. 'Christine is much prettier than me.'

Lots of girls are much prettier than you, Joseph replies in her mind. *But none of them are you.*

Arsinoe smiles. So he would say if he were here. If he could put an arm about her shoulders and squeeze. If he were not in a box, in the ground.

'I miss you, Joseph,' she says, her head resting on the ball of her dress. 'I miss you so much.' And then she falls asleep.

Who knows how long later, Arsinoe wakes with a start. Her arms fly out to her sides, certain for a moment that she will find not ground at all but the water of a bay.

'What a strange dream.' She was a girl, dressed as a boy, on a boat. It had been vivid, as vivid as being there, but as she lies still and tries to remember, it comes apart, driven back by the fading orange light and a soreness in her back from sleeping on the grass. She pushes up onto her elbow with a groan and looks toward Joseph's grave marker.

There is a woman in a long black dress standing behind it.

She scrambles up onto her knee and rubs her eyes, thinking she is still dreaming. But the vision does not waver. The woman in black is darker than a shadow. Arsinoe cannot see her face or the details of her clothing. Only her shape, and her long black hair.

'Who are you?'

The figure raises her skeletal arm and stretches one long finger to point.

Arsinoe turns and looks over the hilltop, toward the harbor. Nothing there but ships in the evening. At least, nothing in that direction that any mainlander would know about.

'No,' Arsinoe says, and the woman's sharp finger extends farther.

'No!' She squeezes her eyes shut. When she opens them, the woman is gone. If indeed she was ever really there.

THE VOLROY

'It was never going to be an amicable meeting,' Pietyr says, seated upon Katharine's sofa. 'No one likes to have power wrested from them. And Luca's choices were . . . unexpected.'

'Unexpected!' Genevieve scoffs as she storms back and forth with her arms crossed. 'They were intentionally antagonizing.'

Katharine sighs. Pietyr has poured her a cup of tea and even added a splash of oleander milk, but she does not want it. She has been listening to him argue with Genevieve since they returned to her rooms after the meeting of the Black Council.

'Intentional or not,' says Pietyr, 'you squawked like an upset bird. Is that how Natalia would have reacted? You have none of your sister's composure, Genevieve. Absolutely none of it.'

Genevieve spins. 'How dare you speak so to me. I am her sister. Her sister, not some errant nephew. And I am the head of the family now. Not your father.'

'I never said it would be my father.'

'Oh, enough of this.' Katharine rises with a huff and goes to the window to throw open the shutters and let in the warm summer air. She breathes it in and looks down. All that sea and sky. The treetops and bright green spaces. All the good people. All hers. 'Can you not see the beauty of these days? The gold in the sunlight? The crown etched into my head?' She turns to them, her smile wide. 'We won! You are too entrenched in the chaos of the Ascension still to see it, but we won. And my reign will not be a time of bitterness and contention.' She steps toward them with her hands out. Pietyr scrunches his brow; Genevieve goes pale as if unsure Katharine is not about to fling a knife at her head.

'It will be a reign of ease and prosperity.' She takes Genevieve's hand, lightly, so she will not flinch. 'And new beginnings.'

'Are you so ready to forget the past?' Genevieve asks.

'I am ready to set old grudges aside. And so should you. I will need the two of you in harmony now to make sure Bree Westwood does not get into any trouble.'

Pietyr stands and straightens his cuffs. He considers shaking Genevieve's hand but at the last moment changes his mind, and they settle on a curt nod.

'The queen is to be commended for her optimism,' he says. 'I hope she is right.'

'I hope so, too,' says Genevieve.

'You will see.' Katharine rises on tiptoe to kiss Pietyr fully on the mouth, her mood lifting along with her words, as though that, too, can be changed by sheer will. 'To set the tone, we will hold a welcome banquet in the square. A warm gesture for the High Priestess and the Westwoods. To signal to the people that the crown is settled.'

Pietyr cocks an eyebrow. 'If Luca and the others will agree to it.'

'Of course they will agree to it,' Katharine says, and laughs. 'I am the queen.'

Katharine invites High Priestess Luca on a tour of the capital, to reacquaint her with it after being so long away. It could be taken as a jibe, she supposes. The out-of-touch High Priestess, with her heart still in Rolanth. But she does not mean it like that.

When she arrives at Indrid Down Temple on her fine black stallion, she and her queensguard find Luca already mounted and waiting beside three priestesses. Katharine's eyes linger on the slivers of exposed blade at each priestess's waist.

'Is it the practice now that all priestesses be armed?'

'Not all,' Luca replies. 'But certainly those who are escorting the High Priestess and the Queen Crowned. Rho insisted.'

'Did she?' Katharine swallows. War-gifted Rho. Somehow Katharine knows that, had the plan to cut off her arms and head after the Quickening come to pass, it would have been Rho doing most of the carving.

And now she serves on the Black Council.

Katharine looks away from the knives and back at Luca.

'You look very well on horseback, High Priestess.'

Luca nods, and her horse dances in place as though it understands. 'They tried to put me on a white mule.' She snorts. 'But I am not that old yet.' Instead of a mule, her mount is a large white stallion. Now Katharine will have to keep their horses at a distance so their stallions will not fight, which is perhaps precisely what Luca intended.

'How are you finding Indrid Down?' Katharine asks as they ride, making their way through High Street past her favorite cheese shop and Genevieve's favorite dressmaker.

'Hotter than I remember,' says Luca. 'And once winter comes, I am sure I will find it colder than I remember.'

'But not more draughty than Rolanth, surely, with its open-air temple and cliffside breezes?' How many times had Natalia hoped through gritted teeth for the damp and draughts to finally kill off old Luca?

'Not as draughty.' Luca cocks her head. 'Nor as light. Nor as lovely. The capital craves brightness and beauty. It is a good thing I appointed Bree to the council. For she is both of those things.'

They skirt the Dowling marketplace, which they are unable to enter with their horses, and Katharine points out stalls of particular quality as Luca smiles and waves to the people. They are thrilled that the High Priestess is back in the capital where she belongs. Those closest reach out to touch the edges of her robes and ask for blessings. Katharine, they ask for nothing. To her they only bow.

'They fear you,' Luca mutters.

'Of course they do. But they will love me, too. Natalia always said the island loves a bloody Ascension. I was the only one who tried to give them that.'

They stop at the bluff where the street rises before gradually sloping to the harbor, and the party members lean on their pommels, admiring the view of the sea in the afternoon light. Far to the north, around the curve of the harbor, the early, wooden skeletons of ships rise on the dry land. They are the ships that Pietyr and the council ordered built for the Martels as payment for Nicolas's death, and Katharine does not mention them.

'I would like to hold a welcome banquet in your honor.' Katharine turns in the saddle as Luca raises her eyebrows. 'To welcome you, and Bree Westwood, and Rho Murtra to the city. So the people might see their new Black Council together as one. We will hold it in the square.'

'How very kind.' Luca looks away again, toward the port. 'Bree will love that. She is always danced off her feet at parties.'

'High Priestess,' one of their escorts says. 'Look. The mist.'

They follow the priestess's pointing arm, out over the water.

It is the mist, rising above the surface. It is not much, really, and could be easily overlooked by a less careful eye. It is just substantial enough that Katharine can see it swirling, and something in her blood tightens while she watches it.

'It is not often visible,' she hears herself say. 'Not from here anyway. Is it often visible in Rolanth?'

'No. Not often.' Luca sighs. 'It is only the Goddess.'

'Yes,' says Katharine. And the curdle in her veins is only the dead queens, who have no love anymore for Her.

'Only the Goddess,' Luca says again. 'Keeping something out, or something in.'

BASTIAN CITY

A night and a day after seeing the oracle at the inn, Jules cannot stop thinking about the prophecy.

If it can even be called that. It was a feeling, the oracle said. Words that came into her mind. *I know only that you were once a queen and may be again.* What a vague bunch of half truths. If that is how it always is with the sight gift, then Jules does not envy them.

'I wouldn't even trade my legion curse for it,' she mutters to Camden, who pricks her ears.

The mountain cat stands up on her hind paws, her forepaws on the ledge of the room's solitary aboveground window, so streaked and spattered with mud that she can barely tell what time of day it is. Jules pats her shoulder.

'Maybe we should have gone with Arsinoe to the mainland after all.'

'How can you say that, after hearing what Mathilde said?'

Jules turns. Emilia is standing in the doorway. Jules did

not hear her approach down the stairs. Nor did she hear the door open. More impressively, neither had Camden.

'I didn't hear Mathilde say anything but nonsense. But I noticed that you didn't seem surprised.'

'That is because she said what I expected.' Emilia gestures toward the low ceiling, the one window. 'This is not the finest room for a queen. But for one who must be concealed it is the best choice.'

Jules scoffs.

'I am no queen.' She tugs at the ends of her short brown hair. 'Look at this. All brown. And these—' She points to her eyes. 'Two different colors and not one of them black. You've met my mother. Madrigal. Not a drop of sacred blood there, I can assure you.'

'I didn't say you were of the queens' line.' Emilia ducks her head, showing the rolled buns at the nape of her neck. Even wandering her own house she appears formal, in brown boots and a knee-length skirt with deep pleats. Clothes on the Vatroses have the look of a uniform, no matter the cut or material.

'Then what are you saying?'

'I am saying that the time of those queens is over.'

Jules blinks. The line of queens has been in place on Fennbirn for all recorded history. 'Is that so?' she murmurs. 'And what about Queen Katharine, then? The one who sits on the throne, with a crown etched into her forehead?'

'Another poisoner puppet.'

'Poisoner or not, she is the Queen Crowned. It is the island's way.'

Emilia crosses her arms. 'What if I told you there is a movement growing of people who feel betrayed by the bloodline? Who will not stand for another poisoner to rule above another poisoner's council?'

'I would say you were lying.' Jules pats Camden on the rump and the cougar hops onto the bed. She lies down facing Emilia with her paws crossed as would a child awaiting a good story. 'Queens have always killed queens, and the island accepts the outcome.'

'But this queen did not kill.'

'She tried. I was there.'

'She failed. She was not the Chosen Queen, and the island knows it. Even some of the northern priestesses.' Emilia strolls to the window and peers through the mud. 'The botched Ascension was a sign. The debacle of the Quickening was a sign. You yourself are a sign. Too many signs to ignore, and now even the pious will stand with us.'

'Us? Who is "us"? Do you believe in these "signs"? Or do you believe in the will of the Goddess?'

'I believe that it is time for change. And that the Goddess's will is for us to make that change.'

THE MAINLAND

Mirabella sips her tea as her eyes drift to the clock. It is full dark, and Arsinoe is still not home from visiting Joseph at the cemetery. Mrs. Chatworth's foot has begun to tap, and Billy's sister, Jane, has arched her eyebrow and sighed twice. Even Billy has gotten up to peer through the curtains.

'I should have gone with her,' he says regretfully.

'It's not as though you could abandon Miss Hollen,' says Jane, and Mirabella sips her tea again. Arsinoe thinks that Mirabella has fallen in with the mainlanders so easily, that she has changed her feathers and joined the flock. In truth, sometimes it is so hard not to scream that she almost cracks her teeth holding her mouth shut.

'Arsinoe has been left to run wild. I know it has not been easy for you girls, coming to a new place,' Mrs. Chatworth says, finally speaking, though her eyes remain fixed on the tablecloth. She never looks at Mirabella when referring to the island or their past. Mirabella does not even know how much about the island Mrs. Chatworth knows. Billy says she knows everything, but if that is true, she seems to have done a fine job of forgetting about it.

'Indeed, it must have been very hard,' she goes on. 'But we cannot be expected to . . . corral her at every turn.'

'Corral?' Mirabella bristles.

'Perhaps that is an unfair term. But the fact remains that my son will not be able to look after her forever. Soon enough, he'll be at university. And then he must make a profitable marriage and start a family of his own.'

Billy winces. Especially at the word 'marriage.'

'University,' Mirabella says to him, and raises her eyebrows. 'You have not told Arsinoe of this.'

'It's not far. A few hours' ride by coach. I'll be home every Saturday and in between terms.'

Mirabella rises from the table, and the other women stare at her above the rims of their teacups.

'Excuse us a moment. I would speak to Billy alone.'

'No, please,' Mrs. Chatworth says, clearly irritated. 'Why should my guest be made to leave the room when I could? Come, Jane, let us retire. I've had quite enough of the tedium of waiting.'

Mirabella steps aside as she and Jane quit the room and walk with straight backs up the stairs.

'I know what you're going to say,' Billy says as soon as he hears both of their bedroom doors shut.

'Do you?'

'It's just that I haven't known how to tell her. Or you.' He looks at her guiltily and ruffles his sandy hair. 'I feel a complete ass, leaving you like this. But I have to go. If we're going to make a life here I need an education. We're rich but not so rich that I can simply be a man of leisure.'

He goes to the window to look again for Arsinoe. 'If only my father would come home.'

'Are you surprised he has not returned already?'

He shrugs. 'After the way I defied him on Fennbirn, I wouldn't be surprised if he sailed all the way around the world before coming back. With stops at every friendly port. Or he could return tomorrow. And when he sees you and Arsinoe . . . that's not a conversation I'm looking forward to having.'

'It seems there are many conversations you are not looking forward to having.'

'Mira, are you cross with me? I haven't seen that look on your face since the day I met you in Rolanth and threatened to skewer you through the neck.'

'Do not be silly.' She softens at the memory. 'I was cross with you nearly every time you cooked for me.'

'Kept you from being poisoned, didn't I?' He grins, but it fades quickly. 'Well, except for that last time.'

'That was no one's fault. But do not change the subject.'

'What subject? I thought we were just waiting for your sister.'

Mirabella goes to the window and snatches the curtains out of his fingers.

'About my sister,' she says. 'How many times have I heard your mother hint about how much happier Arsinoe would be at your country estate? Hidden away from you and away from anyone who might view her as an embarrassment. How many times have they mentioned Christine Hollen as your potential bride?'

'Lots, I suppose.'

'Then when are you going to tell them about you and Arsinoe? That she will not be sent away. That you will not be cowed into marrying someone else.'

Billy lowers his head. He is a handsome young man. Many times Mirabella has thought so. His looks are less dramatic than Joseph's were; he is less like a thunderstorm. He is real and of the earth. He is what her sister needs. Or at least he was. But here on the mainland, he is no longer the daring suitor who risked everything for them. On the island, he was courageous, with an outsider's bravado. Here when girls call him a rogue, they only mean he is trying to get under several skirts at once.

'If you regret bringing us here,' she says carefully, 'if you do not intend to be with Arsinoe, then I will take her someplace else. I am not without skill or cleverness. I can make a life for us.'

Billy stares at her, almost like he does not believe her. But then he takes her hand.

'That's the last thing I want. I will tell them. You have my word. I won't leave her without assurances.'

Before Mirabella can say anything further, he sees movement thought the curtains and exclaims, 'She's here!'

He opens the door and reveals Arsinoe, shivering and soaking wet, on the front step, with what looks to be a dirty fur rolled up beneath her arm. Then Billy embraces her, and the fur barks.

'I found him in an alley after some boys chased him down there with sticks.' Arsinoe holds the dog, squirming, to her chest.

'Poor thing,' says Billy. 'But he's filthy, Arsinoe; my mother will have a fit if you bring him in here.'

'No, see?' she says, and runs her hand over the little dog's back. 'Under all the scum, he's got a pretty brown-and-white coat. I thought we'd clean him up and put a ribbon on him. Give him to your mother and Jane as a peace offering.' She steps farther into the foyer as Billy rubs his forehead and chuckles. Distracted as he is by the dog, he does not notice the haunted look in Arsinoe's eyes. Nor does he note how hard she is shivering, far too hard for someone who has just come in from a warm summer rain.

'Let us take him into the washroom, then,' Mirabella says. 'Quietly.'

Once they are in the washroom, Mirabella sends Billy to heat water for a bath and to fetch extra lamps. When he is gone, she pulls a blanket down from a shelf and wraps her sister in it.

'Now,' she says. 'What is really the matter?'

'Nothing. I saw this dog get chased, and I wanted to save it. It's how I was raised.'

'Yes, yes.' Mirabella smiles softly. 'Poisoner by birth, naturalist at heart. But there is more to this. Why did you stay gone for so long?'

'I fell asleep,' Arsinoe answers, eyebrows down so Mirabella knows she is not telling her everything. But it will have to wait. Billy is returning with the hot water and lamps. So they set the dog in the washbasin, and Mirabella reaches for soap.

'It is a good thing Mrs. Chatworth and Jane are already in bed,' Mirabella says. 'They would be beside themselves if they knew you had taken off your dress in public.'

'It wasn't in public. It was in the graveyard, behind a tree. And besides, I had all these clothes on underneath!'

They finish bathing the dog, who really is quite a lovely fellow underneath all the muck, and towel him dry before Arsinoe carries him up to their bedroom. Billy does not leave her side until they are in the doorway and then leans in to kiss her cheek.

'Don't worry me so much,' he whispers.

'Then don't worry so easily,' Arsinoe whispers back.

'Good night, Billy,' Mirabella says, and closes the door. She goes to Arsinoe's dresser for dry clothes while Arsinoe gets the dog settled into bed.

'Here. Get out of that shirt and into something dry.'

'I'm all right.'

'I am the oldest.' Mirabella holds the nightshirt out. 'Do as I say.'

'Or what? We're not on the island anymore; you're all out of lightning bolts.' But Arsinoe unbuttons the shirt and takes it off, then pulls the quilt off her bed to wrap herself in. 'This place is going to make us soft. Everything so precious and fancy. Look at this wall covering.' She taps her finger against the pattern of raised green velvet. 'It seems like a tapestry, but if you pick at it, it's paper! It peels!'

'Arsinoe, stop that. Mrs. Chatworth will cut your hands off. Besides, according to you, I was always soft. Raised in Rolanth on a fat bed of priestesses.' She looks at her sister's still-shivering shoulders. 'Now tell me what really happened today.'

'Nothing. I fell asleep and I rescued a dog. How was tea with Christine and the governor's girls? Did you manage to put her off Billy?'

Arsinoe blinks innocently and gathers the dog into her arms. Something had happened. Mirabella would know it by the electricity in the air even if it were not written all over Arsinoe's frightened face. But she also knows by the set of her sister's jaw that she will get no more answers tonight.

CENTRA

When Arsinoe falls asleep, she dreams the same dream she had when she was sleeping beside Joseph's grave. Which is odd, as she cannot remember ever having had the same dream twice. In it, she is again on a ship, not a ship like she is accustomed to, but an old ship, with one mast, the kind that merchants used to use and went out of fashion at least a century ago. And again, she is not herself but someone else: a girl dressed as a boy.

Also, she is up very high in the rigging, staring out at fast-moving waves that make her stomach lurch.

'David! Get down from that rigging!'

Yes, yes, let's get down from this rigging, Arsinoe thinks, her own legs weak though the legs of her dream body navigate the ropes and nets without any trouble.

'Richard. You never let me have any fun.'

The girl whose body Arsinoe shares—whose name is actually Daphne, not David—lands on the deck and tugs her tunic down over her leggings. Old-fashioned clothes. Nothing like anything Arsinoe has ever worn, and not terribly comfortable either.

'You shouldn't be here to begin with,' Richard says. 'You know women are bad luck on a ship.'

'Keep your voice down,' Daphne says, with a glance toward the other sailors. 'And it's not as if you would have the nerve to steal the ship without me.'

'Borrowed. Only borrowed.'

The wind flags in the sail as the ship turns back toward the port. Daphne, and by extension, Arsinoe in Daphne's body, looks to the stern where a boy has given up the wheel. He is Henry Redville—*Lord* Henry Redville from the country of Centra—and he makes his way to her and Richard and throws his arms around them.

'How are my two favorite wards?' Henry asks.

'She is not a ward,' says Richard. 'She is a foundling. A foundling, scooped from the sea, the lone survivor of one wreck and sure to be the cursed cause of another with her penchant for sailing in disguise.'

'You know, Richard,' says Daphne, 'when you were small, your nurses said you were sickly and wont to die.'

Arsinoe feels her own ribs squeezed as Henry hugs them together as though to reconcile them by force. And it works. Richard and Daphne laugh.

'I suppose she is not a curse,' says Richard. 'How could she be, when she is already a sea monster stuffed into a baby's skin.'

'And never forget it. Now stop calling me "she." I am still David, in tunic and hose. No more "she" until we're back in the castle.'

The dream moves forward, past the place where she last woke. Yet the strangeness does not abate completely; Arsinoe is still disoriented, and in awe, staring up at the white cliffs overlooking the bay, in a mainland country she has never been to, and in a time she does not know. But it is only a dream, and in any case, she cannot seem to will herself awake.

Daphne, along with Henry (they seem to have left Richard at the port) enter the castle via a hidden passageway through the cliffs, their way guided by lanterns until they reach the end, and Daphne steps behind a hanging curtain to change into her girl's clothes. Off comes the tunic and scratchy hose, and on goes a high-waisted red dress.

Blegh. I change my mind. This dress is even less comfortable than the tunic.

But even worse than that is the long, black wig.

'Daphne. Your wig is askew.' Henry holds out the lantern and tugs the wig on properly. Then he tops it with a terrible veiled headdress. Trapped inside Daphne, Arsinoe grimaces.

As Daphne fumbles with the wig again, Arsinoe tries to look around. She cannot, of course, which is frustrating. But she is asleep and this is only a dream, so she is not bothered too much.

'I'm sorry, Daph,' says Henry. 'Women's wardrobes are truly a mystery to me.'

'The girls in the tavern tell a different story,' she grumbles, and prods him in the ribs.

I believe I would like to hear that story. This boy Henry is nearly as handsome as Joseph. Tall and lean, with straight, thick, brown hair the color of an oiled walnut shell. A pity he had not been the one changing clothes behind the sheet.

In the dream, Daphne and Henry step out of the passageway. In the corner of her vision, Arsinoe sees that they came from a door hidden behind a tapestry of hunting dogs. Daphne smooths the waist of her dark red gown, and Henry adjusts the fall of her white veil. He pulls his hands away quickly at the sound of a voice.

'My lord, your lady mother wishes to see you. To see you both.'

'All right. Where is she?'

'Waiting in her privy chamber, my lord.'

Privy chamber. What exactly is a privy chamber?

Arsinoe watches, carried easily along inside Daphne's body as they make their way to the chamber. She studies the woman they bow to (*must be Henry's lady mother*) as well as the relative plainness of the room. The woman is obviously high-born, dressed in a fine gown in cloth of silver, but the rug beneath their feet is thinner than Arsinoe is used to and the stone walls, very rough.

'Mother, what is it? You look positively gleeful!'

'And I am,' she says as Henry bends to kiss her hand.

'It is good news, then,' says Daphne. 'That is a relief.'

'We have had a letter from the king. Henry is to go to the isle of Fennbirn. He is to be this generation's suitor for the crown, the only one sent in all of Centra.'

'Fennbirn!' *Fennbirn!* Henry looks at Daphne excitedly.

He's a suitor. But why am I dreaming of a suitor and his sister? She feels something in the way that Henry grasps on to Daphne's hand. *Or perhaps NOT a sister.*

'But why me, Mother? Are you certain? Has there been no mistake?'

'We have no reason to think so,' his mother says. 'The letter was signed by the king's own hand and sealed with his seal. And we are always among his favorites at court. This is a boon to your father, in payment for past loyalties.'

Kings. Centran courts. I don't know anything about Centra. Mirabella ought to be dreaming this. She knows everything.

'When do I leave?' Henry asks.

'Soon,' says his mother. 'Very soon. Our young ward Richard will accompany you to the isle and remain there during your suit, as an ally and protection.'

'What about Daphne?'

'Daphne will remain here.'

Henry and Daphne look at each other with wide eyes, and Arsinoe's heart aches for them. It is the same way she looked at Jules when she and Camden sailed away.

'But Mother—'

'No.' His mother takes a breath, and her face brightens. 'Now go and prepare for supper. Your lord father is sorry to miss tonight's celebration, but he will return from court in a week's time to see you off.'

They stand, and his mother kisses Henry on both of his cheeks. Daphne starts to leave with him, but his mother grasps her by the arm.

'I would keep you a moment, Daphne.'

Daphne and Arsinoe sink back into the chair, though Arsinoe's eyes follow Henry as long as they can.

'You knew this day would come,' his mother says. 'That someday, Henry would make a great marriage and increase our lands and our fortune.'

'Of course I did.'

And even though a stranger, Arsinoe can hear the strain in Daphne's voice.

'But I thought he would remain here. That his bride would come, with her lands and titles, and she and Henry would live here.'

'And so she will if he is successful. He will return a king! With a queen, as soon as their reign on Fennbirn is over.'

Inside Daphne, Arsinoe sneers.

'And what am I to do, Lady Redville? Without Henry? Without Richard?'

'You will do what all women do. You will wait for the men to make their ways in the world.'

Ugh.

'Do not despair. You are a foundling, of no noble blood, so there can be no great marriage for you. But you will always have a place in my household as one of my ladies. And I am sure that Henry's queen would have you as a lady as well.'

I suppose it's better than being put out on the street. Which is where my sister and I would be without Billy.

Luckily, the uncomfortable conversation with Henry's mother, Lady Redville, does not last long, and Daphne is able to carry Arsinoe out and back into the hall, where Henry promptly ambushes them.

'Well? Did you change her mind?'

'Me? Why don't you? You're her son! And you didn't say a word.'

His hair is windblown, and though boys seemed older by that age in those old times, to Arsinoe he still looks very young. Too young to be a king-consort. And so unschooled in the ways of the island. She can imagine Billy standing so, talking to his sister, Jane, with a similar thoughtful expression.

'I didn't know what to say,' says Henry. 'She has never tried to separate us before.'

'It is a fool's time to start. When you're being sent so far away, under newly minted favor of the king. And the isle of Fennbirn . . . who knows a thing about it? They say it is full of witches and magic. . . .'

Watch your tongue, foundling. . . .

'You don't believe that,' he says.

'But how would we know? Centra hasn't had a winning suitor for generations. Why is the king sending you anyway? He has plenty of sons!'

'Fennbirn is a prize for nobles, Daph. You know that.'

'That clever look on your face. You want to be king, don't you? You want to be the king of Fennbirn Island.'

'Daphne.' He laughs. 'Who would not? It will be a great adventure. I wish you could come. But I will tell you everything when I return.'

They are quiet for a moment, and that look of separation comes back into Henry's eyes.

He loves her. He loves her, but he's going to go anyway.

'I don't want you to go,' she says suddenly.

'You don't? Daph—' he reaches out, and she turns quickly away. 'Why do you not want me to go?'

'You know why!'

'Do I?'

Do you? Spit it out, then, Daphne. Arsinoe tries to prod, to quicken Daphne's mind. But she is only a dreamer, and this is far, far in the past. Whatever happened, there is no changing it.

'You know that I can protect you just as well as Richard,' Daphne says, and Arsinoe groans.

'I should be going with you. Who will look out for you? Who will make sure that you're safe?'

Henry's hands draw back to his sides. 'I wish you had said something else.'

'What else?'

'You think of me still as a child. How can you not see what I have become? That I am not some tottering little boy.'

'Henry—'

'Well, I am not a boy. I am a man. I will be a king, and I will be a lord. Your lord,' he adds, and Arsinoe likes him a little less.

'Daph. Forgive me. I didn't mean it that way.'

'But that's the way it is,' Daphne snaps. 'Thank you, Lord Henry, for reminding me.'

He storms out, and she spins so fast that Arsinoe is near sick to her stomach. But when she stops, it is to face a mirror, and Arsinoe sees why she is dreaming in the body that she is.

Daphne's hair and eyes are black as night. Even her natural hair, cropped short and barely peeking out from beneath the wig. Daphne may be a foundling, but she is a foundling queen of Fennbirn.

INDRID DOWN TEMPLE

Anxious butterflies tumble in Bree Westwood's stomach as the carriage draws to a stop before Indrid Down Temple. The carriage door swings open, and she looks up, taking it all in: the grandeur of the facade, so fiercely black, with carved gargoyles snarling down. It is not as beautiful as the temple in Rolanth; it lacks the soft, artful touches, but she must admit it is imposing. Struck in the center of the capital like a great black sword into the earth.

'Do you need someone to go in with you, miss?' the driver asks. 'Announce you?'

'No.' Bree steps out of the coach and rolls her shoulders back. 'I am expected.'

Her legs kick out in long strides, the show of confidence easy after years of practice. But she hates the wobbly feeling in her knees and the butterflies still boiling in her belly. She hates that High Priestess Luca summoned her at all, but mostly, she hates that she felt compelled to show up.

When the heavy temple doors close behind her, cutting off the sounds of the city and trapping her along with the breeze, she nearly bolts. She should not have come. Luca should have come to them. She should have come to Westwood House on her knees after what she did to Mirabella. Instead she appointed Bree to the Black Council—along with herself and her pet monster, Rho, of course—and wrote that Bree should join her for tea at the temple before appearing at the Volroy.

'This way, Miss Westwood,' says a tall, reedy priestess with a light blond braid sticking out from her hood. Ice-blond and in the capital: probably an Arron. Indrid Down Temple must be crawling with them. Bree glances at the priestesses sweeping or tending the altar, praying before the great black glass in the floor that they call the Goddess Stone. Their white hoods and black bracelets are supposed to strip them of their names and gifts. But Bree feels like she is walking through a nest of vipers.

She follows the priestess through the temple's interior rooms, past the small open cloister, and down a set of steps into a chamber lit only by torches.

'The High Priestess's rooms are not far.'

Bree stops. 'I will wait for her here.'

'But—'

'Just bring her to me.' She shrugs out of her cloak and slings it across the back of a chair. 'And tell her not to tarry.'

She does not look at the priestess before she goes, so she does not know whether the girl's mouth dropped open. But it probably did. Perhaps telling the High Priestess not to tarry was going a little too far.

Bree considers sitting in the chair, affecting a bored pose as she waits. But the chair faces the door and the hall where Luca would approach from, and angry as she is, Bree knows that were she and Luca to stare at each other for the length of the hall, she would look away first. So instead she wanders the confines of the small stuffy chamber, studying the fragments of ancient mosaic on the floor and the hangings on the wall: poisoner depictions of deaths by boils, and a snake wreathed in poisonous flowers. There are also tapestries of familiars and battles, but they are much, much smaller.

'Bree Westwood. I am glad you have come.'

Bree turns. The High Priestess stands in the doorway with a look of affection on her face, hands folded.

'Of course I came. You named me to the Black Council. Mother was thrilled. She's installed an entire household for me in the north end of the city.'

'Good. And are you finding it comfortable?' Luca steps aside as a priestess arrives carrying a tray of tea and biscuits. She sets it on the table.

'Shall I serve?' the girl asks.

'No.' Luca waves her away. 'I will serve. If you will sit, Bree?'

'I will not.' She lifts her chin. It is a hard thing to refuse Luca, whom she has known and been fond of for most of her life. Whom she has been taught for so long to revere. 'One pot of tea and a seat on the Black Council is not going to make everything better.'

'I see.'

'You joined with them and ordered her execution!'

Luca nods. She pours cups for them both and sweetens her own with honey. 'But she was not executed.'

'No thanks to you. You would have been there when it happened. You would have stood there and watched while Queen Katharine killed her!'

'I know,' Luca says. 'And she would have known. It is that which keeps me up at night, above everything else. That she went into the sea knowing that I abandoned her.'

'Went into the sea? So you believe that she is dead?'

'A storm rose up in the mist, and came for the ship.'

'A storm couldn't kill Mira.'

'That would depend on whose storm it was.'

Bree clenches her teeth. Of course. The Goddess's storm. That is what they say came for the queens. And Luca is the Goddess's most important servant. Loyal only to her, and to her will. 'You are such a wretched old woman.'

Luca's eyes snap to hers and Bree quiets. Those eyes are not old.

'You are angry, Bree. I understand. But dead or not, Mira is gone, and we must make something of what she left behind. With we three on the council, it will be nearly as if she were the one wearing the crown.'

'I should oppose you,' Bree says bitterly. 'I should do it for her.'

'That is not what she would want.'

'You do not know what she would want.'

Luca sighs. 'Then what do you want? What must I do? What amends can I make?' She smiles. 'Or should I pass you over for your mother?'

Bree is well aware that Luca only appointed her to the Black Council as an act of contrition. And perhaps because she would be a more effective thorn in Queen Katharine's side than her mother would be. If she cooperates.

'Elizabeth will stay with us, always,' Bree says. 'The temple will make no more demands on her. And you will allow her to recall her familiar.'

'Priestesses do not have familiars. We do not have gifts. She made her choice.' But Luca's expression is soft. She does not really care about one tiny tufted woodpecker.

'Rho made her choose between taking her priestess vows that very moment or watching her bird be crushed. It was not really a choice. Pepper is small. She hid him before. She can do it again.'

'Very well.'

'Fine.' Bree bends and gathers her cloak.

'You know why I did it, don't you, Bree?' Luca asks.

'Yes, I know.' She looks resentfully around at the musty old temple. 'The island is what matters.'

* * *

Nearly the moment that Bree exits the temple, Elizabeth grabs her and pulls her into the shadows with her one good hand, black bracelet peeking out from beneath her sleeve.

'Elizabeth! I thought you were going to wait at the town house. What are you doing here?'

'Listening,' the priestess replies, and smiles, her cheek dimpling. 'And blending in. None of these priestesses here know me enough to recognize me if I stay quiet and keep my head bowed.' She demonstrates, tucking her chin and widening her eyes until they are large and blank and simple-looking. Then she perks up. 'Now what did the High Priestess say?'

'Just what we expected. She wants to be friends again, so I will do what I am told.'

'And what did you say?'

'I said that I would. As long as you can stay with us. And as long as you can have Pepper back.'

Bree grins, and Elizabeth makes a high-pitched noise and throws her arms around her neck. 'Oh, Bree, thank you! But will you? Will you really do as Luca requires, even after . . . even after what she would have done to Mirabella?'

Bree glances around, but there is no one near to hear them refer to Mirabella by name. 'I may. I will for a time, at least until I find my footing in the capital. But I still intend to make every poisoner suffer. Especially *her*.'

'You must be careful. She is the Queen Crowned. And maybe she won't be so terrible. I've heard she means to welcome you to the city with a banquet.'

'A banquet?'

'To be held later this week, in the square overlooking the harbor.'

Bree looks over her friend's shoulder, toward the sea, imagining the trouble she could cause at a party held in her honor. 'You are a kinder girl than I, Elizabeth, if you think her overtures are genuine.' She sighs. 'Let us go back to the house.'

'I'll meet you there later.' Elizabeth hastily pats her shoulder and then runs off in a flurry of white robes. 'First I'm off to the woods for Pepper!'

THE VOLROY

Pietyr runs his fingers down Katharine's bare back as she lies across his chest.

'Keep doing that,' she whispers. His touch is soothing. Gentle. With his hands on her, she could perhaps fall asleep again, despite the bright light streaming into her bedroom. She slept only a little the night before, unable to still her mind no matter how Pietyr exhausted her body.

Today is the day that Bree Westwood comes to claim her place at the table.

'If I keep doing that, it will lead to more of this.' He rolls on top of her and drags kisses along her throat.

'What do you know about Bree Westwood?'

He stops kissing her and sighs. 'No more than what you know. She is always fashionably dressed. Certainly beautiful, never serious. She flitted about in the wake of your gloomy older sister like an idiot butterfly.' He rolls away and gets out of bed, struts across the room bare and splendid before slipping into a dressing robe.

'Perhaps someone so serious as my sister needed that lightness,' Katharine says, propped up on an elbow. 'Perhaps I do, too, and Bree will become my friend.'

'Or perhaps she is truly an idiot butterfly, never aware of the weight of the events transpiring around her, and now we must suffer her on the Black Council.' Pietyr adds wood to the dying fire and swings a pot of water over it to heat for tea.

Katharine's eyes go blank, her voice empty. 'Never trust her. She will always hate and resent us.'

'Whose words were those?' Pietyr asks. 'Yours or Natalia's? Mine?' He chuckles, and it sounds false. 'Or someone else's?'

She knows who he means. The dead queens clamoring nervously and eagerly in her blood. The words came and went so quickly that not even Katharine is sure.

Pietyr returns to the bed and kneels beside it. He cups her face and trails his fingertips from her neck to her collarbone. 'Do you need them anymore?'

'What do you mean?'

'You are the Queen Crowned. You have what we wanted. What they wanted. And now they can grow quiet and disappear.'

Disappear. In her mind's eye, she sees Pietyr's neck snapping, his head twisted too far around. She can almost hear it, the crunch of bones. *Hush, hush, old sisters. I know you have had enough of disappearing.*

She takes his hand and kisses it, then pushes past him to get out of bed.

'I am only in the crown because of them.' She ties her dressing gown and sits at her table to rub a soothing cream into her dry, scarred hands. 'It was they who brought me back. Who made me strong.'

'I am grateful that they saved you. But it is your time to rule now, Kat, and you have always been a queen, able and blessed.'

Katharine smiles at him from her reflection in her mirror. The young queen it shows is still pale but not so hollow. Not so sunken, and the hair falling around her in loose curls shines brightly black.

'What am I without them? Without the dead queens lending me hints of their gifts, I have nothing. No gift of my own. The dead war queens let me throw their knives. The dead poisoners let me devour their poisons. The dead naturalists make sure that New Sweetheart does not turn on me and bite.'

'New Sweetheart,' he says softly.

'Yes. I figured that out, too. So perhaps they have even made me smarter.'

'You were always clever, Kat. Clever and sweet, in equal measure.' He approaches from behind and squeezes her shoulders. 'I will leave you to prepare.'

'Indeed. We do not want to be late for Bree's first day.'

Katharine orders fresh pink roses to brighten the council chamber, along with plenty of cool water in silver pitchers. She has the tea cart loaded with berries and meringues and other things she has heard that elementals like to eat, and not a single drop of it is poisoned.

'It is more than we could have expected, had things gone another way,' Pietyr says when he sees her preparations. He kisses her hand, and his teeth graze her knuckles, sending pleasurable tingles all the way up her arm. It will be hard to revert to discretion after Pietyr finds her another husband.

The clock ticks, and the other members of the Black Council begin to arrive. Genevieve comes to curtsy and kiss her cheek, so sweet and gentle to Katharine since the crowning. Cousin Lucian bows grandly, perhaps afraid his seat could be traded back to Cousin Allegra at any time. Renata, the priestess Rho Murtra, and High Priestess Luca enter together and sit without a word, though Luca's old eyes twinkle like stars.

Antonin sniffs the dishes on the tea cart.

'Not a drop of poison?' he asks. 'If this is how it will be, I will have to start taking a larger breakfast.'

Together they wait, and wait some more, some standing and chatting quietly, others seated and looking bored. Pietyr has his head propped on forefinger and thumb, staring at the untouched empty chair left specifically for Bree.

'Perhaps her carriage was delayed?' Renata suggests, and glances around meekly. 'Shall we send someone out after her?'

'She will be here.' Every back in the room straightens when Rho speaks. Her voice is nearly too booming for the chamber to contain. 'Her town house is not far. If the carriage failed, she and Elizabeth will walk.'

'Elizabeth?' Genevieve asks. 'Who is Elizabeth? Surely the Westwoods know that they are not allowed an entourage. Surely she has the backbone to come alone.'

'Of course I do!' Bree Westwood calls out, her timing so perfect that Katharine wonders whether she was waiting just outside the door. The heels of her boots ring off the stone, and Katharine glimpses someone behind her, lingering in the hall in a white priestess robe. It must be the priestess Elizabeth. Mirabella's other best friend.

'Perfect,' Katharine whispers, and squeezes her hands tight to quiet the dead queens' grumbling as Bree Westwood blows into the Black Council like a gust of cold air. She has had weeks to prepare for this, her grand arrival. And there is nothing for Katharine to do but be gracious. Bree drops half a curtsy to Katharine, and a very full bow to High Priestess Luca, and then plops into her seat. Her chin is raised, eyes defiant, and hair cascading in bright brown waves, held back by silver combs.

Katharine nods to her.

'Welcome to my council, Bree Westwood. I hope your journey to the capital was not difficult? And if there is anything I can do to ease the transition of your household, do not hesitate to ask.' Bree does not respond, so she goes on. 'I have had a special tea prepared, to welcome you.' She gestures toward the cart.

'No thank you,' Bree says. 'And please do not go to any similar trouble. I doubt if I will ever trust this council enough to eat anything that is in this room.'

The chamber falls silent, except for Antonin, who makes a disgusted sound.

'How then are we supposed to govern together?'

'Reconciling a new council with the old is always difficult,' High Priestess Luca says.

'Or so you have heard,' says Rho. 'The poisoners have grasped on to it for so long, who can really remember?'

For a moment, Katharine wishes she had not dismissed Margaret Beaulin, so she might see war gift against war gift and Rho's face smashed into the table.

'It is so dark in here.' Bree flicks her wrist, and the flames on every candelabra flare, so high that Genevieve must move a vase of pink roses so they will not scorch. 'And so still, without any windows.'

'There is a window.' Katharine looks upward, into the shadows of the high ceiling, where windows were cut out of the stone to circulate the air in case the doors were to be sealed.

'Well, it is so far up that it hardly matters.' Bree slips her summer wrap off her shoulders. Her dress is deep blue embroidered with black, and very elemental, the skirt swaying with movement. The V in her bodice is so deep that Pietyr must be careful to keep from looking.

'If someone else . . .' She pauses. 'Someone with a gift for weather were here, perhaps—we could draw in a decent breeze.'

Katharine notes the delicate pulse in Bree's throat. She notes the largeness of her eyes. The open V of the bodice exposing her heart like a bull's-eye. So many places to sink a knife. Bree Westwood is foolish indeed to speak so when the dead queens are there to hear. To see. They boil so high inside Katharine that she can almost taste their rotten flesh on the back of her tongue.

Quiet, quiet. To kill another queen is one thing. To kill a member of the council . . . Well, she must truly earn such a punishment.

'Shall we to actual council business?' Pietyr cocks an eyebrow. 'There has been unrest amongst the people concerning the bodies of the traitor queens. We keep expecting them to wash ashore, though I have heard some priestesses say it is more likely that the Goddess will keep them.' He looks at Luca, whose mouth has set in a grim line.

'That may be true,' Genevieve says, all too happy to pick up this line of conversation. 'Still, would it be too much to ask for the legion-cursed naturalist to wash ashore? Or the mainland suitor? I would even settle for a few pieces of the Wolf Spring boy.'

'I would settle for the cougar,' Antonin says, and the old Black Council laughs.

'That is enough,' Katharine interjects. But she cannot stop herself from smiling. 'If it will put the people's minds at ease, arrange for boats and small crews to sail out of the harbor to search. Pay them well, and offer an extra reward to any who return with evidence. Whole or in pieces.' She turns toward Luca and Bree. 'Now. Shall we plan your welcome banquet?'

BASTIAN CITY

That night, Emilia takes Jules to a pub, promising that it will remind her of home and that she could even venture to bring Camden, as the proprietors are loyal to the Vatros clan. But the moment that Jules enters, through an entrance down an alley, her hackles rise. It is less a pub than an underground room of stone with a partial dirt floor, and in the many weeks that Jules has been in Bastian, Emilia has never mentioned it. Yet she is obviously a regular, touching the shoulder of nearly everyone she passes and nodding to the two men behind the bar.

'What is this place?'

'We call it "the Bronze Whistle,"' Emilia answers. 'Try the chicken and the wine. Stay clear of the ale, unless Berkley pours it.'

Jules glances at the bartenders. She could not guess which one was Berkley, though both look nice enough, sweating a little and working hard. The tall one with the slight reddish beard catches her watching and gives her a wink.

'They have food here?'

'Of course! Takes a while to get it. We're underneath a manor house. They let us run through their halls and use their kitchens, for a fee.'

'So this is a club, of sorts?'

'Of sorts.'

Emilia leads them through the room, lit a bright gaslight yellow. It is quieter now than when they came in, as people stop talking to gawk and mutter about her cougar. Camden yowls happily at the smell of chicken and jumps onto a tabletop. The girls seated there shout, 'Oi,' and move their mugs out of the way of her sweeping tail.

'Sorry,' Jules mutters, and they cock their eyebrows. She coaxes Camden down and follows Emilia to a corner table, untucking the short hair behind her ears so it can swing past her face. She has not had so many eyes on her since the day in the arena at the Queens' Duel.

'What will you have?' Emilia asks. 'I mean, besides the chicken?'

'The good ale, I suppose.'

Emilia slaps her palms down on the table and turns to a server. 'Three dishes of the chicken and two mugs of Berkley's ale. And a bowl of water, for the cat.'

Camden, never one to skulk on the floor, hops onto the wall bench to wait for dinner. Still so many eyes on them, and just as many watching Jules as the cougar.

'When will they stop staring?'

Emilia pays the boy who brings their ale.

'Maybe when you dance with them. You're a pretty girl, Jules Milone. You can't think that it was only your handsome mainlander would notice that.'

'Joseph wasn't a mainlander. He was one of us.' And he is still in her heart. Anyone who looks at her that way is a fool if they cannot see that Joseph's ghost sits beside her.

Emilia tips her head back and forth. She has made it plain that she does not think much of Joseph, gone so long to the mainland with Billy, but she has never spoken against him. Why would she? He is dead, and it does not matter anymore.

Jules tries to get comfortable in her chair and rests her elbows on the table. The air in the crowded space is close, but not stifling, the freshness aided perhaps by the kitchens being so far away.

'Oh no,' Jules groans.

'What?'

She pushes her chin toward the door, where the oracle Mathilde sits with her eyes on them, her yellow hair braided through with a fat twist of white.

'Ah, Mathilde!' Emilia waves to her. 'Good. Maybe I will get to hear the song of Aethiel after all.'

'Is she really a bard?' Jules asks.

'Of course. She is a seer and a bard. It is possible to be many things at once, Jules Milone. You of all people should know that.'

Jules frowns as the chicken arrives, but her scowl fades as

she smells the steam. The chicken is stewed in a gravy and served with a thick slice of oat bread. She has to yank Camden's plate away to keep her from biting into it while it is still too hot. She blows on both dishes and twists off a small forkful, tender and delicious. Camden, tired of waiting, grabs hers with her forepaw and sloshes most of it onto the table. Then she licks her fur and burned paw pads.

Emilia laughs and shakes her head.

'Having her around is such a danger.'

'Why?'

'I will begin to think I can treat all mountain cats this way. And I'll get ten claws raked down my back.'

Jules snorts. It is not likely. Mountain cats are rare as far south as Bastian City. Camden was the only one even in the forests of Wolf Spring, as far as she knows.

'Jules, look out!'

The knife aimed at her is kitchen cutlery, large and sharp. She leans back as Emilia raises her hands, using her war gift to push the blade off course. Camden ducks, but not far enough, and the knife slices into her back.

When her cougar winces, Jules sees red. She flips her chair and turns. It is not hard to find the one who threw the knife. The man behind the bar. The one who winked. But now his eyes are so wide, they could near fall out and hang on stalks.

'You!' she shouts. Her war gift surges, unbidden, and sends him flying against the wall. Bottles and glasses fall to the floor and shatter. Camden, who was not badly hurt, leaps across the tables and onto the bar, snarling and swiping with her good paw, the cut on her back spattering blood into spilled beer.

'Stop!' Emilia calls. 'Berkley, you idiot. You were supposed to wait until she'd finished eating. And you were not to harm the cat.'

'Was you who harmed the cat. You pushed the knife into her path.' Berkley gets to his feet and brushes at his trousers. He curses when his fingers come away bloody. 'I just mended these.'

Jules turns to Emilia. 'You knew? This was planned?'

'They needed to see your gift. Don't get angry. You lack control.'

'I'll give you control,' Jules growls, and every glass on the bar begins to shake.

No one reacts. Perhaps because they are in the city of the war gifted. But then the murmurs begin, and Jules goes cold, and Camden creeps off the bar to curl around her legs. Near the door on the far side of the room, the oracle Mathilde rises to her feet.

'It is as I said. Juillenne Milone was once a queen. And she may yet be a queen again.'

Jules moans. 'Don't go spreading that nonsense around!'

But in the Bronze Whistle at least, it is too late, and now she knows why they have stared at her since she came in.

'Emilia. Who are these people?'

Emilia grins.

'We are the queen's revolt. And you, Jules, a gifted

naturalist also gifted in war, will be the one to unite us and take the poisoner's place.'

She grabs Emilia by the sleeve.

'How long have you been planning this?'

'The seers have known of your coming for a long time.'

'The seers are fools. They said I should be drowned at birth. Now they say I'm a queen. Or I will be. Or I was once already.'

But Jules's words cast no doubt across the faces in the Whistle. They are too full of hope. In her, they see a chance they have not had in generations. And Jules has heard that there is nothing a warrior loves more than to run into a battle headlong with little chance of victory. That is where the glory is, they say. That is where heroes are made.

Jules has never heard anything quite so stupid.

'Prophecy has many interpretations,' says Mathilde as she crosses the room to stand before them. 'Unfortunately, it is often difficult to know the meaning until after it has come to pass.'

'But it says I was once a queen. I was never.'

'In another life, perhaps,' Mathilde replies. 'Or a less literal interpretation.'

Like when she was briefly 'queen' by using her gift to impersonate Arsinoe's hold over the bear during the Quickening Ceremony. Of course Jules does not mention that. The flames of this madness have been fanned enough already.

'The prophecies were clearer once,' Berkley pipes up, avoiding Jules's eyes. 'Before the bleeding Black Council started drowning all the oracle queens.'

Bitter mutters of agreement ripple through the room. It does not matter that it was an ancient council who passed that decree. Or that the same council may have been populated by those with the war gift. The words 'Black Council' have become synonymous with the poisoners, and poisoners are easy to blame.

'I'm not . . . ,' Jules starts, and then louder, 'I'm not your leader. I can't be. I'm legion cursed. And it's called a curse for a reason.'

'For a foolish reason. You have not gone mad.' Emilia tugs Jules closer. 'What did you think you were here for? That enough time would pass, and we would move you upstairs with a patch to hide your green eye? That we would say you're a cousin and Camden a pet cow?'

'I don't know what I thought.' Jules's heart pounds as she looks into the faces at the Bronze Whistle. The expectations there. The belief. Emilia touches Jules's hair and gently tucks it behind her ear.

'I know you are broken hearted. I know you lost Queen Arsinoe and that boy and you feel like you are nothing without them. But you are wrong.

'Even if you are right, your destiny will find you anyway. Already our whisperers tell us the people have no faith in the poisoner, and the Arrons fight amongst themselves as if tugging on Natalia Arron's bones. By the time we storm the gates of the Volroy, we will have spread tale of you, our Legion Queen, across the entire island. The people will scream your name. And we will take Katharine in chains.'

INDRID DOWN

Katharine oversees the setup for the welcome banquet herself. It must all be perfect. The food, the flowers, the music, and insofar as she can manage it, the company.

'We should have held this indoors,' Genevieve grumbles. 'At the Highbern, like Lucian and I suggested. These clouds . . . What if it rains?'

'Then the elementals will enjoy it all the more,' Pietyr replies. He directs a servant as to where to place the chairs and which arrangements of flowers should go on the head table. 'And stop scowling, Genevieve. People are watching.'

Katharine glances up and sees the curious faces half hidden behind shutters and curtains. She squeezes her scarred wrists and knuckles through her light summer gloves. They ache today, as they have not ached in a long time. As they sometimes do when the dead queens are dormant. She calls for a glass of water, and as she waits, touches the healed black band of ink across her forehead. Her permanent crown, tattooed in the old fashion.

Pietyr leans close to whisper.

'It will be all right, Kat. You are doing the right thing. You must not let the likes of Bree Westwood get to you.'

'It is not truly her that we have to worry about.' Genevieve takes the water from the servant and brings it to the queen. 'It is the High Priestess. Luca is shrewd. Appointing herself to the council. Choosing the Westwood daughter just to make trouble.'

'If Natalia were alive,' Pietyr mutters, 'she would never have dared.'

Katharine raises her chin. 'It was Luca herself who administered the crown. Needles upon needles sinking into my skin. She cannot want to unseat that which she so recently bestowed. She only wants to crow and see if she can drown us out.'

'She wants to see how far she can push you,' says Pietyr.

'But I suppose . . .' Genevieve sighs. 'That is how it always is after an Ascension. After any new appointment to the council. If we stand our ground, eventually she will give up.'

'Queen Katharine.'

A servant, hair covered in baking flour, approaches quickly and takes a knee.

'Pardon the interruption, my queen.'

'Of course. Speak.'

'The feast is prepared. And I was told to tell you . . . to

inform you that the High Priestess is on her way. I don't know why they sent a servant from the kitchens. We're all just very busy and—'

Katharine touches the man's head. 'It is all right. Once the feast is in place, take your ease. Eat.' She looks up at the building before her and gestures to the faces ducked behind the windows. 'All are welcome. As many as the square can hold.'

She steps onto the raised platform and stands before the head table, rubbing flour from the palm of her glove. Genevieve and Pietyr hurry away to see to last touches: the last of the pale ribbon hung from the lamps, the final sprays of pink and purple flowers. Her Black Council waits at the edges of the square and greets the first folk who wander in. Not something they are terribly accustomed to, and the strained expressions of pleasantness stretched across Lucian's and Antonin's faces make Katharine chuckle. Before long, the tables are full and so many people stand between that it is hard for the High Priestess, Rho, and Bree Westwood to make their way through when they arrive in their carriage.

In any case, it seems they are in no great hurry to reach the head table. Luca stops to offer blessing to every person she passes. Even Rho tries to woo the guests, though some will not come close enough for a handshake, and she is near unrecognizable when smiling. Luckily for her, Bree can charm enough for both of them. She is more beautiful than ever with her hair studded with opals. And her bright green summer gown highlights the fact that Katharine may wear only black.

'Wait.' Katharine stops a servant as she passes with a tureen of soup. She dips a spoon and tastes it. 'The little brat had better eat something today. This soup is too good to miss.'

The banquet progresses as banquets do until someone notices a commotion near the harbor. Katharine has almost relaxed enough to sample the desserts when cries of alarm begin to rise.

Pietyr nods to one of the queensguard, and several soldiers push through the crowd. Everyone has turned toward Bardon Harbor. Even the guards. 'Pietyr, what is it?' Katharine asks, and stands.

The mist has risen thick over the water. So thick it might be a cloud, if clouds were known to creep quickly and deliberately toward land. At the sight of it coming closer, those nearest the docks start to back up and then to flee, walking quickly up the hill for higher ground. Katharine glances nervously around the square. There are so many people gathered. If they are not careful, there will be a panic.

She thrusts out her arm and snaps her fingers at High Priestess Luca.

'You and I must go there now.' She walks around the table, and Luca is already out of her chair following. 'Bring horses for me and the High Priestess,' she says loudly. 'And clear a path to the harbor.'

'Make way for the queen! Stand clear!'

In moments, her queensguard has opened the road to them. Katharine's black stallion is ready for her, always nearby and saddled in case of emergency. She half leaps and is half thrown onto his back.

'That was good work,' Luca says when she is mounted and riding beside her. 'Nothing curbs a panic like the courage of a queen. Natalia would be proud.'

'I am too distracted just now to wonder whether you mean that,' Katharine replies. Her eyes are ahead, on the approaching mist. She hears, behind them in the square, Pietyr and the Black Council mounting horses to follow. As they ride to the docks, she holds her stallion to a canter to keep from trampling anyone near the shore, but she need not have bothered. Her figure on horseback is enough to clear a path, hair a black flag and black gown billowing, and the gathered folk part like butter to a hot blade.

'Stay. Do not dismount.' Luca holds her hand out across Katharine's reins. 'The mist does not do this. I do not know what it means.'

'I am the Queen Crowned.' Katharine takes a breath and swings her leg over to land on the dirt. 'I have nothing to fear. It is my mist.' Hers. Theirs. The mist has been the protector of the island ever since it was created by the last and greatest Blue Queen. It will not hurt her. It cannot. It was her bloodline that made it.

'Help me, old sisters.' She reaches out to them with her mind and feels their familiar surge in her veins. Katharine walks toward the shore as the dead queens fill her ears with shrieks. She walks until the sand is wet from the surf, and then they allow her to go no farther.

A wall of white and swirling gray stretches across the harbor from north to south. It has traveled into the shallows, closer than she has ever seen it and continues to advance, moving like the sea creatures do: smoothly and swiftly. The way it darts at times reminds her of a striking shark.

How badly Katharine wants to run. The mist is so thick. If it rushes upon the shore, she is sure it will knock her down and smother her. Choke her. She will die, and find the ghosts of Mirabella and Arsinoe waiting inside the gloom.

'No,' she whispers. 'You must stop.'

The mist pushes forward, and the people behind her scream. Perhaps even the High Priestess. Certainly Genevieve. But before the cloud can touch the earth, it draws back and moves away, back out to sea to dissipate and break apart, gone so quickly, it is hard to believe it was there in the first place.

Katharine hears footsteps as Rho comes to stand at her shoulder, along with Pietyr, backed by a dozen queensguard.

'Queen Katharine, are you unharmed?' He examines her, but she pats his hand and moves him aside. She was not touched.

'What is that?' Rho draws her serrated knife and points into the waves. Something dark and heavy rolls through the water. A dark shape, soon joined by more, cresting and coming toward shore.

Screams and moans of terror sound from all sides as Katharine walks toward the water to see what the mist has brought.

'Keep them quiet,' she orders. 'Keep them back!' The dead sisters hiss and spit; they scratch at her insides and retreat to the darkest corners of her mind. She does not care. Nor does she care when she steps into the water up to the ankles and catches waves across her knees.

The mist has brought her bodies. Ragged, water-logged corpses tossed heavily into the shallows.

Katharine splashes in deeper. The Goddess has answered her prayer. She has brought her the corpses of her sisters and the cursed naturalist. The mainland suitor and the Wolf Spring boy. Her hope to see what is left of Mirabella and Arsinoe is so strong that she convinces herself it is them, even though there are far too many. Far more than she sought. She convinces herself it is them until she turns the first one over and sees a stranger's watery eyes staring back.

As the bodies beach themselves, Katharine searches up and down the sand, looking into one dead face and then another for some spark of recognition. But none are queens.

'Haul them out.' She points to the water. She shouts when her queensguard hesitates to move. 'Haul them out and line them up on the sand!'

It takes several minutes for the task to be completed. Her soldiers grimace, and some will not touch the corpses or enter the water until Rho forces them to at knifepoint. 'My priestesses are braver than you,' Rho barks, and several priestesses hurry into the surf to help, wetting their white robes to the waist.

Katharine and Rho survey the bodies lined up on the

beach. Pieces of their crafts have been brought up as well, bits of curved hull and planks, an oar. Some on shore and others still bobbing in the waves. Scattered tidbits.

'What is this?' Katharine asks, and no one replies. 'Bring me someone who might know.'

Rho shouts to the gathered crowd, and a man comes forward, wringing his hat between his hands. In the face of so much death, he almost forgets to drop to his knee.

'You are familiar with the harbor?'

'I am, my queen.'

'Can you tell me, then, who these people are?'

'They are——' He hesitates, looks up and over the wet shapes laid out. 'They are the searchers. They sailed this morning at your request, to search for the remains of the traitor queens.'

Katharine clenches her jaw.

'Is this all of them?'

'I don't know, my queen. It——it seems so.' He presses his handkerchief to his sweating, balding head and then again to his mouth and nose. The stench of rotting flesh is thick in the heat. But if they sailed that morning, they should not smell at all. Katharine dismisses the man and steps closer to the corpses with Rho.

'All sailed out today, he said,' Rho says in a low voice. 'But some of these bodies are much older, as if——'

'As if they drowned weeks ago.'

Katharine stares down the line of wet, bloated dead, some large, some small, some missing parts. Women and men alike.

Fishers and sailors who were doing her bidding. They had hoped to find Arsinoe and Mirabella facedown in the sea and net themselves a fine reward.

Now they remind Katharine of seals, spread out to lounge on the warm sand. The bravest of the gulls flaps down atop one of the farthest bodies and begins to tear at it like a thief after coin. Then it raises its head and flies away. Someone with the naturalist gift must have told it to wait.

'What could have done all this?' Pietyr turns to the balding man. 'Did they all sail together? Travel as a fleet?'

'No, Master Arron. The Carroway sisters and their brother'—he gestures to three—'they set out in two small craft with crew.' He points to several more. 'Mary Howe and her crew there, she has the elemental gift and a knack for storms. She's never once sailed into bad weather, that one.' Mary Howe lies faceup and freshly dead, her blue shirt buttoned to the throat. What she wore on her bottom half is anyone's guess. The entirety of her lower body is gone. Torn away. Katharine walks to her and leans down, pushes up her shirttails and lifts the torso to better look at the wound. It is ragged and there are errant tooth marks. A shark. The rest of the body is pristine.

'Odd for the shark to leave it so. Odd for a shark to have killed her at all in these waters.'

The bodies lying on the beach tell a strange story. Some are clearly drowned, with purple lips and bloated faces, while others bear signs of harm: a boy with one side of his head cleaved in as if from a heavy, sharp object, another with what looks to be a stab wound to the heart. Some bodies seem to have been dead so long that the flesh falls from them in whitened, water-logged chunks. Yet others, like Mary Howe's, are so fresh she might have died only hours ago.

Katharine kneels and buries her gloved hands deep in the rot of some poor girl, her face unrecognizable.

'Queen Katharine,' Pietyr says.

'What?' She moves to the next body, and the next, turning their heads left and right, inspecting them. *They are a message*, she thinks. They have something to tell her if she will only look hard enough. 'How . . . how did you die . . . ?' she murmurs, and Pietyr puts his hand on her shoulder.

'Kat.'

She stops and looks up, sees all the gathered staring faces. They have watched her pick through the bodies crouched like a crab, her black silk gloves slicked with blood to the elbows.

Reluctantly, Katharine rises.

'I am a poisoner, Pietyr. Taught by Natalia these many years. What do they think? That I am shy to what death does to flesh? That I have never seen a gut burst open?'

Pietyr's mouth draws into a firm line. Even he, an Arron himself, looks slightly green.

Katharine stares out toward the sea. Clear now, calm and shining on a sunny afternoon. Gathered higher on the beach, the people whisper. Too many whispers and voices to identify, but she is able to hear one word above all.

'Undead.'

THE MAINLAND

At first when Mirabella hears Arsinoe muttering in her sleep, she thinks she must be having some scandalous dream about Billy. Mirabella has stayed awake, lying in the dark and listening to Arsinoe's breathing slow. Listening to her drift off. Looking after her as an older sister should after a younger sister is frightened in a graveyard. So when she hears Arsinoe start to murmur happily, she smiles, torn between listening closer and pressing her pillow around her ears. She is reaching for her pillow when Arsinoe says:

'Centra.'

Mirabella sits up and turns toward her sister. She knows that word. She listens closer as the dream goes on, Arsinoe muttering faster and faster, her words becoming harder to hear. Sometimes it is only a snort. Lots of snorts, actually, and Mirabella bites her lip to keep from laughing.

Suddenly, after a moment of quiet, Arsinoe jolts up from her pillow, back straight as a board. Then she slumps and rubs her face with both hands.

'What a dream,' she whispers.

'Arsinoe.' She flinches when Mirabella says her name. 'What was that?'

'It was . . . Why are you awake? Did I wake you?'

'I was not asleep.' Their room is so dark that Arsinoe is only shapes. Hints of bare arms poking out of her pale nightclothes. Mirabella climbs out from underneath her sheets and goes to sit at the foot of Arsinoe's bed. She takes the candle from her bedside table.

Her fire feels close. She can almost sense the heat of it, curling around her ankles like a warm and loyal pet. A small pet now, after weeks on the mainland. Mirabella stares at the wick of the candle and calls the flame. Nothing happens. It is so slow and shy. Each time it takes longer and longer, and the muscle inside her mind goes slack.

'You can always use a match,' Arsinoe says.

'Elementals with gifts of fire do not use matches.' But she sets the candle down. 'What were you dreaming about?'

'Nothing.'

'Are you keeping secrets?'

'No. I'm just not sure I'm ready to tell you I'm losing my mind.'

Mirabella touches the tip of the wick. It is not even warm, and shame creeps up the back of her neck.

'You said, "Centra." Is that what you were dreaming of?'

'You know it?' Arsinoe says, and then, 'Of course you do.

So what do you know about it?'

'Not much.'

'Most people on the island wouldn't even recognize the name.'

Mirabella thinks back to her teachings. To afternoons with Luca in the temple, surrounded by stacks of books. Even all the way back to Willa and the Black Cottage.

'I know that Centra is the name of Fennbirn's ally to the north. Before the mist came. That is all.'

'That's all?'

'What else mattered? All nations that are not Fennbirn are the mainland now.'

'Do you know anything about their history?' Arsinoe asks.

'Nothing,' she replies.

'Think hard. Nothing about a missing Fennbirn queen called Daphne?'

'A missing Fennbirn queen? Of course not. Arsinoe, what are you dreaming of?'

'What about Henry Redville?'

'Arsinoe—' She turns to her in the dark to demand answers. But that name. Henry Redville. 'Redville of Centra,' she says. 'I think he was Queen Illiann's king-consort. Queen Illiann, the last Blue Queen.'

'Queen Illiann.'

'Yes,' Mirabella says. She would say more, but everyone knows of Illiann, the last and greatest Blue Queen, who won a great war with the mainland and whose gift was so strong that she created the very mist that shrouds and protects them to this day. Everyone knows that legend. Even those who resist study as hard as Arsinoe.

Arsinoe gets out of bed and starts to pace, jostling the little dog at the foot of the bed that Mirabella had nearly forgotten about. 'Her king-consort. But he loves Daphne. And if Daphne is nowhere in the history books . . . then did she stay behind or go back to the island to be killed? And if Henry Redville was a real person, then I really am—' She stops and turns back to Mirabella in the dark. 'Dreaming through her eyes.'

'Dreaming through whose eyes?'

'Daphne's.'

'Daphne,' Mirabella says doubtfully. 'The lost Fennbirn queen?'

Arsinoe quiets, and Mirabella finally strikes a match to light the candle, tired of trying to decipher her sister's expressions in the blackness. Yellow-orange light flickers through the room; she touches her candle to the lamp on Arsinoe's bedside table, and the space glows brighter.

Arsinoe's eyes are haunted. But even so, the corner of her mouth is upturned as though she is amused.

'Tell me what you dreamed.'

'I dreamed I was inside someone else.' Arsinoe touches the ends of her hair, down past her shoulder now. She touches her chest and her face, as if to make sure they are still hers. 'Someone who sailed ships on Centra with Henry Redville and had black eyes and hair, just like ours.'

'On Centra,' Mirabella says. 'With Henry Redville. Arsinoe, that was over four hundred years ago.'

'Four hundred . . .' She sits down beside Mirabella on the bed, pulling the dog into her arms when he wakes and begins to whine. 'What does that mean? Why am I dreaming it?'

'It cannot be real. It must not be. Perhaps it is only a memory, from a book you forgot about reading.'

'Maybe,' Arsinoe whispers, but Mirabella can tell she does not think so. 'Except I saw something else first. In the cemetery.'

'What?' Mirabella holds her breath. Finally, her sister is ready to tell her what happened. She has been patient, but her patience had started to wear thin.

'A dark figure. Like a shadow. She had on a crown made of silver and bright blue stones.' Arsinoe goes to her desk and rifles through it for paper and ink. The sound of the pen scratching across it in the dark sends unpleasant twitches down Mirabella's spine. She hands the paper to Mirabella, who looks at it in the candlelight.

'The Blue Queen's crown.'

'I saw the shadow of the Blue Queen,' Arsinoe says. 'And it pointed back to Fennbirn.'

All through breakfast, Mirabella tries to eat as though nothing is wrong. She butters her toast and drops sugar into her tea. Pretends to listen to Mrs. Chatworth and Jane gossip about the governor's wife's birthday party or coo over the little dog and the ribbon on his collar. Only Billy seems aware that anything is amiss, his gaze flitting from the dark circles beneath Arsinoe's eyes to Mirabella's tense fingers and then back again.

They had barely slept. They had simply sat side by side on Arsinoe's bed until the candles had burned down to nubs. Finally, in the early gray hours of predawn, Arsinoe had lain down and let her eyes drift shut. But the moment she closed them, the muttering commenced. Mirabella shook her awake, but every time she slept, it would begin again.

Mirabella does not know what the dreams mean or if they are true visions or simply nightmares. She does not know if Arsinoe really saw the shadow of the Blue Queen, though her hands ache from clinging to the crumpled paper of Arsinoe's drawing. All she knows is what she can feel: that it is the island reaching out for them again.

'A party at the governor's grand estate!' exclaims Jane as if they had not already been talking about it for the last half hour.

'Indeed.' Mrs. Chatworth says, tapping into a soft-boiled egg and feeding a bit to her new pet. At least that idea of Arsinoe's seems to have gone smoothly. 'We will need a new jacket for you, Billy; I saw one in the shops that will do. And Jane, you must wear your new lilac silk. There will be plenty of eligible bachelors there; perhaps I can marry off both of my children in one afternoon!'

At the mention of Billy's marriage, Arsinoe stops eating,

and Mirabella turns to Billy with an arched eyebrow.

He clears his throat.

'I'm not looking for a wife, Mother.'

'Christine Hollen is a fine choice. Everyone in the city knows she has set her cap at you.'

'Mother, did you not hear what I said?'

'And did you not hear what I said?' Mrs. Chatworth asks. 'Your father, it seems, is in no hurry to return from'—she glances sidelong at Mirabella and Arsinoe—'that *place*, and without him our creditors will come calling. The partners will push us out, and before you know it, the estate at Hartford will be gone, and this town house will be gone, and the business will be gone, and we will be ruined! And all you need do to save us is ask for Christine Hollen's hand.'

'If I ask for her foot instead, do you think they'll just give us a loan?' Billy asks, and Arsinoe barks surprised laughter into her napkin.

'May we be excused?' Mirabella asks, and grabs her. 'I am afraid my sister and I have slept poorly. Perhaps a bit of fresh air . . .'

'I'll join you,' Billy says, and starts to rise.

'You will not. You'll stay and come to the shops with Jane and me to be fitted for your jacket. And you.' Mrs. Chatworth fixes her gaze on Mirabella. 'You and your sister are my guests, and how you conduct yourselves reflects on my house. Make sure to take your parasols. And make sure she wears a dress.'

Mirabella assures her that she will, though it will be easier said than done, and pushes Arsinoe gently up the stairs. Not ten minutes later, Billy knocks at their door and pokes his head in.

'I've managed to put my mother off jacket shopping for the time being,' he says, and glances at Arsinoe, who is still dressed in trousers and one of his old shirts.

Mirabella gestures to her sister helplessly. 'She has it in her mind that she should start passing herself off as a boy.'

'It's my fault, I suppose.' He softly closes the door. 'For letting her have so many of my clothes.'

'Don't talk about me like I'm not here,' Arsinoe says from her dresser, where she is rummaging through drawers. 'Billy, would you lend me a pair of your socks? I know how protective you are of them, but you have several dozen pair.'

'And I've lent you at least five pair already. What have you done with those?'

'Does it look like I know?' She tosses long white stockings and other frilly underclothes out of the drawer and onto the floor. 'Just give me the socks, will you, Henry?'

She stops.

'Who's Henry?' Billy asks.

Arsinoe turns and quickly walks past him to search under Mirabella's bed.

'No one,' she says. 'Isn't that your middle name? William Henry Chatworth Junior?' She comes up brandishing black socks.

'You know it isn't,' Billy says. 'Now who is Henry?'

'She will explain later.' Mirabella takes Arsinoe by the shoulder and tugs her through the door, even as she struggles to put on her last shoe. 'If I do not get her out of the house soon, your mother will change her mind and confine us to our room.'

'That was close,' Arsinoe whispers as they walk down the front steps.

Mirabella grasps her by the elbow. 'You are in far better spirits than I would expect, considering.'

'Well, I got more sleep than you did.' Arsinoe ventures a smile, but it fades when Mirabella is unmoved. 'I can't explain it. The dreams are good dreams. They feel safe.'

'And the Blue Queen's shadow? Did she feel safe?'

Arsinoe swallows. 'No. She felt like a threat.'

'So what are we going to do?'

'I don't know. Maybe nothing. Maybe it won't happen again.'

Mirabella takes her sister by the arm. 'Neither you nor I believe that,' she says. 'So you had better take me back to where it started. Let us go back to Joseph's grave.'

'You haven't been back here, have you?' Arsinoe asks as she leads Mirabella down the groomed path of the cemetery.

'No.' Not since the day they erected the grave marker. Mirabella has thought about it and about him, many times, but she has never visited. 'It does not feel that I have the right when she cannot.'

'I don't think Jules would begrudge him visitors.'

'Perhaps. But that is not the only reason. I also do not like to think of him rotting underground when he should be ashes on the wind. Ashes in the water.'

'When he should be alive.'

'Yes,' Mirabella agrees. 'When he should be alive.'

They reach Joseph's grave and step into the shade of the elm trees. It is hard to believe that he is really there, under that dirt, beneath that smooth patch of green grass. Mirabella cannot feel him. But then, they had so few days together. Sometimes she does not trust her own recollection of his eyes or his smile. The sound of his voice. But she had loved him. He had loved Jules, but Mirabella had loved him for those brief few days.

'Why here?' Mirabella asks as Arsinoe drops to a crouch beside the headstone. 'Why at Joseph's grave?'

'I think it started here because he's a piece of the island.' Arsinoe touches the earth. 'I think, with him and me together, she was able to find me. And maybe because of . . .' She makes a fist.

'What?'

'Madrigal said once that low magic was the only kind of magic that worked outside of the island. And maybe because I've done so much of it, the island is able to find me.' She pulls up her sleeve and studies her scars. 'Maybe I burn like a beacon.'

Mirabella's eyes wander over the slashes of raised pink on

her sister's arm. The pocked marks inside her hands. They are different from the bear's claw marks across her face. There is something about them. Something disturbingly useful.

'If that is true, then I like this even less,' Mirabella mutters. 'Low magic has never been trustworthy.'

'It saved me often enough,' Arsinoe says.

'Not without cost. And not only to you.' Mirabella's eyes flicker to the dirt of Joseph's grave. It was an unconscious movement, but Arsinoe sees it and grimaces. 'I did not mean that, Arsinoe. I only mean . . . We should hope the dreams are only dreams.'

'And the shadow queen is only what?'

'Another dream.'

'Mira, I was awake.'

'Barely.' Arsinoe scowls and Mirabella softens her tone. 'Tell me what you dreamed of this morning, when you fell asleep again.'

Arsinoe hesitates, as though she would keep it to herself. When she finally tells her, she keeps her eyes on the dirt.

'I dreamed that I was her again.'

'Who?'

'Daphne.' Arsinoe cocks her head and shrugs, a gesture she has taken up from the mainlanders. 'The lost queen of Fennbirn.'

'There is no lost queen of Fennbirn.'

'Do you want to hear this or not?'

Mirabella exhales and motions for her to continue.

'I dreamed we stole away on a ship bound for Fennbirn. To help Henry Redville in his suit.' She closes her eyes as though remembering and sniffs, searching for scraps of the dream as if they might carry through the memory. 'Her plan is to befriend the queen. To enter into her confidence so she can steer her toward Henry. But I think she's going to want Henry for herself—'

'And then what?' Mirabella interrupts. 'After she stowed away, what happened?'

'Then we were back on Fennbirn. We got off the boat dressed as a boy and made our way to the queen.'

'You met Queen Illiann? You met the Blue Queen?'

Arsinoe nods gravely. 'I have been back there. Back on the island. Back on the docks in Bardon Harbor, and in the Volroy.'

Mirabella turns away, shaking her head. This cannot be real. The more Arsinoe talks, the closer the island feels, as if she could look out past the bay and it would be there, leering back at them.

She squeezes her eyes closed. 'So this . . . missing queen . . . she has met the Blue Queen and not been recognized? How? Did she truly believe Daphne was a boy?'

'No. Illiann saw past that right away. But Daphne moves like a mainlander. She talks like one. And according to everyone on the island, Illiann's sisters have all been dead for a very long time. She's never had to look over her shoulder and guard her crown. She was the Queen Crowned since birth. Not like us.'

'And this Daphne . . . she knows nothing?'

'Nothing,' Arsinoe says sadly. 'She doesn't even know she's an elemental. Her gift has been so long stunted. But I've seen her moods affect the weather. Subtle changes. Her gift is dormant from so many years away from the island, but it's still there.'

'Wait. If Daphne truly is—was—a lost elemental queen, then why is she speaking to you? Why not me?'

Irritation flickers across Arsinoe's face.

'I do not say that because it should be me,' Mirabella explains, 'because I should be chosen. Only that like speaks to like. Elemental to elemental.'

Arsinoe nods. 'I don't know why. Maybe she's more like me than like you. She smuggled herself off Centra by dressing in boy's clothes and sneaking onto a boat to Fennbirn along with Henry's horses. I've never smelled so much manure in one place.

'And then there's the fact that she's essentially an orphan, at the mercy of Henry's family's charity.'

'That makes her like both of us,' says Mirabella with a frown.

'Maybe it's something else, then.' Arsinoe rises to her feet and trails her hand along Joseph's headstone. She pauses on the inscription, on the line that reads, 'A friend to queens and cougars.' Then she clenches her fist. 'The low magic. It has to be the low magic. And I'm marked through.'

She turns toward Mirabella with a devious glint in her

eyes. 'Perhaps if we marked you with it as well. . . .'

'Absolutely not.'

'Well, what do you want me to do, then? Stop dreaming? Stop sleeping?'

Mirabella sighs. She cannot very well ask that. And besides, she knows her sister. Arsinoe will follow this queen to whatever answers and whatever end there may be. No matter the risks.

'Just promise me that you will not keep secrets? That you will tell me everything, no matter what it is.'

THE VOLROY

Katharine walks through the rose garden on the east side of the castle. A small cloistered space, very private, with full bushes of roses of every color. It has been difficult to find a moment of peace in the days since the mist brought the bodies. Everyone is afraid. And no one has answers. Examination of the bodies themselves has yielded no explanations, and the mist continues to behave strangely, rising when it should not rise, thicker and closer to the shore than normal.

Katharine reaches out to cradle a large red bloom in the palm of her hand. It is the dead naturalist queens who have lured her into the garden, craving sunshine and the scent of green, growing things.

But Katharine cannot bloom the rose. She cannot make it grow, any more than she can make it wither and die. The borrowed gifts are not true gifts, after all. The borrowed naturalist gift gives her a sure hand with the royal horses and hounds, but she cannot command them. The borrowed war gift makes her skilled with knives, but it does not let her move them. The dead poisoners let her eat the poison but could not stop the poison from corrupting her.

'Queen Katharine.'

Katharine releases the rose and turns. It is High Priestess Luca with Genevieve, of all people.

'An unlikely pair,' she says as they bow.

'Unlikely indeed,' says Luca. 'Genevieve stepped into my shadow the moment I stepped outside the castle. Almost as if she does not trust me to be alone with the queen.'

Genevieve sighs but says nothing. It is not worth denying.

'We have decided to release the bodies of the searchers for burning,' Luca says.

'But,' says Katharine, 'we still do not know why or how—'

'And we may never. But the bodies will reveal no more secrets. And the families have waited long enough. The longer they are kept, the more time the people will have to murmur wild speculation and incite a panic.'

Katharine frowns, her mind a flicker of images from the day of the banquet. So many bodies rolled onto the sand: fish-bitten and mutilated or pristine and pale. As she thinks, a bee lands upon the back of her hand, and Luca's eyes flicker to it. Katharine lets it crawl a moment and then brushes it off.

'There are still questions unanswered, questions that the people will not just forget.'

'The people will accept the explanation of the temple. That the searchers fell to a tragic accident at sea.'

'And the mist?'

'The mist delivered them home.' Luca looks to Genevieve as though for support, and to Katharine's surprise, she acquiesces.

'People want the soothing answer,' Genevieve says. 'They want the answer that allows them to go on with their everyday lives. Let the temple give a statement. Let the High Priestess wield what influence she has. It is, after all, why we allowed her a seat at the table.'

'Well put,' says Luca, her expression sour.

'Go ahead.' Katharine says, and clenches her jaw. 'But though the people may forget, I will not. I will not forget that my searchers met with violent ends. That they sailed and died within days yet some appeared to have been dead for weeks.'

The High Priestess gazes over the line of rosebushes. She gazes over them for so long that Katharine thinks she will change the subject and comment instead on the blooms or the weather.

'I remember when your sister tried to flee through the mist,' says Luca. 'Do you remember? You were separated by that time, of course, but you must have heard, living here with the Arrons. I was there, when they found them bobbing in their boat. They could not have been gone from Sealhead Cove for more than a night. Yet their little faces were gaunt. And they had drunk all their water.'

Katharine swallows as the High Priestess looks back at her.

'No one spoke of it then. There were too many other things—pressing things—to distract us. But even those who the mist allows to pass through remark on it. Those who sail from the mainland. Those who trade.

'Time and distance do not mean the same things within the mist. Nothing means the same thing within the mist. As much as we would like to know what befell your searchers, we will probably never know.'

And with that the High Priestess bows and walks away.

'She is an irksome old thing,' Genevieve says after Luca is gone. 'But I think she is right. Better to put this incident behind us. The people see the mist as the guardian of the island. For it to behave so alarmingly . . . We are lucky it has been quiet since then. And who knows? This story the High Priestess spins about the mist bringing the bodies home to you, maybe it will work. Maybe it is even true.'

'In case it is not,' says Katharine, 'I would learn more about the mist. Perhaps even about the Blue Queen who created it. Will you look into it for me, Genevieve? Discreetly?'

'If you wish it.' One of the bees hovering near the roses buzzes too close to Genevieve's hair, and she waves her hand at it. Then she cries out when it stings her on the finger.

'Now you have killed it.'

'It stung me!'

'And how many times did you sting me as a child? Stop being such a baby about it.'

Genevieve bows and stalks out of the garden, sucking on her wounded finger. As a poisoner with a strong gift, the venom from the bee's sting will not even cause swelling.

It will not be more than a momentary pain.

Katharine looks back at the roses. The dead naturalist queens always make her feel the calmest, drawing her into the flowers or urging her toward the stables to ride. But the talk of the mist has put all the dead sisters on edge.

'You know as well as I do,' she says to them. 'The mist is not finished.'

THE MAINLAND

In the morning, Arsinoe and Mirabella get ready for the governor's wife's birthday party.

'We must try to be polite,' Mirabella says as she stands behind Arsinoe at their vanity table, trying to pin Arsinoe's short black hair to the sides of her head. 'We must try to smile at Mrs. Chatworth and Miss Jane.'

'I'll try.' Arsinoe coughs as Mirabella puffs loose powder over the redness of her scar, but when she is done, it only looks like a powdered scar. Her mark of the bear refuses to hide.

'We are here on their goodwill. On their charity.'

'I know. It's just . . . harder to move on for some of us.'

In the mirror, Mirabella's face falls. 'I didn't mean that,' Arsinoe says. 'I just meant you're better at pretending to be one of them in a crowd.'

'Only because I am already used to wearing dresses. We should hurry and choose yours. Not the gray. It looks like a potato sack. What about the blue? With the black ribbon at the hem?'

'No,' says Arsinoe. 'No dresses. A jacket and vest will do.'

Mirabella sighs and stops fussing with Arsinoe's hair. 'What did you dream, last night? Do not lie.'

'I dreamed of arranging secret meetings between Henry Redville and Queen Illiann. To give him an advantage before she meets the other suitors at the Disembarking.'

'Met,' Mirabella says with a frown. '*Met*. This is all in the past. None of it can be changed. It is only some trick of the island, some lingering grasp it has on us. And you were the girl again? Daphne?'

'I was.' Arsinoe squints at her sister in the mirror. 'Did you know there are secret passageways hidden behind tapestries hanging in the Volroy?'

'How would I know that? I have never been there, except for the cells. Nor have you.'

'Except that's how I snuck Henry through undetected.'

'Was there anything else about this dream?' Mirabella asks. 'Anything important? Did you see hints of why the Blue Queen would send you these visions? You said you thought Daphne in love with Henry herself. But we know he becomes Queen Illiann's king-consort. Did it seem that Daphne would try to betray Queen Illiann?'

'No. She and Illiann are already close friends. Is that why Illiann is giving me the dreams? Is she teaching me a lesson?'

'I do not know.' Mirabella turns away to dress herself. 'But until the governor's party is over, let us try to forget it.'

Governor Hollen's mansion is just outside the city, a large estate surrounded by trees. As their carriage makes its way up the long circle drive, Arsinoe is reminded of the Black Cottage. The buildings have similar white exteriors and dark timbering, though the brick of the Hollen foundation is a bright red-orange.

'Not bad,' she says, and whistles.

'Hush.' Mrs. Chatworth reaches across the carriage and slaps Arsinoe's shoulder. She has not spoken to her since she came down the stairs wearing trousers and a black vest.

'She was paying them a compliment, Mother,' says Billy. He takes Arsinoe's hand.

'Just keep her to the rear. Show Miss Mirabella to the front. At least she knows how to dress decently.'

In ivory lace and green ribbon, Mirabella hardly looks like a queen at all. But that is what mainland fashion demands. The only thing Mrs. Chatworth complained about was her hair. She wanted ringlets, but Mirabella refused to use the hot metal iron. With her weakening gift, she could be burned, and Arsinoe imagines that for a girl who used to dance with fire, there could be nothing worse.

'Wasn't half the reason you were invited to this party so that people could get a look at us? Christine would have invited Billy, but you and Jane were included to accompany the foreign wards.'

'What is your point, Miss Arsinoe?'

'My point is I'm doing you a favor dressing like this.' She pulls on her lapels, smooths her hair back away from her facial scars. 'Dressed like this, I'm more of an attraction.'

Footmen help them from their carriage and they are shown through the front door into an enormous, high-ceilinged foyer. Some relation of the governor—one of his younger daughters, his niece, perhaps—steps forward to receive them.

Mrs. Chatworth inclines her head.

'May I present Miss Mirabella Rolanth,' she says, 'and her sister Miss Arsinoe.'

At the introduction, the girl's eyes open wide. 'We have heard much! How wonderful to meet you, finally.'

Arsinoe and Mirabella nod and curtsy slightly, and the girl sweeps them through the house.

'I don't know why we had to be Mirabella and Arsinoe *Rolanth*,' Arsinoe whispers as they follow.

'We could not very well be Mirabella and Arsinoe *Wolf Spring*,' Mirabella whispers back.

The governor's girl leaves them at the rear of the house, where a set of wide-open doors leads to the party. Arsinoe whistles again. The sprawling rear lawn boasts a small fountain and a well-kept hedge maze. Tables have been set and adorned with summer flowers, and there is even a stone dance floor and a small band of musicians. On the island, such a celebration would be reserved for a queen or a high festival.

'Some birthday,' Arsinoe says, watching guests as they mill about laughing or clump together with glasses of drink in their hands. Many ladies have opted for wide-brimmed hats instead of parasols.

'Do not be sour,' chides Mirabella. 'Our own birthdays were high-festival affairs as well.'

'We were queens.' She sighs. 'What I wouldn't give for a mug of ale like we used to have at the Lion's Head.'

'Unlikely to find any of that here,' Billy says, and takes her by the arm. 'Tea, certainly. Or champagne.'

'Anything to put in front of my face. We may be foreign curiosities, but I hope they don't mean for us to meet *everyone* at this party.'

'Billy! Over here, Billy!'

They turn. Christine Hollen stands in the center of a group of young women.

Arsinoe grimaces.

'Oh, good, it's Miss Christine.'

'Go,' Mrs. Chatworth says, and prods them not too gently.

Billy clears his throat. 'I suppose we'll have to.' He leads the way, and Arsinoe turns to Mirabella to mouth the word *help*.

'She will not get within an arm's length,' Mirabella says, and snakes her arm through Billy's. 'Do the same on his other side.'

Arsinoe does, though it feels awkward. She cannot help noticing that Mirabella's stride has gotten markedly slinkier. And that with the both of them pressed tight against him, Billy is grinning like an idiot.

'Put on your best smile,' Mirabella says cheerily through her teeth.

'Just like a horse's,' Arsinoe says cheerily through hers.

When they reach her, Christine offers Billy her hand to be kissed, but with both of his arms occupied, her fingers linger idly in the air before fluttering back down to her side. Mirabella glances at Arsinoe and lifts her chin in triumph.

'I am so glad that you and the Misses Rolanth could come.'

'Thank you for the invitation,' says Billy. 'It's a lovely party.'

Christine's smile is not as radiant as usual. She cannot stop looking at the way Mirabella leans against Billy, and with Mirabella there, the poor girl seems to have shrunk three sizes. Arsinoe feels sorry for her and tries to catch her eye to smile for real, but a boy approaches to extend his hand to Mirabella, and Christine's expression brightens.

'Miss Rolanth,' he says. 'Will you dance?'

'Oh yes, you must!' Christine exclaims before Mirabella can respond. 'The band my father chose is absolutely delightful.'

Mirabella looks between the boy and Arsinoe.

'Please,' Christine nudges. 'Billy cannot have thought he could keep you all to himself!'

Mirabella slides her arm free and takes the boy's hand. 'I will be right back.' But she will not be. The boys are already forming a queue beside the stone dance floor.

Arsinoe wonders how well she will fare. The music on the

mainland is so different from the music of home. There are no somber strings and woodwinds like in Rolanth, no cheerful fiddle like Ellis and Luke played in Wolf Spring. This stuff is played mostly on horns, by musicians wearing shirts striped like pulled taffy.

Once Mirabella is gone, Christine wastes no time. She reaches for Billy's empty arm and tugs him to her side, sliding her gaze over Arsinoe's vest and trousers. Then she taps him on the shoulder.

'There is someone here I want you to meet.' She cranes her neck, a perfectly smooth and elegant neck, Arsinoe notes, and points to a young boy racing across the lawn. 'There he is! My little cousin.' They laugh as the child tumbles and pops back up in his tiny, handsome suit. 'He is just the sort of boy that I will have someday. A fine son, for a father to be proud of. Isn't he darling?'

'He is,' Billy agrees.

'He certainly is,' says Arsinoe.

'Isn't that the sort of boy that you would like someday, Billy? A fine boy and a fine woman to raise him.'

Arsinoe snorts unintentionally, and Christine's pretty smile falters.

'Perhaps you should go and dance as well, Miss Arsinoe. That is, if there is anyone here who is willing.'

'Perhaps I should knock you on your—'

'I'm willing.' Billy extricates himself from Christine's grip and slips his arm around Arsinoe's waist. 'And as for a son,

Christine, I think I would prefer a little girl. With a smart mouth. And who only ever wears trousers.'

They walk away together, and Arsinoe cannot resist looking back. Christine's entire face has turned red with fury.

'Well,' Billy says nervously. 'What are they doing?'

'She looks like she's about to scream.' Arsinoe laughs. 'Your mother is not going to be happy about this.'

'My mother will get used to it. She'll have to be content with my agreeing to go to school in the fall.'

'To school?'

'Yes,' Billy says. 'I should have told you sooner.'

'Tell me now.'

He nods and turns them away from the dance floor to find someplace quiet. It takes a while, on an estate the size of the governor's, but finally the sounds of the party are muted, and they stop on a soft knoll of grass between the stables and the carriage house.

'This is nicer.' Arsinoe plops down onto Billy's jacket after he spreads it out for them. 'Some of those people were staring at me so hard, I thought their eyeballs were going to pop past their lids.'

'Here.' He hands her a glass of champagne he had taken off a tray as they passed. 'It's not ale, but it's better than nothing.'

She stares intently at the bubbles.

'Do you think it could be poisoned?'

'It isn't likely.'

'What a pity.'

'I didn't think your gift worked here,' he says.

'I don't think it does.' She downs the glass in one gulp. 'Still a pity.'

He sits down beside her, and for a moment, they recline in the comfort of each other's company. Alas, it does not last long.

'You understand why I have to go to school,' he says.

'Yes. Of course. It's what's done here, isn't it? Go to school and then into business with your father.'

'Unless I'm disinherited,' Billy says, and laughs without much humor.

'Do you think that's why he hasn't come back?'

'No, actually. The fact that he hasn't come back makes me think I have hope. If he's staying away to punish me, then that's a good sign. If he was going to disinherit me, he would just come home and draw up the papers.'

'Are you and your family really going to be all right?' Arsinoe asks. 'About the money, I mean.'

'Yes. No. I don't know.' He grins ruefully and sets his champagne in the grass. 'It'll be fine. I'll figure it out somehow.'

'I wish I could give you all this,' she gestures to the estate. 'But I haven't got it. You went to the island for a queen and a crown and came back with two extra mouths to feed. For Goddess's sake, I'm borrowing your clothes.'

'And you look much better in them than I do. Listen. Don't worry. My father's an arse, but he won't stay gone so long that he ruins us. If there's anything you can rely upon, it's his sense of self-preservation.'

'I'll admit, I sort of dread his return.'

'It'll be all right. But in the meantime, I'll go to school to please Mother.' He touches her chin. 'I promised Joseph and Jules that I would take care of you, didn't I?'

Arsinoe jerks loose.

'Jules should never have asked that. She was just so used to looking after me that she couldn't leave without someone else to take over. You should have said no.'

'I would never have said no, Arsinoe. Jules didn't really need to ask.'

'But maybe then she would have stayed.' Except now that she is here, Arsinoe knows that Jules could never have come to the mainland. The constraint and the ridiculous rules would have driven her mad. And what would have become of Camden, had Jules's gift weakened? She would have become a wild thing, no longer a familiar, in a place where she would have been hunted, or put in a cage.

'Junior, could you ever have belonged on the island?'

He raises his brows.

'I don't know. For you, maybe.'

'But you would have been waiting, to come home.'

'Is that what you're doing? Waiting to go home?'

She shakes her head. There is no home for her on Fennbirn, either. 'It's just . . . very different here. There's a lot to get used to.'

Billy wraps his arms around her and pulls her down beside

him. She rests her head on his shoulder and throws her leg across his.

'I miss Fennbirn, too, you know,' he says. Then he pauses before asking in alarm: 'Do you think the Sandrins have eaten my chicken?'

Arsinoe laughs.

'There are plenty of other chickens to eat besides Harriet. I'm sure she's fine. Spoiled, even. Maybe she spends some of her days at the Milone house, following Cait and Ellis around. Maybe she's met Luke's rooster, Hank, and they've made you some adorable chicken grandchildren.'

'Chicken grandchildren.' He laughs and pulls her closer. 'I think I would like that.'

Arsinoe nuzzles her face into his neck. Even on a hot summer day, she cannot seem to get close enough. Despite living in the same house, they have had so little time alone.

'You know, if your mother finds us like this, she will call it a scandal.'

Billy rolls onto her and grins. 'Then we had better make it scandalous.'

After a very pleasurable while, Arsinoe and Billy drift off in the afternoon sun. And Arsinoe dreams.

She slides into Daphne's body and finds herself at Innisfuil. And there is only one reason for so many to have gathered there: it must be the Beltane Festival.

In the dream, Daphne regards herself in the long polished

mirror. She dresses always as a boy on Fennbirn. Always as she wishes. How fondly she runs her hands over the doublet and hose and the ends of her short hair. The folk of Fennbirn know she is a girl, yet they do not treat her any differently than if she had successfully passed as a boy. Which she does whenever she meets someone from her home country of Centra or Valostra or Salkades. She can dress as she pleases and move freely in all circles, and for the first time in her life, Daphne feels whole.

Arsinoe peers out through Daphne's eyes as she stands beside the Blue Queen: Queen Illiann. Illiann reminds Arsinoe of Mirabella. They are both elementals, for a start, and Illiann is nearly as beautiful, with long black hair shining to her waist and intelligent eyes edged by thick black lashes. She is also just as elegant and assured of her crown as Mirabella was when they first met. So sure that her sisters had been killed as babies that the sight of a black-haired, black-eyed girl from Centra caused not even a flicker of curiosity.

But she is still not as strong as my sister, Arsinoe thinks as attendants dress Illiann for the festival, weaving around her and Daphne so quickly it is a wonder they both do not wind up bound into the same gown. Illiann's elemental gift was for weather and water. A flickering of fire and nothing of earth. Not even the great Blue Queen was master of them all like Mirabella.

'Are you sure I can't smuggle Henry off his ship?' Daphne asks, close to Queen Illiann's ear. 'The suitors miss out on so much of the festival. And Henry loves to watch the mummers.'

Mummers. Arsinoe searches her memory for the old word. *Play actors.*

'Absolutely not.' Illiann smiles. 'The suitors remain on their ships until tonight's Disembarking Ceremony.'

'Even Henry? When he has met you already so many times before?'

Illiann claps her hand across Daphne's mouth, laughing. '*You* are not even supposed to be here,' Illiann says as her attendants clear out of the way, eyes rolling over their smiles.

Inside Daphne's head, Arsinoe laughs along with them. It is still a strange sensation, disembodied yet within a body, the senses so keen that she can smell the sweet perfume on Illiann's palm.

'Such a secret.' Daphne pries the queen's fingers loose. 'I don't see what the trouble is when he will be your husband soon enough.'

'Perhaps. And perhaps not. There are still other suitors to meet tonight.'

'Other suitors. But what are they compared to my Henry? None of them will be as clever or as stout hearted. None of them can calm a horse with a word and a touch.'

'He is lucky to have a friend who is so confident of his virtues.'

A friend. What kind of friend would call him 'her Henry'? And what kind of friend is he to look at Daphne like he does? Open your eyes, Illiann. Don't be made a fool.

Daphne sighs. She looks over Illiann's formal gown. The Blue Queen may be called 'blue' but may still wear only black.

'Are you ready, then? Can we go and see the players, so I can tell Henry about them later?'

With a smile, Illiann affixes her sheer, protective veil across her face and leads the way.

Yuck. Veils. At least we didn't have to wear those. Or a doublet and hose. Goddess bless the girl who invented trousers.

They step out of the tent, and Arsinoe peers around curiously. Innisfuil Valley has not changed much in the four hundred years between Daphne and Illiann's time and Arsinoe's own. The cliffs and the view of Mount Horn remain the same and the lushness of the long grass. The trees are different, though, smaller, and in varieties that no longer exist on that part of the island. They cast a different color and a shifting brand of shade—even the trees suggesting that this part of the island's history was a brighter time than the time of blood and secrets that Arsinoe was born into.

Illiann pulls Daphne up onto a dais. Directly before it, a circle has opened up in the crowd to form an impromptu stage, and as they watch, actors in bright costumes prepare to present a scene for the queen's amusement.

The lead actress steps to the fore and bows.

'We are a troupe from the oracle city of Sunpool. And we present a scene in honor of Queen Illiann's birth.'

It begins, and three young girls wrapped in swaddling cloths of green, gray, and pale blue mime being born to a woman playing a queen with a great, yellow-painted crown atop her head. Another woman, dressed all in shining black, with silver ribbons in her hair, descends upon the queen and wraps her in her arms.

The Goddess, Arsinoe thinks.

The Goddess brings with her one more babe, a beautiful girl in bright blue and black, who bursts out from where she had been hidden in the Goddess's skirts. 'Illiann!' the actors cry. 'Illiann, blessed and blue!' The crowd claps loudly, as does Illiann herself with a soft laugh. The girl playing her twirls in delighted circles and touches each of her 'newborn' sisters on the forehead, and they fall dead to the ground.

If only it were really that easy. That clean. The play ends, and Illiann places a garland of flowers around the neck of the actress she judges to have been the best: the girl who played the birthing queen. But though they received no garlands, every single actress comes to kiss the Blue Queen's robes.

'Why are you looking at me like that?' Illiann asks, and Arsinoe feels Daphne blush.

'It's only . . . you're so different from what I expected. They really love you. You really love them.'

'That is what it is to be a queen.'

'Not where I come from.'

'Is Centra truly such a terrible place? You rarely speak of it fondly. Am I to dread marrying Henry, then, if after my reign we are to return there?' Illiann regards Daphne from the corner of her eye. 'You know, Daphne, that even if I do not choose Henry to be my king-consort, you will always be welcome here.'

'You would let me stay?' Daphne asks.

'Of course. You seem better suited for the island anyway. Perhaps that is why I love you so well and so quickly. You have the novelty and tales of a Centran but the spirit of the island. Though I do not know if you would truly stay if Henry must go.'

Arsinoe wishes for a mirror, to see what Daphne's expression gives away, but then the dream moves ahead, as dreams do, of its own accord, time folding over on itself so that day becomes night and Arsinoe reels at the sudden change.

They are on the cliffs now. Atop the cliffs, overlooking the bay. And from the fires and drums, Arsinoe knows what she is about to witness. She has witnessed it before, from near that same spot, in her red-and-black painted mask.

The Disembarking Ceremony.

Why Daphne is there, Arsinoe does not know. Perhaps because she was ashore already. Perhaps because she has become Illiann's new favorite. It does not matter. Daphne stands behind the queen, so close that Illiann's black skirt billows against the edge of Daphne's doublet. But they are not alone. So many maids and white-and-black-robed priestesses surround them that Arsinoe is surprised none have fallen off the rocks.

'It is nearly time,' one says, and giggles, and even in the darkness lit only by flames, it is easy to see the blush in her cheeks.

So many names pass by Arsinoe's ears: suitors from Bevellet and Valostra and Salkades. Nearly a dozen, far more than the five she had to face at her own ceremony.

'Marcus James Branden,' says one of the maids. 'He has caught everyone's eye. He is the Duke of Bevanne. It is a lesser principality of Salkades, but his family holds great favor with their king and have substantial mining interests. Gold and silver, I think.'

'Marcus James Branden, the Duke of Bevanne.' Illiann grimaces. 'He has so many names.'

'And what is a minor duke compared to Henry?'

'A duke from Salkades,' the maid persists. 'Who commands the finest fleet of ships in the world.'

'So he's rich and has a navy. He'll trudge onto the beach decked out in velvet and slouching from the weight of the coin in his pockets.'

There is some last-minute pushing and prodding as the maids change their minds about one of Illiann's bracelets and replace it with one of lapis lazuli stones. And none of them will stop gossiping, tittering about this or that suitor's piercing eyes, and the pounding hearts of love.

Arsinoe is glad that it is only a dream and her true stomach is not there to be sick.

'When they look at you tonight,' someone exclaims, 'your gift will spark into a flame.'

Arsinoe feels Daphne purse her lips.

'As someone who has been privy to the inner circles of the

women, and of the men,' Daphne says, 'I can tell you that the men on those ships are not talking about Illiann with such rosy-cheeked poetry.'

From the top of the cliffs, all eleven ships are visible in the harbor with flags aloft. It is Illiann's nervous wind, the maids say, but Arsinoe cannot tell if that is true. Illiann looks like she always does. Composed and focused. A queen born to rule.

Then Illiann trembles, and over the bay, spiderweb-thin veins of dry lightning crack across the sky. Daphne gasps, and the queen glances at her with embarrassment.

'I suppose I am a little nervous. Do I look all right, Daphne?'

'Of course you do. You are beautiful. Henry has said many times that you are the most lovely girl he has ever seen.'

Did he really say so? Somehow I doubt it.

The boats launch toward the shore, lit with torches and lanterns, and garlands of flowers that go to waste, as they can hardly be seen in the darkness. They make landfall, and suitors disembark and pass by on the beach below, some nervous boys who mess up their bows, some laughing buffoons like Michael Percy and Tommy Stratford, those poor suitors whom Arsinoe accidentally poisoned.

The ones from Bevellet wear black cloaks hung with gold and carry fat red roses. Those from Valostra are each dressed in different light-wool stripes.

Then it is Henry's turn. He arrives on a launch lit with nine lanterns.

'One lantern for every great county of Centra,' Daphne whispers to Illiann.

'He looks very handsome in that black-and-crimson cape. Though someone should have told him that crimson is for funerals. Shall I wave?'

Daphne chuckles.

'I think he almost winked.'

Illiann chuckles as well and then stops. Below on the beach stands the final suitor. Branden, the Duke of Bevanne.

Arsinoe feels Daphne swallow and begin to fidget as Illiann and Branden stare at each other. He is good-looking, to be sure. One of the best-looking boys that Arsinoe has ever seen, and she grew up with the likes of Joseph Sandrin. But there is something else about him that strikes her, above his looks.

'Illy?' The queen does not respond, and Daphne clears her throat. 'Illy? What is it? Should Henry be worried?'

Henry should be more than worried, Arsinoe thinks. For there is something in Branden's eyes that reminds her distinctly of Queen Katharine's wicked king-consort, Nicolas Martel.

'Arsinoe? Arsinoe!'

She jerks awake to find Billy's hands on her shoulders. They are still on the knoll of grass between the governor's stable and carriage house, and from the look of the sun, not much time has passed. Yet Billy is looking at her crossly, like she slept the whole party away.

'What? What's the matter?'

'You said, "Henry," again.'

Arsinoe sits up and brushes herself off. 'Hmm?' She tries to feign innocence, or perhaps confusion, but the blush creeps onto her face. Her scars must already be dark from it.

'Don't play the fool. And don't play me for one. You called me Henry the other day when you wanted to borrow some socks. Now who is he?'

'Shouldn't we be getting back?' She stands and sees Mirabella approaching from the direction of the house. Billy gets to his feet beside her.

'There you are!' Mirabella calls.

'Arsinoe, stop playing with me. Have you met someone named Henry?'

'No, of course not. Why are you so upset? It was only a dream!'

Mirabella arrives in the midst of their argument and looks from one to the other as Billy picks up his jacket and beats it free of grass.

'If I were to dream and start whimpering and moaning, "Christine, Christine,"' he says, 'I'd wake up to your hands around my throat.'

'Oh no, Billy.' Mirabella touches his shoulder. 'It is nothing like that.'

'Mira.' Arsinoe shakes her head. 'Keep quiet.'

'We said no secrets, sister.'

Arsinoe exhales hard through her nostrils and turns away, the closest thing to permission she can bring herself to give.

'She has been having visions of the past.'

'Visions?' Billy asks. 'I didn't think you had visions. Isn't that . . . some other gift?'

'Not visions. I misspoke. Dreams. She has been dreaming through another queen's eyes. A queen from the Blue Queen's time. And she saw . . .' She pauses, as though searching for a word. 'A specter, a shadow beside Joseph's grave. A shadow that looked like us.'

Arsinoe peeks at Billy from the corner of her eye. He is utterly befuddled.

'But why would she be dreaming that?'

'I love it when you both talk about me as if I weren't here.' Arsinoe casts a glare at them. Then, before either can ask any more questions, she stalks quickly back to the party.

BASTIAN CITY

It does not take long for word of the mist to reach Bastian City from the capital. In the Bronze Whistle, Emilia beats her fist against the table.

'The mist rises and spits drowned bodies onto the shore. Right at the Undead Queen's feet.'

Mathilde leans forward, her arms around a cup of wine. 'They say the corpses were torn apart. Skinned. Aged by years when they had sailed only days before.'

'It is another sign,' says Emilia.

'It's rubbish,' says Jules. 'Fishers got caught up in the same squall, and sharks set upon the wreckage afterward. It's a tragedy, to be sure. But it's not a sign.'

'And what of the aging? The advanced decay?'

'Exaggeration and fear. Or simple misunderstanding. The sea can do strange things to a body. I've seen it myself, back home. And you should know it as well here so near the water.'

Emilia and Mathilde trade weary expressions, and Emilia pounds her fist again.

'Another sign or not, the time is right to move. Half of the people already consider Katharine to be an illegitimate queen, and the other half will say they do if only to get rid of another poisoner.'

'Half and half.' Jules snorts. 'So she has no supporters, then? The whole island is on your side?'

'Even the mist is on our side,' says Emilia, and laughs. She looks to Mathilde. 'It is time. It is finally time to begin.'

'Yes,' says Mathilde. 'A call to arms.'

Both turn and stare at Jules expectantly. As if Jules would stand and shoulder a blade, give a rousing battle cry, and charge straight out of the tavern.

'Don't look at me,' says Jules. 'I already told you what I thought of your prophecy. And where you can stuff it.' She tosses a few roasted nuts into her mouth and chews hard.

Again, Emilia and Mathilde trade glances, and Mathilde slides her hand gently across the table. 'Jules. I understand your reluctance. But there will be no hiding from this. No escape. It will be easier on you and everyone if you choose to embrace it.'

The seer looks so confident. The expression in her eyes is soft and imploring, as if she thinks Jules is simple and if only they talk slower she will understand. As if she does not understand full well the scope of their ridiculous plan. Raising a rebellion in her name. The name of the legion-cursed naturalist. She feels her temper rise into her throat and hates it, that war-gifted aspect of herself.

'Come now, Jules,' says Emilia. 'Haven't I always been a friend to you? Did I not help you save the traitor queens from the Volroy?'

'Don't call them that.'

'Have I not hidden you and fed you all these weeks?'

'So is that it, then?' Jules asks. 'I owe you? Well, perhaps I do, but I can think of a more reasonable payment than leading an army.' She chooses her next words with care. 'You cannot usurp the throne from the rightful line of queens.'

'A failing line,' Emilia says, and points a finger into Jules's face. 'A weakening line. What did they give to us this time? Two defectors and a lesser poisoner. No real queen.'

Jules cannot really argue with that. Even when Arsinoe had determined to fight for the crown, she only wanted to survive. She never wanted to rule. 'Weakening or not,' Jules says, 'the queens are all the island has ever known.'

'And does that make it right?' asks Mathilde.

'Why not show them something new?' Emilia gestures to the ceiling, to the sky. 'You can be a part of that, Jules. You can lead us to it.'

'Lead us to what?' Jules chuckles. Emilia's passion, if not exactly infectious, is certainly something to watch.

'An island where voices outside the capital are heard. A council comprised of people from Sunpool and Wolf Spring, from Highgate. From everywhere. The Legion Queen will not be another queen like the triplet queens. She will be different. She will be a protector for us all.'

'She's an idea,' Jules says. 'And you want me to be her face.'

'I want you to realize that you are her.'

'You want me to rule.'

'No.' Both Emilia and Mathilde shake their heads. 'We want you to lead. We want you to fight. And then we want you to be a part of Fennbirn's future.'

Fennbirn's future without the triplet queens. It is hard to imagine, even though Jules bears no love for Katharine or the poisoners. 'Katharine has been crowned,' she whispers. 'The island won't go against that, no matter how unpopular she is.'

'Let us prove you wrong,' says Mathilde. 'Let us show you. Come with us to the villages and towns. Speak to the people.'

Jules shakes her head.

'Or consider this,' Emilia says casually. 'With Katharine gone and the poisoners out of power, you will no longer be a fugitive. You and your cat could go back to Wolf Spring.'

Jules looks at her as hope leaps into her chest. 'Back to Wolf Spring?' She could go home. Home to Grandma Cait and Ellis. To Luke and even Madrigal. And Aunt Caragh . . . with the poisoners who banished her deposed, Aunt Caragh would go free as well.

'Even if I could go back, I would still be shunned for the curse,' she whispers, but the temptation in her voice is plain.

'Not by your family. You might catch a stone or two to the side of the head, but you would not be carted off in chains.

And eventually, they would come around. They would see that you are still you, and there is no curse at all.'

The corner of Jules's mouth curls upward. The thought of going home again is a sweet dream indeed.

'They'll never follow me. No one will ever really fight beside someone with a legion curse.'

Emilia makes a fist and shakes it, as though the crown is as good as won. 'You let us take care of that.'

In the rear of the Bronze Whistle, the door that leads to the alleyway opens and closes. The trio falls quiet listening to the footsteps, waiting to see whether they will turn up toward the manor house and leave them in peace. But as the footfalls enter the final corridor, they hear the kitchen boy exclaim, 'Mistress Beaulin! We weren't expecting you!'

'Mistress Beaulin,' Mathilde whispers. 'Margaret Beaulin? From the Black Council?'

Emilia glances at Jules, then jerks her head hard toward the bar. Mathilde grabs Jules and drags her quickly behind it, crouched low and out of sight. She presses her finger to her lips as the footsteps pause in the doorway.

Margaret Beaulin. What could she be doing there, Jules wonders. What could she want?

Despite Mathilde's firm grip on her arm, Jules leans out to the edge of the bar and peers around.

Margaret stands in the doorway in black and silver like the queensguard, her clothes still dusty from the road. A tall woman, she occupies nearly the whole frame. Emilia has remained seated, even kicked her chair back to rest her leg against the table. But her fingers brush the long knives she always keeps strapped to her sides.

'Margaret. It didn't take long for you to find me.'

'It was easy enough to guess where you would be.' Margaret steps farther in, eyes darting fondly around the Bronze Whistle. 'They say you've made it your own.'

'Who says?' Emilia asks. 'So I will know whose tongue I must fork.'

'It looks the same as when your mother and I used to come here. When we used to bring you.'

'What are you doing here? Why are you not in the capital, licking an Arron boot?'

'Have you not heard?' Margaret asks, her mouth twisting bitterly. 'The new queen has replaced me on the Black Council.' She walks to Emilia's table. 'Replaced me with a war-gifted priestess, of all things.'

Emilia draws one of her blades. 'If you dare to sit, I will run this through your throat.'

Jules tenses, ready to help, though she knows not how. Emilia's composure is cracking; the tip of her knife shakes and her voice is strained.

'Did you think it would be so easy? Did you think I would help you lick your wounds now that they have finally turned on you?'

'Emilia,' Margaret says softly. 'I came to see you first. Before anyone, because I—'

'Because you knew if I had been the one to find you, you would not have survived the exchange!' She kicks away from the table and stands, her knife still aimed at Margaret's chest. 'You are not welcome here. And you will not speak to me. You left us for them. Now live with that.'

She walks quickly past Margaret and leaves. Jules twitches to follow. Except that Margaret is still standing in the middle of the room.

She stays there for a few long moments. Then she turns and walks quietly out. Mathilde waits until her footsteps have faded completely before emerging from behind the bar, cautious as a rabbit from a hole.

'Put this on,' Mathilde says, and drapes Jules in a red-hooded cloak. 'Keep your head down and return to the Vatros house. I will follow Beaulin and see where she lands. And then I will go find Emilia.'

'You don't think Emilia went home?'

Mathilde shakes her head. 'When Emilia is troubled, she seeks out the quiet. There are not many places she would go; don't worry. I will find her.'

'Why did Margaret Beaulin come here? How does she know Emilia?'

'Before she was a part of the Black Council, Margaret was Emilia's mother's blade-woman. Her war wife. Her lover,' Mathilde explains when Jules's expression stays blank. 'There was a time when they were family.'

Before Jules can ask more, Mathilde strides out on fast, long legs, leaving Jules in the empty tavern. She knows she should do as Mathilde says. But when she passes the kitchen boy, she cannot help asking,

'Which way did Emilia go?'

'That way,' he says, and points. 'Toward the temple.'

'The temple?'

The boy nods knowingly, and Jules pulls her hood down low. She nods her thanks and presses a coin into his hand.

It does not take long for Jules to reach the temple. Even with her head down and keeping to the alleys, she cannot lose it: its impressive height and black-and-white marbled stone is impossible to miss. Emilia took her there once before, not long after she first arrived in the city, yet when she steps inside, it still makes her lips part in wonder.

The temple of Bastian City is so unlike the temple of Wolf Spring that Jules almost cannot reconcile the two as of the same purpose. Wolf Spring Temple is a small one-story circle of white stone, the interior little more than pews and an altar. Beauty is found in its simplicity and in the sprawling, wild gardens that climb across its gates and walls. By contrast, Bastian City Temple is a great hall, with ceilings too high for frescoes. The altar is set back deep as in a cave and twisted through with gold, so that when the sacred candles are lit, the entire altar appears to burn. Embers and rage, waiting to ignite.

Jules finds Emilia before all of that, in the massive chamber that precedes the main room of worship, staring up at the statue of Queen Emmeline. Queen Emmeline, the great war queen, who stands with marble arms raised, her armor depicted atop the flowing folds of her gown. Over her head, marble spears and arrows hang suspended, ready to pierce the hearts of anyone who would enter the temple to do harm.

'That was fast,' Emilia says. 'I thought Margaret would keep you pinned inside the Bronze Whistle for a little longer. Where is Mathilde?'

Jules walks slowly to stand beside Emilia beneath the statue. 'She followed her.'

'Ah, Mathilde.' Emilia smiles ruefully. 'Always so thorough.'

'You never told me you were acquainted with a member of the Black Council.'

'And? There are many people you know whom you have never mentioned.' She sighs, and gestures to Queen Emmeline. 'Isn't she a marvel? A guardian. A sacker of cities. It's strange, is it not, how good the Undead Queen is with her blades? If I did not know any better, I would say she had the war gift as well.'

'If she did, would you let her keep her crown?'

Emilia considers a moment. 'No.'

'Mathilde told me about your mother and Margaret.'

'Oh?' She spins away and pulls her knives from her sides to flip them back and forth, catching them by the hilt and then by the blade. 'But did she tell you everything?'

'Only that they were . . . blade-women? But I don't know exactly what that means.'

'It speaks to the bond between warriors. Margaret

Beaulin was like a mother to me.'

'Where was . . . where was your father?'

'He was there, too.'

'He was there, too?' Jules exclaims. Then she clears her throat. 'I'm sorry. I've just never heard of that.'

'I am not surprised. You naturalists are so conventional. You do not have the fire that we have.'

'You know, you only refer to me as a naturalist when it's convenient for you,' says Jules, and narrows her eyes.

'Yes. And every time I insult them, it is your war gift that retaliates.' She sighs. 'My father was here. Too. A blade-woman does not replace a husband, the father of your children. It is a different kind of bond.'

'Are there blade-men?'

'Yes. Though blade-husbands are rare. But you are missing the point, Jules. Mathilde did not tell you everything.'

'What else is there?'

'When Margaret left to serve the poisoners, it broke my mother's heart. It was that heartbreak that allowed her to fall so ill. It was that heartbreak that killed her.' She spins her knives up into her hands. 'And Margaret Beaulin did not even attend her burning. She did not even send a letter.'

'I'm sorry,' says Jules, and Emilia spits upon the floor. 'Is that why you hate the poisoners so much? Because they stole her from you?'

'I don't need that reason,' Emilia says. 'And they did not "steal" her. She chose to go.'

'I know. I just meant that I know something about being left behind. I learned plenty when Madrigal left me for the mainland.'

'We will leave soon,' Emilia says, slashing at the air. 'To begin the call to arms. You cannot stay in Bastian City now that she is here. The Black Council may have ousted her, but she will still jump at the chance to change their minds, by delivering them their favorite fugitive.' She levels the tip of her knife at Jules's chest and smiles slightly. 'Besides, if I stay, I may end up gutting her in the street.'

'Soon,' Jules whispers. 'How soon?'

'Tonight. It is time. Margaret's arrival is another sign.'

'Maybe a sign you should stay and work things out with her.'

Emilia shakes her head. 'The path is set. Our bards have already begun to sing your tale in towns and villages through the north.'

'My tale?'

'The tale of the strongest naturalist in generations, and the strongest warrior as well. The tale of the girl who bears the legion curse without madness, and who will unite the island under a new crown, and a new way of life. You already have soldiers, Jules Milone. Now they just need to see you, in the flesh.'

Soldiers. Warriors. A prophecy. Jules takes a deep breath as her palms begin to sweat. All of her blood seems to drop into her feet.

'Tonight just seems too fast.'

Emilia sighs. 'Too fast,' she says, and Jules's eyes snap to hers as the spears and arrows over Queen Emmeline's statue begin to rattle. 'When the traitor queens ran away, did they take all your courage with them?'

'I don't lack for courage,' Jules growls. 'But nor do I lack for brains. These stories you're spinning build me up too high. Everyone we meet will be disappointed.'

'When I saw you at the Queens' Duel I was not disappointed.'

'Reluctant people don't make the best figureheads.'

'Reluctant.' Emilia advances and presses her forearm across Jules's neck, forcing her back against the wall. 'Reluctant but curious. You wonder about the truth of the prophecy. Even you want to know how far you can go, if pushed.'

'No, I don't.' Jules pivots and shoves Emilia to the wall, so hard that she slides up, lifted clear off her feet. 'It's a nice story. Something new. The poisoners off the throne. But it's only a story. A dream, and I've dreamed those kinds of dreams before. They don't work out.'

Me on her council and you on her guard. She can hear Joseph's words so clearly it is as if he is there to whisper them into her ear. She backs away from Emilia and is surprised to feel Emilia's hand touch her cheek.

'Come with us, Jules Milone. Let us show you what we can do. And I promise you will start to believe again.'

THE VOLROY

Katharine sits at the head of a long oak table as her Volroy staff present her with samples of fabric. New curtains, they say, for the king-consort's chamber.

'I like this brocade,' she says, and taps one with an abundance of gold thread. In truth, they have shown her so many that she can scarcely tell them apart. And she does not really care enough to choose. But nearly every room in the West Tower must be refurnished and freshened after being so long vacant, and redecorating seems to ease the servants' minds.

She cranes her neck to look past them out the eastward-facing windows. It is a small opening, a mere stone cutout, but she can see the sky, and a bit of the sea in the distance. The vast, empty sea. Since the strange deaths of the sailors sent out to search for her sisters' bodies, few have dared the waters. Only the bravest venture out from the port now and only on the clearest days. There are great profits being made by those few, but their sea-catch and cargo holds are not sufficient to meet the demands of the entire capital. Goods in transit have begun to clog the roads. And the price of fish is so high that Katharine has ordered that the Volroy purchase none of it. Let what comes ashore go to her people instead.

Unfortunately, the gesture did nothing to stem the nervous whispers that wind through the marketplaces daily: that the bodies the mist brought were a warning or that they were a macabre gift for the Undead Queen. Either way, the people are afraid it was a sign of more deaths to come, now that Katharine is on the throne.

'Queen Katharine. Your portrait has been completed. The master painter would like to present it to you.'

'Show him in.' She stands as the servants whisk away the fabric.

'This is a nice surprise,' says Pietyr. All day he has been sitting in the corner, poring over correspondence from the mainland. More payments to be made to Nicolas's family, no doubt. 'We did not expect a completed portrait for at least another week.'

They wait quietly as the painter and his apprentice enter and bow and set the covered portrait and easel in the center of the room.

'Master Bethal.' Katharine steps forward to greet the painter and take his hands. 'How lovely to see you.'

Bethal drops to one knee.

'The honor is mine. It was a great pleasure to paint a queen of such beauty.' He rises and motions to his apprentice to remove the cloth.

Katharine stares at the painting, silent for so long that the smile on Master Bethal's face begins to crack.

'Is something wrong?' He looks from the portrait and back to her.

Pietyr turns toward her.

'Kat?'

The portrait is perfect. The queen in the painting has her same pale, slightly hollow cheek, her same regal neck. Somehow it has managed to portray her smallness and the delicacy of her bones. Even the little coral snake, which when she posed was only a coil of rope, has been transformed into the very likeness of Sweetheart.

'My queen? If you are displeased—'

'No,' she says finally, and Bethal exhales with relief. 'You have captured me utterly. It is so lifelike that I am tempted to ask if my snake also modeled for you in secret.' She steps closer, eye to eye with her image. The eyes are the only things he got wrong. The queen in the portrait's eyes are serene. Pensive. Perhaps a little playful. There is nothing looking out from behind them.

'It will be hung in the throne room immediately.' Pietyr shakes the painter's hand. In the throne room it will go, until her reign is over. Then they will pull it down and take it to be hung in the Hall of Queens.

The last in a long line, she thinks, and unconsciously touches her stomach. Her poison stomach and her poison womb, filled with poisoned blood that killed her first king-consort and may kill every king-consort who comes after.

'What is that?' She points into the painting's background at a table piled high with a poisoned feast: glossy belladonna berries and sugar-crystallized scorpions, a roasted fowl glazed a sinister purple.

But poisoned food is not the only thing on the table. Mixed in with the feast are bones. Long thigh bones and rib cages, tainted with blood and shadow. And on the end, in plain view, is a human skull.

'It is for you,' Bethal stammers. 'Our Undead Queen.'

Katharine frowns, but before she can object, Pietyr caresses her cheek.

'Embrace it. It is what sets you apart. It is your legacy.'

'A prosperous, peaceful reign is the only legacy I need.' But no one will listen. *Queen Katharine, of the poisoner dynasty*, the portrait's plaque will read. And beneath that, *Katharine the Undead*.

On the way to the council chamber, Bree Westwood falls into step beside her.

'Good day,' says Bree as she tries and fails to execute a proper curtsy while walking.

'Good morning, Bree.' Katharine's eyes move over the other girl's burnished brown waves, her pale blue dress embroidered with lilies. 'You are always so effortlessly lovely. I wonder, did you learn those tricks from my sister?'

Bree's eyes widen but only for a moment.

'Or perhaps, my queen, she learned them from me.'

Katharine smiles. The girl has cheek.

Ahead of them, the doors of the Black Council chamber are swung wide. She can see Pietyr inside, his eyebrows raised in wonder at the sight of them walking together. And she hears the fractured murmurings of two sides at odds. It is suddenly too exhausting to bear.

'Will you walk with me a moment, Bree?'

'Of course.'

They take a sharp turn. Inside the chamber, Genevieve rises in alarm, and Katharine halts her with a finger. She knows they are eager to discuss the findings of the autopsies performed on the bodies of the mist victims even though nothing was found. Nothing. No answers. No solutions.

'Some air by the window, perhaps,' says Bree.

The window has been modernized, as some on the lower levels of the Volroy have been, and contains glass, but the panes have been opened to allow in the late-summer breeze. How Katharine misses Greavesdrake. The manor house is much more comfortable. More luxurious in so many ways. But it is nowhere near as grand. It is not the monument that the Volroy is.

Katharine and Bree look out the window together, as companionable as if they are old friends. In the courtyard, beneath the trees, that little priestess of Mirabella's crouches near the hedge, feeding an enormous flock of birds.

'She spends quite a lot of time with birds,' Katharine says. 'I am always seeing this bird or that flying past her. Black ones with smart little tufts on their heads.' Bree stiffens. 'She must have had a strong naturalist gift before she took the bracelets for it to linger so.'

Bree turns, suddenly steely for a girl of so little substance.

'I am trying to figure out why you wanted to walk with me.'

'Perhaps I am tired of council strife.'

'Already? You have only just begun. Should we start to hope that your triplets come even sooner than Queen Camille's?'

The dead queens jerk inside her. *Snap her neck.*

Katharine stiffens until they quiet. 'Perhaps I am afraid.'

'Afraid?'

'Of course. You must think me truly oblivious if you do not think I fear what this mist means. That it has killed my people. We are all, afraid.'

'We are.' Bree looks back out toward the priestess, Elizabeth. 'I have been listening in the square. Word of this spreads across the island like a cry of alarm. It burns like a torch. But underneath that . . .'

'What?'

'They hope that it is nothing. That it will go away. They want to leave it to you and ignore it.'

Katharine laughs softly. 'Well. You must not hate them for that. It is my job.' She leans against the sill. 'It occurs to me, now that you are here, and . . . Elizabeth is here, that I have never had a friend like the friends my sisters had. I had Pietyr. I have Pietyr. But I do not think he counts in the same way.'

'That . . . ,' Bree says, and looks down. 'Surely that cannot be true, Queen Katharine. There are so many Arrons . . . so many poisoners here in the capital.'

Katharine cocks her head. 'No. I had Pietyr. I had Natalia.' Inside her veins, the dead queens tremble; they reach out as though to warm her blood with cold, dead fingers. *And yes,* she thinks, *I have you.*

'Queen Katharine!'

She and Bree turn. Three of her queensguard struggle with a man in a brown shirt at the end of the hall.

'What is this now?' Katharine sighs. She approaches and motions for the queensguard to ease before they cuff him on the back of head and render him unconscious. 'What is happening?'

'He says he comes from Wolf Spring, my queen. He says he must speak with you.'

He looks up at her, breathing hard. Blood leaks down his chin and neck from his lower lip, likely split during the scuffle.

'You did not need to be so rough with him,' Bree snaps from just behind her. 'He is only one man. And unarmed.'

'We take no chances with the safety of the Queen Crowned.'

Katharine steps closer. She leans down and cannot resist wiping the blood from his face with her fingers. The dead queens like it as they like nothing else. Blood from

161

living veins. Pain from living bodies.

'I am here now,' Katharine says. 'And you may speak to me.'

The man licks his lip and glares at her from under his brows. 'I come from Wolf Spring. I fish there. Ten days ago, I was out on a run with my crew, running up the coast after striper. And the mist—' He stops and swallows. 'It took one.'

'Took?'

'It came up out of nowhere and slid onto the deck. I've never seen anything like it. One minute she was there and the next she wasn't, and the look in her eyes . . . I can't forget it.'

Another disappearance. Another taken by the mist. And this time, as far away as Wolf Spring.

Behind Katharine, the rest of the council has drifted out into the hall, drawn by the voices.

'Someone else taken?' Renata Hargrove gasps. 'But why? Why only a fisher? Was she searching for the other queens? Had she anything to do with the Milones?'

'And is there anyone who can corroborate the story?' asks Genevieve. 'What would you have us do, fisher? Send ships to aid your search for one missing crew member? Who is to say he did not push her overboard and is now looking to hide behind the rumors of the mist?'

'I do not think it likely he would come all the way from Wolf Spring to do that.' Rho's white robes swing into view. 'It'd be easy enough to explain as an accident at sea. Why come here, to the capital, and to a queen that Wolf Spring despises, unless it is true?'

'I wouldn't have come if I had any other choice,' the man says angrily. 'No one wanted me to.'

Katharine squeezes her eyes shut as they bicker, gathering close in their tiny factions. Old council separate from new. Poisoner separate from giftless. Giftless separate from elemental, and all removed from Luca, Rho, and the temple.

'Did you sail here?' Katharine asks loudly. The voices behind her quiet, and she opens her eyes. 'Fisher, have you sailed all the way here from Wolf Spring?'

'Yes.'

'I would see your craft.'

Katharine's stallion is saddled, and she rides for the port at Bardon Harbor. Pietyr accompanies her on one side. On the other is the man from Wolf Spring, who is called Maxwell Lane. Some others from the Black Council have come as well: Paola Vend, Antonin, Bree, and of course Rho Murtra to bear witness for the temple. The others, including Luca, remain at the Volroy to grumble and gossip, and Genevieve, determined to become Katharine's eyes and ears, stays behind to listen.

'What good will this do?' Pietyr asks as they trot through the streets. 'What do you think we will find?'

'I am not sure yet, Pietyr.' In truth, she does not expect the boat to provide any answers at all. But the port is gripped by fear and has been since the mist spat the search party onto the sand. The people need to see that their queen is still not afraid.

Ahead, the port is full of docked boats but nearly empty

of people. Only a few sailors busy themselves on their crafts, tying and retying knots, checking sails, cleaning decks, shooing off the seabirds, who seem perplexed by the lack of activity. The birds at least are everywhere, posting atop masts in great patches of shifting feathers or aimlessly waddling along the shore.

'Which is it?' Katharine asks, and Lane points to a small fishing boat with dark green decks, laden with nets.

They dismount on the hill and make their way to the docks. Those who have been working in the port stop to watch, and people from the marketplace farther inland begin to gather as well, drawn by the murmurs of the queen's presence.

'This is the same vessel from which she was taken?'

'It's the only one I own.' He leads them down the dock and boards the boat.

'Where is the rest of your crew?' Rho asks. It is not a large craft, but too big to be sailed alone across such a distance.

'I sent them ashore.' Lane's voice is gruff as he checks knots and runs his hand along the rail. 'They didn't want to be close to the water.'

Nor does Katharine. With every board that creaks beneath her feet, she grows less and less brave. And a glance at the boat tells her that she was right: it will yield no answers. What could she have hoped to find? Remnants of the mist still gripping the hull? The poor girl's blood splashed across the deck?

'Bree,' Katharine whispers, and Bree draws close. 'Do you sense anything amiss here? With the water?'

Bree looks down, along the side of the dock to where the waves lap against the wood and rock. She shakes her head.

'My gift is for fire. The water has never spoken to me. Perhaps if my mother were here . . .'

'Look!'

Back on shore, the gathered crowd stares out at the sea. More voices join the first shout, and a cacophony of cries sends the nearby gulls winging into the air. Katharine turns to see what has their attention, though the dead queens inside her already know.

On the horizon, the mist has risen like a wall.

'Oh, Goddess.' Bree makes a pious gesture, touching her forehead and her heart. 'What does it want?'

'It wants nothing,' Rho replies. 'It is only the mist. Our protector, since the Blue Queen's time.'

Only the mist. Except that Katharine can feel it looking at her. Watching. The mist would speak. It has spoken, by laying bodies at her feet.

'Oi!' someone calls from inland. 'What's that?'

'What is happening?' Pietyr grasps Katharine's hand as the water beneath them quickens. 'The waves . . . The current is coming in harder.'

The boat lurches as the surge hits it, and the ropes holding her strain and squeak. Rho, who had boarded to further inspect the deck, is tossed against the mast.

'Priestess,' Lane says, and tries to help her. She has struck her nose against the pole and come away bloody.

Inside Katharine, the dead queens tug, this time toward the water. It takes only a moment to see why. There is a corpse drifting in toward the boat, facedown.

'Get it out of there. Paola, Pietyr.' Katharine nods to the body. 'Antonin, help them.'

They use gaffs to pierce the flesh and drag the corpse closer. It is unpleasant to watch it bob in the waves, which have slowed now that the body has reached the shallows. It is also unpleasant to watch them drag her up by the hook. But even worse is the sight of her watery, gray eyes when she rolls faceup.

'Allie?' At the sight of her face, Lane leaves Rho and nearly pitches himself over the side. 'Allie!' He pulls the dead girl into his arms and shoves the gaffs away.

'This is your friend?' Antonin asks acidly. 'Who disappeared off the coast of Wolf Spring ten days ago? What kind of stunt is this? What kind of naturalist plot?'

'A fine plot, indeed, if it allows a naturalist to manipulate the mist and the water.' Rho speaks through her own blood, her teeth slicked red. Then she twists her nose back into place.

'Give her over,' says Pietyr, and holds his arms out with a grimace to pull the body onto the dock.

Rho glances toward the shore and the rustling crowd of onlookers. 'Bree.' She jerks her head. 'Block their view.'

'How did she follow me here?' Lane asks helplessly. 'I lost her off the point of Sealhead. Those currents aren't right . . . to carry . . .'

And something more. Though her flesh is slightly bloated and her cheeks fish-bitten, Allie's corpse is far fresher than one would expect after making such a long journey through rough waves.

'She is just like the others,' Pietyr whispers.

Katharine crouches. The girl must have been very pretty once. She touches the dead girl's chin. 'We would keep her here to be examined for a time, to learn what we can of her death. After that, she will be returned to Wolf Spring under royal banner, with more than enough coin to pay for her burning. Do you know the family?'

Lane nods.

'Then this news will sit easier with them, coming from you.'

Katharine's hand hovers over the man's head, but answers are what he needs, not embraces. She nods to Rho and strides back down the dock to return to the horses. Ahead, the crowd has grown, and the people frown at her approach.

'We should disperse them,' Pietyr whispers. 'I will notify the queensguard.'

'It was you!'

Katharine blinks at Maxwell Lane. He has stood, and points at her for all to see.

'You! Undead Queen! You are the curse!'

Pietyr presses against her, as if to be a shield. Rho leaps deftly off the fishing boat and quiets Lane with her hands, too quickly for Katharine to see. Perhaps she merely knocked him unconscious. Perhaps she broke his neck. Either way, it is too late, for the crowd has latched on to the chant.

'Undead Queen! Poisoner! Thief!'

They advance on her as a mob. Some with only fists. Others with knives. Gaffs. Or short thick clubs.

'Queensguard!' Antonin shouts, though the soldiers are already running to intervene, fending off the crowd with swords. They make a wall of themselves and their crossed spears.

'It is all right, Kat. Get past them to the horses.' Pietyr presses her ahead and pulls Bree along in his shadow. Rho has disappeared with Lane back into the boat. Clever. Let the mob forget her. She will be safe.

Katharine keeps her head high. The people do not really hate her, she tells herself. They are only afraid. As they should be. As she is. And when she saves them, when she quiets the mist, they will remember that.

'Cursed queen!'

A clod of mud and filth flies through the air and strikes her chin. It splashes down her neck and into the bodice of her dress.

'Arrest them!' Pietyr growls. 'How dare you!'

More mud flies. And stones. Bree screams and Pietyr puts his arms up to try and shield them all.

Katharine touches the mud on her chest. She listens to the hateful chants of her people.

'Katharine! Run! The queensguard cannot hold them!'

The first of the mob breaks through the line and charges

with a raised club. Katharine draws one of her knives. She shoves Pietyr to one side and hooks the boy around the neck as he comes, plunging the blade up into his throat, up through his shouting tongue. His blood soaks into her glove, and she lifts him high, so strong, much stronger than he is. The dead queens rise to the surface, and Katharine feels as though she has doubled in size, tripled, that she and they are unending.

When the boy ceases to kick, she drops him in a heavy heap. The noise is gone, the crowd silent. Those closest have slid to their knees and peer out around the legs of the queensguard with fearful tears on their cheeks.

'Kat.'

She looks at Pietyr. His hands are raised, palms out. She looks down at the boy, so very young and so very dead, his blood cooling on her arms.

'Pietyr,' she whispers. 'What have I done?'

THE MAINLAND

The night after the party at the governor's estate, Mirabella and Billy sit in the kitchen after the rest of the house has gone to sleep.

'I don't like meeting like this.' He pushes their solitary candle closer to the center of the table and hovers over it, ready to blow it out at the first sound of footsteps. 'You know how she hates it when we talk about her like she's not there. But sometimes—'

'Sometimes we need to talk about her when she is not here.' Mirabella stares into the tiny flame, resolute. But she says nothing more. She does not like it any more than he does.

Upstairs, Arsinoe lies in her bed, sleeping, dreaming through the eyes of another queen. A queen from generations ago, hundreds of years.

'Couldn't they be . . . just dreams?' Billy asks.

'They do not seem like "just dreams."'

'But you've never heard of this happening to any other queen before?'

'No one knows anything about a queen after she leaves the island. Maybe this is common.' The candlelight flickers with her breath. It is hard to resist trying to test her gift, to see if she can push it higher, make it stronger. But she has tried and failed so many times that she is not brave enough to try anymore. 'Besides, Arsinoe and I are different. Our destiny was to be dead. So who knows what lies ahead for us now?'

'I still think it could be nightmares.' Billy rubs his eyes. 'You have both been . . . uprooted . . . strangers in a new place, and she's had a difficult time with my mother and Christine.'

'Billy, I do not think—'

'And before that, the entire bloody, traumatic year. These dreams might pass if we let them.'

He is trying to make it so just because he declares it. She has heard him use the same tone with his mother and other young men. She thinks of it as Billy's 'mainlander' voice. But this is queen's business. Fennbirn business, and when she slides her hand across the table, he is all too happy to take it.

'From what she has told me, Arsinoe is no historian. She says . . .' She pauses, and smiles at the memory. 'She says that Ellis Milone was the historian, so anything she needed to know was stored for safekeeping in his mind.

'Yet she recalled the name of Queen Illiann's king-consort, Henry Redville, and knew where he was from.'

'*Henry Redville*,' Billy grumbles. 'And what sort of man was he?'

'He was a king-consort. A good one. He remained true to the queen. He led a fleet of ships into the last battle.'

'Did he die?'

Mirabella frowns. She gestures to the empty table.

'Does it look like I have my stack of Fennbirn history books with me? And why do you sound like you hope that he did?'

Billy leans back, dragging his forearm across the table.

'You're getting salty. I think you've been spending too much time with your sister.'

She inhales. 'No, I do not think that Henry Redville died. Queen Illiann ruled for another twenty years after the war ended.'

'I didn't mean to snap,' he says. 'I'm just worried about her.'

'I am worried for us all.' She reaches again for his hand. 'If the dreams are only dreams, then how did she know about the king-consort? How did she even know Queen Illiann by name; the whole island only remembers her as the Blue Queen.'

'Maybe from a story Ellis told. Or maybe she heard it somewhere else. You can't be the only queen to know Blue Queen history. Poets must write of it. Your . . . bards must sing of it!'

'That is true. That could be. But I cannot stop thinking . . .' She shakes her head. 'I cannot help feeling like the island is reaching out for Arsinoe, ready to snatch her back.' She stares again into the candle, watches the flame flicker and weaken, mocking, as Billy's eyes spark with curiosity.

'Tell me more about the Blue Queen,' he says. 'Tell me everything. Why was she so important?'

'She created the mist.' Mirabella shrugs. 'That is her legacy. To win the war, she created the mist to shroud and protect the island. She is the one who hid us away and turned us into legend.'

'And now she's after Arsinoe.'

'Arsinoe thinks that the dreams are meant to show her something, about Daphne, the Blue Queen's lost sister. She feels safe in the dreams. The only threat comes from the shadow of the Blue Queen herself.'

Billy leans back and runs his hands roughly through his hair. 'This is madness. I thought we'd left all this behind.'

'It seems not. Low magic is everywhere, and the island has tracked us through Arsinoe's link to it. The last of the magic in the mainland world.'

'Low magic is everywhere. You keep saying that. But I've never seen it.'

'You do not know where to look.' She takes a deep breath. 'Arsinoe says that if I were to let her do a low magic spell with me, the dreams could reach me, as well.'

'Is that wise? To let the island find you, too?'

'Low magic is not for queens. She was a fool to turn to it in the first place. But if it means protecting her, then I will—'

They freeze at a sound from the upper floors. The darkness of the kitchen feels like a cave, and the two of them huddle around their small circle of light. But every shift of the row house is a creak. On blustery nights, the walls sound like they are groaning.

'If you had the dreams, too,' Billy goes on, his voice lower, 'you could help her to—'

Another thump from upstairs, followed by a short cry. Mirabella jumps to her feet with Billy right behind her.

She gathers her skirt, but Billy still passes her on the stairs, taking them by two. They hurry down the hall as quickly as they can, past Jane's room, where Mirabella hears her still faintly snoring.

'Arsinoe.' He opens the door. Arsinoe's cry has become a full-blown fit. She kicks and thrashes in the dark, and Billy yelps as he is caught by an unseen flying elbow.

'I can't see. Get a candle. Arsinoe.' He shakes her. 'She won't wake!'

Mirabella dashes for the bedside table. Her hand closes around a candle; her fingers send matches rolling. Stupid things. She kneels and feels along the rug for them.

'Mira, hurry!'

'I am trying,' she whispers. But the matches have disappeared. She turns toward her frightened sister, but it is too dark to see. 'Curse these matches,' she hisses, and feels her gift rise, an unexpected wave through her blood, out to the tips of her fingers.

The candle lights. It flares up at twice the usual height, so bright it illuminates the room nearly to the corners.

'I—' Mirabella exhales. What the flame has revealed nearly makes her drop the candle.

The shadow is with Arsinoe in the bed. It crouches over her shoulder like a goblin of spilled ink, elongated legs folded over feet that sink into the edge of Arsinoe's pillow. One dark, bony hand is wrapped around Arsinoe's head, holding it fast as her body twists.

'Are you seeing this?' Billy asks.

'You can see it, too?'

He does not respond. The paleness of his face is answer enough.

Slowly, Arsinoe's limbs still, and she begins to wake. The shadow remains until she opens her eyes. When it disappears, it disappears completely: there in one blink and gone in the next.

'Mira?' Arsinoe pushes up onto one elbow. She squints at the brightness of Mirabella's candle, which only now begins to fade along with the easing beats of her heart. 'Billy? What are you doing here? Was I making noises again?'

Mirabella and Billy look at each other. The shadow was real. Not a dream or a vision. And on its head, it wore the whisper of a crown, the same one that Arsinoe had sketched and that Mirabella recognized from a dozen paintings, a dozen woven shrouds. Silver and bright blue stones. The crown of the Blue Queen.

'Was she here?' Arsinoe asks. 'What does she want?'

'Mirabella,' Billy says quietly. 'I think you ought to give the low magic a try.'

Mirabella creeps forward and takes her confused sister by the hand.

'I think you are right.'

Billy, Mrs. Chatworth, Jane, and Mirabella sit at the informal dining table in the room just off the kitchen, sharing a most uncomfortable meal. Mirabella has not touched her sliced ham, instead scribbling away on a piece of paper. The only thing on her mind is the island, and she cannot ignore it, not even to please Mrs. Chatworth.

'I cannot seem to stop drawing her.' Mirabella reaches for a bit of blue chalk, the only drawing tool she could find in that color, even though the blue is all wrong. She turns the paper at an angle and studies it intently. The dark queen made of shadow, her long bony fingers clutching at the air, her grotesque legs tucked under herself. Beneath that drawing is a small stack of others: the shadow queen in other poses, all menacing, all monstrous. So monstrous that Billy's mother has chosen to pretend that they are simply not there.

'Where is Miss Arsinoe?' she asks.

'On an errand,' Billy replies.

'Alone?'

Neither Billy nor Mirabella bother to respond. It is a stupid question. Who else besides those at that very table would be accompanying Arsinoe anywhere?

'It is like I am trying to commit her to memory,' Mirabella says. 'Or perhaps to convince myself that she was indeed real.

That we really saw her.' She slides the topmost drawing across the table. Billy takes it, holding it by the edges.

'Don't know why you'd be trying to do that.' He sets it back down again, so his mother can stop staring pointedly away. 'What could it mean? Why would another Fennbirn queen be haunting you?'

'Haunting us. You saw her, too.'

Mrs. Chatworth makes a pained noise, and Jane pats her forearm.

'And you're certain it is Queen . . .' He searches for the name. 'Illiann? The Blue Queen?'

Mirabella taps her drawing with a forefinger. The rendering of the crown is not perfect. The silverwork is much more intricate and the blue stones, a much brighter blue, but for ink and chalk, it is not half bad. 'I have seen that crown in portraits before. There is no other like it.'

'If she was an elemental, then why wasn't she in one of the murals in the temple? She must've been one of the most impressive and revered of the elemental queens.'

'William Chatworth Junior, this is not proper conversation for the table.'

'Not now, Mother.'

Mirabella glances at Mrs. Chatworth apologetically. But she goes on.

'Blue queens—fourth-borns—are not claimed by a particular gift. They are queens of the people. All of the people.' She stops. 'It is hard to imagine what the island was like before her and before the mist. Had she not hidden us away, we would be entirely different. Perhaps we would be more like you.'

She raises her head. 'You must have some record of this on the mainland. An entire nation disappearing into a fog?'

'No.' Billy frowns. 'Everything known about Fennbirn is thought to be myth. A fable. There are no mentions of it in any historical text. Nothing on the maps. They must have been removed.'

Or he has seen the wrong maps. Mirabella traces her drawings with the tips of her fingers, and they come away stained black. 'This was the queen who turned Fennbirn into legend. What could she want with us now?'

'Ghosts often appear to deal with unfinished business,' says Jane suddenly, and everyone looks at her in surprise.

'Jane!' Mrs. Chatworth gasps.

'I'm sorry, Mother.'

'No, Jane, that's not half bad,' says Billy, and Jane's shoulders wriggle happily, as a bird ruffling her plumage. 'Could that be it, Mira? Unfinished business?'

'I do not see how. She had a thirty-year reign. It began with a war with the mainland, but she won. And then she reigned happily.'

Mrs. Chatworth throws down her napkin and pushes away from the table.

'Enough of this! I will not stand for it in my own house. This talk of witchery and heathen queens.'

'Mother,' Billy chides. 'You sound so old-fashioned.'

'Proper is what I sound. And if Miss Arsinoe is having some sort of . . . episodes, the kindest thing to do for her would be to refer her to a physician, not to let her roam around the city by herself, getting into more trouble.' She stands and smooths her dress. 'Jane, let us retire into the drawing room.'

Jane does as she is bid but casts a rather longing look over her shoulder. After they have gone and the doors between them are shut, Mirabella puts her head in her hands.

'Until last night, I would have agreed with her about the . . . physician. That is something like a healer, yes?'

'Yes. But when she says physician, all she means is a quack who will determine that Arsinoe is suffering from hysteria. They'd lock her away in a sanitorium.' Mirabella grimaces, and Billy glances at her.

'It was chaos in that room last night,' he says. 'So I didn't mention it. But I saw what your gift did up there. I saw that candle light without a match. How did you do it?'

'I did it for her,' Mirabella replies. 'Arsinoe needed me to do it. So I did. Sometimes I think that is my true purpose. Not to be queen, like the Westwoods and Luca convinced me of. But to protect her. Just to protect her.'

THE ROAD FROM BASTIAN CITY

Jules, Camden, Emilia, and Mathilde creep out of Bastian City beneath the cover of dark. They have only the supplies that can be carried on their backs and what money can be stuffed into their pockets. As they pass through the outer wall and move onto the main road, Emilia suddenly stops.

'What is it?' Jules asks, and Emilia bursts into muffled laughter.

'It occurs to me,' she says when she has quieted, 'that in our haste for revolution, we have neglected to decide where to start.'

Jules groans. So does Camden, leaning heavily against her good leg. 'Well? There are not too many choices. Do we head north for Rolanth? Or west toward Wolf Spring?'

'Neither,' says Emilia. 'Word from Rolanth suggests they are still too bitter about their loss, yet also still too loyal to the temple.'

'And why not Wolf Spring? Have your bards made it there yet? What are they saying about the uprising?'

'They may have heard rumors,' Mathilde says. 'But it is still too soon. In my experience, it is best to allow naturalists to warm to ideas slowly.'

'What's that supposed to mean?' Jules asks.

'It means they are fast to say no. Nothing more.'

'It means they still hate the legion curse,' Emilia adds, less kindly. 'Better to avoid Wolf Spring awhile. Dealings with naturalists are uncertain under the best of circumstances. They never want to get involved in anything.'

'Hey,' Jules says. '*I'm* a naturalist.'

'Yes, and you are the only one here who does not really want to rise.'

'Fine. So where, then, are we supposed to start?'

Mathilde adjusts her pack on her shoulders and begins to walk. 'Why not start where we have already begun? My home of Sunpool is with us, as are many of the surrounding villages. They have been preparing for months, for they believe in the prophecy.' She gestures up the road. 'We will go south around the capital and then skirt the mountains to the east. Once we are far enough north, we will begin speaking to the towns. Until the new force meets the existing one.' She looks at them over her shoulder, smile and white braid flashing in the moonlight. 'Then we will circle back for Wolf Spring and Rolanth.'

'At least there is an inn,' Emilia says when they arrive in the village. 'So we will not have to sleep in a barn.'

'A barn might be wiser,' says Jules. 'Easier to run out the

back if they don't like your rabble-rousing and come for us with pitchforks.' She arches an eyebrow at the warrior, but Emilia is too tired to argue much. It has been a long walk on the roads and off the roads, cutting through fields and forests to avoid Indrid Down. All of them are weary, their cloaks and faces stained with dirt, in need of fresh supplies and a good wash. Even tall, elegant Mathilde looks like she wrestled a pig and lost.

'Come on.' Mathilde adjusts her pack and leads them to the inn. Jules glances back up the road toward the place she left Camden dozing in a patch of ferns. The cat will wait there until she is called.

The interior of the inn is not much, just one large room on the ground floor full of tables and wooden benches. A few men and women sit alone or in pairs, hunched over bowls of stew.

'Do you have rooms for rent?' Mathilde asks.

'Wouldn't be much of an inn if we didn't,' replies the girl behind the counter. 'How many will you be needing?'

'Just one, large enough to sleep three.' Mathilde drops a few coins on the counter, and the girl slides them into her palm. 'Does that also buy dinner?'

'Nearly. But you look so worn down that I'll say it does. Another silver will buy you a hot tub of water to wash in.'

Emilia slaps two coins down. 'We'll take two tubs. And we'll eat our meal here in your fine room.'

'As you like.' The girl studies them a moment. But if she finds them odd, two filthy warriors and an oracle bard in a

ed gray-and-yellow cloak, she does not comment on it.
aps as a keeper of an inn she is used to strange travelers.
ough Jules cannot imagine that many choose to stop in this
ny village.

'Are you fleeing from the capital?' the girl asks, and both
les and Emilia tense. 'We've had some folk from there passing
rough after what happened.'

'What happened?' asks Mathilde. 'We have been traveling
r some time. We have not heard.'

'Queen Katharine murdered a boy.'

'Murdered?' Jules gasps. But the girl only cocks her head
nd sighs, as if it is no longer news at all for how many times
she has had to tell it.

'Aye. Right in front of everyone. More bodies had washed
up on the shores of the capital, and the people were panicked.
They started shouting at her and throwing things. One little
boy broke loose and ran at her with something. Probably no
more than a stick, but she sliced his head off, easy as you
please.'

'Where was her queensguard?' Emilia asks.

'Dealing with the grown-sized people I'd imagine.' The
girl's lips curl in disgust. Then she cocks her head again and
slips their coins into her pocket. 'Two tubs will take a while,
but I'll get my boys on it. You can head up to your room now
if you like. I'll have them brought in.' She points up the stairs
behind her. 'First one up those stairs. Or any of them. They're
all empty.'

As soon as they get inside their room, someone knocks the door: the boys delivering the empty tubs.

'Water will take some time,' says the first boy. 'Most folks don't want two.'

'Thank you,' says Emilia, and closes the door behind him. 'I didn't want two either,' she says, turning toward Jules. 'But there's a bug's arse of a chance of me sharing a tub with a mountain cat.'

'Why not just have Camden go last?' Mathilde asks.

'The tub would be cold by then.' Jules takes off her pack and stretches her shoulders. The hot bath will be welcome. The travel has been hard on her poison-damaged legs. Some nights they have throbbed so bad she has felt like screaming, but still she pushed on, not wanting to admit she should stop. She always said that Arsinoe had a stubborn streak a river wide, but really, her own might have been even wider.

'Do you believe what she said?' Jules asks as she sits down on the soft bed. 'Do you think Katharine really murdered some little boy?'

'Maybe she did and maybe she didn't,' replies Emilia. 'It will make it easier to bring this village to our cause, in any case.'

Mathilde unbraids her golden hair and runs her fingers through it to rid it of twigs and leaf bits. 'A queen who kills her own people. One would think she was trying to lose her head.'

'Eh,' Emilia says, a dismissive sound. 'For once, I will not be too hard on her. There was a mob. The boy charged at her with a raised weapon. He had it coming.'

'Had it coming?' Jules asks, and Emilia tips the knife she has been playing with lazily toward her chest.

'You don't threaten the life of a queen and live to tell the tale.' She flips the knife, catches it. 'Taking the life of a queen . . . now that is another matter.'

By the time they descend the stairs and head into the main room for supper, most of the tables are full. It seems to please Emilia and Mathilde: they can hold their meeting right in the inn. No need to try and gather people scattered through the village. But Jules would like to walk straight back up the stairs.

They sit down at a table near the wall, their arrival attracting a few curious glances. The girl from before sets down three cups of ale.

'Stew tonight and some oat bread. If you want more ale than what's in these cups, it'll cost you more coin.'

'What's in the stew?' Jules asks.

'Meat,' the girl replies, and goes to fetch it.

Jules looks around the inn. Nearly everyone in town must have come to the inn for supper, and it makes her wonder whether Emilia and Mathilde had somehow sent word of their coming. But if they had, no one seems particularly interested in them past the first glance. So maybe the meat stew is just very good.

'Do you really think we should start here?' Jules asks. 'We're still not that far from the capital.'

'We're far enough.' Emilia swallows half her cup of ale. 'Sounds like they've got their hands full with a murderous queen. We probably could have walked closer to the border and saved ourselves some time.'

'But look at these people. They're farmers. Tanners. Many too old to fight.'

'That is what rebel soldiers look like.' Emilia's dark eyes sparkle. 'What? You have something better to do? Exile? Fugitive?' She grins and pushes Jules's mug toward her. 'Drink more and think less, Legion Queen.'

'*Don't* call me that.'

'Why not?' Emilia wrinkles her nose at Mathilde. 'That is the one that people seem to have liked the most, isn't it?'

Jules snorts. Who would like such a title? It is as bad as being called 'Undead,' or perhaps even worse. 'You will never convince them that way.'

'They have lived under the poisoners, too. They won't need much convincing.'

Emilia drains her mug and calls loudly for more ale. Her exuberant hand gestures and overall loudness have begun to attract more attention. And as the villagers look toward Emilia, their gazes linger on Jules with something above mere curiosity. As if they sense something that makes her worth staring at.

'Ridiculous,' Jules mutters, too quietly for even her

tablemates to hear. But she would be lying if she said she was not curious too. Every time a stranger looks at her with something like hope, something like hope sparks inside her, and nearly tricks her into breathing again. Nearly, but not quite.

Hope is for fools, she wants to tell them. Not long ago I hoped for everything, and look what has become of me, and those I loved.

'This is never going to work,' Jules says.

'Of course it will,' says Emilia. 'You have not seen how Mathilde can mesmerize with her voice. She'll hold these people in the palm of her hand.'

'It is why I became a bard,' Mathilde says, and smiles.

Emilia prods Jules in the shoulder. 'You do not want it to work.'

'Of course I do. I want to be able to go home. I want Arsinoe to be able to come back and visit us.'

Emilia's voice sinks low. 'Do not speak of that.'

'Why not?'

'If she returns she will want the crown.'

'No, she wouldn't.'

'Yes, she would. It is in her triplet blood. And we are not rising to put the traitor queens back on the throne. We are rising for ourselves. For Fennbirn.'

'Would you have done the same if Katharine had not won?' Jules asks. 'Would you have still tried to overthrow Mirabella? Or Arsinoe?'

'It doesn't matter,' says Emilia softly. 'That is not what happened.'

When the stew arrives, it is good, though perhaps not good enough to attract so many diners on its own. Despite her hunger, Jules cannot manage more than a few bites. Her stomach will not stop buzzing.

'No appetite?' Emilia asks as she licks her bowl.

'I'm going to bring the rest up to the room, for Camden.' They snuck the big cat in near dusk through the rear entrance. The water in the second tub was still warm and fairly clean, and not a single one of them caught a claw to the face when they dunked Camden into it.

'Camden can eat it herself.' Mathilde stands. 'Off this very table.'

'Wait,' Jules stammers as Emilia rises, too. 'What am I supposed to do?'

'All you have to do is be you.' Emilia smiles and draws her long knives. She drags the point beneath Jules's chin, soft as a caress. 'And be ready to use your gifts.'

Mathilde throws back the folds of her gray-and-yellow cloak. Her voice, though soft, seems to fill the room.

'A moment, friends,' she says, and steps before their table. 'I am called Mathilde, from the city of Sunpool far to the west. I am a seer, and I am a bard, and I would tell you a tale, if you will hear it.' She extends an arm toward Emilia, who flashes her blades. 'This is Emilia, a warrior, and witness to the Ascension, to the debacle of the traitor queens and their escape.'

'A band of warriors aided them, or that's the way I heard it,' says a woman in the back. 'Are you one of them?'

'I am,' Emilia replies.

'Then you would fetch a fancy price delivered to the capital tied and trussed.'

'I would. And after we are through, you are welcome to try.'

The woman squints her eye. She has no weapons that Jules can see. But she does have a table full of friends.

As Mathilde recounts Katharine's crimes, most in the room seem curious. They nod when she calls her the Undead Queen, and a few pound their fists on their tables over the murdered boy. But others keep their lips tight. There are loyalists here, to be sure, and if whispers of Emilia's uprising have not reached Katharine by now, they will after tonight.

'We've heard the songs,' a young man calls from the crowd. 'We've heard the tales from other bards in yellow cloaks. A rebellion, they said. Led by a new queen. But there is no new queen. Unless you've plucked the elemental from the bottom of the sea and brought her back to life!'

'Then we would have two Undeads for the price of one!' the woman from the rear calls, and people start to laugh.

'Another poisoner on the throne,' Emilia shouts, and the crowd falls quiet. 'Is that what you want?'

Jules tenses along with everyone else. Eyes dart to Emilia's knives, but no one draws their own. A man with a black cat on his shoulder sits at a table with a boy sharing bread with a sparrow, but past that, Jules sees no evidence of gifts. Perhaps a few elementals, as the wind outside has stilled to nothing.

'Is that what you would have, for another generation?' Emilia narrows her eyes. 'Another corrupt council, surrounded by death? Who will poison us until our blood runs from our mouths, and cuts the heads from children? The triplet queens have been abandoned by the Goddess.'

'But someone with a legion curse has not?' the young man asks. 'That's the queen you speak of, isn't it? The Legion Queen.'

'That is the one we speak of,' says Mathilde.

'A mad queen on the throne?'

'She is not mad.'

'She is not real!' The woman in the rear says, and her table laughs.

'She is real,' Mathilde says, her voice carrying into the farthest corners. 'And she is different. The Legion Queen is no queen of the blood. But she is blessed just the same. Gifted so strongly by the Goddess, so as to be Her champion—*our* champion—who will vanquish the last of the fading queens and beside us will forge a brighter tomorrow.'

It is like Emilia said. Mathilde's words land in the crowd's ears and make them itch with the flicker of possibility. All Jules can do is sit awkwardly as they stare, knowing what they must be thinking, that this small girl cannot be this fabled soldier. It takes all her restraint not to open her mouth and agree with them.

'This little thing?' The woman in the rear of the inn stands and gestures with her mug to Jules, splashing what little ale is left in it across the top of her table. 'This little, vagrant wretch is supposed to be our champion?'

Her friends laugh. But this time, only her friends, and Emilia sheds her cloak and jumps deftly onto a nearby table.

'I have had near enough of you,' Emilia growls.

'Emilia,' Jules whispers.

'The Legion Queen will fight for the people. Even loudmouthed cowards.'

The woman scowls. 'You'll find no cowards here.' She waits until Emilia lowers the tip of her knife and then stands and throws a hidden hatchet she had stuck into the wood of her bench.

Emilia ducks and pushes it off course. It clatters to the ground behind her, harmless, but the warrior lifts her knife to throw. And Jules knows that she will never miss.

'Emilia, don't!' The knife flies, straight for the villager's heart. Jules lurches across the table, hand flung out. She calls to the knife with her gift, fighting against Emilia's good, solid throw. At the last moment, it veers off-course so hard that it winds up stuck fast in the ceiling.

Every face turns to Jules.

'Call her,' Mathilde whispers. 'Call her now.'

Too stunned to disobey, Jules reaches out for Camden, and every eye darts to the stairs as the cougar bursts through the door. She bounds down the steps and leaps over the rail, landing on tables and upending cups and plates, her snarl ferocious until she reaches Jules and stands before her to roar.

'This is the Legion Queen,' Mathilde says to the frozen crowd. 'The strongest naturalist in ten generations. The strongest warrior in two hundred years. She is the one who will fight for all the gifts. She is the one who will change everything.'

THE MAINLAND

The fortune-telling shop that Arsinoe finds has a brass bell over the door. A loud brass bell, and she grimaces as soon as she walks inside. But it seems that the shop is empty. No one there to see her. No one to stare. She reaches up and quiets the bell, and smiles as she thinks of Luke, whose bell back home is not so jarring.

Quietly, she unfurls the cloth sack she brought and begins roaming through shelves. It is easy to find three fat white candles, and into the sack they go, knocking together gently.

'You are not from here.'

Arsinoe spins and finds herself face-to-face with the shopkeeper, a woman in beads and silks, and dark, curling hair.

'No, madam. I've had to travel over half the city to find a shop like yours.'

The shopkeeper laughs.

'That's not what I meant. How can I help you today?'

Without warning, she tugs the cloth sack open and peers inside. Her mouth crooks down. 'White candles. A less interesting purchase than I'd hoped.'

'I also need herbs. And oil.'

'You didn't need to cross the city for those.'

'I suppose I could've swiped the herbs from the kitchen,' says Arsinoe. 'But then my hosts would have complained when their meat was bland. I know you have the herbs here; I can smell them.'

The woman leads her toward the back, where there are racks and racks of dried herbs and mushrooms, kept in jars or bound in bundles with butcher's string. Arsinoe selects which herb she needs, something that will give off plenty of smoke when burned. Something that will lend its aroma but not so strongly as to be distracting. Her hand hovers over a bundle of sage, then she changes her mind and frowns.

Low magic is the only link to the island that the Goddess can hear on the mainland. So Madrigal said. But it would need help to be heard so far away. Here there is no bent-over tree, no sacred valley to whisper her curses into. The oil and the herbs, the flames of the candles would lend her focus, raise her voice over the waves of the sea, all the way back to Fennbirn, perhaps even into the past, to the time of the Blue Queen.

'Have you tried burning amber or resins . . . ?' The shopkeeper reaches up onto a shelf. She hands Arsinoe a chunk that looks like Grandma Cait's nut brittle but smells like an evergreen. 'It will burn longer. Give you more time.' She laughs again at Arsinoe's suspicious face. 'So surprised to find a fortune-teller in a fortune-telling shop. Yes. I know what you're up to.'

She drops more resin into Arsinoe's sack and gestures for her to follow behind a curtain to a smaller room filled with crystals and clear orbs for seers.

'How does a shop like this exist here?' Arsinoe asks.

'It doesn't. Not in the fine parts of town. But as long as we stay buried in the slums, and as long as we provide harmless diversions for the ladies—fortune-telling and séances—they don't run us out.' She unlocks a cabinet and reaches inside.

'Are you . . . from here?'

'I am. But my grandmother . . . wasn't.'

'Do you know who I am?' Arsinoe asks warily.

The woman peers at her.

'I know you are reaching out for answers. And I know that you don't fear the price.' The last bit she said staring through Arsinoe's sleeves, as if she could trace the scars from the low magic cuts. 'Here. The last of what you will need.' She walks to Arsinoe and slides a bottle into her hand: Pretty blue frosted glass stoppered with a cork.

Arsinoe stares at it as she follows her back to the register. 'How much is this?'

'How much do you have?'

She reaches into her trouser pockets, fishes out her handful of coins, and lays them on the counter.

'It is that much,' the shopkeeper says, and sweeps them away.

'It can't be. Just the bottle must be worth more.'

'Take it,' the woman says. 'And take care. Your journey begins. I do not see where it ends. Only that it does.'

Only that it does. The woman's words echo through Arsinoe's head all the way back through the city until she reaches the cemetery and Joseph's grave, where she has arranged to meet Mirabella. The words could mean anything. Or they could be just the mumblings of a fake fortune-teller.

'Did you get everything?'

Arsinoe jumps when Mirabella steps out from behind one of the trees near the path.

'What are you doing, creeping around? You're as bad as Camden on padded feet.' She runs her hand through her growing hair; soon it will be time to cut it again and further horrify Billy's mother. 'Why were you hiding?'

'I was not hiding. I was sitting in the shade.'

'Where's Billy?'

'He left me at the gate. So as not to interfere.'

Arsinoe cranes her neck. The grounds are deserted, as usual. She kneels beside Joseph's grave and begins to unload the contents of her sack.

'I cannot believe I agreed to this.' Mirabella lowers herself onto the grass to help. She takes up the blue bottle and holds it to the light. 'We should have come after dark.'

'The fire would have caused even more attention then.'

Arsinoe sets the three candles in a triangle atop the grass where Joseph lies. But perhaps that is too close. She needs the aid of his island blood, but she does not want to disturb him.

'He would disapprove, you know.'

'I know. And then he'd help us anyway.'

The words catch in her throat, and she and Mirabella look sadly at the grave marker. It is so fresh, so bright among the other, older gravestones on the hill. It is still hard to believe that he is gone.

Together, she and Mirabella lay the other items from the sack on the grass: the pieces of resin, the oil, and finally, Arsinoe's sharp little dagger. Arsinoe uncorks the oil and sniffs. The scent is sweet and herbal. She shakes some onto the ground, then dabs a bit onto her forehead and chest. She does the same to Mirabella, who crinkles her nose.

'Would it be possible to do a banishing spell? Could we use these same things to send the Blue Queen away and get rid of your dreams?'

'Maybe,' Arsinoe replies. 'But somehow, I don't think it would work.' She pauses and looks at her sister a bit guiltily. 'I think I've come to like her. Daphne, I mean.'

Mirabella dabs at the oil in the bottle and rubs it between her fingers. 'What did she show you last night? When you struggled?'

'She showed me her hatred of Duke Branden of Salkades.'

'The handsome suitor? And why does she hate him? Because he is ruining her Henry's chances?'

'No,' Arsinoe says darkly. 'Because he is wicked.'

'Well.' Mirabella adjusts her legs to sit in a more comfortable position. 'You do not have to worry too much. History tells us that Henry Redville becomes Illiann's king-consort. And that Salkades becomes the leader of the losing battle against the island.'

'I didn't know about Salkades.' Arsinoe shoves her lightly. 'Don't spoil it for me.'

The preparations complete, she rubs her hands together and gestures to the candles.

'Can you use your gift to light these?'

'All three?' Mirabella squints doubtfully.

'What about just the resin?'

Mirabella focuses until sweat beads on her temples. It is difficult to watch, when Arsinoe has seen her summon a ball of flame straight into her open palm. With a wish. With a thought. But just when Arsinoe thinks Mirabella will give up, the resin lights and starts to smoke. Mirabella exhales and laughs, and the candles ignite in a rush. Around them, the wind stills. The birds and insects quiet.

'Is this a good sign?' Mirabella asks.

'Any sign is a good sign.' Arsinoe takes up the dagger and cuts a small crescent into the curve of her arm. The sting is familiar, but it does not feel the same as it did beneath the bent-over tree. There is a flatness to it. The pain is thin and bitter as a dirty coin in her mouth. 'Give me your arm.' She cuts Mirabella a crescent to match. The first scar upon her flawless skin.

'What should I do?' Mirabella asks as their blood drips before the candles and sinks into the earth where Joseph lies.

'Reach out to the island with your mind. Let it find you—' Arsinoe starts, and then the shadow of the tree changes.

It grows darker. It grows deeper. It grows legs.

The shadow of the Blue Queen slinks toward them as if made of smoke, if smoke could bend the grass and stamp it down into footprints. When she climbs atop Joseph's headstone and perches there like a hideous crow, Mirabella jerks, perhaps to run away or perhaps to knock her off, but Arsinoe holds her fast.

'What do you want?' Mirabella asks.

The Blue Queen stretches out her arm. She points a finger toward the sea. Toward the island.

'The island.' Arsinoe stares deep into the void of the ancient queen's face. 'We understand. But what do you want? Why am I dreaming as Daphne? What are you trying to tell me, Queen Illiann?'

The Blue Queen makes a sound. A shriek. The groan of a dead jaw yawning open. The sound grows until it becomes a wind, and Arsinoe ducks over the lit candles. But they remain lit. Flickering, as Mirabella uses her gift to push back.

'We are like you,' Mirabella says. 'We are of your line. Tell us what you want from us. Or leave us in peace!'

The screaming wind slows, and the Blue Queen puts her hands to her throat. Her head twists back and forth.

'She can't speak,' says Arsinoe. 'She's trying.'

'Go.' It is a croak. One word. Then again. 'Go.' She claws at her mouth. Points again to Fennbirn. 'Go.'

'We cannot go back.' Mirabella gets to her feet. 'We escaped. We are never going back.' She binds the cut on her arm with a strip of cloth and ties it off with her teeth. Grabs her sister and staunches her blood as well. Without the boost of fresh queensblood, the shadow pales. It slackens. It points one last time and then disappears, taking the wind with it.

'Why did you stop her?' Arsinoe asks as the sounds of birds and insects return to the cemetery. 'She was getting stronger.'

'Maybe that is why I stopped her.'

'But she had more to tell us. I know she did.'

'Arsinoe.' Mirabella snuffs out the candles and stomps the last of the smoking resin. She stuffs everything back into the sack and twists it closed. 'Do you not think that what she wants is for us to go back and be killed? That we were not supposed to get away?'

'But the dreams—'

'The dreams are bait! They are a trap.' Mirabella puts a hand on Arsinoe's shoulder as she looks out toward the bay. 'And even if they are not, it is not worth the risk.'

THE REAPING MOON

ROLANTH

'It was a mistake to come here,' Pietyr says as the carriage approaches the elemental city of Rolanth. 'We should have stayed in Indrid Down.'

'And celebrate the Reaping Moon Festival in the midst of a chanting mob?' Genevieve arches her brow.

'You think there will not be chanting mobs in Rolanth? The entire island has heard about'—he glances apologetically at Katharine—'what happened to that boy.'

'That assassin, you mean. The one whom the queen made an example of.'

The queen and her court are to stay at the finest hotel in Rolanth. The High Priestess herself made the arrangements, in conjunction with Sara Westwood. Katharine drops open the carriage window and takes a deep breath of the crisp northern air. So many white buildings, built into the hills. Limestone and marble, facing the sea, stark against the black basalt cliffs that run up the northeastern coast, that place that they call

Shannon's Blackway. Rolanth is brighter than Indrid Down, with the clear water of the river rushing through the center, and the many green spaces of parks and gardens. Hard to believe that anything could go wrong in such a beautiful place.

She has brought nearly her whole Black Council to ensure it, except for Cousin Lucian, Rho Murtra, and Paola Vend. Some had to stay behind, so it would not appear that they are fleeing. Though that is precisely what they are doing.

When the carriage stops, Genevieve leaps out to see that all has been prepared. Pietyr takes Katharine's hand to escort her into the hotel.

Their room takes up the entirety of the uppermost floor, a lovely space with ivory walls and blue velvet on the bed. Katharine removes her traveling hood and throws it onto an oval table. Then she swings the windows open and leans out.

'Stay away from the windows, Kat.'

Pietyr closes it up and tugs her back to the center of the room.

'How long will you remain angry with me, Pietyr? For what happened to that boy?'

'I am not angry with you.' He unbuttons his jacket and slings it onto a chair. 'I am protective. Though I do wonder why you are not angrier with yourself.'

'I was. I am.'

'Are you? We must brand that poor boy a traitor and not even allow him to be burned, just so we can say that the queen was in the right?'

'I was in the right. He attacked me,' Katharine says, but her voice lacks conviction. The boy had been no real threat. She could have disarmed him. Instead, she put a knife up through his throat. 'Natalia would say it is more important for a queen to be feared than to be loved.'

Pietyr frowns. 'Natalia would never say that. Not in this case.'

Genevieve sweeps into the room, having finished her cursory inspection of the hotel. She glances between them and rolls her eyes at Pietyr.

'Will you never stop telling her she is wrong, nephew? Will you never stop thinking of what is best for your "Kat" and begin to think about what is best for the reign?'

'Murdering subjects is never what is best for the reign. Fear is one thing, but not for a queen as unpopular as this. Heaping fear upon dislike breeds hatred. And hatred makes the people likely to bite.'

Genevieve sighs. 'The people will forget. You have been in the game for so little time, Pietyr. It will be years before your advice is of any value.'

A lump of frustration rises in Katharine's throat. She knows what comes next. Pietyr's pale cheeks will gain color. His teeth will grind. He will shout, and Genevieve will shout back, and Katharine will want her head to explode.

'Genevieve,' she says quickly. 'Go and see to the festival grounds.'

'Yes, Queen Katharine.' She curtsies and leaves, and Pietyr

slams the door so fast it nearly catches the seat of her trousers.

Katharine returns to the window.

'Kat.'

'I am perfectly safe this high up.' She looks out. In Rolanth the sun shines and the sea sparkles. The sky is clear. There is no mist hovering on the water without cause, and there are no missing fishers bobbing in the waves.

Pietyr's hands slide up her arms. His fingers slip into her hair, and she lets her head fall back against his chest. His touch is a balm: it brings her back into her own body.

'It was not you with that boy, was it, Kat? It was them. The dead queens.'

'I do not know.'

'Yes you do. It is just that you do not want to admit it. Why? Do you think I will think you evil?'

'No!'

'Then why?'

'To protect them!' She squeezes his hands. 'As they have protected me. They are a part of me now, Pietyr. And what they give is worth the cost of what they take.'

'Even the life of a young boy?'

Katharine closes her eyes. She sees that young man's face. She sees it in her dreams. But she tries not to think of him while she is awake. The dead queens seem to like it, and that feels so very wrong.

'That will never happen again,' she says. 'Never.'

'How can you be sure? Can you calm them? Can you keep

them from putting you in such danger?'

'You calm them.' She turns and pulls his mouth to hers. 'As you calm me.'

The day of the Reaping Moon Festival, Katharine is to be dressed by Sara and Bree Westwood. No fewer than six servants enter alongside them, bringing dozens of gowns and several boxes of gloves, several cases of jewels, before bowing and departing to give them privacy. Dressing the queen, particularly for one of the high festivals, is a great honor, though one would not know it by the sour looks on Bree's and Sara's faces.

'Mistresses Westwood.'

'My queen.' Sara Westwood curtsies deep, her eyes on the floor. 'We thank the queen for extending this invitation.'

Katharine looks with compassion on the stiffness in the woman's back, and the gray of her hair. It did not used to be so gray. Even as recently as the Queens' Duel, Sara's hair was a bright, vibrant brown.

'I would not think to extend it to anyone else in Rolanth.'

They have brought the one-handed priestess, Elizabeth, with them, as usual, and the girl busies herself straightening dresses and whispering to Bree. At one point, Bree laughs, and Elizabeth prods her jovially with the stump of her wrist. They are good friends, even without Mirabella to bind them together.

'I—' Katharine clears her throat softly. 'I would wear my own gloves.' She holds her arms up. She has already put a pair on, above her dark linen chemise.

'As you like, my queen.' Sara nods curtly and shuts each of the glove cases. 'Though the ones we have brought are more fashionable.'

'I am rather particular about them.'

'Is that why you are standing there in nothing but gloves and your undergarments?' Bree asks. 'Or is it because you do not want us to look upon your scars?' She steps close with a pair made of pretty black lace. 'Everyone knows that your hands were ruined escaping your fate at the Quickening Ceremony. Take the gloves.' She slaps them into Katharine's palm.

Slowly, and feeling their eyes on her every moment, Katharine strips the fabric down her arm. Deep furrows in the skin from poisons being cut in by knife show like inverted veins. Shining pink circles mark the places where old blisters ruptured. And her hands. Her hands are a ruin of rough and patched-together skin, torn and altered from her crawl out of the Breccia Domain.

The lace will not hide that.

'Try these, Queen Katharine.' Elizabeth smiles warmly. 'They are even lovelier.' More lace, but this time stitched over thin black fabric. With a gentle touch, the priestess helps her into them, stretching them carefully as if it might still cause Katharine pain.

Bree, who has been watching with a soft expression, hardens when Katharine looks at her.

'It's good.' She nods and selects a gown: black silk, fitted through the hip.

'She will need a dense cloak for the evening,' says Sara. 'But the low loose skirt will flare nicely in the winds.'

'What about this one, then?' Bree holds another in front of Katharine. 'A similar cut but thicker material and lined.'

'So many choices,' Katharine whispers.

'Yes, well. Some queens are harder to dress than others,' Bree whispers back.

'Are you . . . angry with me, Bree?'

Across the room, Sara and Elizabeth continue sorting through shoes and jewels. Perhaps they truly cannot hear.

'What? You thought I would be sympathetic? Or even a friend? After one moment of civil conversation by a window.' She snorts. 'I thought . . . perhaps. Perhaps you were just a lonely girl, and I should give you a chance. But then I remember that not an hour afterward I watched you put a knife into the throat of one of your own people.' She moves away roughly.

'I was . . . not myself,' Katharine says, keeping her voice low. 'I was afraid.'

'I saw your face. The way you looked. You were not afraid of anything.'

'I regret it. I would take it back. I truly would, but I cannot say that—'

'My queen,' says Sara Westwood, and Katharine turns to find a long strand of fat black pearls in her face. 'These perhaps. I heard once that you favored them.'

'Yes, thank you,' she says, and hears the door open and slam shut behind Bree's rapid exit.

Bree is not in the carriage when it arrives to take Katharine to the festival. Only Sara Westwood and the priestess Elizabeth will accompany her and Pietyr to the grounds of Moorgate Park in the center of the city, but Katharine makes no comment. It is a fast ride along the river. Perhaps too fast, as twice the horses shy and nearly fall.

'They are unused to the steep roads,' says Pietyr.

'It is the winds. Every elemental gift is running high today, and the winds will be wild until dark, when the fires begin.' Sara taps Elizabeth on the shoulder. 'Elizabeth, will you trade places with Master Arron, to be nearer to the horses?'

'Of course.' They trade seats, and the pace of the carriage eases.

'Elizabeth still has some of the naturalist gift about her,' Sara explains.

'That is why I so often see you feeding the birds,' says Katharine, and the priestess smiles.

Outside, Rolanth passes by, decorated with dyed flags hung for the Reaping Moon. Throughout the marketplace, Katharine has seen the flags and banners being sold, dyed in shades of blue and yellow, silver and gold. The more skilled artisans have woven great cloth fish with shining scales in myriad colors, which puff up with the wind when they swallow it. All across the island, folk celebrate the Reaping Moon for the coming harvest, but in Rolanth, it marks the last of the fish runs and the arrival of winter's bluster.

'You must be happy to have your daughter home, Sara.'

'The capital is Bree's home now,' Sara replies, as expected. But Katharine sees through her. She is happy. More than happy—she is relieved. To her, Indrid Down is dark and full of poisoners. Full of death.

The carriage stops, and Katharine's queensguard assembles to escort her onto the festival grounds. Moorgate Park is hung with streamers and flags and many brightly colored sewn fish. Festival-goers laugh and dance throughout, feasting on smoked herring on skewers and drinking spiced wine.

'Queen Katharine.' Genevieve comes to her as soon as she sets foot on the white stone path. 'There is a pleasant place prepared for you, beside the fountain and the canal, where you may observe the festival.'

With Pietyr by her side, Katharine takes her place next to Sara and High Priestess Luca. Servants bring her a cup of warmed wine and three fish on skewers, and the musicians move closer and resume their play. Soon enough, dancers flood the paved stones and even spill onto the grass.

'Pietyr Arron. Will you dance?'

Katharine's mouth drops open at the sight of Bree. She has come from nowhere, slipping through the crowd, to stand before Pietyr and the queen with her hand outstretched. Her festival gown is midnight blue and thread of silver. It leaves her arms and shoulders bare, and hugs her breasts like the two have not seen each other in ages.

Pietyr frowns.

'The queen has only just arrived.'

'Go, Pietyr.' Katharine squeezes his hand. 'You will truly be the envy of every person in attendance.'

'As you wish.' He stands and lets Bree lead him onto the floor. For a few steps, he tries to keep up, but though Pietyr is a wonderful dancer, it is clear he is no match for the limber legs looping between his own. Before long, the other dancers take notice, and whistle encouragement to spur Bree on.

Luca touches Katharine's hand and speaks from the side of her mouth.

'She is only doing it to irritate you. It is her way.'

'I know that. Of course I know that.'

Bree presses against Pietyr's chest and slings a thigh up to his hip. His frown begins to soften. He looks at Katharine desperately. Everyone is looking at her. Genevieve with curious intensity. Sara with nerves and a straight back. The people, ready to grin the moment Katharine starts to cry or shout.

But instead, Katharine laughs.

'Louder! Play louder! Play faster!' She whistles, and Bree stops in surprise. Then she smirks, bows, and begins again. Poor Pietyr breaks out in a sweat, and the crowd cheers. Poor, poor Pietyr. He has never looked so uncomfortable, stiffly resisting all of Bree's advances. It seems an age before the song ends, and Bree bows to Katharine with her hands on her hips, admitting defeat.

Katharine rises and walks through the clapping dancers into Pietyr's arms.

'How dare you do that to me.' He spins her around.

'Did you really not like it?' She twines her leg around his calf. 'I was thinking of asking her to teach me.'

'Teach you . . .' His scowl fails, and he breaks into a smile. 'Do you think she would?' They spin together, and he laughs. It is good to see him laugh.

'Even so close to you, I am cold,' he says as wind ruffles his collar. 'Sometimes I envy these elementals, for their resistance to the weather.'

'Yes,' Katharine mutters. The cold does not bother her as much. Some of the dead queens carried the elemental gift, and what she borrows from them is enough to shield her from it. 'The fires will begin soon, and then the winds will quiet, like Sara said—'

A scream cuts through the music.

'What is it?' asks Pietyr. He glances quizzically at Genevieve, who may have a better view from the queen's table.

But Katharine knows. She and the dead sisters feel it, even before the panic breaks out beside the river. They feel it before the mist rises out of the water and stretches across the ground.

'Get the people out of here, Pietyr.'

'It is too late.'

The panic begins, and Pietyr throws himself across the queen as they are battered by fleeing bodies. High Priestess Luca is on her feet, trying to direct the crowds to the south and west. People fall and are trampled. They are swallowed up by the mist, come to the center of the city via the river. Katharine wonders where they will be found again. Or if they will be found at all.

'Queen Katharine.' Genevieve takes her by the arm. 'We must get you back to the hotel.'

At the hotel, shut up safely inside with queensguard posted around the building, the members of the Black Council gather in the queen's room. It takes a while for them all to arrive, and every time the door opens, Katharine sighs with relief. Luca and Bree and Antonin are there. Genevieve and Pietyr were the first to the hotel with her. Renata Hargrove scurries through the door last, shivering in a gray cloak, and after several moments, Katharine begins to panic, worried about Cousin Lucian until she remembers that he remained in Indrid Down, with Paola Vend and the priestess Rho.

'How many are gone?' Katharine asks. 'How many were taken?'

None can say. Eyes come to rest on Renata, since she was the last to arrive.

'It is too early to tell, Queen Katharine. Not all have been found. And when I was running . . . it was still happening.'

But it is over now. Katharine was at the window the moment they reached the top floor, scanning the city for Moorgate Park. She saw the mist, spread out in thick white fingers. Saw it hover over the festival grounds and hesitate at the edges of the city streets. The air was still full of people's screams, the sound made small by the distance, and somehow even more frightening.

'It receded,' she says, and Renata shudders. 'I watched it from the window. It returned to the river and back out to sea to disappear.'

'It took them so quickly.' Antonin pours tainted brandy for himself and the other poisoners, and drinks it all down at once, his hand shaking. 'And the way their screams cut off . . . like they were being choked.'

'Some passed through the mist unharmed,' Luca notes. 'But others . . .'

'Others we will find torn to pieces and decomposed. Bobbing in Bardon Harbor when we return to the capital.' Genevieve pours more brandy. She is so rattled that she even pours a cup of untainted wine for Luca.

'Do you think Lucian and Paola are all right?' Antonin asks. 'Is it happening there as well? Or only here?'

'Rho is there,' Luca says vaguely, as if that makes all the difference.

Katharine turns to Bree.

'Bree. Are your mother and Elizabeth safe? Did they get out of the park unharmed?'

'They did. They were right beside me. I left them to come here, and they went on to seek refuge at the temple.'

'The temple,' Katharine murmurs. 'Good.' No doubt many sought refuge there. Most of the city would flee toward it. Perhaps on the way, they would stop by the hotel with torches and raised fists. They would have a good enough reason.

She wanders away from the group, back toward the

window. The area surrounding the festival grounds is quiet now. Deserted. But the rest of the city seethes with frightened activity.

She feels Pietyr's hands on her shoulders.

'Do you know what this is, Kat? Do you know what it wants?'

'No, Pietyr.' She shakes her head miserably.

'Do *they*?'

At the mention of the dead queens, she jerks loose and darts a glance of warning between him and the nearby ears of the council.

'If they do, they have not told me.'

They have not told her, but they are racing through her blood like spooked fish. They make it impossible to think. Impossible to stand still.

'What must be done?' She holds her hands out to Genevieve. To Luca. She turns to Antonin and Renata and even Bree. But no one answers. Finally, Katharine clenches her fists and shrieks. 'What must be done?'

'We do not know.' Luca scrunches her wizened old shoulders. 'You may as well ask the air. Or the Goddess. Nothing like this has happened within our lifetimes. Nothing like this has ever happened before.'

Katharine stares at the floor. As she dressed that morning, she had not noticed the pattern of the rug beneath her feet. It is a weaving of Queen Illiann, the Blue Queen, standing atop the black basalt cliffs with her arms outstretched and black hair billowing like a cloud. In the sea, the mainland ships wreck against her waves, and between them, the mist rises like a shroud. Katharine glares at it. It is as though she is being mocked by the mist's very creator.

'Is this where it happened? Here on Shannon's Blackway? Was the mist created here?' She turns on Genevieve. 'If it was, you should have known, and we should never have come to Rolanth!'

'Battles were fought up and down the coast,' Genevieve stammers. 'But the mist was created at Bardon Harbor. Not here. She is depicted here perhaps because she was an elemental—'

'And you have learned nothing else? About her. About this?' She gestures to the mist in the weaving, but Genevieve shakes her head. It is all legend. Another ancient secret that the island keeps.

Katharine frowns. She wills the dead queens to help her, to guide her, but they remain agitated and silent.

'Get reports,' she says finally. 'Find out who is missing. Take accounts from those the mist touched but did not harm. Pietyr, Renata, and'—she searches their faces—'Bree will do this. The people of Rolanth will speak to her and to you, if you are with her.'

She nods to Antonin. 'Antonin, take the queensguard back to the park. Secure it and then disperse soldiers through the city to provide aid.'

'Yes, Queen Katharine.'

They go without complaint, relieved to have a task.

'And what of us?' Genevieve looks between herself and Luca.

Katharine strips off the pretty lace gloves that the Westwoods gave her. She tears the black pearls off over her head and squeezes them between her fingers.

'Genevieve, I need you to send for an oracle.'

'An oracle?'

'Write to Sunpool. Tell them to send their best. Their most gifted. Tell them if they can offer an insight into the mist, they will have a seat on the Black Council as their reward.'

'A council seat?' Genevieve blinks. 'Are you sure?'

'Just do it!'

'Right away, Queen Katharine.' She leaves and closes the door softly behind her. Katharine looks at Luca and pours a glass of tainted brandy.

'You must be thrilled. My reign is going so poorly.'

'I would be,' says Luca as Katharine drinks, 'if it were going poorly only for you.'

Katharine snorts.

'Well, then. What can the temple do to help?'

'The temple is full of old scholars. We can comb the libraries and the histories, see what we can find.' She steps up beside the queen and knocks their cups together. 'And we can pray.'

THE ROAD FROM BASTIAN CITY

By the time Jules, Emilia, and Mathilde leave the village, heading north along the foothills of the Seawatch Mountains, the mood at the inn has changed. After that first night, when they saw Jules guide the knives and saw Camden leap across tables so fiercely, they began to look at her with awe. So much awe that, when they bid farewell to the innkeeper, Jules is almost sure the girl will bow. Though in the end, all she does is a hasty curtsy.

'We'll spread the word,' the girl says. 'And we'll be ready when you call.' She holds out a parcel, and Camden sniffs the air. 'May I?' she asks, and Jules nods. The girl unwraps the fish and lets Camden take it gently between her teeth. 'Farewell,' she says.

'Farewell.'

'For now,' says Emilia, and they walk on.

Jules watches Camden up the road, where she has lain down to tear at the fish and purr. 'Reminds me of how it was in Wolf

Spring. When Arsinoe had her bear. We couldn't walk into a pub without someone shoving a trout into our arms.'

'Get used to it,' says Emilia. 'It is better, is it not? Having them feed your cat instead of spit in your hair for the curse?'

'It is.' The looks on their faces when they saw her use her gifts, *her gifts*, both of them. Not disgust or even fear. Only hope. All thanks to a silly prophecy and a couple of bards who could carry a fine tune. Still, it felt good. More than that, it had started to feel right.

They pass through three more towns on the road north, and in every village, Emilia and Mathilde find ears willing to listen. They meet in secret, in taverns and country houses. In dark, dusty barns and beside the soft banks of rivers. The people come carrying pitchforks and shovels as though they would be weapons. They see the warrior who has a cougar familiar, and they start to believe.

'What did I tell you?' Emilia says, turning the roasting rabbit on the spit above their campfire as Camden's mouth waters. 'They believe. They want change as badly as we do.'

'But can we win?' Jules turns her own rabbit, a much larger and meatier one than Emilia's. 'With an army of farmers and fishers and all of different gifts? They aren't soldiers, and they're as like to fight one another as they are to fight the queensguard.'

'We can win,' says Mathilde. 'With enough of the island at our back, we can win.'

In the back of her mind, Jules hears the whisper that the

queens are sacred. But she stamps out the thought. Queens are sacred. But these poisoner queens have failed them. They have corrupted the line. Especially Katharine.

'You should go easier on the exaggerations next time, Mathilde,' Emilia says, but across the flames, the seer only grins.

'Why? The crowds love to hear the grand tales. The grander, the better. So what if Jules did not really kill fifty soldiers during the escape from the Volroy cells? So what if her war gift cannot halt one hundred arrows?'

'Nothing as long as they never want a demonstration,' Jules says, and Emilia laughs. 'You and the other bards are going to make people think I'm twelve feet tall.'

Mathilde chuckles, and tears a small loaf of bread into four chunks. She tosses them one each, and Jules takes up Camden's share to press against the side of the rabbit to soak up the juices.

'That is the last of the bread,' Mathilde says. 'We will have to go without for a few days. There is nothing between us and the foot of the mountains now.' Nothing, unless they turn south and make for the glen and the Black Cottage. Jules strips off a piece of meat and chews it as she snaps off a quarter haunch for Camden. It is not enough for the cougar. They will have to hunt again before dusk, but with her gift, game is easy to find. This sweet rabbit practically hopped into her arms.

'Up.' Emilia stands and nudges Jules with her foot. 'Time to train. You are right about one thing: if we are to carry this off you must truly look like a better warrior than I am.'

Jules pats Camden on the head and tells her to stay near the fire. If the big cat comes along, she will only wind up pinning Emilia to the cold ground.

They find a small clearing in the trees, and Emilia tosses her a sword. Jules has graduated from the bluntness of sparring sticks.

'How much time will we need to train the soldiers?' Jules asks as their blades cross.

'More than we have.'

'But—' Jules parries. 'We can't send farmers against armored queensguard. Not without the right training.'

'We can with the right leader. Now pay attention or I am going to slice off your arm.' They cross blades again. Attack and parry. Nothing fancy. No flair. No heart. 'But you are right about one thing. They are farmers. Tradespeople. They are not soldiers, and many of them will die.'

'But why? If we wait—'

'Because people die in war.' Emilia advances in a flurry. 'They die for what is right. And if you are to lead them, you'll have to let go of your naturalist weakness!'

Jules thrusts her palm into Emilia's belly. Her war gift sends Emilia flying into a tree and knocks the wind right out of her.

'Oh!' Jules runs to her and kneels. 'I didn't mean for you to hit the tree.'

'It's all right.' Emilia takes Jules's hand and kisses the knuckles. 'I kind of liked it.'

At the edge of the clearing, Camden grunts.

'Cam? I told you to stay with Mathilde.'

The cat grunts again and twitches her tail irritably. When she turns and dashes back the way she came, Jules knows well enough to follow.

At first, it seems that nothing is amiss. Mathilde is seated before the fire, nearly as they left her. It is not until Camden puts a paw up onto Mathilde's shoulder that they see: the seer is stiff with a vision.

'Mathilde?' Jules approaches cautiously. 'Emilia, what do we do?'

'Do not disturb her.' The warrior squats low and quickly moves nearby weapons and rocks. 'When she comes out of it, she may jerk. Keep her from running into the flames, and keep her from falling and striking her head.'

She makes it sound worse than it is. When the vision is over, Mathilde simply twitches and blinks. Then a thin rivulet of blood leaks from her nose.

'Here.' Emilia presses a wad of cloth to it.

'Are you all right?' Jules asks.

'I am fine. Did it last for long?'

'Not long. Camden told us to come back, and then it was only a few minutes.'

Mathilde sniffs and reaches out to scratch Camden behind the ears. 'Good cat.' She dabs at the blood; it has already stopped.

'What did you see?' asks Emilia.

Mathilde turns to Jules, her eyes large and sorrowful. 'I

think I saw your mother. I think she is in danger, at the Black Cottage.'

After Mathilde's vision, Jules and Emilia wasted no time breaking camp and making their way toward the Black Cottage. The travel was slow in the dark, and by sunrise, their legs are too weary to increase the pace by much.

'Perhaps she was wrong,' Emilia says. 'Or perhaps the vision wants us to go to the Black Cottage for some other purpose and is trying to lure us there.'

Jules glances at Mathilde, who avoids her eyes. Behind her, Camden swings her tail back and forth, swatting Emilia in the legs. It seems an age that they travel along in silence: another uncomfortable night's camp in the mountains and another morning of walking, before the smoke from the Black Cottage chimney rises into view.

Jules looks down across the meadow at the dark, pitched roofs, the crossed timbering. The door to the stable is open, and a small flock of chickens meanders around near the stream. Nothing seems out of sorts.

'We may not be welcome here,' Jules warns them. 'Old Willa might try to toss us out on our ears.'

'Old Willa.' Emilia grins. 'Sounds like I'll like her.'

They walk on, out of the trees, and a large black crow dives from the branches. It flaps its wings hard in Mathilde's face and caws loudly into Camden's.

'Aria!' Jules holds her hand out to her companions, to

keep them from harming the bird.

'You know this bird?' Mathilde asks.

'She's my mother's.'

They hurry across the grass, already brown from hard frosts, and Jules leaps up the cottage steps, casting an eye toward the crow perched atop the roof's edge. 'Wait here,' she says, and she and Camden go inside alone.

Instantly, Caragh's brown hound, Juniper, barrels into Camden's side and licks her face.

Caragh comes to the door, and Jules walks into her arms.

'I hope you don't mean to lick my face like that.'

'Your cougar doesn't seem to mind,' Caragh says, and chuckles. She draws back, holds Jules at arm's length. She studies every inch of her, from the tips of her toes to the ends of her cut brown hair. The tightness of her fingers speaks of how badly she wants to pull Jules close. 'What are you doing here?'

'Madrigal,' Jules says quickly. 'We saw Aria, and my friend'—she nods to Mathilde—'had a vision. Is she here? Is she safe?'

Caragh nods at Juniper, and the hound stops frantically pawing at Camden. Then she sighs. She is lovely as always, even in an apron and her brown-gold hair tied messily with a piece of twine. But her eyes are heavy.

'Pesky crow,' she says softly. 'Always flying off places.'

'She flapped around happily and then tried to peck my eyes out. Just like Madrigal would have done. Where is she?'

A shadow crosses her aunt's face. 'Let's go and see her. She will want to hear all your news. Juniper will sit with your friends, to make sure that Willa does not chase them off with a pitchfork when she returns from the barn.'

Quietly, Jules follows her aunt past the drawing room and the kitchen, down the long hall to the same room where Arsinoe recovered from the bolt that Katharine shot into her back.

Madrigal is in the bed. That alone is a strange enough sight. Though Madrigal was lazy about many things, she never overslept or lingered under blankets. She wanted too much of the world to lose one minute of daylight. But even more a shock is how small she looks, lessened by the sheer size of her belly, pregnant with a child by Matthew Sandrin. Joseph's older brother.

'Madrigal. What are you doing here?'

Her mother pushes against her pillows, and Caragh moves past Jules to help, sitting her up and slipping another pillow behind her back. The uncharacteristically sisterly gesture makes Jules go cold.

'I could ask you the same.' Madrigal pats the quilt, and Jules goes closer. 'Returned to the island and no word? When did you get back? Where have you been?'

'I actually never left. I've been in Bastian City, with the warriors.'

'You could've gotten a message to us.' Madrigal pauses at a tapping; Aria the crow is at the window, and Caragh goes to let the bird in. She flies once around the room and lands on the top corner bedpost.

'I didn't want to make any more trouble for Grandma Cait and Ellis. I figured they had enough on their hands just dealing with my reputation.'

'Liar. You know your grandparents can handle that and more. They're worried. They're wondering. The fields are terrible. And Luke. When poor Luke heard the rumors about the Legion Queen, he wept.'

'The rumors have reached you, then?'

'They have reached us. But where is Arsinoe? And Joseph? Billy and the elemental?'

Jules shifts her weight to lean against Camden.

'Arsinoe, Billy, and Mirabella made it to the mainland. I guess that's where they are now. As for Joseph . . .' She stops, and Madrigal places a hand atop her stomach. 'He's dead. But I think you probably guessed that.'

'He looked very bad when you left us by the river,' says Caragh. 'But I hoped. I'm so sorry, Jules.'

'I'm sorry, too,' adds Madrigal. 'He was a good boy.'

He was more than that, but Jules clears her throat.

'I'm sorry I made Luke cry. I guess I should have found a way to tell everyone.'

'Oh, Luke cries at the drop of a hat.' Madrigal waves her hand and wipes quickly at her eyes. She is pale, and that crow of hers is never so close by.

'Now what's wrong? Why are you in bed? I didn't think

the baby would come until winter.'

'He won't,' says Caragh. 'Willa and I are making sure of it.'

Jules glances around the room. It has a strange, stale smell she does not remember and on the corner dresser is a tray of dirty cups and a plate of half-eaten root vegetables and greens.

'Nettle leaf tea,' Caragh explains. 'And fanroot. If she eats it every day, it will ease the early contractions.'

'A waste of time. Trying to hold this baby in. He won't come until he's ready, and he will be perfectly safe.'

'What do you mean?' Jules asks.

Caragh sighs. She has heard this tale many times before. 'Your mother saw a vision in a fire, when she was dabbling with Arsinoe and her low magic.'

'At the bent-over tree, you mean?'

'Yes,' Madrigal interrupts. 'I saw a vision in the fire that day, a fire stoked by queensblood, in that sacred space. So I know it is true.' She pauses and looks at Jules, her face a mix of stubbornness and regret. 'I saw my son born alive. Strong and red and screaming. And sitting atop my dead gray corpse.'

THE MAINLAND

Mirabella and Arsinoe sit together at a table in a quiet tearoom. It is not the most popular establishment in the city—the biscuits are dry and there are stains on the tablecloth—but at least they have some privacy and do not have to be seated in some dark corner because Arsinoe still refuses to wear dresses.

Since their encounter with Queen Illiann's shadow in the graveyard, they have had to find places besides the Chatworth house to talk. Billy's mother has been pushed to her limit, and on any day may try to put them out on the street.

'I want to seek more low magic,' Arsinoe says, but Mirabella shakes her head and rubs the scab on her forearm.

'No more. She wants us to go back to the island. More low magic will only make her stronger.'

'You don't know that; you're just afraid. And so am I. But I can't take much more of these dreams. Every time I close my eyes, I'm someone else. I'm Daphne. And I'm tired.'

'You are curious,' says Mirabella. 'I see you, Arsinoe. You are more and more drawn into the dreams. Her bait is working.' The door to the shop opens, and Arsinoe glances toward the entrance. A woman and her two small children have come inside. Two little girls, holding hands and pointing at which biscuits they would like on the display.

'After this is over, I would like to become a teacher,' Mirabella says. 'I like children. Though I have had little interaction with them.'

'Why would you?' Arsinoe asks crossly. 'Queens whelp babies, but we don't raise them.'

'Do not say "whelp."' Mirabella frowns. 'You know I hate it when you say "whelp."'

'*Whelp*, that's not my problem.' Arsinoe crunches through a biscuit, slouched down so far that crumbs are able to fall directly into her collar. 'Though if you become a teacher, what would I do?'

'You could do the same.'

'I'd be a terrible teacher.'

'Only at first.'

Arsinoe studies the children, so well-behaved, their brown hair in ringlets. 'I'd rather make clothes or work in a pub. I'm no use in a kitchen, but I can sew, a little. Ellis taught me how. And Luke.'

Mirabella looks down at her hands. 'If you do the low magic again, I am afraid of what will happen. I am afraid we will lose all this.'

'All what?'

'Our lives. This future.'

Arsinoe sees the way her sister looks at the children. With a kind of hopeful despair. The way someone looks at something they can never possibly have.

'What if there's something wrong on the island?' Arsinoe asks.

'Then let them sort it out. As they tried to sort us out. As they would again, the moment we set foot back in that place.'

Arsinoe sighs.

'I have to find a way to stop the dreams,' she whispers. 'Or solve them. I have to, or they will drive me mad. But after that,' she reaches across the table and takes Mirabella's hand. 'There will be time. We can have a future here, I promise.'

Mirabella does not respond, and Arsinoe leans back and slides down into her chair.

'You promise,' says Mirabella. 'Except that it will never be over. Because the island is not something we can escape.'

That night, Arsinoe fights sleep. For Mirabella and for Billy, she fights the dreams. She has her own life now and if she wants to keep it, Mirabella is right. She has to let go of the island and make the dreams stop.

She turns and peers through the darkness at her sister's still form. Mirabella makes not a peep when she sleeps. No moans. Certainly no snoring. A queen through and through. And to think, Arsinoe once thought Mirabella would fart cyclones.

'Mira? Are you awake?' Arsinoe waits but gets no response. She takes a deep breath and shuts her eyes.

The dream begins as they always do: nestled snug down inside Daphne's mind. Seeing through Daphne's eyes. Hearing through Daphne's ears.

As the dream takes hold and Arsinoe finds herself seated at a table in the Volroy, it is only the thought of Mirabella that allows her to keep her resolve. It would be so easy not to fight, to be Daphne for one more night, one more fortnight, another month . . . or to simply stay dreaming until her story ends. Except that the dreams have begun to feel less like an escape and more like a distraction, dulling her senses so she is oblivious as the ax swings down.

In the dream, Daphne sits beside Richard, Daphne and Henry's pale, skinny friend from Centra, and glares up at the head table, where Queen Illiann and Duke Branden sit with their heads close together.

'I do not understand it, Richard,' Daphne says. 'There is no reason why Henry should lose. He has beaten all comers at the joust, at hawking and archery. He commands a ship even better than I do!'

'You see Henry differently,' Richard replies.

'What is that supposed to mean?'

She takes a swallow of ale, good ale, not like Arsinoe has had on the mainland.

'Anyone with two eyes can see that Henry is twice the man that rogue from Salkades is.'

'I believe that Henry is a match for any man,' says Richard. 'But not every woman is a match for him.'

Daphne peers up at Illiann. Neither she nor Arsinoe know what he is talking about. Illiann is a beauty. Such long black hair and soft, even features. Eyes as dark as Daphne's own but wider, larger, and more thickly lashed. 'How can you say that? She is lovely.'

As Richard laughs, Arsinoe begins to squirm in Daphne's mind. It is not easy, separating herself from the form she inhabits. It is actually so hard, she would be sweating if only she had a body to sweat with.

'Why are you laughing?'

'I always laugh when my friends are fools. Daphne, have you really never noticed the way that Henry looks at you? All those tavern girls back at Torrenside were a lie. All for show. For as long as I have known him, Henry has cared for only one girl above all the rest. You.'

Finally, someone said it. The thing that had been obvious from the moment Arsinoe had started dreaming, and she pauses her struggle to free herself from the dream in order to watch.

'That's not true,' Daphne says. 'That's ridiculous.'

'Is it?' Richard shakes his head and chuckles again.

'Yes it is.' Daphne pushes away from the table and stalks out into the quiet corridor.

Get back in there. Sit down and listen. But inside Daphne, Arsinoe feels the turmoil as the realization takes hold. As she remembers every interaction she and Henry have ever had and begins to see them in a different way. The poor girl. Arsinoe wishes she had her own arms to pat her comfortingly on the back with.

'Is something troubling you, Lady Daphne?'

Daphne turns, and together she and Arsinoe narrow their eyes. Duke Branden has made his way into the hall after them.

'Not at all, my lord. I am only taking a little air. Please, return to the queen and your meal.'

'She will wait.' He smiles lopsidedly. Such a handsome man. Even Arsinoe's intense dislike of him cannot completely override it. 'Why do you never wear dresses?' He advances a step, then another. 'You are a lovely enough thing.'

'On Fennbirn one can be lovely without the aid of a dress.'

Arsinoe notices the shuffle in his stride. He has had too much wine.

He's drunk far too often. Even Illiann cannot be blind to that. And nor is Daphne. Arsinoe feels alarm spike through her as the duke moves closer, pushing her further into the shadowy corridor.

'But you,' he says, 'were raised in the civilized world. And so you should behave as a proper woman.'

'Proper?' Daphne asks.

'Were you one of my sisters, I would have you whipped. Were you one of my serfs, I would have you burned.'

'Then it's a good thing I am neither.'

Arsinoe's pulse quickens as she watches the duke edge ever

closer. *Get out of here, Daphne!* But she does not, and in two fast movements, Branden has them pinned against the wall.

For a moment, Daphne is so shocked that she freezes, and inside her, Arsinoe does the same. The feeling of Branden's hands roaming beneath Daphne's tunic is so wrong and disgusting that it nearly causes Arsinoe to wake.

'Do not touch me!'

'Why? It is no great secret what you have underneath. You have shown it to all, dressed as a man.'

'I thought you were pious,' Daphne objects. 'And courteous to women.'

'Courtesy does not extend to whores.'

Kill him! Kick him! Inside Daphne's mind, Arsinoe tries to move her limbs. To bring her knee up hard in the place where it would pain him most. But she cannot make Daphne's body fight any more than she can stop the tears that blur their vision.

'Daphne? Are you all right?'

Branden moves away at the sound of Richard's voice.

'I heard a bit of a scuffle.'

Branden glares between Richard and Daphne and back again before he laughs. He leaves the hall as quickly as he arrived. When he walks past Richard, he shoves the thin young man into the wall.

'Centrans,' he mutters. 'Whores and weaklings.'

In the dream, Daphne and Richard move to comfort each other, but Arsinoe balks.

NO.

ENOUGH OF THIS.

Anger at Branden fuels her frustration with the dream. She twists and thrashes, screams so hard she must be screaming for real; her attempt to break the dream will probably be thwarted not by the shadow of Queen Illiann but by Mrs. Chatworth and Jane shrieking in panic after she wakes the house.

For a moment, her thrashing does not work. Until she jerks her arm and Daphne's arm jerks right along with it.

That is all it takes. The dream goes dark.

'Hello?' She can hear herself breathing. She looks down in the dark and sees that she is herself again, Arsinoe, right down to the scarred face and borrowed trousers.

This is a dream of a different sort. But equally as vivid; she inhales and smells the familiar, damp scent of Fennbirn earth.

'Did I break the dream?' she wonders aloud. 'Why didn't I wake? Can I wake?'

Something in the shadows slides coolly past her shoulder, and she pedals backward, not caring that she cannot see the terrain. She knows that touch even though she has never felt it. The shadow of the Blue Queen.

Light breaks through, and Arsinoe blinks. They are on the island. In the clearing, beside the bent-over tree.

'Did you choose this place? Or did I?'

The shadow of Queen Illiann stands before her, motionless. Then it puts a hand to its throat. Points a thin finger, as it did that day next to Joseph's grave. As it has every time she has seen it.

'Go to where you can speak. I know. But we are on the island now'—she stomps her foot against the dirt—'so spit it out.'

It repeats the motion, more and more agitated until it is shaking so hard that the crown of silver and blue shifts atop its head. It drags dark fingers across where its mouth would be.

'Stop doing that!' Arsinoe shouts. 'Just tell me what you want! Why am I dreaming through Daphne's eyes? Why won't you speak to my sister?' She sticks out her arm and bares the crescent scar. 'She worked the same low magic as me. So why isn't she dreaming?'

But no matter what she asks, the Blue Queen says nothing. Only continues the frustrating pantomime: throat, mouth, point.

'Go to the island. But why do you want us to go there? What am I supposed to see?'

The shadow stops. Then it points again, very slowly.

Arsinoe turns. Above the trees of the Wolf Spring meadow is the summit of Mount Horn, the great mountain of Fennbirn that looks down upon Innisfuil Valley and houses the Black Cottage at its base.

'You can't really see that from here,' Arsinoe says. 'And I should know.'

The shadow claws at its mouth.

'You mean the mountain?'

The shadow relaxes, and Arsinoe exhales. 'You want me to go to Mount Horn? And what will I find there?'

In answer, the dark queen slides toward her. She drags across the ground and across the half-submerged sacred stones. Arsinoe steps back until she feels the hanging branches of the bent-over tree. She does not know what she fears most: Queen Illiann or it.

The Blue Queen draws closer, and as she comes, the darkness melts away at the edges until it is completely gone, and Arsinoe stands face to face with Daphne.

Daphne, the Blue Queen. Not Illiann.

'Daphne! It's been you the whole time? How . . . Why are you wearing Illiann's crown?'

She smiles at her, a smile Arsinoe has seen only through a looking glass. She touches her mouth, shakes her head.

'Right, right. You still can't speak.'

Daphne cocks her head, and the dream shifts again, this time only a flash, a rush of colors. But it is all nightmare. Blood and swords and bodies rotting on the ground. Camden with her fur stained red. Jules—

'Jules!'

She jerks awake and finds Mirabella and Billy leaned over her. Mirabella holding her shoulders while Billy holds a candle so close it is likely to singe her eyebrows.

'Arsinoe,' Mirabella gasps. 'What is it?'

'Jules.' Arsinoe swallows. The dream is still thick around

her. She half expects to look into the corner and see Daphne standing there in Queen Illiann's crown.

'Billy?' They hear his sister, Jane, call out from down the hall. 'Is everything all right?'

'It's fine, Jane. Just a nightmare. Go back to sleep.'

Arsinoe breaks away from him and swings her rubbery legs out of bed. 'It wasn't just a nightmare. It was a message.'

'What message?' he asks. 'What did you see?'

'I saw Jules. On a battlefield. With Katharine.'

'A battlefield?' Mirabella's brow knits. 'The island has not seen a battlefield in a hundred years.'

'I know what I saw.'

'You do not have the sight gift—'

'I know what I saw,' Arsinoe snaps.

'All right. But it was still only a nightmare.'

Billy and Mirabella exchange that look, the one she has come to hate, that says they are worried and she is losing her mind. If she tries to tell them now, about Daphne, about the message, they will never believe her. Worse, they might try to stop her. So even though her heart is halfway into her throat, she forces herself to be calm.

'It felt very real,' she says.

'I'm sure that it did. Was it like . . . the other dreams you've had?' Billy sets down the candle. He pours her a cup of water from the pitcher on her bedside table.

'No. Not really.'

Arsinoe drinks down the water and runs her fingers

through her hair. The dream of Jules felt like a warning. A consequence if she does not do what Daphne wants.

'Are you . . . going to be all right?' Billy asks.

'I guess so,' she says.

'Can you go back to sleep? We can talk more in the morning.'

Arsinoe nods, and begins to think of ways to pay for a boat back to the island.

THE VOLROY

After the attack of the mist in Rolanth, Katharine and her court quickly returned to Indrid Down. No one, not even Antonin and Genevieve, who love the capital as their own mother, really wanted to return. But there was nowhere else to go.

'They have still not found all of those who went missing,' Katharine says, lying in Pietyr's arms in the safety of her rooms. 'How long will it take? Or does the mist mean to keep them?'

Pietyr kisses the top of her head.

'I do not know, Kat. But whoever is found, and in whatever state, should be brought to the capital immediately. There are bound to be wild tales. And we will want to verify them.'

'We have to find a way to fight the mist, Pietyr. They think I am the cause of it!' All the way back to the Volroy, they had been dogged by whispers and shifting eyes. The mist or the queen, the people cannot decide who they ought to fear most. But they have decided who to blame.

'Pietyr.' She slides her fingertips between the buttons of his shirt to feel his heartbeat, and the warmth of his skin. 'What if the mist is right?'

'What do you mean?'

'What if I am not supposed to be in the crown? What if it was not meant to be me and I stole it, like the people are saying?'

Pietyr props his head on his elbow, his ice-blue eyes soft, for once.

'No one knows why the mist is doing this. When people are afraid, they grasp on to the easiest answer.'

'But what if it was supposed to be Mirabella? Or even'—she makes a sour face—'Arsinoe?'

'Then it would be them. The crown of Fennbirn cannot be stolen. It must be won, and you won it.'

'By default. Because I was the only one who wanted it. I am the queen because they abandoned us and allowed me to be.'

'That is right.' He brushes a lock of black hair from her neck. 'You are the Queen Crowned because you fought when they did not. Because you would have killed them as a queen does. You are not the one who does not belong in the crown.' He looks down to her chest, to the center of her.

'The dead queens. They are the ones who were never meant for it.'

'Do not start that again, Pietyr. They are the only reason I am anything. Without them . . . you would have killed me.'

'I know.' He squeezes his eyes shut. 'I know that. But if the mist, and the Goddess behind it, is displeased, they are the only reason I can think of.'

'Why? They are also her daughters.'

'Yes. But the dead queens had their chance, Katharine. They had it, and the island chose them for extinction.'

Inside Katharine, the dead queens are silent. She can feel them there, in her blood and in her mind, clinging to her like bats to the walls of a cave. Their silence speaks to her of sadness. Old sadness and pain. Part of her would tell Pietyr to stop. To be quiet and not to hurt them anymore.

'They take care of me,' she whispers. 'They care for me, and I owe them the same care.' She strokes her own skin. But for the mist to quiet, must she really let them go? 'Perhaps . . . if they could be gotten out . . . if they could be laid to rest . . . that would not be cruel?'

'No.' Pietyr takes her hand and kisses it. 'That would not be cruel at all.'

The next morning, Genevieve comes to escort her to the council chamber. Pietyr has already gone, down to the library to try to find a way to exorcise the dead queens from Katharine. If he does not find it there, he will try the library at Greavesdrake. And if that fails, Katharine has given him permission to discreetly go to the temple scholars. He was so eager to be off and so pleased with her for making the right choice. He called her brave. Good-hearted.

'Genevieve, what word have you received from Sunpool? When is the oracle to arrive?'

'I mean to address that in council this morning, Queen Katharine.'

They pass by the open doors of the throne room, and Katharine glances inside. There is no one there except for a smattering of queensguard. So few people come to her for governance that they are able to restrict them to certain days of the week.

'Is something odd going on?' Katharine asks. 'Should I not have sent Pietyr on that errand this morning?'

'Nothing odd,' Genevieve replies. 'Or if there is, it is nothing that cannot be handled without my nephew.'

Inside the Black Council chamber, everyone has already assembled. Even Bree, who has proven to be chronically late. When they see Katharine, they stand, and the mood in the room is so tense that she does not bother sitting down.

'Tell me.'

She waits, watching as the responsibility to speak passes through the room in sighs and shuffling feet. Antonin and Cousin Lucian look away. Bree pretends she has not heard. Only Rho and Luca raise their eyebrows, and finally, Luca takes a deep breath.

'There is an uprising in the north.'

'An uprising?'

'Someone claiming to be Juillenne Milone is traveling through the north country raising an army to rebel against the crown.'

The words strike Katharine cold.

'A rebellion? Fennbirn does not have rebellions.'

'Perhaps this will be the first.'

'How do you know this?'

Luca and Rho glance at each other.

'Reports first reached us in Rolanth,' says Rho. 'The rebels were supposedly seen there, to the west, and there have been rumors of Jules Milone as far as the villages south of Innisfuil.'

'Jules Milone drowned with my sisters,' says Katharine, and every eye falls. They know as well as she what it will imply if the naturalist is found to be alive and well.

Beside her, Genevieve clears her throat.

'We think they are heading to Sunpool, and that is why the oracles have denied our request for a seer. They have allied with the rebellion.'

The room closes in around Katharine until it is hard to breathe.

'The legion-cursed naturalist is alive.'

'Or someone who is pretending to be her.'

'And the city of the oracles has taken her side?' Katharine scans the faces of her council. 'Who else?'

'Bastian City, perhaps,' says Genevieve. 'The Milone girl is calling herself the Legion Queen.'

The Legion Queen. The queen of multiple gifts, who will unite the island under one banner. If they only knew. It strikes Katharine as almost funny. The people yearn for a queen with a two-gift curse, when they already have a queen with all of them.

'So now I must fight a war for my crown and the mist as well?' She grinds her teeth. 'And I suppose that the rebels are using that to their advantage. Spreading word that the attacking mist is my fault?'

'They say it rises against you,' says Luca. 'They are using it as a sign.'

Katharine sinks into her chair.

'Well,' she says. 'You are my Black Council. My advisers. This is the part where you are supposed to advise.'

'I say embrace it.' Rho Murtra places her knuckles upon the table. 'Wage a war. Use it to quiet the unrest. Nothing calms the people more than having something to fight against.'

'You would say that,' Antonin spits. 'War gifted. Always spoiling for a battle.'

'And why not, if it's a winning battle? The queensguard army is in fine shape, despite languishing under soft poisoner leadership. It can rout a band of rebels made up of farmers and fishers.'

'Even if those rebels are backed by every warrior in Bastian City?'

Katharine slaps her hand down, and their arguing ceases.

'There is still too much I do not know. About the mist. About the Blue Queen. And now about these rebels and Juillenne Milone, if that is indeed who she is.' She turns to Genevieve. 'I need an oracle.'

'I told you, my queen, none will come. They have refused us.'

'They cannot refuse the crown!' Katharine barks. 'Send the queensguard and arrest one! And bring her back here for questioning.' She presses one hand to her cold belly, where she can feel the dead queens beginning to quicken. 'Then we will know what to do.'

THE BLACK COTTAGE

'Well?' Jules asks as she and Camden help Caragh brew another of the endless pots of nettle leaf tea. 'How bad is it?'

At the counter, chopping herbs and trying to keep cougar breath from blowing them everywhere, Caragh frowns. 'It's not good, Jules. Every day she bleeds. And every day it's harder to stem the pains.'

'How long will it be before it's safe for the baby to come?'

'Maybe it is not only the baby we should be worrying about.'

Jules swings the hot water kettle away from the fire and wraps the handle in cloth. 'Don't tell me you believe that low magic nonsense.'

'Whatever you think about the rightness or wrongness of it, low magic exists,' Caragh says. 'And my sister has become the closest thing that the island has to a master of it.'

'Maybe. But this time she's wrong. Have you heard her

talking about the baby? She keeps calling it "he." A boy. When we all know that Milone women only bear girls. Two girls.'

'The old Milone rule,' Caragh says softly. 'The old Milone curse. We have more than our fair share of those, don't we?'

Jules brings the pot, and Caragh ties the herbs in cheesecloth and drops the bundle in. The nettle tea will be bitter enough to pucker Madrigal's cheeks, but Willa says that they cannot add even one drop of honey.

'We thought you were dead,' Caragh says quietly. 'Or at least gone. And then Worcester came with strange news: the mist was rising without cause and leaving dead bodies in its wake. Rumors of a legion-cursed naturalist who would go to war.' Caragh narrows her eyes. 'I didn't believe it was you, of course. I thought it must be an impostor. But your mother knew it had to be true.'

'How did she know?' Jules asks.

'Perhaps she knows her daughter.'

'She doesn't know me. You know me. You raised me.'

'And then she raised you,' says Caragh. 'After I came here.' She reaches out and tucks Jules's short hair behind her ear. 'You even look like a queen these days.'

Jules brushes her away with a smile. 'I never thought we would get this far. Even when Mathilde's crazy stories started to work and people started to believe . . . and then, maybe I started to believe.'

'Madrigal would say that is what destiny feels like.'

'How do you know what Madrigal would say?'

'She's my sister, Jules. Thinking she's dying has made her almost sweet. She's trying to make amends. So am I, in case she's right.' Caragh looks at her meaningfully, but Jules just sticks her lip out and blows hair away from her forehead. The baby will be fine, and Madrigal will be up to her old tricks in no time.

She gathers a cup and saucer and assembles Madrigal's afternoon tea service, piling on a few of the almond biscuits she likes, the only thing that Willa will consent to her eating alongside the tea.

Halfway down the sunlit hall, Jules hears Emilia's laughter bubble out from Madrigal's room. It is a pretty sound, and her unwell mother sounds in good spirits, laughing back. But for some reason, the fur on Camden's tail begins to puff with apprehension.

When Jules enters, all is innocent. Emilia has just returned from foraging in the woods, her hands black with dirt, her burlap sack heavy with roots and herbs.

'What did you find?' Jules asks.

'Big patch of fanroot.' Emilia reaches into the bag and pulls some out, a pale tuberous root still attached to its bright green leaves shaped like tiny fans. Hence its name. 'I will go out again after dinner. Willa says it will keep well enough in the cellar. Before long, the frost and snow will get to the leaves, and it will be that much harder to find.'

'More fanroot. How delicious,' says Madrigal sarcastically.

'What brings you in to see my mother?' asks Jules, and Emilia shrugs.

'We got on well together, after you left us for the queens at Bardon Harbor. Your mother understands the virtue of the war gift and the possibilities of your so-called legion curse.'

Jules sets the tray of tea down beside Madrigal's bed. She pours some of the bitter liquid into the cup and points to it. Then she takes Emilia by the arm and pulls her out of the room and down the hall.

'What?' Emilia asks. 'What is the matter?'

'I know why you were in my mother's room.'

'Yes. I told you. Because it is nice to converse with someone who understands our cause—'

'And because of the binding.'

'What?'

'The low magic binding. The blood. You know my mother bound my legion curse with her blood, and you know that if she dies, the war-gifted side will be let loose. Which is exactly what you've always wanted.'

For a moment, Emilia stares at Jules wordlessly. Then her eyes darken, and she steps up close.

'I would never want that. She is your mother! Have you forgotten that I had a mother who died?'

'No,' Jules says quickly, ashamed to admit that, for the moment, she had. 'This war is everything to you; that's all I know.'

She braces, sure that Emilia will use her war gift to shove her, to explode in her face. But instead, her shoulders slump.

'It is not everything.'

She turns and stalks off, and though Camden trots halfway down the hall after her, Jules cannot bring herself to.

'Jules?' Madrigal calls. 'Is everything all right?'

'Everything's fine.' Jules returns to her mother's room and puts the neglected cup of nettle leaf tea into her hands. 'Now drink.'

Madrigal takes a sip. 'You are a good daughter, Jules Milone.'

'A good daughter.' Jules snorts. 'I've only been as good a daughter as you have been a mother.' She looks at Madrigal, still small, beneath her enormous, swollen belly. 'Maybe we both should have tried harder.'

Madrigal purses her lips. 'Your friend Emilia is very fond of you.'

'Of course she is. I'm her pet queen. Ridiculous as that sounds.'

'I think it's more than that.'

'Are you pleased? This is what you wanted, isn't it? For me to go to the warriors and learn their side of my gift? Embrace some great destiny?'

Her mother frowns at the tone that has crept into her voice. Jules had not meant for it to, but nor can she help it. It has been this way between them for too long to change, even in the face of illness.

'Maybe once,' Madrigal says. 'That was what I wanted. But now I'm dying, Jules. And I would just very much like for us to be able to go home.'

'And we will. Or you and the baby will, and with luck I'll follow, someday.'

'I heard what you said out there, in the hall. But it isn't true. The binding must be cut from my vein with a blade. If I die having this baby, you will remain bound, until you choose to release it.' She stares into her teacup. 'I may be a bad mother, but I wouldn't have placed a binding on you that could be broken if I died by accident.'

'That's not what I—'

'Never mind. I've left things with Cait. Thinned blood from shallow cuts. And she knows how to—'

Madrigal groans and grasps the sides of her stomach. The cup tumbles into the bed and tea stains the quilt dark.

'Madrigal?'

'Call Willa. Call Caragh.'

Jules shouts for them. Moments later, Willa limps into the room, hurrying without her cane, and shoves Jules out of the way. Willa presses her hands into Madrigal's stomach and pulls back the blankets. There is blood, and water.

'What do we do?' Jules asks.

'Get your aunt from the barn. Tell her to prepare for a birth.' Willa lays Madrigal back onto the pillow with strong arms and uses gentle fingers to caress her cheeks. 'There is no stopping it now.'

As Madrigal's labor intensifies, Jules and Camden wait with Emilia in the sitting room, staring into the fire.

'Is that normal?' Jules asks when Madrigal starts to scream. Emilia raises her brows.

'I do not know. The war gifted often scream during birth, but it is usually more of a bellow. Like an elk.' She makes a fist. 'Like triumph.'

Madrigal's cries do not sound like triumph.

'Here.' Mathilde comes to them from the kitchen, carrying cups of watered wine.

'Where have you been?'

'Away. Keeping busy. Oracles are no comfort during times like these when we cannot foresee the outcome.' She takes a swallow from Emilia's cup before handing it over. 'And even sometimes when we can.'

The door to Madrigal's room opens and shuts, and Willa comes hurriedly down the hall. Her face is impassive. Calm. But the gray braid near the nape of her neck is wet with sweat.

'What's happening?' Jules asks. 'Are they . . . will they be all right?'

Willa ignores her and goes in to retrieve something from the kitchen. She returns in moments with a tray. It is covered over with cloth, but Jules sees the shine of silver underneath. Blades.

'Willa?'

'It will be over quickly, one way or the other.' She says nothing more, and they hear the door open and shut again.

'It will be all right, Jules,' Emilia says. 'Who better to deliver a baby than the Midwives of the Black Cottage?'

'I will go outside and start a fire,' says Mathilde. 'I will pray for her.'

The door down the hall opens again, and Aria the crow comes flying out of the room in a panic. Her poor caw sounds raw to the ear, and she batters her wings against the walls.

'Should we let her outside?' Emilia asks.

Jules looks to Camden, and the big cat deftly stalks the crow until she is close enough to pounce, then traps the bird softly in her jaws. She lies down on the rug, purring as Aria stops flapping and calms, her little beak wide open to pant.

'I'll get her some water.' Emilia pauses on the way and looks gravely at Jules. 'You should perhaps go and be with your mother.'

Jules walks down the hallway on legs made of wood. And she does not have Camden to lean on, since she stayed back on the rug with Aria.

She turns the knob and swings the door open. Her knees nearly buckle when she sees Caragh slick with bright red blood.

'Jules,' Caragh says, and gently moves her back into the hall.

'Is it over? Was he born?'

Caragh wipes her hands.

'He will not come out.'

'Jules! I want my Jules!'

At her mother's cry, Jules pushes past her aunt and bursts back into the room. Madrigal is covered, her legs squirming beneath the blankets in pain. Willa stands to the side of the bed, wiping her hands on a towel.

'She has lost a lot of blood,' says the Midwife. 'Not making much sense.'

Jules goes to the bed and takes Madrigal's hand.

'How are you doing?'

'As well as I expected to.' She smiles. She is almost unrecognizable under so much paleness and sweat, thinner everywhere but in the belly. She resembles a gray corpse, like the one she said she saw in her vision. 'I did a wrong taking Matthew from my own sister. Making the charm to keep him.'

'Nothing more wrong than what you always do,' Jules says, and presses a cool, wet cloth to her forehead.

Madrigal laughs breathlessly.

'Should I apologize? Is there time?'

'There's plenty of time,' says Caragh, 'when you're up and out of this bed. I'll accept that apology, with you down on one knee.'

Madrigal laughs harder.

'You know you're nothing like me, Jules. You're like her. So tough. So mean.' She touches Jules's cheek with her fingertips. 'Except that you're crying.'

Jules sniffs. She had not realized. 'Just hurry up, Madrigal, will you? I'm tired of waiting for this baby.'

Madrigal nods. She looks past Jules to Willa, who has uncovered her tray of knives.

'Will it be fast?' Madrigal asks.

'It will be fast, child.'

'What are you going to do?' Jules asks, eyes wide. 'Will she survive it?'

Willa frowns. 'I do not know.'

'It'll be all right, my Jules. I'm paying the price of my low magic.' Madrigal lays back. 'Put him on my chest when it's over. So I might see him a moment.'

'Madrigal?' Jules stumbles backward as Willa approaches the bed. 'Mother?'

Her eyes are blurry, but had they been clear, Caragh would have still been hard to see. She moved so fast. One second Willa was leaned over Madrigal's belly, and the other, she had been shoved out into the hall and the door locked behind her.

'Caragh,' Madrigal says. 'What are you doing?'

'Maddie, you have to push now.'

'No. Let Willa back in here. I'm tired. Go with Jules into the kitchen. Or outside.'

But Caragh does not listen. She takes up position at the foot of the bed and puts her hand on her sister's knee.

'Madrigal, push. You aren't done yet.'

'I can't.'

'Aunt Caragh,' Jules says quietly, 'maybe let her rest a minute.'

'She rests, she dies.' She slaps Madrigal across the hip. 'Push!'

'I can't!'

'Yes you can, you silly brat! You just think you can't because of some foolish vision! Now get up and push!'

Madrigal forces herself up onto her elbows. She bares her teeth. There is so much blood in the bed. So much sweat on her face.

'What do you care? You'll have everything you wanted! My baby. My Jules. You'll have my children and Matthew back, too, so why don't you cut him out of me and leave me alone!'

The room falls quiet. The only sound is Madrigal's labored breathing until Caragh reaches out and sends everything on her table crashing to the floor. A pitcher and bowls of water, bloody cloth, sharpened knives, herbs, and tea, it all clatters and splashes and breaks into pieces.

'I don't want your baby! I want you! I want my sister to live, and you want it, too.' Her hound bays miserably as she dives for the floor, and the discarded knives, pressing a blade into her arm. 'If the low magic wants a price, then I'll pay it.'

'Stop! Caragh, stop. I'll do it. I'll push.'

'You'll live,' Caragh says. 'You'll live because I won't have it any other way.'

It is not easy. Madrigal is already weak and has lost so much blood. But in the hours before dawn, Jules's baby brother is born. Madrigal names him Fennbirn, for the island. Fennbirn Milone. Fenn, for short. She names him and then loses consciousness with him on her chest. But she lives.

In the days after the baby is born, Jules lingers at the Black Cottage, watching her mother and aunt become close again. Whether it will last is anyone's guess, but it is still nice to see.

'Jules Milone,' Emilia says as they walk through the north woods with Camden, 'how long do you intend for us to stay here staring at that baby?'

'He's a good baby to stare at. You don't think he's good-looking?'

'He is handsome enough. Though I don't like his name. Fennbirn. If she would call him "Fenn," why not "Fen*ton*"? So many boys are already named for the island.'

'But none called Milone.'

Emilia makes a face like she is wondering what is so great about that, until Camden pricks her ears and grunts. Emilia puts her hand on the hilt of her sword. They are walking in search of Braddock, Arsinoe's false-familiar bear.

'Why are we out here looking for a bear?' Emilia asks.

'This is the last thing I need to do before we go. Arsinoe would want me to see him. She would want me to make sure he's all right.'

'How do you know he is still friendly? He was not your familiar. He was not even really her familiar.'

Jules grins. She does not know if they will be able to find him. Caragh said she had not seen him in weeks, and thought he might have followed the fish upstream. She also said he grew wilder by the day.

'Don't worry.' Jules looks over her shoulder and winks. 'I won't let him hurt you.'

Emilia blushes but glances around cautiously.

'With her gone, isn't he only a bear now?'

'He will never be only a bear. He was a queen's bear. And there he is.' They have reached the widest part of the stream, and out in the middle of it, splashing down hard with his front paws, is a very handsome, shiny-coated great brown bear.

'Is he fishing? Or trying to smash a fish flat?' Emilia asks. She partially draws her sword as Camden bounds out of the ferns, startling Braddock up onto his hind legs. Then the cougar grunts, and he comes back down so she can rub her head against his chest.

Emilia sheaths her sword. Jules unwraps an oatcake that Willa baked and tears a chunk for Emilia. 'If he bites my hand, I am going to—'

'You're going to what?'

'Run away, I suppose.' She holds out the cake, and Braddock takes it. Then he takes the rest from Jules and snuffles around in her pockets before raising his head, and bobbing it in the direction of the trees behind them.

'He's looking for Arsinoe.' Jules pats his shoulder. She uses her gift to soothe him, and soon enough he and Camden are playing happily in the stream.

'There,' says Emilia. 'Now you have seen to the bear, and your new baby brother, and your mother is well. And now we can go.'

Jules turns and watches Braddock as he drinks from the stream, as he splashes and kicks pebbles. She is sorry to say goodbye to him, but he is happy there. And safe. Days must pass when he does not wonder at all where Arsinoe is. *It will be a long time*, Jules thinks, *before I have those days.*

She and Emilia return to the Black Cottage and find Caragh sitting on the porch with the baby in her arms.

'Back so soon,' Caragh says. 'How is Braddock?'

'Well,' says Jules.

'Large,' says Emilia. She holds her hands out for Fenn, and Caragh gently gives him over. 'Where is his mother?'

'Gone.'

'Gone? What do you mean, "gone"?'

'Gone to tell Matthew he has a son. To bring him back here so that they can take Fenn home together. She borrowed my brown mare and left is what I mean.'

Jules turns toward the bridle path, the one that passes through the Greenwood and winds down toward Wolf Spring. 'It's only been a week since the birth.'

'And no easy birth at that. But you know Madrigal. She's up and around, nearly fast as a queen. And restless already.'

Emilia shifts the baby in her arms.

'What about this little lad's feeding?'

'Willa knows how to manage with goat's milk. She won't be gone long.'

'She's not . . . leaving us again?' Jules asks.

'Not this time.' Caragh stands and takes the baby back. 'This time I think she will stay.'

GREAVESDRAKE MANOR

Q ueen Katharine is wandering the west grounds of
Greavesdrake Manor when Bree arrives in the shadow of
the great house. Or where the house's shadow would be if there
were enough sun to cast one.

'Queen Katharine.' Bree curtsies. 'Why have you called me
here and not the Volroy?'

'I like it here,' Katharine replies. 'There are fewer eyes and
ears. Now that Natalia is gone and I am gone, Greavesdrake
stands hollow, with only the barest staff to tend its upkeep.'

'It is Genevieve's house now, is it not?'

'Yes. And Antonin's. Even Pietyr's, in a way, if he would
seek to claim a piece.' She gazes up at the red brick, the black
roof. She looks out at the alder trees and the long green swath
of grass where she and her king-consort Nicolas had once
practiced archery.

'I suppose it does not feel the same without her,' says Bree.
'Some people leave too much space behind when they are gone.'

They stand in silence a moment, and Katharine shivers against a cold wind.

'Such a chill day. There was a spattering of snowflakes earlier. Did you see any in town?'

Bree shakes her head.

'I would almost wish that my sister were here,' says Katharine, 'if only so she could clear these gray clouds away.'

Bree chuckles. 'She was strong. The strongest I have ever seen. But she still couldn't change the seasons.'

Katharine blows into her hands. Elemental Bree could stand outside all day, but the queen will soon need to go inside. Of all the gifts she borrows from the dead sisters, the elemental gift seems to be the weakest. Perhaps even they are loyal to the wonder of Mirabella. Or perhaps there were simply fewer elementals who lost.

'Katharine,' says Bree, dropping for the first time the formal address. 'What do you wish of me?'

Katharine sighs and leads the way around the paved path back to the front of the house.

'The oracle will be brought to me any day now. I would know how the council seats from Rolanth feel about that.'

'I do not speak for the High Priestess. And I would not speak for Rho. But I think they would say they think it wise. You must know all you can if the rumors of the uprising are true.'

'And if they are, whose side will you take?' Katharine asks quickly.

'After the Ascension, there is only one side,' Bree replies, unrattled. 'The queen's side.'

'I thought you would blame me for what happened in Rolanth. Would you take the queen's side, even against the mist? Against the Goddess?'

'Who is to say who is more of the Goddess? The line of the queens is her line, and it was the queens who gave us the mist. So . . .' She stops and shakes her head. 'These are questions for a priestess. Where is Elizabeth when I need her?'

'I must admit I thought you might bring her along. You two are never far apart. But I will not hold you to these oaths, Bree Westwood. I know that whatever comes of this rebellion, the High Priestess will decide the allegiance of Rolanth.'

'Rolanth is not Luca's lapdog. Nor is it mine. But for my part, I think you have grown into the crown very well. Better than I thought. It has been difficult, but I can't imagine Mira—any queen doing better.'

They round the house, and Katharine signals for Bree's horse.

'Is that all, my queen?'

'That is all.'

Bree glances up at the dark walls and windows. 'Why are you really here instead of at the Volroy?'

'Just why I said. And also to retrieve something I will need for the oracle when she arrives.'

Bree turns and is helped into the saddle by a groom. Her horse snorts and dances in place.

'When she does arrive, you should question her before the whole council. The people will no doubt hear of it, and they like to know that the High Priestess has the ear of the crown.'

'I will consider it.'

Bree lifts a rein to wheel her horse back to the city. 'There are plenty of poisons in the Volroy, are there not?'

Katharine smiles.

'Not like these.'

Not long after Bree leaves, Genevieve and Pietyr arrive, nearly at the same time though not together—Genevieve in a coach from the Volroy and Pietyr on horseback, coming to scour the Greavesdrake library for insights into the dead queens. Still, when Edmund, Natalia's good and loyal butler, tells them that the queen is upstairs, both make their way to Natalia's old study.

'Pietyr, Genevieve.' Katharine turns to greet them but only partway. Her arms remain inside the open doors of one of Natalia's cabinets. 'Is there news? Has the oracle been brought?'

'Not yet.' Genevieve comes into the room and runs her hand over Natalia's favorite wingback chair.

'I do not know what is keeping them. The captain of the queensguard sent word that they arrested her nearly a week ago.'

'The weather in the mountains is bound to slow their progress.'

'You do not come in here often, do you, Genevieve?'

'No. Not often.'

'I can tell.' Katharine wrinkles her nose. 'It smells musty. Perhaps Edmund could open the windows for an hour or so per day.'

Neither Genevieve nor Pietyr comment. They are so silent that Katharine turns around, thinking they have gone. But there they are. Standing beside Natalia's old chair as if they are staring at her ghost seated in it.

'I wish she were here,' says Katharine.

'So do I.' Genevieve squeezes the leather. 'I asked Rho Murtra what it was like to find that mainlander standing over her body. I asked what it felt like to kill him for it. Made her describe it to me in every detail. And still it was not enough.'

Her fingers dig deeper into the leather. 'Leave it to the war priestess to carve him up. When poison was what he deserved. Someday, I will cross the sea and find his entire family. Poison them with something from the room here. Watch every last one of them kick and bleed from the eyes. His wife. His siblings. His children. And especially the suitor Billy Chatworth.'

'That would be a worthy errand,' Pietyr says quietly.

'Someday,' says Katharine. 'But not today. Today, I would have you help me find a proper poison to loosen the oracle's tongue.' She points to the cabinets she has not looked through yet, and the Arrons set to work.

'I do not know what you hope to learn.' Genevieve's finger softly rattles a row of bottles. 'I have met only two oracles before, but both had gifts so weak, they could hardly be called gifts at all. A few correct predictions, a hazy vision, all garbled with doublespeak.' She chews on her cheek. 'If only there were a poison to sharpen one's gift.'

Katharine laughs, her head so far into a particularly deep shelf that the sound echoes. 'If there had been such a poison, I would have nowhere near as many scars.'

'Kat,' Pietyr whispers, so suddenly close that she startles and hits her head. He is always so silent. She should make him start wearing more of that cologne she likes, so she can tell when he is coming.

'I am starting to find passages on the queens. So many different texts, it is difficult to keep track of them all, and I am only taking the volumes I most need to avoid suspicion.'

Katharine carefully extricates herself from the cabinet and looks into his excited eyes. Over his shoulder, Genevieve is not listening, occupied with an open book of poison notes in one hand and a bottle of yellow powder in another.

'There are passages about the dead sisters?'

'Not many. I did not really start to gain ground until I looked past them, into cases of spiritual possession.'

'Spiritual possession!' she hisses, and pulls him down low.

'That is, in essence, what they are.'

'They are more than that, Pietyr. They are queens.'

'Yes, but separating them from you may work in much the same way—'

She squares her shoulders and returns to her cabinet.

'I cannot entertain this right now.'

'But I thought we agreed——'

'Yes, but . . . not now, Pietyr! With a rebellion rising under Jules Milone? I cannot let them go right when I might need them.' When he starts to argue further, she reaches up and takes his face in her hands. 'Not now. Not yet.' Then she looks away before he can begin to doubt.

'Very well, my love.' He steps away, voice terse. 'Another day. Today, however, you should be wearing an apron. And better gloves than these. Borrowed gifts or no, some of the poisons in this room could still mean your death.'

'This reminds me,' Genevieve calls from across the study. 'We should have the poison room at the Volroy restocked. Even some of these here in Natalia's private collection are better than what the castle has on hand.'

'Not a terrible idea.' Pietyr pulls one of Natalia's journals from her desk. 'Though there are more pressing things to deal with just now.'

'Yes, yes, nephew. Like raising more soldiers for the royal army. But Rho Murtra is seeing to that. And a poisoner should never settle for substandard poisons. Most of the restocking we could pull from the inventory here at Greavesdrake. Our poison room has always been better anyway.'

Katharine touches the bottles affectionately. Most of the labels were written in Natalia's own hand. Some contain Natalia's own special concoctions.

'I should have a cabinet made specifically for Natalia's creations. With silver fastenings and a glass door. The last poisons of a great poisoner.'

She and Genevieve smile at each other. Pietyr turns and taps a page from the notebook.

'It says here that Natalia once crafted a poison that induced an agreeable delirium.'

'That might work.' Katharine turns to the shelves as Pietyr comes to scan them. He plucks it from near the top: a tall purple bottle. 'Is it preserved?'

'If it was not, she would not have kept it.'

'Does the delirium outpace the agreeable portion?' Genevieve asks. 'What do the notes say?'

'She designed it specifically for interrogation.' He gives the murky liquid a gentle shake and removes the stopper to sniff. 'Sharply herbal and very alcoholic. With a fungal note, right at the end.'

'There is so little of it left,' says Katharine.

'But I think she would want you to use it. She would want them used for you and for some important purpose.' He looks back down at Natalia's notes. 'I would say we could try to duplicate the recipe, but that is risky. We have only one chance to administer it.'

'Why? It does not result in immunity?'

'No,' he says. 'It results in death.'

The next morning, Katharine, Pietyr, and Genevieve ride back to the Volroy together after a night spent at Greavesdrake. It was refreshing, to have a whole evening in quiet, with familiar, discreet servants and warm cups of Edmund's mangrove tea. A whole night with Pietyr in her old bedroom.

The carriage crests the hill, and Katharine looks upon the massive twin spires. Once, it was a true fortress, the capital not much more than the palace and what could fit inside the border wall. Now Indrid Down stretches far inland, north, west, and east to the harbor. What remains of the wall is barely visible at this distance, so low and worn down and overgrown with moss. Its stone torn out long ago and used to build up other things.

When they arrive through the large open gates, Katharine knows that the oracle has arrived. It is the only reason she can think of for Rho to meet the carriage.

'They have brought the oracle,' Katharine says as she steps out.

'Yes.'

'How long ago?'

'Two hours, perhaps,' Rho answers. 'Her journey was long, so Luca ordered her housed in the East Tower with a hot meal and a bath.'

Genevieve snorts. 'Not to the cells, then?'

'It is Theodora Lermont,' Rho says by way of explanation. 'An elder. Respected by all in Sunpool. They say that visions bubble forth from her like water in a brook.'

'Like water in a brook.' Genevieve frowns. 'This will all turn out to be a very great waste of time.'

'It will be all right, Genevieve,' says Katharine, and takes

Pietyr's arm. 'I would not have her put in the cells anyway. Give her a chance to be loyal. Summon her to the throne room.'

She walks with Pietyr through the castle, the weight of the poison a comfort in her pocket.

'Let them doubt,' Pietyr says softly. 'The oracles know things about the island that even the temple does not. Bringing her here was a wise decision.'

Katharine nods. 'I hope so, Pietyr.'

When they enter the throne room, they are alone except for the servants who tend and clean. But it does not take long for the Black Council to relocate from the chamber, and soon all are seated at their long table to her right. Bree catches her eye, pleased she has decided to question the oracle before them all. Cousin Lucian, on the other hand, clears his throat.

'Has the oracle been sent for? Should we not meet first? To discuss what to ask?'

'We will meet after. To discuss what is said.' Katharine motions with her chin. It is perhaps a less respectful gesture than he is accustomed to, for his eyes narrow. But Katharine does not care. Her mind is on the oracle, and besides, he is not *her* cousin.

Theodora Lermont, of the famed Lermont family of oracles, enters the throne room in a gown of pale yellows and grays. She is older, not as old as the High Priestess, but still older than Natalia. She is very spry, and the bath and meal have served her well. One would never guess she had just been dragged all the way across the island at a fevered pace.

'Theodora Lermont,' Katharine says after the seer has bowed deeply. 'You are most welcome at the Volroy. I hope that your journey was not arduous?'

'It was long, Queen Katharine. But not arduous.' She turns to face the Black Council and nods a greeting to the High Priestess. 'Luca. I am glad to see you are well. It's been many years.'

'It has.' Luca chuckles. 'And not all of those years have been kind.'

Katharine smiles passively at their exchange. She does not like the seer's eyes. There is an emptiness there, or perhaps a resolve.

'Do you know why I asked you here?'

The seer smiles. 'I am afraid, my queen, that that is not how the sight gift works.'

Katharine laughs politely, along with most of her council. Theodora Lermont has no tell, but Katharine knows she is lying.

'Then tell me, seer, how does it work? What use can you be to your queen?'

'I can cast the bones.' Theodora reaches into the folds of her gray skirt and produces a small leather pouch affixed to her belt. Inside will be knuckle bones, and the bones of a bird, feathers, and stones carved with runes. 'See your fortune. Tell your future.'

'It is hard to be respectful of the sight gift when it comes dressed as a charlatan and with a bag of child's toys,' says

Genevieve, and Theodora's eyes glitter with outrage.

'But respect it we will.' Katharine shushes Genevieve with a finger. 'Respect it, we do. I would be honored if you would cast the bones for me. But later. Knowing my future is useful, but it is not why you are here. What do you know of the naturalist girl called Juillenne Milone?'

The oracle lowers her eyes, and Katharine glances at Pietyr, who nods subtly.

'Everyone has heard of the legion-cursed naturalist,' replies Theodora. 'After she attacked you in the Wolf Spring forest, word spread quickly. And after she appeared in the midst of the duel, her fame continued to grow.'

'And now?'

'Now she gathers people to her cause.'

'So it is truly Jules Milone?'

Theodora shakes her head.

'That, my queen, I have not seen.'

'But you have seen that her cause is my crown.' The seer looks up at her gravely, and Katharine leans forward, that the woman may have a better view of the black band tattooed into her forehead. 'How can that be? How can she seek to replace me with herself, when she is not a queen? Not of the bloodline of the Goddess?'

'Some say that the Goddess has abandoned the queens' bloodline.'

'Is that what the prophecy says?' Pietyr asks, and Theodora's eyes dart between them. 'We have heard there is a prophecy.'

'Jules Milone was once a queen, and she may be a queen again.'

The Black Council begins to mutter, making gestures of disbelief.

'*Or*,' the oracle goes on, 'she may be our doom.'

Katharine straightens. A sharp intake of breath sounds from the council table. But Theodora Lermont only shrugs.

'Our queen or our doom,' she says. 'Or both at once. And if that is to be then none will stop her. Not the Black Council. Not the High Priestess.' She levels her eyes at Katharine. 'Not you.'

Katharine touches her stomach as the dead queens wail. The crown is all they want. All they are. If she were to lose it, they would leave her. They would seep out of her pores, and then what would she have? How would she get it back?

'What does she have to do with the mist?' Katharine asks sharply. 'Is she the cause of the mist rising?'

'The mist?' Theodora's brows raise. 'I know not.'

'Can you at least tell me how Jules Milone can bear the legion curse without losing her mind?'

'I cannot speak to that either.'

Katharine throws up her hands. She looks at the council, at Bree and Luca. She has tried. They must be able to see that.

'I am sorry, Queen Katharine. I'm sorry to displease you.'

Katharine turns her wrist against the bottle of Natalia's poison, hidden in her sleeve.

'You have not displeased me. Return to the room we have prepared for you. Rest. I will join you later this evening to have my fortune read. I am looking forward to it.'

Theodora bows low and turns to leave. Katharine studies her every movement, wondering if the woman's sight gift has shown her the queen's true intentions. It does not seem so.

'Is that all?' Cousin Lucian asks. 'Is that all we have waited for?'

'No, it is not all,' Katharine says. She motions to Pietyr and he comes to her instantly.

'Have guards placed outside her door. Let her wander, if she will, but do not let her leave the Volroy. I will have my answers, Lucian. We will all have them.'

That evening, Katharine goes to the oracle's room with dinner in covered silver platters.

'Queen Katharine.' Theodora bows deeply. 'It is an honor to dine with you. Will others from the Black Council join us?'

'Not tonight,' Katharine says, thinking of Bree and for some reason feeling guilty. 'Tonight, I would keep my oracle all to myself.'

They sit, and the servants reveal the dishes: a pretty, pale soup of autumn squash, golden roasted hens bundled full of aromatic herbs and a dessert of custard swirled through with a fruit preserve. The servants fill their cups with wine and water and slice the bread. Then they go and close the door tightly behind them.

'I would have asked my companion, Pietyr Renard, to join us or Genevieve Arron. They have ever been fascinated by the sight gift. But they have also grown up as poisoners, and their faces turn so sour in the presence of untainted food.' Katharine gestures to the plates. 'I find it terribly rude. But I cannot seem to break them of it.'

'The poisoner gift has grown strong. Even the babies are born with immunities now. To come into your gift and be impervious to the deadliest toxins . . . They have every right to be proud. It is a sacred thing.'

'Like all gifts are sacred,' Katharine says quickly. 'I would instill in them a healthier respect of those other gifts.'

'Shall I throw the bones for you?' Theodora asks.

'After supper, perhaps. We do not want the food to get cold.' Katharine motions for her guest to begin, feeling the weight of the poison tucked into her sleeve.

Theodora stares at her. She is no fool. She knows what is coming. After a long moment, she takes up a piece of bread and dips it into the soup.

'I am sorry I was not of more use.' She turns to the hen and picks meat from the breast with her fingers.

'That is all right. You will be.'

The woman eats as slowly as she can, afraid of every bite. But she swallows and swallows again. Such brave consumption. It is a wonder to watch, even if the meal is not poisoned yet.

'You know I never wanted a troubled reign.' Katharine takes up her silver and begins to eat her own portion. 'I am not the monster that you have heard about. Not undead, like they say. It was my sisters who were the traitors. Pretenders in black dresses—or trousers, as the case may be.

'But the island never gave me a chance. They rose up as soon as I had my crown. The mist coming for me like the Goddess herself.' Katharine skewers a bite of hen. 'Well, let her take the naturalist's side. It was not by the Goddess's will that I was crowned anyway.'

'If not hers,' Theodora asks, 'then whose?'

In her lap, Katharine positions the bottle of poison. Then she reaches for her wine.

'Have the oracles truly allied themselves with the rebellion?'

'I know of no such allegiance,' Theodora says, and purses her lips.

'Then why did you refuse to come? Why was I forced to drag you here?'

'Perhaps because everyone on the island is afraid of you.' She takes another bite of soup and bread.

Katharine shifts the poison at the edge of her sleeve. Agreeable delirium, in a purple bottle. Agreeable delirium, and death.

'You have such kind eyes, Mistress Lermont. I wish you were telling me the truth.' She takes a drink and sets her wine back on the table, passing her hand over the tops of Theodora's cups. She has gotten better at it, and the poison slides down unseen to mingle with the water and wine. It is so easy that Katharine slips poison into every dish, tainting the bowl of squash soup and adding several shimmering drops to the custard. So much poison in the meal that the delirium begins to strike before the dessert is even touched, and Theodora starts to laugh.

'Is something funny?'

'No.' She dabs at her forehead with her sleeve and calms to take a swallow of water. 'It's only so strange that we are afraid of you. The stories that they tell—the Undead Queen—but you are such a small thing. And young. Nearly a child.'

'All queens are young in the crown at some point. You would think Jules Milone and her cronies would know that. But perhaps it is not even the true Jules Milone. Perhaps the real Jules Milone drowned in the Goddess's storm with my sisters.'

'No, it is her. I have seen her myself in the visions. One green eye and one blue, with a mountain cat in her shadow. Some have said that, when she ascends the throne, her blue eye will darken to black, but that is just nonsense.'

'It is nonsense that she may be queen at all when she is not a queen. When she will bear no triplets.' Katharine drains her wine and pours more. She herself may bear no triplets, and the thought makes the hen in her mouth taste like wood.

Theodora shrugs. 'The prophecy says, "once a queen and may be a queen again." It's never easy to interpret. But the people believe. She is a naturalist and she is war gifted. And both of her gifts are as strong as a queen's.'

'How?' Katharine asks. 'How is she as strong as a queen when she is legion cursed? Why is she not mad?'

The oracle looks at her seriously. Then she erupts into peals of laughter. It is uneven, this poison. And Katharine has no idea how long it will last.

'But you are a pretty girl,' Theodora says, and cackles. 'And you are sweet and kind and have given me a comfortable room. You speak of the gifts with equal reverence.' Her left eye narrows. 'Did you really buy the High Priestess with a council seat?'

Katharine pushes the custard bowl forward. 'Take some dessert to ease the wine in your stomach. I think you have had too much.'

'Yes, yes.' Theodora swallows a large spoonful. 'Forgive me.'

'Why do the people seek to overthrow me?'

'They fear that you are wrong. That you were never meant to rule.'

'But Juillenne Milone was?'

'Perhaps anyone is better than a poisoner.'

'And if she goes mad? Can you foresee that, whether she will lose her mind?'

Theodora puts her elbow on the table. She is beginning to look tired. Her head hangs. It seems harder for her to swallow even the custard.

'I can't see that. But the low magic will hold. Her mother bound it, you see. In blood. So the curse is held in check and both gifts are allowed to flourish.'

Katharine leans back. She has seen this mother before. In

Wolf Spring during the Midsummer Festival. She stood by the water as they released the garlands into the harbor, before Katharine issued the challenge of the Queens' Hunt. Madrigal Milone, her name was. Very young to be mother to a daughter of sixteen years. Very pretty to be a mother to a girl as plain as Jules.

'If the mother dies, will the curse come to fullness?'

The oracle opens her eyes wide.

'None can say. No one with the legion curse has ever lived so long unharmed by it. Some wish for the binding to be cut. Some say it will make her even stronger.'

'Where is Jules Milone now?' Katharine asks, but Theodora shakes her head. Perhaps she truly does not know. Or perhaps even Natalia's poisons have limits. 'Where is her mother?'

Theodora's eyes lose focus, and her face goes slack, a glimpse of the true sight gift at work. 'If you go now, you will catch her in the mountains, riding south toward Wolf Spring.' The vision ends, and Theodora blinks as though confused.

Katharine calls out over her shoulder, and a servant opens the door. 'Go to the Black Council. Tell them to send our fastest messengers and best hunters toward the mountains with a bounty on Madrigal Milone's head. A nice, fat bounty if she is brought to me alive.'

When the servant is gone, Katharine faces Theodora, whose eyes swim circles. The poison has begun its final, grotesque turn, inducing highs and lows, grins and terror. 'Is there anything else you can tell me? About the mist? Why does it rise? Why has it turned on its own island?'

The oracle looks down and listens. She presses her hands to her temples and leaves behind smears of custard. 'The Blue Queen has come. The Blue Queen! Queen Illiann!'

'Why?' Katharine asks. 'What does she want?' But the oracle can say no more. She only weeps and shrieks. The poison has become a spectacle, and Katharine pours them both more wine. 'Take a sip,' she says gently.

'I do not think I can.'

'You can.' Katharine takes up the cup. She moves to sit beside Theodora and helps her to hold it, pressing her hands over the woman's cold fingers. 'It will make it easier.'

'You did this,' Theodora says. Then she gasps, twisting with laughter that is like the bray of a mule.

Katharine holds her shoulders tightly. 'I did this. So I will stay and talk with you until it is finished.'

THE REBELLION

THE MAINLAND

It takes Arsinoe longer than she would like to gather the money she needs to hire a ship to the island. But finally, the day has come. After squirreling away coins earned by donning a cap and acting as a delivery person and twice being tempted to swipe just one of Mrs. Chatworth's brooches to sell, she stands alone before the harbor and prepares to board a boat. No Mirabella this time and no Billy. They will be safer here.

'And I won't be gone long,' she whispers, and clenches the coin in her fist.

On the docks, she slips through the workers, looking for some idle captain. The day is busy, the port full of too many men, and not a woman to be seen. She keeps her head down and cap low, but at least she is not in Daphne's time and does not have to worry about the superstition of having a girl on board. She stuffs her money deep in her pocket and walks past the slips. It does not need to be a great boat. Or even a large boat. This time, she is not trying to fight her way out of the mist. Any available captain and crew who are willing to sail in whatever direction she chooses will do.

She would even settle for a dinghy and a good pair of rowing arms.

'Excuse me, sir.'

The man in the green wool coat turns around sharply, though he had not been doing anything but stuffing his pipe.

'What is it, lad?' He recoils at her face or perhaps just the scars across it. 'Or miss. What can I do for you, miss?'

'I need to book a passage,' she says. 'For a short sail.'

'A short sail to where?'

Arsinoe hesitates.

'I need to book passage for a short sail with a *discreet* crew.'

He squints. When she does not budge, he chomps the end of his unlit pipe.

'My boys and I will take you, but you'll have to come back tomorrow.'

'Tomorrow?'

'Aye. I've nets to repair this afternoon. If you come back tomorrow, around the same time, we should have unloaded the catch, and I'll keep the crew around.'

Arsinoe searches the docks. So many other boats, but some are far too grand, and others have become deserted in the short time she has been there. She pulls all of her money out of her pockets.

'If I give you everything I have, will you round up a small

crew and take me now? It won't take long to get where I'm going. I promise.'

'I don't know. . . . Just what's your hurry, miss?'

But before she can manage a lie, she hears Billy's familiar whistle.

'If he says no, tell him I'll pay him double.'

Billy and Mirabella walk confidently down the dock. The captain straightens as he shakes Billy's hand and Billy introduces himself.

'Care to tell me what's going on, young Master Chatworth?' The captain looks at Arsinoe suspiciously. 'Is she not supposed to be sailing?'

Arsinoe glares at him and spits into the water.

'Not alone, I'm afraid,' Billy says. 'I am her fiancé, and this is her sister, and we will all be sailing together.' He puts more money into the captain's hand, and the man shrugs his shoulders.

'I'll gather my crew.'

Once they are alone, Arsinoe pushes Billy and Mirabella back up the dock.

'What are you doing?'

'Coming with you,' Mirabella says, and shoves a satchel into her chest. 'And we at least remembered to pack.'

'If I'd have packed, you'd have known what I was doing. And didn't you tell me this was a bad idea?'

'It is a bad idea. Once we get on that island, we will probably never get off again.' Mirabella takes her by the shoulders.

'Please. Do not go. Because you know we cannot let you go alone.'

'That's why I didn't tell you. I'm not going back to stay. I'm sneaking on, making my way to Mount Horn to find out what Daphne and the Blue Queen want, and then I'm coming back here.'

'If you can come back,' says Billy, studying the state of the fishing boat they have booked passage on. 'Last time Mira had to fight a Goddess's storm, remember?'

'It won't be like last time.'

'How do you know?'

'I just do.'

'That is not an answer. Which is why we are going with you.' Mirabella gathers her skirt and jumps down over the rail. 'And to make sure you keep your word. Sneak on, sneak off.'

'Sneak on, sneak off,' Arsinoe mutters, and boards the boat.

The ship sailed in less than an hour. At first, the small crew of fishers was cross, but their mood was soon lifted by the sight of the extra coin and the relative ease of the journey. Also by the presence of Mirabella's pretty face.

Arsinoe peers over the side to watch the waves crash against the hull as she and Mirabella stand on the deck. There is not much to the boat. It is certainly nothing compared to the large vessel they arrived on.

'Is your gift back to fullness yet?' she asks. 'Can you feel it?'

'No. And even if we reach the island, who knows how long that will take to happen. Or if it will happen at all. There are many things we deserter queens do not know.' She pulls Arsinoe back upright. 'But what I do know is we have nothing to fight another storm with. So you had better hope the mist lets us pass right through.'

'It will,' Arsinoe says. Billy has directed the crew to sail southeast out of the bay. It is not the direction that they came from, but it does not matter. The island's magic will find them if it wants them.

'I suppose you're angry with me,' Arsinoe says.

'I suppose I am.' Mirabella's mouth is drawn tight, and the more she speaks, the more her anger leaks out. 'Sneaking off like that. Preparing to leave without a word. Treating this like it is a game when it could get us all killed.'

'I know it's not a game. I didn't tell you because I didn't want you to come. You didn't have to.'

'Yes I did.'

'No you didn't. I survived sixteen years without your mothering. I survived a bolt to the back. A poisoning.'

'You are a poisoner.'

'I didn't know that. I survived being struck by lightning by you!' She pokes her sister in the shoulder with a forefinger. 'I saved your life at the duel. I broke us out of the cells! So if you want to talk about who saves whom—'

Mirabella laughs and shoves her lightly.

'You are a brat. And you would have drowned when the

first of her waves hit.' Her smile fades. 'But . . . I am not only coming along to look after you. Though I am sure I will have to do that.' Arsinoe makes a face. 'I am coming along because if you are right, and there truly is something amiss on the island, it is . . . our responsibility, is it not? To do what we can. We are still of there; we are still its queens.'

'No we're not,' Arsinoe says glumly. 'It's thinking like that that's going to get us killed.'

'Are you still dreaming of Daphne?'

She shakes her head. There have been no dreams since she decided to return to Fennbirn. It is that as much as anything that tells her she is on the right track.

'Have you started to dream?'

'No,' Mirabella replies. 'She is still speaking only to you.' She crosses her arms and nods to Billy as he approaches from the other side of the rail. 'So you know, this is probably a trap. She is probably going to deliver us right into our little sister's clutches.'

'Have a little faith,' Arsinoe says as Mirabella walks away.

'Two queens die. That is just how it is.'

'Don't say that!' Arsinoe calls after her, then turns back to the rail and pounds it with her fist. 'Why does she say that?'

'I think she was joking.' Billy leans against the rail. He shells a nut and holds it out.

'No, thank you. Where did you get those?'

'The captain had them. We paid him so much for an afternoon sail that I think he feels he should provide refreshments.'

'You're in a fine mood. Aren't you going to lecture me, too?'
He shrugs.

'I trust Mirabella to take care of that. She'll make a very fine sister-in-law one day. Keep you in line for me.'

Arsinoe scoffs. Then she slides her fingers into the hair at his temple. It is longer now than when they first met, long enough to blow in the strong sea wind. He called her his fiancée when they arranged for the boat. Only a lie, she knew, but it still gave her a pleasurable burst of excitement in the pit of her stomach.

'I'm sorry for dragging you into this. Dragging you away from your mother and sister.'

'Don't be. I told them I was returning to find my father and bring him home. They couldn't have been more thrilled.' He smiles, perhaps a little bitter. 'But it is dangerous, Arsinoe. And you're a fool for trying to do it alone.'

'Dangerous.' She curls her lip.

'Fennbirn is dangerous. You can't deny that. Not after what we've lost.'

'It's just as safe on the island as it is back there.' She jerks her head toward the mainland.

'You can't be comparing the two. We don't force our girls to compete to the death—'

'Maybe not. But if I stayed there without you looking out for me, I might be killed. Girls like me must be killed there every day.'

'Arsinoe . . .'

'Maybe not executed. But dead anyway. Somewhere right now, a girl like me is being locked away to be forgotten about or thrown onto the streets to starve. Pushed down so far that no one will care what happens to her.' She swallows. 'I'd rather have Katharine's knife in my back.'

Billy blinks and pushes himself up off the railing.

'I don't know how we're supposed to make a future there, with you feeling that way.'

'I don't mean that I can't—' She stops. There is danger in both places. Danger everywhere. But on the sea, sailing for the island, it feels like sailing home. 'Maybe I'm just a part of the island, and you're just a part of the mainland.'

They stand together, shocked. She wishes she could take it back. But even if she did, it would still be true.

He threads his fingers through hers.

'What if we were somewhere else, then?'

'Somewhere else?'

'Somewhere else entirely. If you could pass through the mist and be somewhere new, where would you want to go?'

She has to think only a moment.

'Centra.'

'Centra. Good. I've heard it's lovely, and I've never been there. We could sail there, after this business is finished. After my father returns and we're no longer in danger of losing the estate. We could go to Centra and be entirely new.'

Arsinoe smiles. 'That sounds nice. It reminds me of what Joseph used to say to me and Jules. About our happy ending.'

Even though this is not the same ship, her eyes go to that place on the deck where Joseph lay dead in Jules's arms. She can still almost see him, that pale shape, the blood so washed away by seawater that it made it even harder to believe he was gone. *Jules on my queensguard and him on my council.*

She wraps her arms around Billy and holds him tight. Over his shoulder, the sky is still clear. But it will not be long before they reach the mist.

THE BLACK COTTAGE

Jules, Caragh, and Emilia stand at the front windows of the Black Cottage, watching Mathilde stare into the small fire she has built on the ground. The first snow fell that morning. Clearing out the skies, Mathilde said. Making it a good night for visions. A good night to see their way ahead, now that they are leaving to continue their journey.

'Where's Willa?' Jules asks. 'In with Fenn?'

'Probably,' Caragh replies. 'She does love that baby. More than that, though, she dislikes the sight gift. Having an oracle here makes her uneasy.'

In the yard, the fire melts the young snow in an even circle, and Mathilde crouches on toes and knees and the tips of her fingers. Sometimes it seems that she speaks to the flames. Other times that she sings. They cannot hear her through the glass or see what it is that she sees. To Jules, Caragh, and Emilia, the flames are only flames.

'You are sure you will be all right?' Emilia asks. 'You two

with the little one, until Jules's mother returns?'

'I should think so. We're both Midwives.'

Emilia rolls her shoulder, favoring a bruise that Jules gave her as they practiced sword-craft with thick sticks as the snow fell all around them.

Caragh reaches down and slaps her brown hound on the rump. 'Let's get into the kitchen and start the stew for dinner. And I would speak to my niece a moment.'

Emilia nudges Jules. 'Go. I am going into the woods after grouse. You could send some my way, if your gift reaches that far.' She grins, but it changes quickly to a frown. 'On second thought, don't. I can't shoot them when they come hopping into my lap.'

'Why don't you take Camden? She could use the run.'

Emilia nods. Her dark hair is loose and rumpled; it looks as restless and ready to be off as the rest of her. 'Fine. But make something delicious. It won't be much longer that I will be able to get a meal from you. My queen.'

'Stop calling me that.'

Emilia swats her playfully. 'I think you are starting to like it.'

Out by the fire, Mathilde blows into the smoke and feeds the flames with herbs and blue-burning amber. She shakes her hair back off her shoulders, the braid of white stiff and separate in the cold evening air.

In the kitchen, Caragh tears a large fillet of smoked fish into pieces.

'Dinner tonight, courtesy of Braddock.'

'Oh? He caught it just for us, did he?'

Caragh snorts.

'No. And to be honest it is starting to be harder to get it away from him.' She gestures to the counter, and Jules sets to chopping vegetables.

'How long do you think it will be until Madrigal returns?' Jules asks.

Caragh's only response is a gentle raising of eyebrows. 'Will you go to the larder for butter and cream?'

'You have more faith in her than I do.' Jules sets the butter and cream pitcher on the counter so Caragh can add it to the stockpot. She watches her aunt closely, but all she does is reach up into a cabinet for a sack of flour. Maybe for biscuits. 'You shouldn't have let her go.'

'Jules,' Caragh says, her voice sharp. 'Who am I to tell my sister what she can and cannot do? Where she can and cannot go?' She starts to measure flour and lard. 'Your Emilia is in a hurry. I wonder if that is how all warriors are. So eager to fight.'

'Grandma Cait always said I had the worst temper she had ever seen.'

'So she did.'

They look at each other, remembering broken plates and screaming fits. Wondering what could be attributed to the bound war gift and what was just a child needing to shout.

'So,' Jules says. 'What is this word you need to have with me?' She sweeps the chopped vegetables into her hand and adds them to the stew hanging over the fire along with a measure of fish broth. But when she turns back, her aunt is frozen, staring blankly down at the knife on her cutting board. 'Aunt Caragh?'

'I don't know how to tell you this, Jules, so I am just going to tell you. There was a second prophecy after the oracle saw your legion curse that night.' Caragh straightens and looks into her eyes. 'After the oracle saw your legion curse, she told us to drown you. Or to leave you out in the woods for the animals to find. That is just what is done, when the curse is discovered. But Madrigal refused. She wailed. I wailed. The oracle tried to take you out of your mother's arms. And when she did, she had another vision.'

'Another vision?'

'Different than the one before.' Caragh's brow knits. 'Her discovery of your legion curse was like a healer finding a cracked bone or a rider finding a swollen pastern on a horse. The second time was like a trance.' She looks at Jules gravely. 'She said you would be the fall of the island.'

For a moment, Jules thinks she has misheard.

'The fall of the island? Me?' She laughs. 'That's ridiculous.'

'That's what she said.'

'Well, it must be a joke.'

'It could mean nothing. Prophecies mean a lot of things. Often never the things people think they do.'

Jules reaches for a potato and starts cutting it into chunks. The fall of the island. Her blade slows. 'Or it has already come to pass. I was there when the Ascension Year failed. When the line of queens broke. I was there to help them escape. That must have been what the prophecy meant.'

'It must have been. And now you will lead an army against Katharine, who is despised by even the mist that protects us.'

'Yes,' Jules whispers.

'Unless you are wrong,' says Caragh, 'and the mist truly rises in response to you.'

Jules stops. The prophecy must be wrong. The rebellion must be right. It must be, because despite herself it has won her heart and given her hope.

She peers out the window at Mathilde.

'Mathilde told me something back in Bastian City. She said that the oracle who saw my curse never returned.'

Caragh adds more to the stew. Her mouth tightens.

'Did Cait kill her?' Jules asks. 'Did she kill her to keep her quiet?'

'Yes,' Caragh replies.

'How?'

'The how doesn't matter any more than where we buried her. She will never be found. We offered to pay. Everything we had. But she wouldn't take it.'

Jules holds her knife tightly so it will not begin to shake. So her war gift will not bury it up to the handle in the wall of the Black Cottage. She cannot look at her aunt. She cannot think of Cait. So much darkness around her birth. So much death.

'You always told me how blessed I was.'

'You were. That was our crime, Jules. Not yours. I never wanted to tell you. I didn't want you to bear it.'

'Someone always pays.'

Caragh and Juniper jump away from Mathilde, suddenly in the doorway.

'Mathilde!' Jules exhales. 'I nearly put this knife through your head.'

The seer's eyes are empty. Juniper creeps close and sniffs her. She paws at her knee, then jumps up against the oracle's chest.

'Oh,' Mathilde says, and grasps the dog's shoulders.

'Are you all right?'

'I am fine. Where is Emilia?'

'She's out hunting with Camden.'

'Get her back. Get them both back. I have had a vision. We must call up the rebels now and fall back to Sunpool.' She pushes Juniper gently to the ground and comes to take Jules by the wrists. 'She knows. The queen knows. And she is coming.'

'How? How does she know?'

'She knows because she has your mother.'

AT SEA

'How much farther?' the captain asks.

'Not far,' Billy replies, but he sounds uncertain. They have sailed through the afternoon and into evening, and still there is no sign of the island.

'Have we sailed for too long?' Arsinoe asks. 'Is the mist not coming for us?'

'You would know better than I would,' Mirabella replies. 'You have sailed into it much more than I have.'

And Billy would know best of all, having sailed into it and through many more times than either of them.

'I thought you said this would be a few hours,' the captain says. 'For what you paid, I've let it go on, but now, we have to turn back.'

'A little farther!' Arsinoe walks to the fore, leans out and over. 'I'll know it when I see it!'

'See what? There's nothing out here to see! No land in this direction until you run straight into Valostra.'

Billy joins her and Mirabella by the railing. 'I can't keep them out here much longer. We will have to turn and sail for home. Try again tomorrow.'

Arsinoe grits her teeth. He is trying to sound regretful, but his tone is full of relief.

'Look!' Mirabella lifts her hand and points. Though the horizon had been clear a moment ago, the mist stands up ahead, pale white from sea to sky. Under their feet, the little boat surges, and they hear the captain and his skeleton crew mutter in confusion.

'A squall? We'll have to go around.'

'No.' Arsinoe waves her arm forward. 'Straight through. Straight through!'

They plunge into the mist.

It is so thick that Arsinoe cannot see Mirabella though she is standing right beside her, and she is certain that if she breathes it in, it will stick inside her lungs and make her choke.

'What's happening?' The captain shouts as inside the mist, the wind dies. 'Check the sails!' Mirabella and Billy grasp each of Arsinoe's hands.

'This . . . isn't like what it usually is,' Billy whispers. But nor is it like when they fled. The mist is thick and pure white. No thunder or rain, and the water so still that the boat barely bobs. But it is taking too long.

Something large splashes just off to their port side, and Arsinoe shivers, imagining it is the dark queen taking form within the mist. In her ears, every wave is the slithering of the shadow's mermaid tail, coil after coil of it rolling through the deep, murky water.

'Where do you think it will take us?' Mirabella asks. For the mist can take them anywhere.

'I never thought about it,' Arsinoe admits. 'I guess maybe I thought I'd pass through and be looking at Wolf Spring.'

'And I thought of Rolanth. When the truth is we could emerge and find ourselves staring up at the twin spires of the Volroy.'

'Or we could not emerge at all,' Billy offers.

Arsinoe swallows. Everyone on board has fallen silent. Even the boat has ceased to creak.

Daphne. What have you lured me into?

'There,' Mirabella says, but the mist is too opaque to see where she points or whether she points at all. 'Do you see that?'

Arsinoe turns. She looks up and gasps. The Blue Queen is directly above them. A black shape that cuts through the white.

'Has she always been there?' Billy murmurs as she raises her long sinewy arms. And the mist dissipates.

The three of them exhale and lean against the railing. They laugh with relief.

'What in the world was that?' the captain asks.

'They did not see her.' Mirabella looks up at the now empty sky.

'Good. If they had, they'd have taken her for a witch and

probably thrown us overboard. Look.' Arsinoe gestures ahead. Across the water lies the shores of what can only be Fennbirn Island.

'Where did that come from?' one of the fishers asks.

'Never mind,' says Billy. 'It's what we were looking for.'

Arsinoe claps him on the back as he goes to make arrangements with the captain to get them ashore. Though they just sailed through the mist, they are already too close to identify what part of the island they have come upon. But it does not really matter. Daphne must have brought them there for a reason, and there are no black spires in sight.

After speaking with the captain, Billy returns with a dubious expression.

'Here's a complication. There are no small crafts or rowboats on board and not a dock in sight. Do we pick a direction and sail to the nearest port or—'

'No.' With the island so close, Arsinoe cannot wait any longer. 'Have him take us as far into the shallows as he can. Then we'll swim.'

'Arsinoe, it's freezing! And you have no idea how far we are from the nearest town.'

'So we'll start a fire.'

Billy sputters. 'What about Mira? She can't swim in that corset and all those petticoats. She'll drown!'

'Actually,' Mirabella says, staring over the side, 'I do not think I will drown.'

Arsinoe leans over. Her sister is shifting the current in small swirls that as she watches grow into contrary little waves.

Mirabella turns and shouts to the captain.

'Take us in as far as you can!' She looks at Arsinoe and Billy, her smile broad, the happiest Arsinoe has seen her in months. 'And you two. Prepare for the easiest swim of your lives.'

Though the crew initially objects to Arsinoe and Mirabella swimming, they eventually bring the boat into the shallows. So far, in fact, that Arsinoe has to tell them to stop, for fear they will beach and have to come ashore themselves.

As soon as they drop anchor, Mirabella dives over the side. Her splash brings the crew shouting and leaning over, too late to try and stop her.

'Thank you, captain,' Arsinoe says, and shakes his hand. 'I am truly grateful for your service. But now I had better get after my sister.' She steps up onto the rail and crouches. 'Billy, don't forget the bags!'

She jumps in, never that much of a swimmer, and her jaw instantly locks from the cold. Her arms and legs seize up as well, so she can barely grab for the satchel that Billy throws into the water.

Another splash, and she hears him shout and curse her for such a stupid idea. But then Mirabella's current takes hold and ferries them toward shore.

'Pretend to swim,' she says, teeth chattering. 'Or it'll look strange.'

'I'm too cold to even pretend, you arse,' he says, and a

moment later their toes drag against the sand.

Miserably freezing, they join Mirabella on the beach and wave to the slack-jawed fishers on the boat.

'What must they think of what they found?' Mirabella asks.

'Doesn't matter,' Arsinoe replies. 'They won't be able to find it again if they try. Not unless they're meant to.' She turns and looks past the beach to the dense green moss and flat, gray stone.

'Good Goddess, I've missed this terrible place.'

INDRID DOWN TEMPLE

With tired eyes, Pietyr cracks open yet another book from the many shelves of the temple library. He has been there since before dawn after creeping out of Katharine's bed and onto the back of a cranky, half-awake horse. Riding through the dark streets to slip into the library with a lamp and a sheaf of paper. Hours later, the paper is mostly blank. He has not come across much about the dead queens or even about exorcism, and when he does, he must be careful what he writes in case someone were to find the notes.

He leans back and stretches, and the light of one of the small windows catches him in the eye. He has no idea what time it is. It could be near midday. He bends over the book, scours a few pages, and shuts it again. Part of him wants to quit. It is not as though getting rid of the dead queens is something that Katharine wants. Not when they have convinced her how much she needs them.

But she does not need them. They forced her hand to take

that young boy's life. Their existence is an affront to the Goddess. It is their presence that has caused the mist to rise. It must be.

If he does not find a way to stop them, they will cost Katharine everything.

He takes the book back to its shelf. The library on the lower level of the temple is not large. The entirety of it could be fit into a corner of the one at Greavesdrake. But it is well stocked. The texts here are ancient and preserved nicely, not a speck of dust on the spines and no whiff of mold even near the binding. Some of the pages actually smell rather like fresh parchment simply from being so rarely read. He was sure he would find something here. But every tale of spiritual possession he has come across has been written about shallowly. Treatments simply alluded to and sometimes the outcome not mentioned at all.

Pietyr sighs and gathers up his paper and fading lamp. Perhaps there is no way.

'They said you have been here a long time.'

He turns.

'High Priestess. How do you manage to be so quiet with all those rustling robes?'

'Years of practice. What brings you to our library, Pietyr?'

'I did not know anyone saw me come in. What are you doing here?'

'The temple has been tasked with uncovering the truth of the mist.' She opens her hands and looks around at the shelves. 'I came to learn of the progress.'

Pietyr cocks an eyebrow. If there was progress made, there was none to be told of that morning. He had been the only person in the library since he arrived.

'Are you also here on an errand for the queen?' Luca asks.

'No. I am here on behalf of myself.'

'You know you can confide in me, Pietyr. She is as much my queen now as she is yours.'

'That is not true,' he says, and straightens. 'That will never be true.'

'All of our fates are tied to hers. You cannot keep her all to yourself. Not anymore.' She raises her arm and folds one side of him in soft, white robes; squeezes his shoulder; and guides him back to the table, where they sit.

Perhaps it is because he is in need of sleep or perhaps it is due to simple frustration, but after a moment, he says, 'I am not here on behalf of Katharine. I have been looking into another solution to the mist.' He rubs his throbbing temples. 'Examining any possibility. Sometimes I think I have found something useful, and then it falls apart.'

'It has been a long time since I took a deep dive into these old shelves.' Luca nods. 'But I well remember how it felt: an aching back, dry eyes. So many words turning circles in my head.'

'Have you ever—' he starts, and hesitates. Old Luca is shrewd. If he tells her what he seeks, all of Katharine's secrets about the dead queens may be laid bare. But it is true what she said. Her fate, the fate of the Black Council, the very tradition of the island, and their way of life are all tied to Katharine. So let Luca figure it out. Even if she were to know, she could do nothing.

'In all your years in service to the temple,' he says, 'have you ever come across an instance of spiritual possession?'

'Spiritual possession? What an odd question.'

'Forgive me.' He waves his hand, casually. 'I am exhausted. It was just something I happened upon this morning, and there was so little written about it . . . the entry was so vague. I suppose it piqued my curiosity.'

Luca drums her fingers on the table.

'I have never seen a case of it, only heard reports. None could ever be confirmed, which would explain the incomplete writings. The temple does not generally interfere in such things. The only thing for it is prayer, and usually a merciful execution.'

Pietyr exhales. Merciful execution. That is a dead end, and a bleak one.

'Of course,' the High Priestess goes on, 'knowing that, many sufferers do not seek the aid of the temple. They go elsewhere. To those who practice low magic.'

'Low magic is a desecration of the Goddess's gifts.'

'They are desperate. Who knows? Sometimes it may work. Though the temple could never condone its use.'

Low magic. It is not the answer he hoped for. To practice low magic is a danger even to those who are well versed in it.

He knows nearly nothing of what it entails.

'Blast,' he says, looking at his hand and seeing a smear of ink. 'Is it everywhere?'

'Just a bit on the cheek and the bridge of your nose.' Luca points and helps him to rub it off.

'What time is it?'

'Not yet midday.'

'Is the queen awake?'

'She was not when I left. Up too late celebrating. She is overjoyed to have the mother of Juillenne Milone locked up in the Volroy cells.' She pats him on the knee and stands. 'You had best find someplace to get some sleep. As soon as she rises, she will want to question the prisoner. And then there will be decisions to make.'

THE VOLROY

Katharine sits before her dressing table and rubs soothing oil into her temples and hands. For once, everything is proceeding as she hoped. The visions of the dead oracle Theodora Lermont proved true, and Katharine's soldiers found Jules's mother as she rode south through the mountains. She arrived the night before, arms tied behind her back and a sack over her head. Now she sits cozily in the cells below the castle.

'A lovely morning,' Katharine says to her maid Giselle.

'It is, my queen.'

'Only the dark, blue expanse of the sea. No mist, no screams . . . no one running into the Volroy to tell me that more bodies have washed ashore.' She takes a deep breath as Giselle gently brushes her hair. 'How long has it been since we had any ill news?'

'Since before the oracle was brought.'

'Yes. Since before the oracle was brought.' Since she has

begun to pursue the legion-cursed pretender. The quiet mist must be a sign. She must be doing the right thing.

Katharine reaches for a bottle of perfume and shoves away from the table so quickly that she knocks Giselle down onto the carpet.

'Queen Katharine? What's the matter?'

Katharine stares in horror at her right hand. It is dead. Wrinkled and decaying to the wrist. She makes a fist and watches the skin stretch and crack.

'Mistress?'

'Giselle, my hand!'

The maid takes it and turns it over.

'I see no cut, nothing to cause a sting.' She strokes Katharine's palm and presses her lips to it, those pretty red lips to that wet, rotten skin. 'There. Is that better?'

Katharine tries to smile. The maid sees nothing. And indeed, when Katharine looks again, her hand is just her hand, pale and scarred but alive as usual.

'You still treat me as a child.'

'To me, you will always be a little bit a child.'

'Just the same,' the queen says, 'I think I will finish up by myself. Would you go and see that my council is roused?'

Giselle curtsies deep and leaves her alone. As much as she is ever alone.

'What was that?' she asks the dead queens. 'A warning? A mistake?' But though she can feel them listening, they do not respond. 'Or was it a threat?'

Katharine sits back down before her mirror, and with shaking fingers, lifts the styled black waves from her shoulders to tie with a length of ribbon.

'Pietyr is right. After this battle is won, I will find a way to lay you to rest.' She slides her hands into black gloves. 'Perhaps I truly will.'

Before Katharine goes into the Volroy cells, she calls for Pietyr and Bree and the High Priestess. It takes them time to assemble, having been exhausted by revelry the night before. Pietyr is the last to arrive, and he does so looking wretched.

'Such tired faces,' she says as they lean against the wall. 'Perhaps I should go alone to see the Legion Queen's mother.'

'We are fine.' Luca straightens her shoulders. 'Some of your council should be there for the questioning.'

'Very well. Try not to vomit in the corridor.' She turns and leads the way, relishing the cold rush of stale air closing over her head. She has always liked this part of the Volroy, from the first time that Natalia brought her there to help with the poisoning of prisoners to the last time she descended to show her sisters her crown.

They reach the cell and guards place extra torches to illuminate the straw-covered floor. Madrigal Milone sits with her back pressed to the rear wall. Or at least Katharine assumes it is Madrigal Milone. The guards have not taken the sack off her head. Beside her, another sack lies on the straw, with something inside flapping weakly. The naturalist's familiar, no doubt.

'Go in,' Katharine says. 'Remove the bag. Both of them.'

Jules's mother groans when the guard tears it away.

'Now unbind her hands.'

They do, and the prisoner rubs her wrists. They will need treatment. They have been rubbed raw to the point of bleeding. Finally, the guard dumps the last bag into the straw, and a crow tumbles out. Instead of flying, it hops on wobbly legs into the naturalist's lap.

'You are indeed Madrigal Milone,' says Katharine, leaning forward. 'Even under all that dirt, your pretty face is unmistakable.'

'Where am I?'

'In the cells beneath the Volroy. Where your daughter was, not long ago.' Katharine lets the woman ponder that as she blinks at her new surroundings. At the walls of dark, cool stone that collect dampness in the corners and the wisps of stale straw on the floor. It is not the same cell that held Jules and her cougar. That one was many floors down. But it does not matter. Every cell in the Volroy holds an equal amount of terror and the same dank smell.

'What am I doing here?'

'Asking too many questions,' says Pietyr irritably.

'Forgive him,' Katharine says as Pietyr studies the naturalist warily. 'He has a headache and got little sleep.'

Madrigal does not respond. She continues to rub her wrists, and stretch her fingers.

'Will you not speak?'

She jerks her head toward Pietyr. 'He just said I was talking too much.'

'Why were you in the mountains?' Katharine asks.

'I was on an errand for my mother. Your soldiers jumped me with no explanation.' She looks at Luca. 'I thought I was being robbed. Or killed.'

Katharine and Luca look at each other skeptically, and in the uncertain silence, the crow hops out of Madrigal's lap to pace back and forth before the cell bars.

'I think your bird would like to leave you,' says Bree.

'Of course she would. She's a survivor. And she's never been much of a familiar.' Madrigal's eyes linger on the bars as well, and Katharine frowns. The mother is not like the daughter. Jules Milone is fierce. Too much loyalty and not enough brains. But Madrigal . . . perhaps Madrigal could be used.

'What can you tell me about your daughter, Juillenne?'

'Only what you already know. That she's legion cursed with naturalist and war. That she escaped with Ar—' She stops. 'With the other queens and disappeared.'

'You have not seen her since?' Pietyr asks.

'No.'

'You think her dead, then?'

'Yes.'

'You are lying.'

Katharine puts a hand on Pietyr's arm. 'What do you know about the Legion Queen?'

'I don't know anything about that,' Madrigal says, with the

barest hint of a smile. 'We don't get much news in Wolf Spring. I confess that, the day of the escape, I was the one who freed the bear. After Jules and . . . *the others* sailed away into the storm, I brought him back north and released him into the woods there.'

'Hmm.' Katharine touches her chin with a gloved finger. 'The day of the escape was the last day I saw her, too. Down here in these cells. When I came to poison my sister Arsinoe to death. When I frightened them so badly that they chose to die at sea instead.'

'If you're convinced that my daughter is alive, then what makes you think the other queens aren't also?'

Katharine's eyes glitter, and Madrigal recoils. The dead queens do not like her. They would stomp down hard on her pretty black bird and leave nothing but a red mess and feathers.

'Tell me about the blood binding.'

'How do you know about that?'

'The same way we knew how to find you,' says Katharine. 'We questioned someone. Unfortunately, that someone did not survive the questioning. So speak. If Jules is dead, like you say, then it will not matter.'

'Very well.' Madrigal draws her knees up to her chest. 'We discovered Jules's curse when she was a baby, and I was told to drown her or leave her in the forest. But I couldn't. So I bound the legion curse through low magic. Bound it in my blood. To keep it from harming Jules and keep her from being found out.'

'But she was found out,' says Katharine. 'And she is legion cursed. It seems your low magic is not very strong.'

'Or Jules's gifts are so great that they overcame it.'

'Hmph,' says Pietyr. 'You must truly want to die.'

Katharine wraps her fingers around the bars. 'You know she is alive. You were riding from the north, where her rebel army is. We have spies. We have seen.'

'If that's true, then why haven't you stopped her?'

Katharine's hand slides down her side; she raises her boot and reaches for the small knives she always keeps there.

Madrigal crouches against the back wall. 'Spill my blood and the binding is broken. Whatever remains to hold my Jules in check will disappear. And if you're afraid of her now, wait until you see what she can really do.'

'I am a poisoner,' Katharine snaps, her hand drifting away from the knife. 'I will poison you so your insides boil, but not a drop of blood will be lost. It will not be clean, but it will be contained.'

'That won't work either. Murder by poison counts as blood spilled. That's how it is with low magic.'

'Is that true?' Bree asks. 'Or is she lying?'

Madrigal smiles a pretty, crooked smile.

'Maybe it is, or maybe I am. None of you know for sure. You exalted Arrons have had no cause to use low magic. And you, High Priestess . . . I know you would never touch it.'

'She is only trying to scare us,' says Bree.

'Is it working?' Madrigal asks. 'Are you willing to chance

it? I have been using low magic all my life. I know its ways as well as its ways can be known.'

Katharine grits her teeth. She is not sure yet. For now, let the woman remain locked up in the dark cells. Quietly, she turns on her heel and leads the others back above ground.

'Well,' she says. 'You are my advisers, so what do you advise?'

Bree crosses her arms and speaks hesitantly. 'We should learn what we can about the low magic binding. Send for experts, if any will come forward.'

'None will,' says Katharine. 'And if they do, none will know more than the Milone woman knows herself. High Priestess, what do you think?'

Luca takes a deep breath. 'Rho has been assessing the queensguard. There are near five thousand trained soldiers in and around the capital, and another thousand standing at Prynn. More are waiting to be called up and trained. You have what you need to crush a rebellion, even one supported by a lesser number of war gifted and oracles. But that is not what I think you should do.'

'Am I to wait, then? For spring and the naturalist to march on the capital?'

'You have her mother,' Luca says. 'I think you should arrange a trade. Without Jules Milone, the rebellion will fold.'

Katharine stares at the High Priestess as she considers. She would avoid a battle if she could. Even though the dead queens clamor for it. To stand directly in the midst of it with blood on her arms. In her teeth.

'I could not execute her. That would only entrench the rebels further. I would have to hold Jules Milone here, under charge of treason, and then offer a sentence of mercy.' Her eyes narrow. 'Would she truly trade the rebellion for her mother?'

'It is worth a try. And I know Cait Milone. If you hand down a sentence of mercy, she will accept it, and Wolf Spring will take its cue from her. What does the Goddess say? Do you feel her hand in this?'

Katharine cocks her head. 'Should I not be asking you that?'

'You are the Goddess on earth, Queen Katharine. I am only her voice to the people.'

At her words, the dead queens twist through Katharine's insides, spreading the ash-gray of corpses through her body until she can practically taste it.

'I have never felt the Goddess,' says Katharine. 'She turned her back on me so I have acted in kind. Is that why the mist rises? Because a queen sits the throne who will not kneel?'

'The Goddess does not demand your loyalty. She does not need it any more than she needs our understanding.'

'Curse the Blue Queen,' Katharine mutters under her breath. 'If not for the mist, the people would not be so desperate. What went so right for her that she was able to perform such a feat?'

'It was not what went right,' Luca says, 'but what went wrong. Queen Illiann created the mist to protect the island from an invasion. A spurned suitor who returned to wage a war. Have you never studied the murals of the queens in our temples? A queen can do great things when she must.'

Katharine sighs and turns to Pietyr, who nods. She will ride north, then, and make the trade. If the cursed naturalist will agree to it.

SUNPOOL

Arsinoe, Mirabella, and Billy navigate the sloping, mossy cliffs of the coastline, trying to reach high ground. Arsinoe, in her hurry, slips and knocks her knee against exposed rock. But she is not the one in the lead: Mirabella has nearly crested the hill. She has pulled her hair free of its pins, and Arsinoe suspects that she has called a little of the wind that whips through it. She has never seen anyone look so triumphant, even in a muddy, blue, salt water–stained mainlander dress.

'I thought she said it would take some time for her gift to return,' says Billy breathlessly. 'But she could move the water the moment we arrived.'

'Well, you know Mira. Always the pessimist.'

Mirabella's current made their swim to shore so easy that they each have energy to spare for the walk. And after they reached land, she conjured a blazing fire so they would be warm and dry while they did it.

'Do you know where we are?' Billy asks, and adjusts his pack on his shoulder.

Arsinoe looks inland, upward. The behemoth of Mount Horn sits to the east. Not terribly far.

'We're west of the mountains. Away from Wolf Spring. Away from Rolanth. A whole island between us and our baby sister.' It is probably the best place for Daphne to bring them. Secluded and secret, where they will not likely be seen.

'And we have to climb that?' He nods to the peak. 'Not all the way, I hope.'

'I hope not either.'

She hurries ahead to where Mirabella has stopped at the top of the hill.

'Look,' Mirabella says. 'Is that what I think it is?'

Across the rolling hills lies the white-walled city of Sunpool. The oracles' city.

'Why would the mist bring us here?' Mirabella asks. 'I do not like the idea of being so close to so many seers.'

'Nor do I,' Arsinoe says distractedly. 'But I have always wanted to see Sunpool.' And this is a very fine view of it: the sprawling, white castle and the built-up wall, white buildings nestled so tightly together that the whole of it looks like a cluster of sea-bleached coral. They say when the sunset strikes, the city appears to burn. Though there is no evidence of that on a day as cold and gray as this.

Billy catches up and peers at it.

'What did that used to be?'

'Sunpool. The city of oracles,' Mirabella replies.

'And it used to be grand,' Arsinoe adds. 'Before the gift weakened and the numbers dwindled. Before the people started to fear the sight as near a curse.' In reality, the once proud, white walls are crumbling, chunks of stone rolled away to wear down to roundness and be covered with moss. The central castle, though still sprawling, is covered in vine and the dirt of centuries. But it is still easy to see what it was.

'The seers are weak and few,' says Arsinoe. 'I think we're safe enough, even close as we are. Probably the perfect place to buy supplies and a hot meal. A forgotten city for a secret quest.'

Billy reaches for coin in his pocket. He takes his pack off his shoulder and considers the goods inside.

'Maybe I should go alone and get what we need. You two are still a little too recognizable, even in those colorful clothes.'

'Agreed,' says Arsinoe as Mirabella reluctantly drapes a gray scarf over her hair.

They walk toward the city, stopping at the crest of every hill to make sure to avoid main roads. Arsinoe and Mirabella fall into easy chatter, so that Billy has to tug on their arms when he notices something odd.

'Didn't you say this place was nearly deserted?'

'Not many live here anymore, that's true.'

'Well, that doesn't look deserted to me.' He points to Sunpool, and Arsinoe and Mirabella shield their hands from imagined brightness, as if that were responsible for what they see.

Hundreds of people crowd the streets. Disorganized, harried-looking people, pushing handcarts and carrying packs of supplies.

'Is it a . . . marketplace?' Arsinoe asks.

Mirabella points to the east.

'Look. On the roads. More are coming.' It is not a steady stream, but it seems an uncommon number for a city not known to have a large share of visitors. As they watch, someone releases a messenger bird from one of the castle's uppermost windows.

'That bird is flying awfully fast,' says Arsinoe. 'And awfully straight. What is a naturalist doing in Sunpool?' She tugs Billy around and rummages through his pack for another scarf, this one to wrap around her scarred face and mouth.

He looks at her doubtfully.

'I know there's a chill in the air, but that still looks unseasonable.'

'Maybe I have a cough.' She tugs the scarf up over the tip of her nose. Curiosity has gotten the better of her; she cannot be left outside the city now. 'Let's go in and see what's happening.'

Inside, they find a hive of activity. Mirabella and Arsinoe are careful to keep their hair and faces partially obscured, but there is little need. The constant flow of new arrivals means strangers are aplenty, and everyone is on the way to this place or that. No one looks at each other for very long.

'Should I go try to find out what's happening?' Billy asks.

Mirabella takes him by the arm. 'No. That will only draw

attention to you. Just keep moving. And listening.'

They make their way through the wide main road. Only a few people seem to know Sunpool well enough to provide direction, and many of them are dressed in gray and yellow. Oracle colors. Mirabella carefully maneuvers them away from every gray or yellow cloak they see, until Arsinoe's ears prick at the mention of Wolf Spring:

'They're running grain stores up the coast. Should be here any day.'

'But no fighters?'

'A few have come on their own. Less than I'd expected. Maybe she'll bring them with her when she arrives.'

Fighters. Grain stores. And everyone through the gates seems armed, or armed after a fashion, with clubs and shovels. Mirabella taps her on the shoulder and ducks into a tavern. Arsinoe pulls Billy in after her.

'We have stumbled into an army camp,' Mirabella whispers furiously as she leads them to the rear. 'I am less and less certain of your Daphne bringing you here for a simple solitary quest!'

'It changes nothing. I'm still headed up that mountain as soon as I have the food and clothes to make it.' Thinking of food, her stomach growls. There are bowls of stew on many of the tables and cups of wine and ale. Loaves of golden, soft-looking bread.

'I'll go and get us some,' Billy says, following her eyes. 'We can eat standing up and then go back out and try to barter. Though I don't know how much luck we'll have.' He slides through the tables to the bar. There is nowhere to sit. Hardly anywhere to stand. And without Billy, Arsinoe and Mirabella huddle together, two black-haired girls in mainland clothes and no shadow large enough to hide in.

It seems forever until he returns, carrying bowls of stew and trying not to spill, one fat chunk of bread floating in each. They eat in silence, eyes on their food, Mirabella with her head bowed. Arsinoe sneaks bites in between lowering and raising the scarf that covers her nose.

They are nearly finished when people start to hurry past the tavern windows.

'What's happening?' Arsinoe asks as the door flies open and the inside of the pub begins to rapidly empty.

Billy runs out of patience and grabs a man by the shoulder.

'Oi. What's happening? Where's everyone going?'

'She's here. I think she's here!' The fellow points to the street and runs after the crowd.

'She.' Mirabella and Arsinoe lock eyes. She. The queen? They set their bowls onto the nearest empty table and go to the window. So many have crowded around the tavern that seeing is impossible.

Frustrated, Arsinoe turns to the barkeep.

'Plenty of coin if you'll permit us to your upstairs windows.' She nudges Billy, who gets it out of his pockets.

'As you like,' the barkeep replies. She chuckles a little as she wipes out a cup. 'Though if it really is the Legion Queen, you'll have plenty more chances to get a view.' She jerks her head over her shoulder, through to the kitchen. They hurry, running quickly past the near-empty pot of stew and up the flight of stairs to the woman's private room.

'The Legion Queen,' Arsinoe mutters. 'Who . . .' A thought flashes into her mind, but that is impossible. 'It can't be . . .'

Mirabella reaches the window first. It is not that high, but the view is substantially better than the one from below. The gate of the city is open, and the first riders are coming through.

'Riders only, no carriage. And no black. It cannot be an Arron caravan.'

Arsinoe presses her nose to the cold, dusty glass. There is no black at all. Not even the horses.

Then she sees the mountain cat, curled onto the rump of a large bay workhorse. Her dark tail-tip twitches, and she nervously swats with her good paw at anyone who gets too close.

'Good Goddess,' Arsinoe exclaims. 'It is her. It's Jules.'

'I know you want to see her. But getting to her without being recognized might be just too difficult.' Mirabella keeps a firm hand on Arsinoe's sleeve as they follow Jules's party through the city, alongside the most fervent of the crowd.

'It might be impossible, full stop,' Billy adds. 'Seems she's not just Jules now. She's "the Legion Queen," whatever that is.'

'She's still Jules. She'll see me. She'll know I'm here.'

But when they arrive at the castle, the gate comes down and leaves Arsinoe, and everyone else, outside.

'So I'll wait.' She crosses her arms. 'I'll duck down in the bushes, and she'll have to come out sometime. You two go back toward the shops and try to buy what we need. It won't be long.'

Mirabella and Billy look at her doubtfully. So she shoves them out into the street.

But she was wrong about her wait being short. It seems an age before anyone comes back out of the castle. And when someone finally does, it is not Jules or Camden, like she hopes. Though it is still someone she recognizes: Emilia Vatros, the warrior girl who aided their escape from the capital.

'She was helpful once,' Arsinoe whispers, and takes her chance. She throws a pebble at the girl's back. It hits her in the head. Not a great throw, from cold, aching fingers.

Emilia whirls. It takes her no time at all to discover the source of the pebble.

'Yes!' Arsinoe motions for her to come. 'It's me!' She motions again, and Emilia's eyes slide right over her hidden in the shrubs before she turns around and walks away. So much for that. If only Camden would come out, with her superior hearing and far superior nose. At this rate, it will grow dark before she gets a real chance.

Emilia's hand reaches out from behind her and covers her mouth. She drags Arsinoe back so fast that her feet scarcely touch the ground.

'What are you doing here?' She presses cold metal against Arsinoe's scars. 'I should cut your throat. Carve you up so that no one will recognize you!' For a moment, Arsinoe thinks she really will, but then Emilia shoves her forward onto the grass.

'What's the matter with you?' Arsinoe flips over and scrambles up.

'Why have you returned?'

'None of your business. Right now, I'm here to see Jules.'

'See her?' Emilia spits upon the ground. 'See her and complicate things. Contend for the crown that is meant to be hers.'

'I don't want any crown.' Arsinoe holds up her hands. Angry as she is about Emilia's greeting, she does not have Jules's hot temper. She keeps her head. She knows what the war-gifted girl can do if given the excuse.

'Then why did you come back, poisoner?'

'I think that's something I'll tell her. And I'm not only a poisoner. I'm a naturalist. Like she is.'

The warrior's eyes narrow. The last time they met, things had happened too quickly, and it had been too dark for Arsinoe to notice how severe Emilia is. The deep brown of her hair and eyebrows, the thick eyelashes. The tightness of the twin buns at the nape of her neck. All the weaponry at her belt and tucked into her tall boots. She does remember the fierce red lining of her cape and how it flashed like a new wound when they ran.

'If you interfere, it will not be easy for you.'

'I don't know what's going on here. And as long as Jules is safe, I don't care. I have business of my own, on the mountain.'

Emilia purses her lips. 'On the mountain? What sort of business?'

'The secret sort. The queens' sort.'

'Queens? So the elemental is here as well.' Her eyes flicker to the bushes, the trees, the corners of the castle walls. 'And you just happened to find your way to Sunpool and the Legion Queen.'

'When we got to Sunpool, it was the first I'd heard of the Legion Queen.'

'And what about the mist?'

'The mist?' Arsinoe asks, confused. 'It let us pass. It brought us here.' She shrugs as Emilia studies her.

'Wait.'

The warrior goes back through the shrubs, and a moment later, returns with a burlap sack.

'Put this over your head. Don't ask questions.'

Minutes later, Arsinoe is shoved, stumbling, through the unfamiliar castle. She has no idea where she is after the first three turns, and the sack over her head reeks of mildew. But finally, they stop, and Emilia knocks on a door.

'Jules. Someone to see you.'

'Who?'

Once inside, Emilia can hardly get the burlap off before Camden has her paws on Arsinoe's chest.

'Oof!' Arsinoe groans as the cat rubs her whiskers against her cheeks. 'It's nice to see you, too, you big stinky cat.'

'Arsinoe!'

Jules flies against them both, so excited that for a moment Arsinoe cannot tell whether it is only the cougar who is licking her.

They draw back but hold each other at the elbows. Jules peers around her, at Emilia, who is positively scowling.

'Emilia, look! Where did you find her?' She beams into Arsinoe's face. 'Where did you come from?'

'The same place you left me.'

They smile, and the silence stretches out. There is too much to say. Finally, Jules looks past her, searching for someone.

'Emilia, is Mathilde still with the Lermonts?'

'Yes.'

'Who are the Lermonts?' Arsinoe asks.

'The Lermont family of oracles,' says Jules. 'They're really all who remain, as far as old oracle families go. Our friend Mathilde is a relation of theirs.' Her face falls. 'She's with them now, in mourning. We learned when we arrived—Katharine has poisoned their matriarch.'

'Why would she do that?' Arsinoe asks, and Jules swallows.

Emilia steps between them and takes Arsinoe's arm. 'There is much to explain. On both sides. Where is the elemental?'

'Mirabella and Billy are in the marketplace.'

'I will go and have them brought up.' Emilia leaves, only turning to glare once more at Arsinoe before she closes the door behind her.

'I can't believe you're here,' Jules says.

'I can't believe it either.' Arsinoe touches the ends of Jules's hair, just below her chin. Shorter even than Arsinoe's own now. 'You cut your hair.' Her brow knits. 'Jules, what are you doing here? Why are they calling you the Legion Queen?'

Jules goes to the window. The room they are in is sparsely furnished. Only a rug and a trunk and a table and chairs. A makeshift bed.

'Have you been through Sunpool? Seen what's happening?'

'Yes.' Arsinoe goes to stand beside her. 'Looks like someone's raising an army. I guess that's you?'

Jules raises her eyebrows. 'Seems to be.'

Arsinoe exhales. 'This has to be a long story.'

'Full of bards and prophecy and even a birth.'

'I suppose you'd better tell me all of it.'

They sit down together, and Arsinoe listens as Jules recounts what her life has been since she left them that day. The mourning and hiding and longing for home. The prophecy and her war gift. The rebellion.

'I knew you would get into trouble without me,' she says when Jules is finished, and Jules snorts. Outside the window, the sounds of the army assembling in the city are plain. 'And now you're going to war.'

'There's no choice anymore now that she has Madrigal.'

'But are you ready? Madrigal wouldn't want you to sacrifice yourself.' Arsinoe sighs. 'What am I saying? Of course she would.'

'Whether she would or not, there's Fenn to think about. He's going to need his mother.'

'And you would fight a war for this?' Arsinoe asks.

'That's not the only reason.' Jules stands and her bad leg drags just enough for Arsinoe to notice. The mark of the poison. 'We went from town to town. Village to village. You should have seen their faces, Arsinoe. The hope. The belief, in me. They want Katharine gone and the poisoners out of power. After what she's done and the fear of the mist, I want that, too.'

Camden rests her head on Arsinoe's knee to be pet.

'Am I wrong?' Jules asks. 'You're a queen, as much as you'd like to deny it. Is it wrong, what we're doing? To overthrow her?'

Arsinoe looks down at the cougar. She has always been a familiar fit for a queen. Jules has always been strong enough. An image flashes in her mind of the nightmare Daphne imparted: Jules on a battlefield and Camden's fur red with blood. She clenches her teeth and swallows hard.

Is that why I'm here? To stop this? To help her?

'All these people are coming together because of you, Jules. So I don't think I can tell you what to do anymore. No matter how much I would like to.' She scratches Camden between the ears. 'And you're going to rule after it's over?'

'No. I mean, not really. They're calling me the Legion Queen, but that's just the start of something new. Something better, for all of us that we can decide together.' She looks at Arsinoe hopefully. 'Unless . . . ?'

'No,' Arsinoe says simply. 'Not me. Not Mira.'

Jules nods. 'And . . . you don't believe the prophecy?'

'The one that says you'll be the island's queen or the island's doom? I don't know, Jules. But between the two, I know which one we should try for.'

Emilia locates Mirabella and Billy and brings them to the castle, so quickly and with so much ducking into bushes that Mirabella feels like some kind of a spy.

'We would not have needed to hide in the shrubs if you had allowed me to put a sack over your head,' says Emilia, watching Mirabella pluck thorns from her sleeve.

'No one is putting sacks over our heads,' Mirabella hisses.

'Whatever you say, *Queen* Mirabella.'

'Where is Arsinoe? You haven't done anything to her?' Billy asks.

'Of course not. My own queen wouldn't allow it.'

When they return to the castle gate, Mirabella tries to look up at the tall, white tower overgrown with half-dead vines. But Emilia pushes her head down and shoves her inside the moment the gate is open.

'Where are you taking us?'

'To your sister.' The warrior prods them through the keep and to a small set of winding stairs. They go up and up and around and around until Mirabella thinks she will be sick. Finally, they reach an open door and find Arsinoe inside.

'There you are!' Arsinoe grasps Mirabella's shoulder and then slips her fingers into Billy's hair. 'Did you find supplies?'

'Some decent clothes for mountaineering,' says Billy. 'But that's about it.'

'Good. You are reunited.' Emilia salutes them from the door. 'Rest well. We will decide what to do with you later.'

'Are we prisoners here?' Mirabella asks as the key turns in the lock.

'Not really,' says Arsinoe. 'Don't worry. I've seen Jules, and she's still Jules. Warriors are probably always like this.'

'What's happening?' Billy asks. 'All through the market-places people were talking about Jules Milone, the Legion Queen, and her rebellion.'

'And about Katharine,' Mirabella says.

'And about the mist,' says Arsinoe. 'No doubt you heard that in the marketplaces, too. The mist, rising and swallowing people whole. Spitting them back out in the sea to wash up later on.'

Mirabella and Billy trade a glance. They had heard that. Mirabella had hoped it was not true.

'It's all starting to make sense now, isn't it?' Arsinoe says, pacing slowly across the small space.

'It is?' Billy asks.

'The mist rises, and we see the shadow of the queen who created it,' Mirabella whispers. 'But why is it rising? It is our guardian. Our shield.'

'Maybe it's failing,' says Arsinoe. 'Maybe that's why I've been dreaming in her time. Daphne's time and the Blue Queen's.'

'To find out how it was made,' Mirabella says.

'Or how it could be unmade.' Arsinoe turns to them. 'I knew we weren't coming home to rule. Though if I'm being honest, I wasn't *certain*. But now I know.'

'Know what?' Billy asks.

'I think I'm here to stop the mist.'

THE VOLROY

High in her rooms in the West Tower, Katharine locks herself away with a glass of wine full of floating poison berries. It has been days since she dispatched a messenger to seek out the rebels and convey her message, and that morning, the mist rose again. The infernal mist, bobbing on the water just past the northern outcropping of rocks of Bardon Harbor. She takes a large swallow of wine and curls her lip. She can go only so fast. The mist must be patient, and neither she nor the dead sisters appreciate having it loom over her shoulder. Since it appeared again, she has not looked outside nor taken any visitors. Her mood has turned from gray to black, and the change is not caused only by the mist.

The idea of sparing Jules Milone—of granting her mercy or even making peace—sticks inside Katharine's throat. To rise against the line of queens should not be tolerated.

The leaders of the rebellion should be flayed in the square. We should take their skin in slow strips.

Katharine puts down the poisoned wine. Flaying is not the work of a poisoner. Flaying is the work of a war queen. Or queens who have been dead too long to know better.

Her door opens, and her maid announces Pietyr and the priestess of the council, Rho Murtra.

'Rho.' Katharine nods a greeting as the taller woman bows. 'How strange to see you here.'

'When you did not come to the council chamber, I tired of waiting.'

Ignoring her, she holds her hand out to Pietyr, who comes and kisses her on the mouth.

'Pietyr. Have you found me a low magic practitioner to unravel the Milone woman's blood-binding?'

'Not yet, Kat. None will come forward.'

She knew that none would. She knew that, as usual, none would volunteer to help her.

'Queen Katharine,' says Rho. 'I have a report on the naturalist's rebellion, if that interests you.'

'Of course.'

'They are falling back through the mountains.'

'How many?'

'Impossible to get an accurate count. They are coming from everywhere: ten from one village, a dozen from another. Streaming across the north country like ants. Unfortunately, none seems to have a direct line to Jules Milone.'

Katharine folds her arms.

'I would settle this uprising as quickly as possible. How

long before she receives my message? How long before I can expect a response?'

'Any messenger she sends back will have to go through mountainous country, in winter weather.' Rho sucks her cheek. 'A response rider will take more than a week, even if she changes horses.'

'How then is she able to communicate so well to so many small bands of rebels?' Pietyr asks as his hand slips around Katharine's waist.

'We think they have naturalists in their ranks,' Rho replies, eyeing his arm about the queen. 'They send birds and all manner of beasts with their orders. And with the naturalist gift, birds fly swift and direct.'

'If only we had one who could be relied upon,' Pietyr whispers, his lips brushing against the queen's ear.

'Stop trying to irritate my war adviser.' Katharine turns and bites him, and he chuckles and moves away.

'My queen, perhaps we do have a naturalist who could be relied upon.' Rho calls to the maid. 'Send for Bree Westwood.'

It does not take long for Bree to arrive, and when she does, her eyes dart between Rho and the queen.

'What is going on?'

'The queen requires a naturalist to ferry messages between her and the rebel uprising. Can you think of anyone?'

'A naturalist?'

'Someone who can use a bird. And be discreet.'

'Would she do it?' Katharine asks, realizing who they mean.

Bree presses her lips together.

'If it is not dangerous for the bird, then I am sure Elizabeth would gladly be of service to the crown.'

'It should not be dangerous at all!' says Katharine. 'Only a summons to a meeting, on neutral ground, for a prisoner exchange. We are trying to avoid a war, not start one.'

'Very well. I will speak with her immediately.'

Bree finds Elizabeth in the kitchens, helping a few of the servants to prepare the evening's meal, using a clever attachment on her left-side stump to chop vegetables. As soon as she sees Bree, her ruddy face lights up. She quickly excuses herself, detaching the blade and wiping her hand on a cloth.

'I didn't expect to see you so soon. Did the Black Council disband early?'

'Come with me.' Bree leads Elizabeth down the corridor until they step outside, skirting the side of the castle and the drains for kitchen and rain runoff. 'The queen did not feel like attending the council today. Her mind is on the rebellion in the north. Where is Pepper?'

Elizabeth stills and they listen. Soon, they hear him loudly drilling into some unlucky nearby tree.

'I love that sound.'

'Really?'

'It soothes me. You've no idea how often I would like to drill my nose into a tree in winter, especially here in the bleak, closed-off capital.'

'Elizabeth,' Bree begins, and looks up into the branches. 'Can you use Pepper to send letters?'

'I suppose so. I've never tried. I send him to fetch things for me sometimes: tools or even wild ingredients for one recipe or another.'

'How far can he go?'

'He's a very good flier.'

'I mean, how far can he go and still . . . hear you?'

'Far, I would imagine.' Elizabeth's brow knits, finally realizing this is not an idle line of questioning. 'If our bond was breakable, I think it would've broken when I sent him away to take the bracelets. It must've been stretched taut. But he came back when I called.'

'The queen wants him to find the rebel camp. She wants him to find Jules Milone and deliver a message to her. Can he do that?'

'He doesn't know Jules Milone.'

'But could he find the camp?'

'It would . . .' Elizabeth pauses, her eyes on the trees. Perhaps sensing that he is being discussed, Pepper has come closer and clings to the trunk directly in front of them, his tufted head cocked.

'Would it be dangerous?' Bree asks. 'Would the rebels be likely to hurt him?'

'You know as well as I do that it would depend on who he found.'

'Could you send another bird, then?'

Elizabeth shakes her head. 'My gift is not that strong. I have only used it with Pepper. I am out of practice.' She looks so sad and frightened that Bree takes her by the shoulders.

'You do not have to do this. I can simply tell the queen that it is impossible.'

'Do you want me to do it?'

'I do not want a war.' Bree exhales. 'And I think . . . I *think* that Katharine is sincere in her offer to trade Jules Milone for her mother. Whether or not she will really spare her life afterward is anyone's guess.'

Elizabeth holds out her arms and the woodpecker hops off his tree and swoops into them. He is a watchful, silent bird, very good at hiding. Perhaps he will be all right.

'Tell the queen to write her message. I'll tie it close against his leg.' She strokes his back, and he pecks her robes affectionately. 'Then I'll feed him a good meal and send him off.'

When Pietyr descends into the cells beneath the Volroy, the guards there barely acknowledge him. They are not the best of the queen's army, but they do not need to be. So few prisoners rank high enough to warrant being tossed down below. Only murderers. Traitorous queens. Rebels. Or a rebel's mother.

Pietyr stops outside the bars of Madrigal Milone's cell. She is unbound and seated on the bench beside the wall. Her crow perches on her knee, eating from the palm of her hand what he assumes is the last of Madrigal's meager breakfast.

'Hello, Mistress Milone.'

'Hello, Master Arron. You ought to do something about the food here. It's upsetting the stomach of my bird, and she's quite hardy.'

Pietyr smiles. 'I will see what I can do.'

'And what can I do for you? You can't be here on account of my pretty face, dragged here like I was with a sack over my head.' She touches the ends of her hair hanging limply down her arms in strings.

Pietyr steps as close to the bars as he dares. He listens for any passing guards and hears none.

'I came to ask you about low magic.'

Madrigal rolls her eyes.

'I told you, there's no way to kill me without unbinding the legion curse.'

'I think you are lying. I do not think you are the kind of person who would weave the kind of spell where the only way out is through your death.'

'I didn't say it was the only way,' she says, and laughs. A pretty sound in the dark space. 'I could work my own unbinding whenever I like. Perhaps I will when you let me out of here, just so your Katharine can really see what she's up against!'

Pietyr crosses his arms. Something about Madrigal Milone is immediately unlikable. Perhaps it is the recklessness in her lovely eyes. Or perhaps it is the fear in them. He wants to turn around and leave her to rot, and he would, if he had any other choice.

'I need something from you, Madrigal Milone. And if you are wise enough to give it to me, I will give you something in return.'

'What could you possibly have that I would want?'

'How about a fighting chance? Katharine intends to march you out before your daughter's rebel army. She intends to trade you for her. And I can tell by the look in your eyes that you know it is a trade your daughter will accept.

'If you can tell me what I need to know, I will give you a chance to avoid the trade. To flee.'

'How?'

'I will be the one to deliver you. I can cut your bindings when Juillenne is close enough to see. And you can run.'

'That's not much of a chance.'

'It is the best I can give.'

Madrigal gets up and walks to him. She wraps her hands around the bars and considers, staring at her feet. Her crow flies onto her shoulder and starts to peck and worry at her hair, but she does not move. So strange, the naturalists are, to have a bird beak clicking and twisting like that and not even seem to notice.

'If Jules does trade for me, what will Katharine do with her?'

'She will be merciful. She will spend the rest of her days down here. And if she outlives the reign, perhaps one day she will be released.'

'Do you believe that?' Madrigal asks. 'Do you trust her?'

'What matters is that you trust me. Tell me what you know about spiritual possession.'

'Spiritual possession?'

'Yes,' Pietyr snaps. 'How would you use low magic to separate a dead spirit from a living body?'

Her eyes flash, piqued by sudden curiosity. 'You'll have to tell me exactly what's happened. Or I'll be of no help.'

Pietyr grinds his teeth. Hinting at Katharine's secret to another member of the Black Council is one thing. But to confide in a naturalist traitor?

'Never,' he mutters, and walks away. Madrigal follows him along the bars.

'It's the queen, isn't it? That's why she's so strong. Why her gift seems so varied. She's borrowing it from the dead.'

He stops and turns. He knows the look in his eyes must tell her she is right. But instead of laughing or shouting it to the rooftop, Madrigal's mouth drops open in awe.

'Whose idea was that? Natalia Arron's? That woman was clever indeed—'

'It was no one's idea. It was an accident!' His hands shoot through the bars to hold her fast. 'The night of the Quickening Ceremony, Katharine fell down into the Breccia Domain. We all thought her dead. But she came back. Only she did not come back alone.'

Madrigal's eyes cloud a moment. Then she gasps.

'The Breccia! You mean—'

'That is precisely what I mean.'

'How many?'

Pietyr hangs his head, remembering Katharine falling. Remembering pushing her.

'As many as could get their dead hooks in, I suppose.'

'Two legion queens,' Madrigal says thoughtfully. 'Maybe the oracle was wrong. Maybe my Jules is not the island's ruin after all.'

Pietyr glares at her. 'Tell me: can they be gotten out?'

'I'm not sure.' Madrigal turns around to pace slowly. 'This is queensblood we are talking about. Queens and queensblood. Does she know you're planning this?'

'Yes. She knows. She wants them out, too.'

'Hmph,' she snorts, unconvinced even though he looked her straight in the eye. 'If you say so.'

She walks to the wall and crouches, pressing her hands against the cold, damp stone of the floor. 'The queens were down there, trapped, all this time.' She chuckles. 'No wonder they put forth such a charge to get her on the throne.'

'Do you know how to do it or not?'

Madrigal swivels to face him. 'You'll have to put them back where you found them.'

'Back into the Breccia Domain?'

'Yes.'

'And how am I supposed to do that? Katharine will never go back there.'

'I thought you said she wanted this?'

'She does,' he says. 'But she does not always know it.'

Madrigal crosses her arms. She mutters something about sacred spaces, a bent tree, how her spellcraft would be more focused were she not beneath the accursed Volroy.

'You'll have to *make* a Breccia Domain, then. A circle of stones from there should work. Put the dead ones back into the stones and then dump the stones back into the crevasse. The stones must touch, from end to end. And do not leave that circle until you are sure they have all been gotten out.'

'Is that it? Is that all?'

'No.' Madrigal smiles. 'But I will tell you the rest when we are set to make the trade and you have cut me free.'

The poisoner in him would like to get it out of her now, lash her to a rack, and administer scorpion venom until she could barely speak for all her screaming. But that would eventually attract attention.

'You know there is a chance that Katharine will not survive this.'

'What?'

Madrigal raises her eyebrows. 'Surely you must've considered that she may not be alive at all, except for them. She may truly be undead, and the moment she is emptied of the last of the queens, her body will break and shrivel up. Just like it would had they not intervened in the first place.'

Pietyr freezes. For a moment, the Volroy cells are gone, and they are deep down in the heart of the island. There is no light. Only the smell of cold rot. And the feel of bony fingers wrapped around his ankle.

'You poor thing,' Madrigal says. 'You truly love her. Hasn't anyone ever told you?'

'Yes, yes,' he says as he stalks away. 'Only a fool would love a queen.'

Once upstairs, he intends to saddle a horse for Greavesdrake, to go there for a night and think. Instead, he wanders into the throne room, where he hears Katharine along with Bree Westwood and the one-handed priestess.

'Pietyr,' says Katharine when she sees him enter, 'you are just in time. Our good Elizabeth has consented to send her familiar, Pepper, to the naturalist rebel with a message. I was just considering calling Rho to determine the best place for the prisoner exchange.'

'Why can you not summon the rebel here?' he asks, still dazed from his conversation below.

'I do not think she would come. Or if she did, she may bring her entire upstart army, and I would spare the capital that. Besides, I want to march with some of my new soldiers.' She has the parchment out and has written a few lines. There is room for only a few more. It is a small roll, cut for the leg of a small bird.

Pietyr looks at the woodpecker clinging docilely to the priestess's shoulder. Can he really be so fast? Can such a tiny thing truly make it into the north country in winter to find a rebel camp?

'Innisfuil Valley,' he hears himself say. 'It is a neutral location, far enough from the capital and from any Bastian

City reinforcements. And those devoted to the temple will look upon it as a good sign when a successful trade is held there.'

Katharine considers, then bends to scribble on the parchment. She rolls it up and hands it to Elizabeth, and they watch with quiet wonder as the little bird sticks his leg out to receive it.

'I never imagined you would send your own familiar, Elizabeth,' Katharine says. 'I thought you would send a hawk or some other strange bird. I am truly grateful.'

'We are happy to be of service,' the priestess replies. 'Happy to help avoid a war.'

Katharine smiles at Pietyr. He feels himself smiling back. It will not be long before they depart to march on Innisfuil Valley. Innisfuil Valley—and the Breccia Domain.

SUNPOOL

In the small courtyard at the rear of the castle, Mirabella watches the warrior Emilia Vatros and naturalist Jules Milone train together on the war gift. It does not look much like training: Emilia has brought a cord of wood, and the two are chopping it together. But as they work, the swing of their axes changes perceptibly; they swing straighter and faster, until the logs seem to split themselves.

The Legion Queen. That is what they call Jules now, this rebellion that Mirabella and Arsinoe have so conveniently stumbled into. The people bestowed the title of queen so quickly. So lightly. As if it never carried any weight at all.

'Take care!' Emilia shouts when Jules's blade misses. She wrenches it out by the handle and swats her. 'Just because it feels like nothing to move, does not mean it isn't dangerous. It's still an ax. Mind it!'

Jules nods and begins again. She takes direction well.

She does not seem like the same girl Mirabella met those few times before. The simmering anger is gone, and her stance is such that she seems much taller than she really is. Even the cat seems larger and more confident, lying draped across the waiting wood with her tail flicking lazily back and forth.

Jules looks different. She is different. But she is still not a queen.

'A break,' Jules says, and Mirabella steps out and claps softly. She joins Jules beside the cougar as she drinks a cup of water.

'You are doing very well.'

Jules crooks her lip.

'Thanks. I feel as wobbly as a young colt.'

'Your war-gifted friend is clever, to combine training with a necessary chore.'

'Always work to be done when you're raising a rebellion,' says Jules. She holds out the cup. 'Water?'

'No thank you.'

'Arsinoe won't tell me much about why you all are back here. Only that you're headed up the slope of Mount Horn.'

Mirabella nods.

'I am sure she would tell you if she knew more herself.'

Jules looks down at her hands. 'She says you're going back as soon as your business is finished.'

'I am relieved that she would say so,' Mirabella says, and exhales. 'Part of me feared that the moment she saw you, she would vow to stay forever, no matter the danger.'

'You shouldn't have let her come, you know. You should've made her stay away.'

'I do know. Just as you know how impossible that would have been, without the use of ropes and chains.'

Jules smiles grudgingly, and Mirabella feels a surge of fondness. For ten years, all the years between the Black Cottage and the Ascension, Jules was the one who looked after Arsinoe. She saved her life on the day of the Queens' Hunt. Saved them all on the day of the duel. But she still does not like to meet Mirabella's eye.

'Arsinoe says you buried him instead of burning.'

'Yes,' Mirabella replies. 'That is how they do it there. He rests atop a green hill, looking out at the sea.'

Tears gather at the corners of Jules's eyes, and the cougar comes to lean against her legs.

'I wish I could see it.'

'Maybe you can, someday.'

'Well.' Jules blinks. 'Someday seems like a far-off thing. Anyway, I'm glad Arsinoe and Billy were there. And you. I'm glad someone was there who loved him.'

'You loved him more. I always knew that. And he loved you.' Mirabella shakes her head. 'He never really loved me.'

For a moment, Jules is silent. Then she turns and looks at her, dead-on.

'You must think I'm really small, to think that would make me glad.'

'I only meant—'

'You should get back inside, Mirabella. Even with that cloak and those clothes, it won't take anyone long to figure out who you are if they get a good look at you.'

Jules picks up her ax and resumes chopping wood, even though Emilia has disappeared. Mirabella lingers, but Jules never again glances her way. Finally, she throws up her hands and leaves, not back into the castle as ordered but farther into the courtyard, where it wraps around to the rear.

She walks across the grass and climbs over stones that have fallen from the wall, intrepidly making her way to the top.

When she reaches it, the wind catches her cloak and presses it tight about her, like an embrace. How she longs to throw her hood back so the breeze can rake cold fingers through her hair. But she knows what Jules and Emilia would think of that. Besides, they are right. It is better for everyone if their presence remains a secret.

Still, she cannot resist calling a little more wind to swirl around her body. A few more clouds to darken the sky. The nearness of her gift, the ease and strength of it, is the only joy returning to the island has brought. Everything else—the rebellion, the Legion Queen—has only shown how unneeded she was. How easily replaced.

She is not even part of Arsinoe's quest to stop the mist.

I am my sister's keeper. Her protector.

But is that enough? For a girl who would have been queen? The people speak of Jules already as if a legend: a naturalist with a gift as strong as a queen's.

No elemental queen in history has mastered all the elements so fully as I. Yet there will be no mural to remember me. Not even my name will endure.

She lets the wind die and thinks of Bree and Elizabeth. Her friends and her home, that she may never see again.

And then, as if it were a wish or a prayer, a black-and-white tufted woodpecker flies into her stomach, so hard she feels the slight puncture of his beak.

'Pepper!' She gathers the little bird in the crook of her arm and looks into his bright black eyes. He is panting and afraid. 'Pepper? Is that really you?' But of course it is. She has no relationship with any other bird. She strokes his chest and looks around, hoping to catch a glimpse of Elizabeth ducked down behind a rock. But he is alone. Elizabeth sent him away the day she took her priestess vows, to keep him from being crushed by horrible, brutal Rho.

'Have you been alone in the north country all this time?' she asks, and holds him up to her face. 'Poor Pepper. What luck to find me here. What luck that you saw me.'

In response, the woodpecker lifts his wing and thrusts out one tiny leg. A tiny leg with a roll of parchment tied to it.

Bartering for supplies in the midst of a rebellion is not the easiest thing on the island, but Billy manages to do it. Somehow, despite limited funds and the fact that everyone in the marketplace is hoarding goods for the cause, he secures them warm clothing, climbing tools, and what is hopefully plenty of dried meat for the leg of the journey above the snow line.

'There now,' he says to Arsinoe happily. 'Ready to depart. Now aren't you glad you brought me?'

'I suppose I am.'

He shrugs.

'Negotiation. Buying things. They're the only skills of value my father ever taught me. Though you could say that my success is mostly due to charisma, and you can't really teach that.'

'How long do you think it'll take you to find him?'

'I don't know. After we've finished on the mountain, I thought I'd sail around to the capital. I won't go in,' he adds, seeing her expression. 'I'll send a letter or a messenger.' He sighs. 'I'll wager that he isn't even here.'

'Where, then?'

'Sailing around the world. Having a grand holiday in Salkades, maybe. Drinking wine and teaching me a lesson about life without him and the price of disobedience.'

'He would put that hardship on your mother and Jane?'

Billy shrugs again, and Arsinoe spots Emilia passing in the street.

'There goes Emilia.'

'She doesn't seem to have seen us.'

'Oh, she saw us,' Arsinoe says. And sure enough, the warrior drops down into the alley behind them only a minute later.

'You both should return to the castle.'

'We are. We're done here.'

Emilia smiles a smile that never reaches her eyes. 'Then allow me to escort you.'

She circles around and leads them through the side streets, taking shortcuts through rear alleys and jumping stacks of old crates. It is so quiet a route that Billy has to dodge a bucket of waste that someone empties out of an upstairs window.

'That was close,' he says, and brushes off his shoulder. 'This poor old city seems overrun. Strangers taking up residence in abandoned homes and buildings. How must the oracles and the local residents feel about your army's sudden presence?'

'Many of them are oracles, as you said,' Emilia replies. 'They knew we were coming. And they would have vengeance, too, for the murder of Theodora Lermont. They are with us, or we wouldn't have come.'

'Have you come here before?' asks Arsinoe. 'You seem to know your way around.'

'I have been here with Mathilde, when we were younger. Though I would know it just as well had I only scouted it the first night. It is an aspect of the gift. We find our feet quickly in new places.'

Arsinoe thinks back to their journey to Indrid Down, the way Jules was able to memorize the map with such ease.

'A warrior and a poisoner in naturalist's skins,' she murmurs. 'None of us are ever who we think we are.'

'Hurry along.' Emilia prods her in the side. 'Stop muttering.'

'Why don't you like me?' Arsinoe asks, annoyed and rubbing her ribs from the poke.

'Not like you?' Emilia laughs. 'Why would I not like you? You inspire such loyalty. Someone or another is always looking out for you. Protecting you. Giving their lives for you.'

'You think I'm going to get Jules hurt.'

They stop and face each other.

'I think your being here will ruin her chances,' says Emilia. 'I think you would restore the line of queens. I think you would put her back down, in Wolf Spring or in hiding forever. Perhaps on the mainland, like you.

'But I will tell you one thing *Queen* Arsinoe: Juillenne Milone is not your servant. She is not your helpmeet nor only your friend. She is our queen, the queen that the island needs, and I will be there beside her when she fulfills that promise.'

'That's more than one thing,' Arsinoe says, and pokes her in the chest. 'And who promised? Did she promise? Or are you and your blond friend Mathilde pushing her into something she's not ready for? It's not up to me to speak for Jules, and I have no right to decide her path.'

'Indeed, you do not.'

'But neither do you. And if your cause ends up getting Jules hurt or worse . . .'

'What?' Emilia draws a short blade, and Arsinoe feels the chill of the metal against her neck. 'What will you do?'

'I guess I'll poison you.'

Emilia's eyes narrow, and Billy steps quickly between them.

'Now, now, ladies, let's not dally in such idle conversation. We should get back to the castle, like you said.'

They separate, pushing off each other. The rest of the walk to the castle is silent.

When they reach the gate, the oracle Mathilde is there waiting.

'Thank the Goddess, where have you been? We have had a message.'

'What kind of message?' Emilia asks, and pushes ahead, hurrying inside and bounding up the stairs to Jules's rooms. Arsinoe follows and finds Jules inside pacing, with Mirabella seated at a table behind her feeding what looks to be a woodpecker.

'What's happening?' Arsinoe asks. 'Whose woodpecker is that?'

'The bird arrived with a message,' Mathilde explains. 'Queen Katharine is taking Jules's mother and marching to Innisfuil with a force of soldiers.'

Arsinoe looks to Jules, who looks back with large eyes.

'She wants to trade her for me.'

The room falls silent as they stare at each other, until Emilia stomps her foot.

'You cannot!' she exclaims.

'I have to,' Jules says softly.

'You can't! You are the Legion Queen. You are more important than one life.'

'Not my mother's life!' Jules growls. 'Not anyone's.'

'Wait, Jules.' Arsinoe holds her hands up before Emilia can say anything more. 'Even if you would trade, do you really think Katharine would honor it? She could take you both. Or take you and kill Madrigal anyway.'

'Then what do we do?' Jules asks.

'We came to fight,' says Emilia. 'We will march out and meet her.'

'We do not have the numbers,' Mathilde says quietly. 'If we march now, they will have an advantage of four to one. Perhaps more.'

'Then what are you going to do if Katharine decides to advance on Sunpool?' Billy asks curiously.

'If they advance now, we must winter in the mountains. Hide. Let them hunt for us through the snow if they will. Let the island grow even more restless as the mist rises and the Undead Queen fails to protect them from it.'

'Why would we leave the stronghold of Sunpool for the mountains?' Emilia asks furiously.

'Because the walls have yet to be repaired. The city yet to be fortified. Because we are not ready.'

'We have to do something now!' Jules shouts, and Camden hisses. 'She has my mother!'

'Katharine will not kill her. It is only a tactic,' Emilia says, her tone steady.

Jules's eyes narrow. 'Then it's a good tactic.'

'I don't think it's a tactic at all,' says Arsinoe, with a glance to Mirabella. 'Our baby sister doesn't bluff.'

Jules stills and buries her hand in her cougar's fur. 'Ambush,' she says after a moment. 'If we will lose in a battle and we can't trust the trade, an ambush is the only way to save my mother.' She looks to Emilia. 'How many warriors have come from Bastian City?'

'Only a few dozen. The rest are entrenched, waiting for word.'

'That's more than enough.'

'More than enough against the queen's force?' Mathilde asks. 'She is bound to bring at least a thousand.'

'We're not going to fight them. We're going to divert and strike them.'

Emilia shakes her head. 'What diversion would be strong enough? It will not work.'

'It will work!' Jules points to Mirabella and then to Arsinoe. 'If we use them!'

Mirabella's eyes widen, and the woodpecker flies to her shoulder as Jules stalks toward her.

'She can call weather and lightning. Spook the horses, blow them over. She can burn them up, and in the chaos the warriors can strike. We will grab my mother and be gone before they know which way to chase us.'

'No,' says Emilia. 'The people will hear of it. They will know the traitor queens have returned.'

'So let them,' Jules says. 'Let them see that the queens stand with me. Let them see that they stand *behind* me. They'll see us united against Katharine and more will join us.'

Emilia nods, grudgingly. 'You think more like a warrior every day.'

Jules turns from Mirabella, who has risen to her feet, to Arsinoe, and Arsinoe looks between Jules and her sister.

This is not why they came back. But how can she turn Jules away when she needs them so badly?

'Please? Please, Arsinoe? Mirabella? Delay your trip to the mountain until we return. Until my mother is safe.' She grasps Arsinoe by the shoulders and squeezes.

'All right, Jules,' Arsinoe says. 'We'll go with you.'

That night, the room that Arsinoe shares with Mirabella and Billy is quiet as the three of them prepare for bed.

'Mirabella, did you get something to eat?' Arsinoe asks to break through the quiet.

'Some cheese and bread.'

'Did you need something more? I can see if there's any stew—'

'No.'

Arsinoe stares at her sister as Mirabella folds back the blankets on her makeshift cot. Her shoulders are straight and stiff, her movements brusque.

'Mira, are you angry with me?'

'Why would I be angry with you?' Mirabella asks, and finally turns. 'You have only promised our involvement in a war.'

'You don't want to fight? You won't help?'

'Of course I will help. You volunteered me.' And then she goes back to her blankets, slapping down the flat pillow with the back of her hand.

'I'm sorry,' Arsinoe stammers. 'I thought it's what you would want to do. I thought it was the right thing.'

'I thought the right thing was going to the mountain,' Billy says, sliding out of his jacket. 'I thought we weren't going to get involved.'

'You're mad at me, too?'

'You spoke for all of us, Arsinoe,' Mirabella says. 'You decided, without discussion.'

'Billy, you don't have to go,' Arsinoe starts, and instantly realizes it is the wrong thing to say. She has never seen him look at her like that. Like she has hurt him and does not understand him at all.

'I can tell Jules that you've changed your minds,' she whispers.

'We're going.' Billy sits down on his blankets to remove his shoes and stacks them loudly beside the wall. 'We just aren't speaking to you until it's over.'

'Fine.' Arsinoe shrugs. 'Then I'll leave you alone. I'll go sleep with Jules.'

'Good,' Mirabella says as she gets into bed. 'Go and discuss your battle plans.'

INDRID DOWN

Rho has assembled the soldiers in the inner ward of the Volroy grounds so that Katharine may survey them before riding out. Every one appears focused, straight backed, and clean of dress. The spears and shields held at rest are perfectly aligned. The only irregularities are the horses moving within the mounted cavalry: a swish of a tail or a stomping foot. They are, for all appearances, a true army.

'Kat? Are you ready?'

She turns and finds Pietyr, looking so handsome in a queensguard commander's uniform that she would like to delay the march for a few minutes and tear him right out of it.

'Nearly,' she says. 'I have sent one of my maids back into my room for something.'

'Genevieve is still pouting about being left behind,' Pietyr mutters. 'Expect to hear about it before we depart.' He leans down and kisses the curve of her neck. 'What is your maid fetching you?'

'A keepsake,' Katharine says, and smiles as the maid appears, carrying a small black lacquered box that usually sits beside Sweetheart's cage. When the maid reaches them, Katharine opens it and takes out the only thing she keeps inside: Arsinoe's mask.

'I stripped it from her after I shot her during the Queens' Hunt.' She runs her fingers down the cheek, so smooth and cold to the touch and painted so fiercely with red slashes. 'Do you think it will fit?'

'I think if you wear it,' Pietyr says, 'you will drive the naturalist to do something foolish.'

'Perhaps you are right.' She slips it into the sleeve of her cloak. 'But I will bring it anyway. For luck.'

Genevieve brings Katharine's black stallion and holds him while she mounts. He is outfitted handsomely in silver armor, his reins strung with the poisoner flags. Rho rides up beside her, and Katharine holds her horse firm as he dances in place.

'How many are here?'

'Five hundred,' Rho replies. 'One hundred horsed. Another thousand are garrisoned in Prynn and ready to march should something go wrong. But I do not think we will need them.'

'Good. Where is Madrigal Milone?'

'They are bringing her up now. I'll see to it.' Rho rides away, and Genevieve looks up from checking Katharine's stirrups and cinch.

'If my sister were here, I would ride beside her. Since she is not, I should ride beside you. It is what she would want.'

'What she would want is for you to do what you do best. Stay. Be my eyes and my ears here. Pietyr and Antonin will look after the Arron interests in the field.'

'Pietyr and Antonin,' Genevieve mutters. 'There should be an Arron woman at the head of your armies. Instead, you choose a priestess.'

'If Natalia were here, she would have chosen Margaret Beaulin. She was no fool; she knew how to put the war gift to use.'

Genevieve lifts her chin toward the other council members on horseback: Pietyr and Antonin, waiting on thick, black chargers, and Bree Westwood, on a light brown mare.

'Why her, then?'

'The priestess who sends my messages will be more comfortable if she is there.' She looks through the ranks for Elizabeth in her white-and-black robe but does not see her. Perhaps she will join them as they ride.

'But . . . Bree Westwood!'

Katharine groans.

'Perhaps I am bringing Bree Westwood in the hopes that she will die.' She presses a heel to her horse's side to move him off. Though she is no longer poisoning Katharine to the brink of a scream, Genevieve can still put a strain on a perfectly good day.

Katharine turns her horse in a slow circle, watching his breath puff in a small cloud as they pass the waiting soldiers. Innisfuil Valley will be frozen and covered in snow. A clean, white field for her army to tromp through. In her veins, the dead queens call for blood; they show it to her in vulgar images of snow stained red. Cold mud and flesh churned into each other.

'Quiet, quiet,' she murmurs, and flexes her fists, wondering what she would find if she looked inside her gloves. Live, pale fingers? Or black, rotten ones?

She catches Pietyr's eye and he smiles at her just as Rho returns, half dragging and half escorting their prisoner.

'Bind her hands and put her on a horse. A sweet palfrey, who will not be easily startled.'

'What of the bird?' Rho holds up a burlap sack. It beats like a heart as the crow inside flaps nervous wings. 'I could put it in a cage. Leave it here. She will not die without it.'

'How can you trade me without my familiar?' Madrigal asks, and jerks out of Rho's grasp. She is filthy from the cells, but still her loveliness shines through. Even past her resentful, miserable scowl. Katharine has always thought of naturalists as a rugged sort, suited for working with their hands and bathing every other week. But this one is not like that. This one has been pampered.

'Or maybe you don't really mean to trade me?'

Katharine takes a deep breath.

'Keep your crow in line. If I allow her to come and she tries to fly, I will put a bolt in her chest myself. Do you understand?'

Madrigal nods. Rho reaches into the sack and pulls the crow out flapping. Once released, she dives directly for Madrigal's arms and stays there.

'Tether them together,' Katharine orders. 'Give it just enough room to hop from hand to shoulder.'

'You'll never get my Jules,' Madrigal says after she has been put onto her horse. 'If you truly hoped to, you should have kidnapped someone else. My daughter doesn't even like me. She is not even going to show up.'

SUNPOOL

'You've chosen the warriors who are going with you?'

'Yes. Well, Emilia did.'

Arsinoe and Jules sit together before the hearth, watching the fire crackle and burn.

'It's been a bit of a wonder—' Arsinoe tears into a chunk of bread and drags it through the stew broth left from her dinner. When she had shown up at Jules's door after being ousted (or ousting herself) from the room she shared with Billy and Mirabella, Jules had immediately called for more food. 'Watching Emilia these last days. She's . . . hard not to listen to.'

'She does know how to give orders.' The corner of Jules's mouth crooks upward. 'You don't like her.'

'I don't trust her,' Arsinoe corrects. 'But she cares about you.'

Jules bends and spoons up the last of the stew to drop onto Arsinoe's plate.

'Sorry there's not much. And sorry there's no poison in it.'

'Hmph. I'm not enough of a poisoner to miss it. Though you're right about the quantity.' The loaf of bread was small, and she could have only a plate and a half of the stew, but it is good. Rich and full of root vegetables and meat.

'Thank you for coming with me,' Jules says.

'Don't thank me,' Arsinoe replies. 'Thank Mirabella, and Billy. Me, you never even had to ask.'

'I didn't think I'd ever see you again,' Jules says, and Arsinoe feels Camden's tail wrap affectionately around her ankle.

'I always knew I'd see you.' Arsinoe sips from a cup of warmed watered wine. 'Somehow, I knew.'

Jules smiles and takes up her own cup. They knock them together and drink awhile, watching the fire.

'So what do you think you'll find up the mountain?'

'I've no idea. I'm just going to learn what I can.' She glances at Jules from the corner of her eye. 'You're not afraid, about tomorrow? Or worried, about any of this?'

'The only thing I'm afraid of,' Jules says, 'the only thing I regret, is that I can't do this alone. That others have to risk themselves with me.'

Arsinoe sighs. 'More has changed than just your hair,' she jokes, and Jules laughs and punches her.

'This quest you're going on,' Jules says, 'it isn't dangerous, is it?'

'Oh, don't start that again. You're the Legion Queen now.

It's not your job to look out for me, not that it ever was. But I sure did appreciate it.'

She sets her plate on the floor for Camden to lick and heaves up out of the chair.

'Where are you going?' Jules asks.

'Big day tomorrow. Don't you think we ought to get some sleep?'

'I suppose so. Though someday I'd like to hear more. About what it's like on the mainland.'

Arsinoe smiles. 'Someday I'll tell you.'

That night, Arsinoe dreams a Blue Queen dream for the first time since deciding to return to the island. But is not like the other dreams.

This dream is of the mist. And of the bodies inside it. Torn apart. Choked. Rotting. This dream is a blanket of white closing in around her friends, around Jules and Camden, and Billy and Mirabella, blotting out the island and carving up everything it touches.

It ends with the shadow queen crouched on her chest, her long cold fingers pressed against Arsinoe's head. She does not speak. She still cannot. But Arsinoe knows what she means.

INNISFUIL VALLEY

The queen's army sets up camp on the eastern side of the valley, spreading tents and horses and soldiers like black ants across the snow-dusted field and all the way through the cliffs to the frozen beach. Antonin and Rho send scouts up the cliffside. Nothing that moves through the valley will escape their attention, and no crafty rebel force can creep up on them from behind.

'There has never been a war like this,' Pietyr says, staring out at the soldiers, some of whom seem no more than girls still in their freckles. 'A rebel against a queen. It has been a long time since we have seen war of any kind. So who knows what to expect?'

'This is not a war, Pietyr,' says Katharine. 'This is a trade. It will not come to fighting.'

'You seem very certain.' He brushes his knuckles across her cheekbone. 'Are you all right here, Kat? So close to the Breccia Domain?'

Her mouth crooks. 'I wondered about that. That deep, dark place.' Her eyes flicker toward the southern woods. 'I can feel it opening and closing like a mouth. And they feel it, too.' His hand slides into hers. He feels the cold of her even through the gloves. 'Part of them is still down there, Pietyr. Part of them always will be.'

'Do you want to go to it?'

'Never. I will never return to it again. I could never be sure . . . whether I would be able to stand or if I would dive straight down inside.'

She sighs, and he feels her press close, his wicked little Kat whom he cannot get enough of.

'Come,' she says, her breath hot in his ear. 'Close the tent flap and lie with me awhile. No one will notice we are gone. No one will interrupt us once they hear the sounds that I am making.'

'I cannot, my pet.' He steps out of her reaching embrace, though he would much rather fall into it. He must be careful, so close to carrying out his plans. With Katharine wrapped around him, he forgets how to think, and the last time they were together, he devoured her so desperately, he was sure he had given away his fears. 'Rho will bellow if I do not help with the soldiers.'

He takes her gloved hand and turns it over to kiss the bare skin of her wrist, to feel her pulse against his lips. She says she is fine so near the Breccia, but she is not. With the source of them close by, they have changed her; he can feel their influence turning her sharp, like she was during the Ascension when they sought the crown. The closer they marched to Innisfuil, the more she barked at the soldiers. The more poison she ate at meals. The more she hunted with her horse and crossbow. He saw her shoot down a hawk in flight with perfect war-gift aim. He watched her skin a rabbit like removing a glove, and lick the blood from her fingers.

He backs out of the tent, leaving Katharine to rest or pout, and turns and runs directly into the High Priestess.

'Luca! Forgive me.'

'It is all right. I am nothing if not sturdy. Is the queen inside?'

'Yes,' he says, and steps out of the way. But Luca seems to change her mind.

'Walk with me a moment, will you, Pietyr?'

As she leads him through the encampment she pauses every few steps to lay a blessing on the head of this person or that, soldiers who touch her robes as they pass or simply drop to one knee.

'What is wrong, Master Arron? You have seen these blessings before.'

'Of course. They just . . . remind me of who you are. I suppose in our close quarters on the Black Council, you have become less the High Priestess and more Luca to me.'

'I have lost my mystique.' Luca laughs. 'Well. In the capital, none of these soldiers would do more than step out of my way. But all regain their faith in the face of a coming battle.'

'Queen Katharine is still sure it will not be a fight.'

'And I hope she is correct.'

'But you do not think she is.'

Luca bites her lower lip and tilts her head thoughtfully. 'I think this rebellion has come too far to end without a battle.' She folds her hands. 'Did you ever discover a solution for the problem we discussed? The problem of spiritual possession?'

'It was not a problem. Only a curiosity.'

'Ah.'

They pass by the priestess's tent and come upon Bree and Elizabeth. Bree nods when she sees him, but when she looks upon Luca, her lips press together in a firm line.

'Is that—?' Pietyr asks, and points to a small black-and-white woodpecker climbing about on Elizabeth's robes.

'It is!' Elizabeth scoops him up and shows him to Pietyr happily. 'He rejoined us this morning, flew into my chest so hard he nearly pierced my heart!'

'He seems very . . . proud of himself.'

The bird, once again in Elizabeth's lap, crawls up and down her legs excitedly and makes small chirping sounds.

'He has been like this since he returned,' says Bree. 'We have fed and watered him, but he will not be calm. Perhaps he is proud.'

'No. He's trying to tell me something.' Elizabeth reaches down to stroke his back, and he pecks her hard between the fingers. 'Ouch! And he's getting very upset that I'm not understanding what it is.'

Pietyr glances at Luca, who has fallen silent, watching the bird. 'Well, I am sure you will figure it out.'

SUNPOOL

Just after dawn, Jules and Arsinoe stand together near the city gate, the stone of the square stretched out before them. The edges are crowded with what appears to be the entire rebellion, risen early to see their leader off.

'Seems like I should be more tired,' Jules says. 'We hardly got a wink of sleep.'

'Nor me,' says Arsinoe as Camden yawns. Soon enough, Emilia and Mathilde will arrive with the small band of warriors and Mirabella and Billy, who have gone to the stable with them.

Jules lets go of a shaky exhale and looks Arsinoe up and down. Arsinoe tugs at her cloak and the coat underneath.

'You look like a real mainlander in Billy's clothes.'

'Ha. Can you believe they nearly fit?' Arsinoe holds up her arms. Then she frowns. 'Listen, Jules, I can't go with you after Madrigal.'

'What? Arsinoe—'

'I've got to go on. I've got to go up the mountain. I can't explain it. I just know I have to.'

'Can't it wait even a few more days? We'll ride fast through the pass to the valley—'

'No. I'm sorry. If there'd been more time . . . if I'd told you more of what I'd seen . . . what I'd dreamed, maybe you'd understand.' She puts a hand on her friend's shoulder. 'But it will be fine, Jules. You don't really need me anyway. Mira is more than enough.'

Jules frowns. 'It would just feel better having you there with me.'

'I know. I wish . . . ,' Arsinoe starts, but does not know how to finish.

'Are you sure? I can't wait around for you to change your mind.'

Hoofbeats clatter, and the warriors trot into the square, with Emilia leading on a horse as red as blood. A dozen warriors ride behind her, and Mathilde and Billy ride beside. Mirabella brings up the rear on a dappled gray, looking oddly uncomfortable on horseback.

'Fifteen,' Arsinoe says. 'You can bet Katharine will bring fifteen hundred.'

'We won't need that number. It is an ambush, not a battle, remember?' Jules and Arsinoe go forward to meet her mount, a stunning black gelding with four white stockings and a crescent on his forehead.

'Isn't that Katharine's horse?'

Jules takes the reins and grins as she leaps onto his back.

'The same one I stole the day of the hunt.' She pats his neck. 'And still every bit as game as when he carried you half-dead through the mountains.'

'How fitting.' Arsinoe strokes his nose. 'You should give him a name.'

'Or maybe I'll just ask Katharine what it is.'

Emilia rides up close. 'Another scout has returned,' she says. 'Katharine has reached the valley and set up camp. She has put the war-gifted priestess Rho Murtra at the head of her army.'

'A fine thing,' Mathilde adds sarcastically, 'ousting the warrior on the council and replacing her with a warrior priestess who, by the laws of the temple, should not acknowledge her gift. We are not the only ones shedding the old ways.'

The horses shift, and Arsinoe is jostled out of the way, farther from Jules as she greets her warriors. On the edges of the square, the rest of her army waits, silent. A united army, of many gifts. Soldiers with hawks on their shoulders. Others with flickers of flame darting across their knuckles. And many with the seers' steely eyes and bright white braids.

'She should bring more,' says Arsinoe as Mirabella and Billy maneuver their horses to stand close by.

'No, the seer is right,' says Mirabella. 'They are not ready and still too few. If they stood before the queensguard now, most would die.' She turns her eager horse in a tight circle. With her hair obscured by the scarf and hood, and in her mainlander clothes, she could truly be anyone.

'They're whispering about you now that you ride with the Legion Queen,' Billy notes. 'Wondering who you are. Why don't you take the hood down and show them?'

Mirabella shakes her head. 'Emilia is still unsure. She wants me to stay hidden unless I am forced to show myself.' She glances at Arsinoe pointedly. 'And I agree with her.'

'Arsinoe, do you want help into the saddle?' Billy asks.

'I'm not coming,' Arsinoe says, and winces.

'What?'

'I'm sorry. I'm sorry for getting you into this, first volunteering and then not going myself, but I have to go to the mountain. I saw her again last night. The shadow. She made me dream of the mist and showed me what it could do.'

Mirabella and Billy look at each other, and Billy shrugs and slides down from his horse.

'Then I'm not going either,' he says. 'I'm coming with you.'

Mirabella presses her lips together, and Arsinoe holds her breath. Jules's plan will not work without her.

'I will still go,' Mirabella says finally.

'Are you sure?' Arsinoe asks, and exhales.

'Yes. You go and take care of the mist. I will take care of our little sister.' She looks at Arsinoe with a gentle expression. 'And I will look after Jules. I promise.'

'Look after yourself, too,' Arsinoe says. 'If our sister sees you—'

'I have not been poisoned this time. This time, if she sees

me it will be different. *Very* different.'

Emilia wheels her horse and canters around the group in a tight circle; the riders put heels to their mounts and make for the gate.

'Time to go,' Mirabella says, and clicks to the dappled gray awkwardly.

'I never knew you couldn't ride.'

'I can,' she calls over her shoulder as she bounces away. 'I just spent more time in carriages!'

Arsinoe grunts as Camden jumps up and puts her paws on Arsinoe's chest. Jules has turned back and rides toward her and Billy with a regretful face.

'You'll be left behind,' says Billy.

'I'm their leader. They can't go far without me.' Jules smiles. She is afraid, but she is also exhilarated. She will ride hard to catch up. She will charge the field. She has become a warrior. 'Are you two sure you'll be all right? I've heard Mount Horn is . . . an unforgiving place.'

'Are you sure *you'll* be all right?' Arsinoe asks, but instead of answering, Jules reaches into her saddlebag and pulls out a knife. She tosses it to Arsinoe handle first.

'Take your bear with you at least,' she says, and rides away. Camden gives Arsinoe's cheek another lick before running off after Jules.

After the ambush party is gone, the square empties. The rebels return to their work, preparing weapons and storing food. Repairing the city that has worn down and crumbled over the centuries. It is strange to watch them return so quickly to their task, while Arsinoe stares after Jules and Mirabella until long after they are out of sight. Finally, she and Billy gather up their packs. No one pays them any mind, even when the scarf slips down and reveals Arsinoe's scars.

They leave through the main gate and keep the mountain in their sights. Billy rummages in his pack and pulls out a small bundle of papers.

'I've been looking over maps—well, what maps I could find here—and trying to determine the best route to take,' he says. 'A girl who lives in a village near the western foot says there are caves and a good-sized one if we follow the trail along this stream.' He riffles through the papers and holds up a map of Mount Horn. 'The last stretch will be a slightly difficult climb, but I think it's our best shot. Will that be far enough up to satisfy the Blue Queen, do you think?'

'I don't know,' Arsinoe replies, studying the route. The cave he indicates is still farther up the mountain than she wanted to go. 'I hope so.'

'I can't believe you almost let me go with Jules and Mira. Why didn't you ask me to stay?'

'I didn't think of it. And I figured you were still angry.'

'Is that it? Or are you just trying to politely get rid of me? You keep trying to leave me behind; should I be taking the hint?'

'No, I—'

'Because I don't want to keep on where I'm not wanted.'

'Of course I—' She growls in frustration, and they are both suddenly very aware she is still holding the knife that Jules gave her.

'What are you going to do?' he asks. 'Gut me?'

'Of course not. I don't know what I'm doing. I don't know what lies at the top of that mountain. But I do know that it's all for the hope of something else. A future somewhere, with you. And I'm sorry I can't say that when I'm not holding you at knifepoint. All right?'

'All right,' he says, and grins. His grin changes to a grimace as she uses the knife to cut into her palm. 'And now you're slicing your hand open.'

'I'm calling Braddock, like Jules suggested.' She walks to the nearest tree and smears her blood against the bark.

'Will that even work, after all this time?'

Arsinoe smiles. She was not sure whether it would either. But the moment her blood touches the tree she feels him. Somewhere not too far away, she feels him lift his big brown head and sniff the air.

INNISFUIL VALLEY

Pietyr creeps away to the Breccia Domain toward evening, when the sun is fading to a winter orange but while there is still plenty of light to see by. And even then, he steps carefully, wary of the treacherous pit. The heart of the island, it is called, but it truly is more like a mouth. A fissure in the earth made of mouths and eyes and ears to hear him coming.

The Breccia Domain lies before him in the clearing, looking innocent, but he is not fooled.

'You had your chance to eat me the last time we met,' he says, tying a rope around his waist. 'This time, I will eat my fill of you instead.' He winds the rope around the sturdiest tree he can find and then around another for good measure.

The tools tucked into his belt should serve him well enough: a trowel and hammer, a handheld pick, and a sack to carry the rocks. Madrigal did not say how large the stones should be nor how large a circle he would require. She was not much of a low magic teacher.

He braces his feet against the edge and takes a deep breath. With his head above ground, he still smells clean air and fresh snow. As usual, there is no birdsong. No sound of any kind except his nervous breathing and thumping heartbeat. He wraps his anchor rope around his arm three times, and the Breccia seems to yawn open to receive him.

'Not this time, you wicked pit.'

Pietyr stands over the edge, secured to the trees, and swings his hammer against the stones.

It takes longer than he hoped. So long that he loses the sun and must labor in the dark. His shoulders shaking, he finally dislodges a final piece of rock and drops it into his sack. He does not have enough. But it is all he is capable of.

After securing the stones in his tent, he slips through the camp, past soldiers' cookfires, to find the tent where Madrigal is kept.

'I need to speak to the prisoner,' he says. The guard nods and steps just outside. 'Give us some space.'

'Yes, Master Arron.'

'His name isn't Arron, though, is it?' Madrigal sings from inside. 'It's Renard.'

Pietyr ducks into the tent and scowls at her in the lamplight. 'The Arron in me is what counts. I need you to tell me the rest of the spell.'

She holds up her hands, still bound.

'I do not care,' he snaps. 'You have my word; I will try when the time comes. But in case something goes wrong, I need to know the rest. I could get only a few stones. Not enough for a full circle. Not one touching end to end. So what do I do?'

'Get more?' Madrigal raises her eyebrows, then sighs. 'Very well. Close the circle with something else. Start staining rope with your blood. Set the stones inside the rope and it should do.'

'Then what?'

'Get the queen inside the circle. Carve this rune'—she traces it lightly in the earth—'into your hand—'

'I will never remember that.'

'Fine. Give me a knife.' She cocks her head, exasperated, when he hesitates. 'Just a small one.'

He hands one to her.

'Now give me your palm.'

He gasps as she slices into it, making curving cuts that fill with red.

'There. Just reopen those scabs when the time is right. Press the blood to her skin. Carve the same mark into her. And return every last ghost into the stones.'

'I do not want to cut her.'

'You don't have a choice. Queensblood is the key. It makes all the difference. Believe me.'

THE WESTERN WOODS

Mirabella and Jules wait together deep in the woods that border Innisfuil Valley to the west. The warriors, and even Mathilde, have gone ahead, disappearing into the bare winter trees on foot to scout and spy on Katharine's army. Leaving them to do nothing but wait and listen to the horses munch grain in their feed bags.

'They should be back by now,' Jules says from atop Katharine's black gelding.

'There is a lot of ground between here and the valley. It takes time to cover on foot. Even more when one is trying to tread quietly.'

'How would you know?' Jules asks.

'I would not.' Mirabella shrugs. 'I was only trying to make you feel better.'

'No doubt you think them all fools, following me here. Calling me a queen on the basis of faith and a prophecy murky as a mud puddle.'

Mirabella chooses her words with care. Jules Milone is as feisty as Arsinoe, only feisty of a different sort. Less impulsive but more easily offended.

'All prophecy is . . . ambiguous.'

'Ambiguous. Murky. "May be a queen again."' She snorts. '"May be." Can't they ever say anything for certain?' She pauses to listen for the sound of anyone returning. 'It must really stick in your craw. Them referring to me as a queen. Even a queen in title only.'

Mirabella swallows. To be a Fennbirn queen was to be of the line. A queen in the blood. That was what she had always been told, and taught by the temple.

'It bothers me, too, to be honest,' says Jules, reading her silence. 'Feels like the High Priestess is going to come and knock me on the back of the head.'

She turns toward some unheard sound, unheard to Mirabella at least, as the mountain cat's ears perk up as well. Soon enough, though, the footsteps are plain. Six of their party, returning through the trees with Emilia and Mathilde in the lead.

'Well?' Jules asks.

'She has made camp on the eastern edge of the valley, butted up to the cliffs and spilled out onto the beach,' Emilia says. 'Scouts are positioned up high, to the north and south as far as the cliffs allow. But we saw no sign of anyone in the western woods. Nor past the west edge of the valley. It is almost like she truly intends to trade. Pity for her.'

The warriors behind Emilia smile. They are armed with

swords, throwing knives, and crossbows. Three carry longbows larger than any Mirabella has ever seen. She does not need to ask to know that the others have remained in the woods, ready and waiting to strike.

'There is no perfect place to ambush,' Emilia goes on. 'We will have to draw her out of the clearing somehow and into the trees. You will have to play the bait, Jules.'

'I can do that.'

'I know. And I will do it with you.'

'Did you see my mother in the camp?'

'Only the tent where she's being kept,' Emilia replies. 'And Mathilde thought she heard the croaking of a crow.'

'Aria.' Jules glances at Mirabella and explains. 'Her familiar.'

'What about me?' Mirabella asks.

'We have found a place for you to the south. Up a tree, if you can manage.'

'I have been up trees before.'

Emilia cocks her eyebrow. 'There will be no quick escape from there if something goes wrong.'

'I will not need one.'

'Then go. One hour to take positions before we send a bird to the poisoner to let her know we are here.'

Mirabella looks at Jules. Despite the band of warriors and the strong mountain cat by her side, Jules is afraid. Legion cursed or not, she is outnumbered, and Katharine is a true queen. A fierce queen, to hear the tales told now, who might no longer freeze at the sight of Jules like she did in the arena the day of the duel.

Seeing Mirabella's look, Jules puts on a brave smile. 'It'll be all right. Go with Mathilde.'

'Take care, Jules. Arsinoe will have my head if I let any harm befall you or Camden.'

'It won't come to that. We ambush the trade and run, like we planned. You be careful yourself. Arsinoe'll have my head, too, if you don't return with us.'

Mirabella nods and goes with Mathilde into the trees. The seer is fast of foot and so silent that she makes Mirabella feel like a herd of goats, snapping twigs and crunching leaves as she moves. Finally, they reach the tree. It is a good tree for climbing, with broad, well-spaced branches.

'If you brace in the second fork, you will have the best view,' says Mathilde.

Mirabella grasps the lowest branch. 'This is too far. I won't be able to see properly.'

'Emilia wants you to stay hidden. So stay hidden if you can. She thinks the warriors are quick enough and stealthy enough to save Jules's mother without your help.'

Mirabella arches her brow.

'For what it is worth,' Mathilde says, 'I don't agree. I have scented the wind today, and it reeks of blood.'

'So,' Mirabella sputters, 'what do I do?'

'Be ready.' The seer turns and disappears between the trunks. Mirabella sniffs the air, detects nothing in it but crisp, cold snow.

'Oracles,' she mutters, and climbs into the tree.

MOUNT HORN

Braddock finds Arsinoe and Billy at the foot of the mountain. He emerges from behind the scrub brush with an exuberant roar and frightens Billy so badly that he falls backward onto the grass.

'Braddock,' he squeaks. 'Is it him? It is him, isn't it?' But there is no time to wonder as the bear promptly steps over him and lumbers to Arsinoe to press his nose happily into her scabby palm.

'Braddock!' She wraps her arms around his neck and strokes the fur between his ears. 'You found us! And a good thing, too. I was starting to feel faint.' She had painted trees with her blood every mile or so since they departed from Sunpool.

'Does he remember me as well?' Billy asks, brushing himself off.

'He didn't eat you. I think that's a good sign.'

Cautiously, Billy approaches and lays a hand on the bear's rump. A trembling hand. Braddock he may be, but he is still a great brown bear and large as a horse.

'He looks wonderful, doesn't he?' She stuffs her face into his shiny coat. 'Caragh must be helping him fish and forage. Not bad eating with a naturalist around, is it, boy?'

'It's good to see him,' Billy says, casting an eye up the mountain. 'But he might not be able to stay with us for long. The path up to the cave might be too hard. And . . . Stop doing that,' he adds as he watches Arsinoe feed the bear more than a day's ration of dried meat.

'I have to reward him for coming. It's winter, you know; he would much rather be in his den or in the warm stable at the Black Cottage snoozing with the mule.'

'Fine but no more. He can hunt for himself, but we need food for the journey back to Sunpool.' He waits for a response, but she only snuggles farther into her bear. 'Arsinoe, there will be a journey back, won't there? You never really told me what's waiting for us at the top of this mountain.'

'That's because I don't know. I'm not keeping some great secret. All I know is that Daphne wants me there. That she'll speak to me.'

'Which could mean a hundred things.'

'Are you regretting not going with Mira and Jules?'

'No, of course not.'

They continue with the bear in tow, making their way through the trees, upward and upward toward the snow line. The path in the lower elevation is not that difficult, and Braddock keeps up easily and finds plenty of cold berries to forage along the way. That night, they stop at a broad stretch of the trail and build a small fire. Braddock lies down and lets Arsinoe and even Billy cuddle up in his side.

'On second thought,' says Billy, 'maybe we will try to bring him all the way. It'll only get harder to light a fire, and he's sure to stay plenty warm.' He slides an arm around her, careful not to jostle the bear too much. 'We should have kept Mira back, too. We could be toasty and dry all the way to the cave.'

'Do you think she's all right?' Arsinoe asks. 'Do you think they both are?'

'I think if they weren't, we'd have heard Mira's storm all the way across the mountain.'

Arsinoe glances up at the peak of Mount Horn. She hopes the cave will be good enough for Daphne, and they will not have to go any farther. If they rise early and climb hard, they may reach it by nightfall and not have to camp on the steeper mountainside.

'Do you know what I'm afraid of?' she asks.

'What?'

'I'm afraid to reach this cave and find nothing inside. That it was all a joke. A ploy to bring us back here. Or a trick of my own mind.'

'Funny'—he kisses her head—'that's what I would like to happen. But I don't think that it will.'

Arsinoe snuggles closer to him, entwining their legs, and lets her hands roam until he inhales sharply.

'Arsinoe!' He grins. 'Not in front of the bear.'

She grins back. 'The bear doesn't mind.'

But as soon as their movements disturb him, Braddock gets up with a grunt and goes to lie someplace else.

INNISFUIL VALLEY

'How many cavalry soldiers can you knock from their horses with your gift?'

'I don't know,' Jules asks. 'How many can you?'

Emilia shrugs. 'Two. Perhaps three if their seat is no good. Certainly not a hundred, which is how many horses she seems to have brought.'

They lie on their backs in the snow, watching the clouds go by overhead. It is a clear, quiet day. Either not many of the queen's soldiers are elementals, or none of them is the least bit nervous. As for Mirabella, somewhere up a tree to the southeast, well, she knows how to mask her gift.

'If this goes wrong, Emilia, you have to promise to let me go through with the trade.' Jules turns her head. But Emilia will not look at her.

'I will not promise that.'

'She's my mother. And my little brother needs her.'

Emilia half rolls onto her shoulder and stretches her

neck back to peer toward the valley.

'The others should be in position now.' Camden growls, and the warrior grins, reaches down and scratches her shoulder. 'Even your cat wants to fight. Like she is touched with the war gift as well. If you trade yourself, what am I supposed to do with her?'

'Hold her back. Don't let her follow.'

Emilia and Camden regard each other. The cougar seems fairly sure she would win that argument.

'It's time,' Emilia says. 'Send a bird to the queen. Let her know you are here.'

The bird that the rebels send is a hawk. Unmistakable in its message, it swoops low through the army camp, every so often sounding its sharp, piercing cry. When Katharine emerges from her tent, it flies directly onto her arm, the insolent thing.

She grits her teeth and strokes its chest feathers as its talons needle through her glove. Then she tosses it back up into the air and watches it fly, back to the west end of the meadow.

'Horses?' Pietyr asks as he comes up behind her buttoning his shirt and queensguard coat. 'Or shall we go on foot?'

'Horses,' she replies. The dead war queens have lent her plenty of their gift today, and she will be ready for anything.

With the arrival of the hawk, her queensguard comes alive, arming themselves and falling into formation. Though many of her soldiers are older than she, some are old enough to have served under the last queen, and she walks through them with a sense of pride. They are hers now. She reaches out and rattles a spear held in a girl's shaking wrist.

'No need for courage today.' She smiles. 'You are simply an escort for queen and prisoner.'

She mounts her horse, who looks twice his normal size in light armor, and takes a long shield to hold on her right. Madrigal will ride to her left and Pietyr, on Madrigal's far side.

'Keep the army to the rear,' she says to Rho, who holds her horse's bridle. 'Do not seem a threat. We do not want Jules Milone to turn tail and run.'

She takes up her reins, and Pietyr rides close, tucking a sharp knife into his belt.

'Are you all right, Kat? Are you ready?'

'Yes,' she says without looking at him. Perhaps she should have left him behind. In Pietyr's eyes and beneath his gaze, she is Kat, little Katharine. Only herself. And she cannot be that today, not until the trade is over.

The crowd parts as the prisoner is brought near. Madrigal Milone sits astride an old gray mare, her hands bound behind her back. Her crow familiar rests docilely on her shoulder, still tethered to her wrist.

'Are you looking forward to seeing your daughter?' Katharine asks.

'More than you should be.'

Katharine leans over and pushes the woman's hair out of her eyes. She tucks it behind her ear and smooths it down, revealing some of that unsinkable prettiness. She is so lovely but of so little substance. Only a regular-sized woman despite that beauty. Though they were of similar height, Natalia would have towered over Madrigal Milone and covered her in shadow.

'Do not be afraid,' she says gently when Madrigal flinches. 'I will not hurt you. I swear that it is not why we have come.'

'You can't hurt me,' Madrigal mutters.

Katharine clicks at the mare and tugs her along, keeping her close enough that Madrigal's toe occasionally bumps into her heel. She looks over her shoulder where her army stands waiting.

'No.'

Turned around, she sees it before anyone: the mist, rising over the water of Longmorrow Bay.

'Not now! Pietyr!'

He twists in the saddle, just as the soldiers farthest away on the beach begin to scream.

The mist spreads, slow and thick through the path between the cliffs and into the meadow. She watches it creep up over the cliff tops, watches it swallow her lookouts.

'Kat, what do we do?'

'It does not matter,' Katharine replies as her army breaks ranks and scatters.

From her perch up in the tree, Mirabella sees the mist roll out over the sand of the beach and crawl up the sides of the cliffs. At first she thinks it is only a storm. Some quirk of the weather. But as it swallows the first soldier and the next and the next, and she hears them scream . . .

'The mist,' she whispers.

She grasps on to the branches so hard the cold bark splits the skin of her hands. Her heart beats loudly as she watches the mist swirl over the terrified soldiers. To cloak them? To protect them?

A shrill shriek draws her eye as the mist rolls back, revealing a body twisted in two and pulled apart. The snow between the torso and legs is littered with entrails and spreading red.

She does not know what to do. The mist has wound nearly the length of the valley, leaving some and maiming others, causing panic and confusion, and swirling westward, toward Katharine and Jules.

If Mirabella stays her hand, it may all be resolved. The Undead Queen and the Legion Queen destroyed in one stroke. Perhaps that is what the Blue Queen wants. What the island wants. Perhaps she was brought there only to witness.

'No.' Mirabella slides down the trunk. She jumps from the lowest branch and winces as her ankle rolls.

All those innocent soldiers. The servants. The priestesses she saw in their white robes. She does not know what is wrong with the mist. But she knows that it is wrong.

Mirabella runs as fast as she can toward the sounds of screaming, calling the wind and the storm up behind her.

* * *

Katharine can only watch as her army comes apart. As the mist darts through them like wispy fingers, mangling them or swallowing them whole.

The entire camp is in shambles: turned-over tents, horses running loose to trample through supply stores or over the tops of people the mist has taken and spun around.

'Katharine! We have to get you to safety!' Pietyr shouts.

'What safety?' Her head turns at the sound of hoofbeats. Rho is leading a band of cavalry, galloping for the cover of the trees. The priestess's face is hard as stone. Angry as Katharine is that there is no form to truly fight. The mist is almost upon them, creeping around to the sides. *How can it move so quickly without seeming to move at all?*

'Ride!' Pietyr calls to her. 'Follow Rho!'

He kicks his horse hard. He does not see the arm of white billow between them until it is too late.

'Pietyr!'

'It's blocking us in!' Madrigal screeches. 'Don't you see? We have to run!'

'Where?' Katharine drags her closer, the dead war queens infusing her with strength enough to pull Madrigal from her horse and across Katharine's pommel. 'Right for the western woods? Right into your waiting rebels' arms?'

'Are you mad? People are dying!'

'But not us!' Katharine drops her shield and draws a long knife out of her boot. The mist is everywhere. She cannot see anything in all the white. Not even the silhouette of a tree trunk. Her horse's hooves prance and kick up wisps like smoke. They are pocketed inside it, and she need only wait for it to rush into her lungs. Will she feel it then, pull her heart out through her mouth? Or twist her arms from their sockets?

'Madrigal? Mother!'

Katharine whirls as the mist around them thins. Jules Milone and her cougar stand at the edge of the trees. Her hand is raised.

'I've come to trade.'

'No!' Madrigal shouts. 'No, Jules, get out of here!' She tries to burst out of Katharine's grip, but Katharine's fingers are locked tight.

'You cannot run yet!' Katharine cries. 'Not yet!'

'Let go of me!' In a flurry of black feathers, Madrigal sends her crow at Katharine's face.

'Mother, stop struggling!' Jules calls, and Katharine looks at her through the haze. She is not alone. Mirabella is running up behind her. She is dressed in mainlander clothes, blue and gray, none of the black of queens. But her regal face is unmistakable.

At the sight of Mirabella, the dead queens surge through Katharine's blood. Their rage is so pure that it turns her vision red, even through the white of the mist. She cannot calm them or speak to them, and when Madrigal's bird flaps again in her face, the dead queens lash out. Katharine does not remember that she had drawn her knife until the blade is already buried deep in Madrigal's neck.

'No,' she whispers as the blood begins to pour from the wound. She looks into Madrigal's wide, surprised eyes. 'I did not mean . . .' She presses her hand against the blood, but it is no use. The veins of Madrigal's throat have been cut. Severed. Horrified, Katharine lets go, and Madrigal's body tumbles limply to the ground, her panicked crow still tethered to the dying woman's wrist.

The next thing Katharine hears is an otherworldly scream. The next thing she feels is herself blown backward to land hard upon the snow and her horse rolling over her foot.

When Madrigal falls, Mirabella dashes past Jules to try and catch her. She sends her storm out into the mist ahead, pushes wind through her fingertips, and feels the clouds gather over the valley.

She pushes harder, and the mist is blown back, creating a path for her straight to Madrigal. She is still strides away when an unseen force hits her from behind, throwing her forward hard to bounce against the ground. For an instant, everything is dark, and her storm begins to fizzle. But she shakes her head clear and goes on, scrambling on her hands and knees.

Not far ahead, Katharine is on the ground, struggling beneath her horse. The horse itself is dead or knocked cold by the unseen blast. Mirabella ignores her and hurries to Jules's mother, lying in a bloody heap, her arm lifted by a crow desperately trying to fly away.

She kneels beside the woman and turns her over. Madrigal's

eyes roll toward her, white and panicked as blood pours out of her neck.

'It is all right, Madrigal. Do not move now.' Not knowing what else to do, she quickly unties the crow and lets her fly. It seems a relief, to the bird and Madrigal both. 'We have to get you out of here.'

'No. She's—' Blood bubbles over her lips. She says more, but it is nearly impossible to understand. 'She is full of them.'

'Full of what? Who is?'

'Full of dead,' Madrigal gurgles, and grasps on to Mirabella's shoulder. She spits blood into the snow, presses her hand into it. 'Stop her . . . Jules . . .'

'Hush now.'

The storm above rumbles, and rain falls hard onto the snow, driving it down and melting it as it does the same to the mist. Her wind drowns out the sound of thunder as it clears the valley of white, revealing stunned soldiers on their hands and knees.

As the valley becomes visible once again, Mirabella turns back to Jules and the rebels, to see if they were hurt by the blast. But Jules is fine. Standing alone, with her hands thrust down in fists.

'Madrigal, we have to go,' Mirabella says. But when she tries to lift her, she is heavy and dead in her arms.

Jules screams again, as her war gift explodes into the meadow. It sends Katharine's horse flying over the top of her to land behind. Mirabella gasps. The blast came from her. Both of the violent blasts came from Jules. Mirabella stands and tries to use her gift to further push back the mist when she hears Emilia shout.

'Mirabella, look out!'

Mirabella turns. Too late, she sees the fallen form of Jules's familiar, lying limp at her feet, taken out by Jules's own attack. Her war gift is out of control. It will not spare even her friends.

'Run!' Emilia screams, but not before Mirabella is thrown sideways into a tree.

Blackness swims before her eyes. She struggles to her elbows and squints. Jules has been taken to the ground. Emilia has pinned her and strikes her hard on the back of the head.

'Cover!' Emilia shrieks. 'Give us cover, elemental!'

'Cover,' Mirabella grumbles, blinking her aching eyes. With her jarred, the storm has begun to fray at the edges, but she pulls it back together, her gift singing in her veins after so many months on the mainland unused. Her lightning strike lands in the valley, cutting off the queen's army from pursuing any retreating rebels. There is no mistaking it for natural weather, and every eye in the meadow seeks out the source.

Katharine stares at Mirabella as Mirabella stares back. Katharine can no longer feel the ache in the leg that was trapped under her horse. She no longer cares whether the mist has retreated all the way into the sea. She does not even see it when the warriors and the oracle in a yellow cloak come to spirit away the legion-cursed naturalist and her fallen cougar. All that matters is Mirabella.

'Come to me.' Katharine holds out her hand. 'Come to me, sister!'

Mirabella backs away into the trees until she is far enough to turn and run. But she need not even do that. The mist and her lightning have taken the fight out of the queensguard. Not a one of them is brave enough now to follow. Not even Rho.

'Kat!' Pietyr rides to her and leaps from the saddle. He takes her by the shoulders and presses his forehead against hers. 'Kat, thank the Goddess. I thought I had lost you. I thought you were lost in it.' He tugs gently, and she moans. 'You there,' he barks, and points to the soldiers and then her horse. 'Get him up! Get him off the queen!'

They roll him up, and he kicks out his front legs—he is not dead, after all—and Pietyr drags her out of the way.

'What happened?' he asks. 'Kat, are you truly all right?'

'They made me kill her,' she whispers as she braces against him and struggles to her feet. 'The fools. They used my hand and cut the legion curse loose.'

'Oh, Kat.' Pietyr holds her tight as the shock wears slowly off. She is cold, all over, and herself again, the dead queens gone, perhaps ashamed or perhaps merely sated by Madrigal's blood.

Katharine surveys the meadow and all her wet soldiers. Some lie dead, torn apart by the mist, and she is sure that many are missing. But most appear unharmed. Pietyr is unharmed.

Rho and twenty-five of her cavalry emerge from the trees.

Jules Milone and the rebels are gone. Even Madrigal's body is gone, dragged away in the chaos.

'My sister has returned,' Katharine says dazedly. 'Mirabella is alive.'

MOUNT HORN

'Aren't you glad we brought him now?' Arsinoe asks Billy as they ascend along a steep slope of icy rock, their hands buried in the warm fur of Braddock's rump.

'Yes.' He stretches his neck to get a view of something other than bear tail. 'You don't think the trail is becoming too narrow?'

'He'll let us know. He'll stop.'

'And how will we get around, then? How will he get down?'

Arsinoe squints as fat snowflakes start to fly by. 'We'll climb over the top of him and help him to back up. Is it hard to breathe? It seems harder to breathe.'

She sucks in cold air. They are far enough up the mountain that the air could truly be thinner, but she thinks it is only her nerves. They have been above the snow line for the better part of the morning, making slow progress. The cave cannot be much farther.

'I think I see it.' Billy jumps, and she grabs his arm to make sure he does not lose his balance and fall over the edge. 'We're almost there. Are you all right? You're looking green.'

'I don't know what it is about this place. I used to climb the high hills of Wolf Spring and look down all the time. But I think if I looked over the edge now I'd pass right out.'

'Don't look, then.' He presses her against the cliff face protectively. 'Just keep moving and focus on the bear behind.'

'It's hard to miss,' Arsinoe says, and he laughs.

They trudge along, and after what feels like an age, Arsinoe lifts her head to peek over Braddock. She does not see any sign of a cave, and the snow is falling harder, blotting everything out.

'I thought you said you saw it!'

'I thought I did!' He wipes his eyes free of ice and tries to look again. 'This mountain doesn't want us to— Whoops!'

Braddock turns into the cave so quickly that they both fall forward onto their hands. But they waste no time scrambling inside, and Billy digs the stash of firewood from his pack and lays it out, deep in the cave where the wind does not reach. He strikes a match with trembling fingers and touches it to the wood. It goes out.

'Oh, I wish Mira were here,' Billy grumbles, and Braddock seems to agree. He snuffles doubtfully at the fire and shakes snow from his back. 'Don't get the wood wet, you big oaf!'

'Billy!'

'You know I love him. But I'm freezing.' He strikes another match and another, until finally the curls of bark and kindling begin to catch. The cave brightens with a warm yellow glow, and they can see the length of it. The cave opening is large, plenty of room to sleep a bear and several people. It tapers to the rear until it disappears in shadow, far down into the depths of Mount Horn.

'All right,' Billy says as they huddle close to the fire warming their hands. 'What do we do now?'

Arsinoe walks farther into the cave. She listens to the hollow sound of her boots against the cave floor. Listens to the silence, and the lack of echoes. The way the wind dies and disappears. This cave is like the ancient clearing near the bent-over tree. It is like the chasm of the Breccia Domain. Another one of the many places on Fennbirn where the Goddess's eye is always open, though this is perhaps the greatest: stone stretched into the sky and struck deep in the earth, to press against the Goddess's pulse.

'This is the right place.'

After a time, they fall asleep beside the fire. Even the bear. Before Arsinoe drifts off, she murmurs, 'I'm here, Daphne.'

And Daphne is there as well, with something else to show her.

In the dream, Daphne stands before a mirror dressed all in black. The light from the candles is low, and she wears Queen Illiann's veil over her face. She holds two cups, and behind her, in the reflection, Arsinoe sees Duke Branden, seated on a bed.

I know what is in his cup. Daphne, what are you doing?

'Illy, what is taking so long?' Brandon asks, and Daphne

nearly spills the poison, her hands are shaking so badly.

They are in a room in the Volroy that Arsinoe has never seen before, and Daphne is dressed as the queen.

You're taking it into your own hands. Luring him off somewhere quiet, to kill him. Is this how Henry became king-consort? Was it all you?

Impatient, Brandon rises and comes to wrap his arms around her waist. 'We will be married soon.' Arsinoe's skin crawls. 'Could you not wait?'

Thankfully, Daphne twists out of his grasp. She steps quickly away and then turns, thrusting out the poisoned wine.

Well, that's not at all obvious. And to think the Arrons make it look so easy.

Branden hesitates. This was a foolish plan. He must suspect her, with her strange silence and trembling wrist. But then he sighs and takes the cup.

'A moment alone together,' he says. 'Before the ceremonies and the crowds.' He raises the cup to his lips, and Daphne and Arsinoe hold their breath.

'But that will be our life, I suppose,' he says without drinking. 'Or rather, your life that I am party to. No one has explained my duties as king, after all. Am I to oversee the servants? Manage certain accounts to the crown? Or is my only function to get you with child? Except that is not attributed to me either. Whatever grows in your belly is the fruit of your . . . Goddess.'

At the last word, something changes in his tone, and he looks at her and smiles.

He knows.

'Your first mistake was refusing to touch me,' he says. 'All Illiann does when we are alone is paw at me like a whore.'

'Don't call her that! Don't you ever call her that,' Daphne growls as he reaches out and yanks the veil from her face. But Branden does not respond. He simply sniffs the cup.

'Whatever it is it cannot be detected by scent. Far better than anything you Centrans could have crafted. So you must have gotten it from one of these heathens.'

He steps closer.

'What would it have done? Made me choke? Made blood pour from my eyes and nose?'

Daphne, run.

'Why don't we find out?'

Daphne shouts as he grips the back of her head and pushes the cup to her lips. She claws at him as the poison splashes against her neck and chin, and she and Arsinoe fight together in panic. It is a strange sensation, being so afraid of the poison. But in Daphne's body, Arsinoe may become the first poisoner to know what it feels like to die by it.

Is this what causes the war, then? Between the island and Salkades? Was it the murder of the queen's dear friend?

Arsinoe searches Branden's eyes and sees pure glee. Glee and something worse. Something near lust. The sight of it adds shame to her fear. An odd mix of shame and rage, that he would enjoy doing this to Daphne so much.

Inside the dream, Arsinoe twists and screams like she did before, trying to break it. She does not want to know. She does not want to live it. The cup that grinds against Daphne's teeth grinds against Arsinoe's. Branden's hands around Daphne's throat make it impossible for Arsinoe to breathe.

'You will drink it,' he barks into her face. 'You will drink it in the end!' His long fingers pry her lips apart, and he tips the poison to her mouth.

'Get away from her!' The shout came in tandem from Henry's and Illiann's throats. Startled, Branden lets go, and Daphne falls to her knees. She drags a pitcher down from the bedside table and splashes water against her face and neck, flushing out her mouth and spitting onto the floor.

'Get away from her,' Illiann orders as Henry draws his sword.

'Are you going to allow them to treat me this way, Illy? I am your chosen king.'

'King-consort,' she corrects. 'And perhaps you are not.'

'Illiann,' he says, his voice soft, cajoling. 'You don't understand.'

'I understand all,' she says. 'I am the queen.' She folds her hands atop her skirt. 'Lord Redville. Please escort the Duke of Bevanne down to the cells.'

'Don't be ridiculous. You cannot imprison me! I am not one of your subjects. My father and my cousin the king will never allow it.'

'I care not what the king of Salkades thinks of what I do on my island. Lord Redville, take him.'

Daphne and Arsinoe watch silently as Henry points his sword at Branden's chest.

'Don't struggle. It'll be better.'

'Very well.' Branden lowers his head and steps past Henry, but at the last moment, reaches for the iron beside the fire. He spins and swings it, landing a glancing blow across Henry's jaw.

Henry!

Blood runs from a deep cut, and Henry falls to the floor as Branden raises the iron over his head.

'No!' Daphne and Illiann scream, their hands out as if to stop the attack.

Arsinoe feels something explode from the center of her. A flow of heat and a sense of elation.

One moment Branden was about to bludgeon Henry to death, and the next, the fire had set him ablaze.

Henry scrambles away as Branden falls screaming to roll across the rug. The fire goes out quickly, perhaps with Illiann's help, but the damage is done.

'Send for a healer,' says Illiann, but Branden struggles to his feet, looking in horror at the burns across his arm and chest. He touches the black blisters on his face.

'Stay away from me, witch! Look what you've done! I'll see you all dead for it. Fennbirn and Centra together will burn!'

Arsinoe startles awake with a deep intake of breath. She is

herself again, lying on the stone floor of the deep, cold cave. The fire has burned down, but there is still light enough to see Billy and Braddock sleeping safely curled together.

She sits up and rubs her face, shaken from the dream, from the sensation of the poison running down her neck, and from the feel of Branden's hands around it. She gets to her feet and rummages in Billy's bag for another small piece of dry wood to add to the fire.

'Is that what you needed to say?' she whispers to the cave. 'Is that why you brought me here? To confess?'

'To confess what?' Billy asks groggily, up on one elbow.

'It was her fault,' Arsinoe replies. 'Daphne was the one who started the war between Fennbirn and Salkades.'

Something moves in the darkness at the rear of the cave, where it grows small and falls down into the heart of the mountain.

Billy scrambles back against Braddock, who wakes and lifts his head with a grunt.

'What was that?'

'I don't know,' Arsinoe says. Except that she does. She can see the shadow of the Blue Queen in her mind, scratching and dragging her way up the steep stone walls. She can see it so clearly that, when the ink-black arm slides around the rocks, she is not even surprised.

The shadow is just as hideous in the mountain as it was on the mainland. Elongated legs, thin bony fingers. The grotesque crown of silver and blue stones set atop her eyeless head.

'Is that her?' Billy asks breathlessly. 'The Blue Queen?'

'No. It has never really been the Blue Queen.' She takes one step, all that she can manage on shaking legs. 'It was your fault, wasn't it, Daphne?'

The shadow slips forward. Arsinoe stands her ground as its jaws strain open, stretching the blackness apart like rotten skin.

'Yes,' the shadow says through softened lips, her words thick and spoken with a swollen tongue. 'This was my doing. This and everything after. The war. The mist.' She looks down at herself. Long black fingers. A form that shifts like smoke. She reaches up to her face, and Arsinoe and Billy grimace as she pulls at the skin, tearing away strips of shadow to drop to the cave floor. She rakes down her arms, across her chest, until some semblance of Daphne shows through in a familiar inky eye and living skin.

'That night,' she goes on, her voice clearer and more the voice Arsinoe knows from the dreams, 'I changed everything. I made a true enemy of the Duke of Bevanne and in so doing made an enemy of Salkades. And I discovered who I really was.'

'A lost queen,' Arsinoe says. 'One of Illiann's sisters.'

'Yes. I was one of those sisters drowned or exposed or smothered by the Midwife. The other elemental queen, given a name I will never know. But it didn't matter. To Illiann and Henry, I was only Daphne.'

Daphne moves closer to the fire, picking off bits of shadow

like scabs. 'She kept my secret after we discovered it that night. She even helped me develop my gift. She wasn't driven to kill me like the old stories say. Not any more than you were.

'I didn't believe her at first. In Centra, kings made overtures of mercy often, only to change their minds on a whim and put their rival's head to the block. But Illiann was different.'

'Daphne,' Arsinoe says. 'Why did you want us to come here?'

Daphne stares soberly into the fire. She pulls a long strip of shadow from her neck and drops it into the flames to sizzle.

'The mist is rising against the island,' she says. 'I would show you how to stop it. Because its creation was my fault.'

THE FATE OF THE BLUE QUEEN

It is strange to see Daphne outside of the dreams, a dead queen half-covered in shadow. And older. This Daphne is a full-grown woman. Her hair is long and lines lightly crease her face.

'Your boy is handsome,' she says, looking at Billy as he stands protectively in front of the bear. 'He reminds me of my Henry.'

'Henry Redville,' Arsinoe says. 'The king-consort of Queen Illiann.'

'The king-consort of the Blue Queen,' Daphne corrects her.

'What does that mean? What do we do about the mist? How do we keep it from rising?'

With every new question, Daphne shakes her head. 'No.'

Arsinoe's eyes narrow. She must remember that the Daphne before her is not the Daphne from her dreams. This Daphne has been long dead, and Arsinoe must remember that she knows her not at all.

'Why did you send me the dreams? Why did you show me your life?'

'So you would know us. So you would love us. To call you home.'

'Is that what you want? For one of us to come home to take the crown from Katharine?'

'A queen crowned cannot be uncrowned,' Daphne replies.

Arsinoe nods to the silver and blue stones. 'Then how did you come to wear Illiann's?'

Daphne grimaces, baring teeth that are still tipped in shadow.

'Don't,' Billy murmurs. 'Don't make her angry.'

'I'll make her whatever I need to make her to learn what we came for. People are dying. The mist is killing them. And if she won't speak, maybe we ought to be talking to Illiann.'

Daphne rounds on her and despite her irritation, Arsinoe gasps.

'You can't talk to Illiann,' Daphne says, crooked finger pointed to Arsinoe's chest.

'Why not?'

'Because Illiann is not Illiann. Illiann is the mist.'

'You mean she made the mist,' Arsinoe says.

'No. I mean she *became* it.'

Became the mist? Arsinoe blinks. 'That couldn't be. It had to be some kind of spell. Some elemental trick—'

Daphne springs forward, elongated fingers wrapped around the sides of Arsinoe's head. 'No tricks,' she hisses, and presses her thumbs over Arsinoe's eyes.

'Let go of her!' Billy shouts, and Braddock roars and swipes his paw furiously. But the fire flares up like a wall, burning them both and sending them reeling backward out into the snow. Even long dead, the elemental is still an elemental.

Arsinoe squeals and squirms. But Daphne's cold grip is like a vise.

'See,' Daphne whispers, and shakes her hard, sending a jolt through Arsinoe's entire body. And Arsinoe sees.

Daphne and Illiann stand atop the cliffs over Bardon Harbor in the driving rain. It is night, but the waves are lit bright orange and yellow by the fires in the burning boats. Some torched, others struck by Illiann's lightning. Farther out, the sea is dark, but each illuminating flash reveals the horror of the battle: Selkan ships like a swarm upon the waves.

'There are too many!' Daphne shouts over the thunder. 'Too many here, too many in Rolanth.' Salkades has besieged the entire eastern side of the island. Fennbirn will be overrun.

All this, Arsinoe sees in flashes. As she struggles against the shadow queen, she sees the ships and feels the rain sting her cheeks.

'My storm is not done yet,' Illiann calls. 'I can roll them under the waves. All of them.'

'You can't,' Daphne cries. 'Henry is out there!'

Arsinoe twists her arm up between her and Daphne's chests and wrenches it down hard, forcing Daphne to let go.

'Stop!' Arsinoe strikes out blindly with her fists. 'Just stop!'

But Daphne leaps on her again, cold hands pressed to her ears, over her eyes, leaking into her mind.

Illiann falls from the cliffs, screaming, her storm still surging over the harbor. She falls, down to break upon the rocks, but when she does, her body is lost to the white. To the mist that bursts out from the foot of the cliffs and across the sea, to spread across the water north and south, choking the invaders as Illiann would have done with her own waves.

'There is no place on the island for sisters,' Daphne says, still clutching her. 'We tried, she and I, but we failed. My elemental sister had to die to create the mist.' She releases Arsinoe's head and drags her close by the collar. 'And yours must die to unmake it.'

Arsinoe shoves her away. 'No. You're lying. Queen Illiann ruled for decades more. She had the next triplets.'

'*I* had the next triplets,' Daphne says, her eyes ablaze. 'I stepped into her life. Stepped into her crown, with Henry by my side. "Daphne" died at sea, in the battle. And out of grief, the queen was not seen publicly for a long time. Or at least not without a veil.'

'No. Someone had to know.'

'Many knew. But Fennbirn needed a queen. And soon the island's secrets are lost to time. Like my real name.'

Arsinoe trembles, sick from the sight of Illiann falling to her death and from the thought that Mirabella—

'There has to be another way.' Except there does not and wanting one will not make it so.

'Now you know why I did not call to Mirabella.'

'Don't you say her name,' Arsinoe growls. 'And stay away from me! You're a liar! You're a murderer!'

'Murderer—?'

She advances on Daphne, her anger driving back the fear, and Daphne retreats farther into the cave. Farther and farther, and every shadow she steps into clings to her skin until she is back in the dark. Grotesque once more.

'We aren't like you, me and my sister! And for the island or not, I will never hurt her!'

'Arsinoe? Are you all right?'

She looks back. With Daphne gone, the fire has died, and Billy and Braddock stare at her from the cave entrance.

'What did you hear?' she asks.

'Everything.'

'Then you know it was nonsense.' She goes back to the fire and gathers their supplies. 'Let's just get back to Sunpool.'

INNISFUIL VALLEY

'Mirabella has returned,' says Katharine, once she and Pietyr are inside the relative safety of her tent. 'And if she is here, it is a sure bet that Arsinoe is lurking somewhere as well.'

'It does not matter, Kat. They are defectors. Traitors. You are the Queen Crowned. The people will fight for you; they will never follow them—'

Katharine scoffs. 'The same way they would never follow a naturalist with the legion curse? They will follow anyone if it means the end of me.'

In the camp, the queensguard searches for survivors of the mist. They are good soldiers and shed themselves quickly of their fear, righting tents and catching horses. Rho has not stopped barking orders since she returned the queen to her quarters.

Katharine peeks through the tent flap. 'So many dead.' She hugs herself tightly. 'I just wanted to be a good queen.'

'Oh, Kat.' Pietyr takes her in his arms. 'You are a good queen. All you have done is your duty, and it is neither right nor fair that you should be hated for it.'

'Hated,' she whispers. 'And feared.' Slowly, she strips her gloves from her hands and flexes her fingers. They are alive. Covered in scars but alive, and hers again. 'The dead queens wielded the knife that cut the legion curse from Madrigal Milone. This was as much their fault as the mist's.' She drops her hands. 'And it was mine, for not listening to you sooner. For not trying harder to control them.'

The tent flap bursts open, around High Priestess Luca. Unharmed by the mist and unruffled as ever.

'A moment of the queen's time?'

'Of course, High Priestess.' Pietyr walks to the table for a cup of poisoned wine. 'How pleased we are to see you have survived the spread of the mist.'

The old woman's mouth twists wryly. 'No doubt just as pleased as you are about certain other survivals.'

'What do you want?' Katharine asks. 'To turn in your council seat? Change sides again and run back to your precious Mirabella?'

Luca stares at the crown inked into Katharine's forehead. How bitterly she must regret placing it there. But place it she did.

'A queen once crowned,' Luca says, 'is crowned forever.'

'So you mean to stay? You will not join the temple to the rebellion?'

'The temple would never join with a rebellion,' Luca snaps. 'Not with a rogue queen at its head and certainly not with one who is legion cursed. I will serve on the Black Council for as long as is Queen Katharine's pleasure.' She folds her hands over her white robes. 'But I have come to speak to you about Mirabella.'

'High Priestess, my soldiers are routed. Many wounded or still missing. We are fighting a war on two fronts already, with the naturalist and with the very mist itself. So as much as it might displease her, my sister may just have to wait.'

Luca sighs and glances at Pietyr. 'Is there any wine in this tent that is not tainted?'

'Of course.' He reaches for a cup and pours from a green bottle. 'Here you are.'

'Thank you.' She sips and turns to Katharine. 'Do not think of your sisters and the rebels as separate problems. They are one and the same. Traitors or not, with both of them standing beside Jules Milone, the Legion Queen's rebellion is too strong. It will gain more support. Maybe even enough to take Indrid Down.'

'So what do we do? I will kill them both, as is my right. But when? Not now in the middle of—'

'I would suggest another course,' Luca says. 'Consider why Mirabella would support Jules Milone? She is a queen in the blood. She, even more than most, understands that the crown cannot be worn by just anyone.'

'She supports the naturalist because Arsinoe supports

the naturalist,' Pietyr says, and Luca nods, her eyes full of meaning. 'But you think she is unconvinced.'

Luca takes a large swallow from her cup and walks around them to refill it. 'I know my Mira. I raised her. What Natalia Arron was to you, Katharine, I was to her. And she would not in good conscience support the wresting of a crown from a rightful queen.'

'And in her eyes, I am a rightful queen?'

'She and Arsinoe fled,' Luca says. 'Abdicated. If not you, then who else?'

'Even if she does feel that way,' Pietyr interjects. 'What of it? She stands with the rebels.' He narrows his eyes. 'You think she can be brought over.'

'No.' Katharine glares at her. 'Never.'

'Do not be so quick to dismiss the idea,' says Luca. 'I have done what I can with the temple, to restore the faith of the people in the Goddess and her rightful queen, but it is not enough. If Jules Milone is seen to have the backing of both of the other queens, you will not win this war.'

Katharine clenches her jaw. She grasps her wrists and rubs at them through her gloves. 'I felt the blast of that legion-cursed gift. I may not win either way.'

'What are you truly suggesting, High Priestess?' Pietyr asks with disgust. 'That Katharine extend an invitation to Mirabella? To rule together, side by side?'

'Of course not. I am asking that the queen allow her sister to return and fight for her, as a loyal subject and ally.'

'You will never get her to submit to that,' he spits, but old Luca only smiles.

'I will get her to agree. But I do not have much time. I ask for your permission.' She looks to Katharine.

Mirabella returned. And still so regal, so arrogant in those mainlander clothes. She could never be loyal. Never be trusted. But it is worth a try.

'I will welcome my sister back with open arms,' Katharine says. 'In exchange for her allegiance.'

The High Priestess bows; she takes Katharine's hands and kisses them.

'How will you find her?'

'I have my ways,' says Luca. 'But I must hurry before those ways are too far off to catch up with.' She smiles at them again and ducks out of the tent.

'For someone so old, she is certainly quick.' Pietyr sets his cup down and refills it for a third time. 'Maybe she is lying about her years.' He takes a swallow and pauses. 'Welcoming another queen into the capital, with no threat of death over her head . . . Katharine, this has never been done.'

'Many things we have done have never been done,' she replies. 'This one gives me hope.'

'Hope?'

Katharine lifts her scarred hand and clenches it in a shaking fist. The dead queens know what she is thinking. She can feel their fear and their anger and their dead fingers clutching at her to soothe and plead.

You made me kill Madrigal Milone. You loosed the curse, the one thing I did not want to do.

They say that they are sorry. They promise to be calm. But she is not angry with them. They cannot help being what they are.

You will be at peace, dead sisters. You have done what you set out to do. And with you gone, perhaps the mist will quiet. With you gone, perhaps all will be well.

Katharine looks at Pietyr, eyes shining. 'If Mirabella will fight for me, then I will have need of no one else. I can put the dead sisters to rest.'

'Katharine. Are you certain?'

'I am.'

He smiles and sighs a sigh that relaxes his whole form. 'I am proud of you, Kat. And I think I have found a way.'

THE WESTERN WOODS

Mirabella is only a few miles into the woods, retreating after Emilia and the other rebels, who have rushed ahead carrying an unconscious Jules, when Pepper flies past her.

'Pepper,' she gasps, and stops.

The little bird flits from her shoulder to a tree and back again, all the while making high-pitched, piping calls. Mirabella looks around just in time to see them come through the trees on the back of an unsaddled horse.

'Bree! Elizabeth!' she cries, and they dismount and run. When they crash into her, she catches one in each arm and immediately begins to weep. 'What are you doing here?'

'I am on her council.' Bree gasps and buries her face in Mirabella's hair. Poor Elizabeth cannot even speak. All she can manage are tiny squeaks in between great heaving sobs, the squeaks not too dissimilar to her woodpecker's.

'Calm, Elizabeth.'

'Can't be calm. Mira!' She grins, face wet. 'I might vomit.'

Mirabella and Bree laugh. 'Take slow, deep breaths. You should not have followed me.'

'How could we not?' Bree asks. 'When we saw you . . . Everyone said you were dead, but I knew it could not be. Not the way they told it. Not in a storm.'

'But it almost was.' She smooths Bree's hair back from her cheek. So beautiful, still. And somehow, she seems to have grown. The Bree she remembered did not have such somber eyes, did not own such an austere gray-blue dress.

'Now I know what Pepper was trying so hard to tell me,' says Elizabeth, her breath lighter. 'He found you, didn't he? He saw you when he brought word to the rebels.'

'He flew into me so hard his beak tore my clothes.'

'And what clothes they are,' says Bree, stepping back to study her. 'A far cry from island black.'

'Who cares?' Elizabeth says. 'We have trunks and trunks of it to change her into. You are back, aren't you, Mira? Back for good?'

'That is an excellent question.'

Bree and Elizabeth twist in her arms—as Luca appears through the trees on a tall white mare.

'They were so desperate to see you,' she says, 'that they did not turn around to see if they were being followed.'

'I am sorry, Mira.' Bree takes her hand. 'We were not careful.'

Elizabeth steps in front of them and throws out her arms.

'Stay away from her, High Priestess! Please!'

Luca's brows raise. 'Such dramatics. I am not here to hurt her.'

'Why should we believe that,' Bree growls, 'when you were ready to have her executed?'

Mirabella wipes her cheeks and forces herself to stare at Luca. At the woman who she had once thought to be her greatest protector. Luca's eyes are soft as they travel over her face. Soft near to trembling, and Mirabella feels the same old urge: to take Luca's hands, to help her walk, to find her someplace comfortable to take her ease. But all of that is over.

'What do you want, Luca?'

'To speak to you,' she says. 'Only to speak to you.'

'Very well.'

Luca nods gently to Bree and Elizabeth. 'You girls should return to camp before you are missed.'

'No.' They grasp Mirabella by the sleeves. 'We can't go so soon,' Elizabeth cries. 'Will we see you again?'

Mirabella touches each of their cheeks. 'I do not know. I do not mean to stay.' She pulls them in, holds them tight. 'But she is right. You should go now and be safe.'

'No,' Bree says. 'We will wait for her just beyond those trees. Where we cannot overhear but will still see if she tries anything. Come, Elizabeth.' They go, but reluctantly, fingers trailing along Mirabella's hands and their eyes stuck solidly to Luca.

'They love you very much, those girls,' Luca says

when they are a safe distance away.

'Do not say you love me, too. Or I will call a thunderbolt down on your head.'

'I would prefer a water spirit, if it is all the same to you. Like the first time we met.'

'Stop it, Luca. You cannot fool me anymore. What do you want?'

'I want you to come home.' She gathers her reins and leans against the pommel of her saddle. 'I have spoken to the queen, and she will welcome you, if you turn away from the rebellion and put your support behind the crown.'

Mirabella blinks. What madness is this? Such that she cannot even muster a laugh.

'The people cannot see this rebellion as a rebellion of queen against queen,' Luca goes on. 'If they do, with you and Arsinoe on one side and Katharine on the other, Queen Katharine will lose. But with you beside the crown, they will see the rebellion for what it really is: a doomed enterprise led by an abomination.'

'What about Arsinoe?' Mirabella asks. 'She is a queen as well. And she will never leave Jules.'

'With you and Katharine standing together, Arsinoe will not matter. She has never mattered.'

'She matters to me,' Mirabella says, but the High Priestess does not respond. 'And you believe her? You believe Katharine, that she will not have me executed? When we last met, she did not seem the kind of queen who was partial to mercy.'

'That was the Ascension.' Luca straightens as her horse

paws, made nervous by the current in the air. 'She is the Queen Crowned now. And she is a good one. Bree is on her council, as well as Rho and I.'

'A council seat. Is that what it took for you to stand by while she poisoned me before the capital? Is that all it took?'

'You would not fight,' Luca says, her anger showing. 'I blame *you* for that. Though it still would have broken me to see you die and not be able to save you. But I would have done it for the island. It would have been my duty. As it is still yours.'

Mirabella shakes her head. 'I am not a queen anymore. Nor is Arsinoe. You have my word that I will not interfere in this island business. But that is all I will give. Katharine will have to fight her own battles.'

'Fight her own battles? They are Fennbirn's battles. You saw the mist; you saw what she faces. And you saw, too, the legion curse at work. The monster the rebels would put on the throne.'

'Jules Milone is no monster!'

'Her own people had to knock her unconscious. Perhaps once, she was able to control it. But now that the curse is unbound, her mind will not be spared. You have been brought back for a reason.'

'Arsinoe was brought back for a reason. And when that is known, we are leaving. The island let us go. She will not have us again.' She half turns away. 'Go back now, Luca, and try to save your queen.'

'You cannot just shed your responsibilities.' Luca looks over her mainlander clothes. 'You cannot put on a costume and become something else. You are a queen of Fennbirn island. A queen of the line, whether you have turned your back on the Goddess or not.'

Mirabella steels her heart and walks away. Even after all that has passed between them, it is difficult to go. Past one tree and then the next, farther and farther from Bree. From Elizabeth. Part of her wants to stop and spend more time arguing. To let Luca try to change her mind.

'Arsinoe will never turn against Jules,' she calls out. 'And I will never turn against Arsinoe. She is my sister. I love her.'

'I know that,' Luca calls back. 'But I think you are forgetting that once you loved them both.'

SUNPOOL

Arsinoe pauses for a brief rest on the top of a mossy rise. Just beyond, not more than an hour's jog, is Sunpool.

'Finally.' Billy stops beside her and leans down, hands braced against his knees. 'I didn't know how much longer I could keep up that pace.'

Arsinoe shields her eyes and peers at the city, wondering if Jules and Mirabella have returned.

'They'll be all right,' Billy says. 'I've never known one as tough as Jules, and with Mira there . . . they were safer than we were scaling the mountain. You'll see.'

Arsinoe nods and gets moving again, the jog easy as they go downhill. Braddock is no longer with them; they said goodbye at the edge of the woods.

Sunpool's gates stand open as the rebels continue to welcome new arrivals, but the stream of them has slowed. The moment she is inside, she knows that something is different.

'They're staring at you,' Billy says as Arsinoe tucks her

scarf up tight over her scars. Every pair of eyes in the square seems to be watching with solemn curiosity. 'Why?'

'I don't know,' she says as they hurry toward the castle. 'But somehow, I get the feeling that I could have brought Braddock.'

When they reach the castle, they are allowed inside without escort, and the ball of worry that has hovered in Arsinoe's stomach since leaving the cave grows heavier. When she hears the cries and shouting, it goes cold.

'What is that?' she asks, and takes the stairs by two. She finds Emilia and Mathilde in a room on one of the upper floors, pacing before a closed door. Camden is standing up against the wood, mewling miserably.

'Emilia? What's going on? What's wrong with Camden?' Arsinoe bounds inside, and Emilia thrusts a finger into her chest. But before she can utter anything aside from a growl, Mathilde drags her off. 'Mathilde, who's in there?'

'Jules is in there.'

'Why—'

'The legion curse has come unbound. Madrigal is dead. Killed by Katharine. And Jules . . .' She stops and lets Arsinoe listen to the sounds coming from behind the door. Screams. Guttural bellows. The impact of objects striking the walls hard enough to rattle them. And the terrible, terrible sound of fingernails dragging against the stone.

'You should let the cat go in with her,' Arsinoe says numbly.

'She will hurt the cat. They will hurt each other.'

That cannot be true. Slowly, Arsinoe walks toward the cougar. Jules and Camden are joined. They would never—

She shouts as Camden turns and attacks, raking claws across Arsinoe's hand. The blood comes fast and spatters across the floor.

Billy and Mathilde drag her back, and he takes out a handkerchief and presses it to the cuts.

Arsinoe stars at the cat in disbelief as Camden hisses and spits.

'What's wrong with her?' Billy asks.

'The curse. It is affecting her, too.'

'You, poisoner,' Emilia snaps. 'You must calm them.'

'How?'

'There must be some tonic, some sedative. You must make it.'

'I'm not that kind of a poisoner,' Arsinoe says, but even as the words leave her mouth, her mind returns to the pages of the book of poisons she borrowed from Luke's shop.

'You must be of some use!' Emilia shouts.

Billy steps between them. 'You quiet down. If there's anything Arsinoe can do, she'll do it. But she doesn't need your barking and threats. Where's Mirabella?'

Emilia bares her teeth. She could skewer Billy like a cube of goat meat, but he does not waver. 'Probably wandering the streets, basking in the adoration of the people. She showed herself during the attack. The queens' secret is out. So you may as well lose that ridiculous scarf. Not that it was doing much anyway.'

Arsinoe turns to Mathilde. 'Are there still healer's stores here in the castle?'

'No. But there is a shop in the marketplace. I will take you.'

The shop is not far. Mathilde takes Arsinoe and Billy to it and gently moves the old proprietor to the side of the counter. Both she and Arsinoe frown when he bows.

'Old habits,' Arsinoe mutters, and then she gets to work, gathering bowls and ingredients with her uninjured hand, her mind focused and relaxed, so confident in the movements that it is almost like watching someone else navigate her body.

'Do you know what you're doing?' Billy whispers.

Arsinoe shrugs. 'Seem to.' She opens a jar and sniffs. Elder flower. Not what she needs, but it does remind her to set Billy aside near the shopkeep. Most of the stock will be for healing, but some jars are bound to contain true poisons.

She pauses a moment and chews a fingernail, thinking of how best to administer the sedative. A salve perhaps? Something to rub into the skin? Though who was to say she would be able to get close enough to do the rubbing. Something to load into a dart, then? Or to coat the edge of a blade?

'No,' she murmurs. No matter what condition Jules is in, the thought of shooting her or cutting her makes Arsinoe sick to her stomach.

'Down the hatch it is,' she says, and begins. She grabs bundles of pale skullcap and strips the petals. Grinds root of valerian into a paste. Pushes the whole mess through a sieve with oil made from betel nut. At the last moment, she squeezes her fist, letting several thick droplets of blood fall from Camden's scratches into the oil. 'I need to thin it out with liquor.'

'A sedation?' The shopkeep nods and fetches a bottle down from a shelf. 'Try this and a little sugar. Helps it go down.'

She uncorks the bottle and sniffs. It smells like Grandma Cait's terrible anise cookies.

'That'll do.' She pours it into the bowl and adds sugar, then transfers the mixture into a bottle and caps it. 'Are you a poisoner, shopkeep?'

'No, my queen. I'm of no particular gift. Where did you learn the craft, if I may ask? Not many poisoners down in Wolf Spring.'

'I learned it nowhere, I guess.'

'So it's true you are a poisoner, then. There was rumor after the Ascension that you had been a poisoner in naturalist garb.' He nods knowingly. 'Amongst the healers, we hoped it was so. That maybe there had risen a poisoner somewhere who could be something other than wicked and corrupt.'

'I'm still no queen.' Arsinoe tucks the bottle into her sleeve. 'But I thank you for the use of your shop.'

By the time they return to the castle, to Emilia guarding the locked door, they are out of breath.

'I thought you would never arrive.'

'Was it so long?' Arsinoe asks as Emilia picks up the end of a rope. The rope is attached to a noose that she has managed to loop around Camden's neck. 'That can't have been easy.'

'Or safe,' Billy adds.

'The hard part comes now,' Emilia says, looping the length of rope around her hand. 'Are you ready?'

'Should you—' Billy takes her arm. 'Should you really go in there alone? I know it's Jules, but . . . it doesn't sound like Jules.'

'It will in a few minutes.' Arsinoe pulls out the bottle of greenish liquid. 'All right, Emilia.'

'Pay no attention to her eyes,' Emilia says gravely. 'It is only broken blood vessels.'

Arsinoe heads for the door, and Emilia jerks back on the rope. The sight of poor Camden struggling at the end of it, snarling and charging, reaching with her claws, makes her want to weep.

She turns the key in the lock and slips inside, closing it up and locking it tight again. Then she stops. And listens. Her belly pressed to the wall.

'Jules. It's me.' She cannot hear anything. The screaming and crashing, even Camden's struggles outside have stopped. She cannot even hear Jules breathing.

'Arsinoe.'

'Yes.' She sighs and turns around. 'Thank the Goddess, Jules—' The plank of wood flies straight for her throat. She dives and hits the floor hard, covering her head and sliding through debris. Every piece of furniture is broken, bashed into pieces and strewn about, the remains so small that she cannot tell whether she is looking at what is left of a bed or a chair or a table.

And pressed against the opposite wall is Jules. They have managed to bind her arms and legs with heavy chain. Twisted and on the floor, small as always, she does not look a threat. Except for the hatred on her face and her bloodred eyes.

Only the burst vessels, Arsinoe thinks. But if it is, she has burst every one. Not a speck of white remains. Just pure, bright red, her pretty blue and green irises set in the centers like gems.

'Arsinoe, help me.'

'That's what I'm here to do, Jules.'

'Help me!' she screams, and Arsinoe is blown back. Her head strikes against the stones hard enough to bounce, and her vision wavers. Using every ounce of courage, she scrambles across the floor and grasps Jules by the neck. She wraps her legs around her, too, and pulls out the bottle.

'This will not taste good,' she says, and forces it between Jules's teeth, pink with blood. It takes Arsinoe a moment to realize that Jules has bitten part of her own lips off.

'Oh, Jules,' she whispers, and squeezes her tight. When the bottle is empty, she hooks both arms around Jules's chest and hangs on as she convulses. By the time it is over, Arsinoe is weeping harder than she has ever wept in her life, but Jules's eyes are closed. She is asleep.

The door to the room opens, and Camden bounds inside to lie beside Jules and lick her face. She licks Arsinoe's hand, too, and grunts at her, as though ashamed.

'It's all right, cat.'

'It worked,' she says to Billy at the door between Emilia and Mathilde.

'We know. Camden stopped fighting. Just all of a sudden, she stopped fighting the rope.'

Emilia shoves her way inside, wiping tears from her face and neck. She takes Jules from Arsinoe and nestles her onto her lap.

'Don't take off the chains,' Arsinoe says. She starts to get up, and Emilia grasps her by the wrist.

'Thank you, Arsinoe.'

'You're welcome.'

'Even if she didn't do it for you,' Billy says, and puts his arm around Arsinoe's shoulders as they leave. 'Are you all right? She didn't hurt you?'

'No.' She kisses his fingers. 'But I need to go and find my sister.'

'Of course. I'll . . . stay here. Keep an eye on Jules for you.'

She finds Mirabella in the rear cloister, seated on a stone bench with a cloth of cheese and bread. Daphne's words echo through her mind. *My elemental sister had to die to make the mist. And yours must die to unmake it.*

'Arsinoe!' Mirabella sees her and comes quickly. 'You are safe! And Billy?'

'He's fine. Braddock, too. We brought him along.'

'To Sunpool?'

'No. To the mountain.' She presses her hand to her temple. She is exhausted, and still there is more to do. Find a way to ease Jules's legion curse. Inform the people of Sunpool not to hunt for bear in the nearby woods. And kill her sister. 'No,' she whispers. 'Never. Not even for the entire island.'

'What for the entire island?'

Mirabella leads her back to the bench and they sit. She stuffs bread and cheese into Arsinoe's hands. How Arsinoe would like to tell her what Daphne said, if only to promise that they will find another way. But until she finds one, she thinks it is best not to.

'Have you seen Jules?' Mirabella asks. 'Is she still . . . ?'

'I crafted a tonic. A sedative. She's resting now.'

'Good,' Mirabella says. 'I knew she would be fine.'

'She's not fine. She's not better.' Arsinoe starts to cry again, and Mirabella pulls her close. 'I don't know what to do.' Arsinoe gasps. 'She's not even Jules: her eyes are full of blood. She doesn't even know me.'

Mirabella rocks her gently, and Arsinoe clings to her.

'Everything is going wrong, Mira, and I don't know what to do.'

'No, no, no,' Emilia says to the people gathered in the street before the castle. 'Our Legion Queen is well. She was injured in the attack by Katharine the Undead but only slightly. She is shut up now in grief for her mother, who was murdered by the Undead Queen herself.'

'And what of the elemental? The naturalist?'

'They have long been allies of Juillenne Milone. But they have abdicated, and that abdication stands. Be patient, friends, and be ready. Continue your work. They have struck first blood, but we shall have answer for it soon enough.'

Mirabella watches from behind the cracked open door. When Emilia comes back inside, she jumps at the sight of her in the shadows.

'They strip us of our proper title,' Mirabella says. 'The elemental? The naturalist? Do we not even have names anymore?'

'No names that matter. No titles of importance. Isn't that the way you wanted it?' Emilia stalks deeper into the fortress, her gait fast and lithe but no trouble for Mirabella to keep up with.

'It is. It is only strange to hear. You are a very fine orator. No doubt you had plenty of practice, spreading the legend these past months.'

'Was there something you wanted, Mirabella? I am very busy, as you can see. Walls to fortify. Grain to unload. And this afternoon, the queen's mother to burn.'

'But Jules is not yet out of her room. You would burn Madrigal before she is well enough to say a proper goodbye?'

Emilia stops. She turns and presses Mirabella backward, down into a shadowy corridor until her back is against the stones, and Emilia's hand is hot on her shoulder.

'Out with it, then,' Emilia snaps.

'I want to know what your plans are now.'

'Now what?'

'Now that everything is changed. Jules is . . . unwell. I have not been able to speak to my sister for days because all she has done is concoct more potions and tonics to help her. Yet you tell these people—who risk their lives and have left their homes—that she is unhurt and in mourning?'

'Jules will be fine. She will be our queen.'

'Perhaps once,' Mirabella hisses. 'But you and I both saw what we saw at Innisfuil. You cannot put that on the throne. Let us take her away to the mainland. The curse may be eased, away from the island.'

'No.' Emilia presses a finger to Mirabella's chest. 'Your sister would never allow it.'

'Arsinoe will do anything that might help.'

'And what of the mist? Since the day the temple took you, they have said that you were for the island. Its great protector. Will you leave us to it after what we both saw?'

'But when did the mist start to rise, Emilia? Was it the moment Katharine stepped into the crown? Or was it weeks and weeks later, when you sought to elevate Jules above her station?'

Emilia bares her teeth, and Mirabella braces for anything: a strike to the head or an unseen blade slipped between her ribs. But in the end, the warrior merely spits on the ground and walks away, and Mirabella lets out her breath.

It takes a few moments to collect herself before she can go up to the room they have designated as hers. It was meant to be shared with Arsinoe, but since she returned from the mountain, Arsinoe has not slept there, if she has slept at all.

She turns her head at a knock, and Billy pokes his head in.

'Have you seen Arsinoe? She's not with Jules.'

'No. And even when I seek her out, she does not want to see me. Has she . . . Is she angry with me because of what I let happen to Jules?'

'Of course not. What happened to Jules was not your fault. She's relieved that you're safe. It'll be better once Jules is better.' He smiles, covering up the words that echo through both of their heads.

But we are not leaving anytime soon.

'Do you need anything?' he asks.

'No. Thank you.'

He closes the door, and Mirabella hears a familiar trill come from the window.

'Pepper.'

The little woodpecker flies from the stone sill to her shoulder and pokes a bit at her hair. Then he sticks out his leg. Another note has been tied to him, this time labeled with an M in familiar scrawling script. She unrolls it and reads.

We have spoken with the queen, and we too believe she is true. We have departed for Indrid Down. The decision is yours, but we will be here if you need us.
-B&E

Mirabella takes a deep breath. She strokes the wood-pecker's chest feathers. Then she sets the message down, unrolled, upon the table.

GREAVESDRAKE MANOR

Pietyr lays the stones he took from the Breccia Domain onto the floor of Katharine's old bedroom, inside the circle of thin rope he has soaked with his own blood.

'The rope looks so fragile,' says Katharine as another stone knocks hollowly against the wood.

'It should not matter. That it is joined from end to end is what is important.' He had been soaking and staining it little by little, day by day, until the entire length was crimson and brown. Stiff to the touch. He has little more blood to spare, but spare he must when he reopens the rune that Madrigal carved into his palm.

Katharine wanders toward the windows. Her hand slips over the back of the sofa and over the desk. All her old, childhood things.

'Do you think Mirabella is on her way to me?' she asks softly.

'I do not know, Kat.'

'Do you think if she comes, Arsinoe might come, too? That they might stand behind me, united?'

'I do not know, Kat.'

Pietyr steps back, surveying his work. He wishes bitterly that Madrigal had not died. He does not know what he is doing. Perhaps she lied to him, and he is not doing anything at all. Katharine cocks her head at his crude circle, the ends of the rope set apart to allow them to step inside.

'Is that it?'

'Seems to be. Do you feel anything?'

Katharine rubs her arms and grimaces. 'Only for the stones. They do not like them. They do not want them here.'

He looks at her. Fetching and queenly in black riding breeches, a smart black jacket, ready to do as he instructs.

'Do you trust me, Kat?'

She looks up at him in surprise. 'Of course I do.'

'Even after . . .' he says, and looks down in shame.

'Even after,' she says, and smiles. Her smile, not the dead queens'. They were his doing—he was the one who pushed her down and let them in—but now he will make it right. He holds out his hand and leads her inside the circle. When he joins the ends of the rope, he thinks he feels something ripple through the room. Some slight shift in the air. Then it disappears, and he is not sure.

Perhaps he should have chosen another place to perform the ritual. The temple, perhaps, before the Goddess Stone. Or somewhere on the grounds of the Volroy. Sacred spaces.

But Madrigal never mentioned any particular place, and Greavesdrake was somewhere private, where they would not be interrupted. The place where they first met. And to Katharine, the place that still feels the most like home. Greavesdrake has been the seat of Arron power for a hundred years. It must be good enough.

'Will it hurt, Pietyr?' she whispers.

'I think so.' He shows her the rune cut into his palm. 'You are not afraid of that?'

She shakes her head, but her eyes are full of fear, even as she keeps her voice resolute.

'After that boy by the harbor,' she murmurs. 'After Madrigal. We have no choice.'

He bends down to kiss her hand and slides a blade from his belt.

The first cut is the hardest. Seeing her pale skin split and the red run through her fingers. But he works quickly, and she makes not a sound, the room so quiet that he can hear the first drops strike the floor.

With her rune complete, he releases her wrist and turns to his own. Cutting through the scabs burns and he bites his lip, but though he cuts, not enough blood comes. The strength of his poisoner gift has healed them too well, and he will have to cut deeper.

'Pietyr,' Katharine says. 'I feel strange.'

'Strange?' he asks, and she falls to her knees.

'Katharine!'

He falls beside her and holds up her arm. Dark veins stand beneath the skin, and the blood that pours out of her is less red than burgundy.

'They are afraid. They do not want to leave me.'

'Do not listen to them.' He cups her cheek and nearly recoils at the gray rot spread across her face. 'They are only fighting,' he says, but in his mind, he remembers Madrigal's warning.

Surely you must've considered that she may not be alive at all, except for them. She may truly be undead, and the moment she is emptied of the last of the queens, her body will break and shrivel up. Just like it would have had they not intervened in the first place.

'I am with you, Kat. You will be fine.'

Katharine screams and doubles over, and he presses his cut rune against hers, locking their hands together. The shock that goes through him sends him onto his back. And one of the Breccia stones rolls out of the circle.

'Pietyr, it hurts.'

'Hold on, Kat.' He grinds his teeth. Her blood splashes darkly onto the stones, and her screams fill the room. Another shock passes through him as the queens scratch for purchase inside Katharine, and his leg jerks, sending another stone rolling. He squeezes his eyes shut.

'So cold,' Katharine moans.

'You do not need them. Hold on.'

'I can't.'

'You can.'

'I won't.'

He opens his eyes as she lets go of his hand.

'Katharine?'

Every bit of exposed skin is gray and mottled black: the dead queens risen to the surface. He pushes himself up onto his elbows as she licks clean the wound in her hand and kicks the stones aside, clacking them together like marbles. Perhaps he did not know enough of low magic. Perhaps it was foolish for him to try. Or perhaps it would not have worked, even if Madrigal had done it herself.

'I had to,' he whispers as the dead queens stalk toward him wearing Katharine's body like a costume. 'I had to, for her.'

'You had to,' they say, and lift him to his feet. He looks into her eyes, searching, and what he sees makes him want to scream. But it dies in his throat as they press their lips to his, flooding him with black and cold, filling him up with them until his blood has nowhere else to run except straight from his ears and eyes.

THE SEAWATCH MOUNTAINS

On the side of a road that curves eastward through the mountains, Mirabella raises her arm and flags down a passing coach.

'Have you room for another passenger?' she asks. 'I have coin enough.' She holds it out in a small purse, and the driver weighs it in her hand before nodding.

'You a naturalist?' she asks, gesturing to Mirabella's hood.

Mirabella smiles and tucks the woodpecker deeper into her collar.

'No. I am only borrowing him.'

'Aye. Get on in, then. We're going all the way to the capital, if that suits you.'

'That suits me fine,' she says, and opens the door. 'For I am expected there.'

To be concluded . . .

ACKNOWLEDGMENTS

And here we are, at the end of book three. Just one more now, and that bittersweet feeling is creeping in. Right away I want to thank the readers of this series along with the team at HarperTeen for giving me the chance to write the last chapter of the queens' story (even though I may come to regret knowing what happens to them!). Without you, Mirabella, Arsinoe, and Katharine's tale would have ended at the close of *One Dark Throne*, their destinies settled but futures unknown. Now, for better or worse, I'll get to know. So thank you, thank you for the opportunity.

An even larger thanks than usual this time to my editor, Alexandra Cooper. The editing was amazing (duh, it always is!) but I am particularly grateful for your dedication to this series, and this book. Thank you for going above and beyond.

Thanks to my ever-incredible agent, Adriann Ranta-Zurhellen, who never fails to be awesome and who never steers me wrong. Please never leave me. I will need a support group. Also thank you to the entire team at Foundry Media with a hearty wave to Richie Kern!

Thank you to Olivia Russo, publicity wunderkind, and the fastest responder to emails I ever did see. Thank you also to the whole publicity team at BookSparks: Crystal Patriarche and Liane Worthington and Savannah Harrelson. You guys are just plain rad and wonderful.

Thank you to the marketing and art teams at HarperCollins: the awesome Audrey Diestelkamp, Bess Braswell (once again, sorry for putting that arrow into that character with your name, Bess), Aurora Parlagreco, John Dismukes, and Virginia Allyn. These books are gorgeous and the art and marketing that goes into them . . . WOW.

Alyssa Miele, thanks for doing a little bit of everything! Thank you to Jon Howard, for the support and the final touches. Thank you to Robin Roy for meticulous copyediting.

Thank you to Allison Devereux and Kirsten Wolf at the Mackenzie Wolf Agency.

And thanks as always to my parents, who buy copies for all the relatives, and my brother, who put a *Three Dark Crowns* sticker on his guitar. Thanks to Susan Murray, who is solidly Team Camden.

And to Dylan Zoerb, for luck.